A Louisiana CHRISTMAS to Remember

*Three Heartwarming, Interconnected Stories
of Faith, Love, and Restoration*

BETSY ST. AMANT
MORGAN TARPLEY SMITH
LENORA WORTH

BARBOUR
PUBLISHING

A Louisiana Snow ©2023 by Morgan Tarpley Smith
Restoring Christmas ©2023 by Betsy St. Amant
A Christmas Reunion ©2023 by Lenora Worth

Print ISBN 978–1-63609–647-6

Adobe Digital Edition (.epub) 978–1-63609–648-3

This book is a work of fiction. Names, characters, places, and incidents are either products of the author's imagination or used fictitiously. Any similarity to actual people, organizations, and/or events is purely coincidental.

Published by Barbour Publishing, Inc., 1810 Barbour Drive, Uhrichsville, Ohio 44683, www.barbourbooks.com

Our mission is to inspire the world with the life-changing message of the Bible.

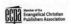
Member of the
Evangelical Christian
Publishers Association

Printed in the United States of America.

A Louisiana Snow

Morgan Tarpley Smith

DEDICATION

For Brooke,
the Serena to my Mattie.

And to those in small towns everywhere.
I'll always be a small-town girl at heart, no matter where I live.

Author's Note

Reader, thank you for joining Mattie and Paul on their journey to love, forgiveness, and a deeper connection to God. I pray you are encouraged in your faith and uplifted in your spirit.

I also hope you enjoy these stories set in fictional Moreau, which is loosely based on the lovely town of Natchitoches, the oldest European settlement in Louisiana. The town was founded by a French explorer in 1714, and in the late 1700s, my ancestors were married there.

Lenora, Betsy, and I are proud Louisiana girls who wanted to bring some of the warmth, humor, and spirit of our home state's Southern culture to the page. This collection idea began with a 2021 social media post. An avid reader of Christian fiction was compiling a list of Christmas books set in all fifty US states and hadn't listed one for Louisiana. I couldn't think of a single title, and someone commented, "Why don't you write one?"

Not long afterward, Lenora and Betsy were graciously on board, and the characters of Mattie, Jolene, Adale, and Granny drifted into our lives like a Louisiana snow. We had the best time planning and writing these stories and adding to our Pinterest board too.

I'd like to thank my coauthors for their support, prayers, laughter, and wisdom and for saying yes to my random message about writing a Louisiana book. I'd also like to thank my amazing agent, Tamela Hancock Murray, for believing in me and this project, and the wonderful staff at Barbour, especially editor Rebecca Germany, for giving our stories a home.

Other thanks go to my writing partner and dear friend, Carole Lehr Johnson, and my writing mentors, Johnnie Alexander, Becky Melby, and Melanie Dobson. I couldn't do this writing life without them and the support of my family and friends. Thank you to my husband, Steven, and son, Gareth, and to my mom, Mellanie, and mother-in-law, Jennifer, who are faithful first readers and cheerleaders.

Thank you to God, who sparks my creative spirit and teaches me through these stories. To God be the glory. And may we always remember to simply come in faith and adore Him.

"O come all ye faithful. . ."

Chapter One

Three weeks before Christmas
Moreau, Louisiana

Mattie Hayes froze, her fingers warm around a latte, and stared at the flurries of white outside the window of Le Petit French Press coffee shop, the sight briefly restoring faith to her disheartened state of mind.

"No way!" she whispered under her breath, then swiveled to face the counter, where the owner, her best friend Serena, prepared a hot drink for a customer. "Serena!"

Serena raised her head and grinned. "Look at that. A Louisiana snow."

With a deep breath, Mattie took in the wintry scene. "Looks like we won't be wearing shorts this Christmas."

Serena topped off a latte with a flourish of whipped cream. "Yeah, it'll be winter coats this year."

"It's always a surprise which one," Mattie added with a grin.

"How's the Christmas market coming along?" Serena nodded toward Mattie. "Come on, top reporter at the *Moreau Gazette*. Give me the scoop."

"The only reporter, you mean."

Serena laughed. "Okay, *star* reporter, tell me about the market."

Mattie glanced at the falling snow, then back at her friend. "I hope snow is the icing on the cake for us. We've got to raise the money to restore the chapel."

In her mind's eye she saw the hurricane damage to the beautiful historic church where her ancestors—the Lavignes—had been married two centuries ago. The hurricane that past August had been the worst to hit their town since she was a kid.

"Cameron is delivering the market stalls tomorrow," Mattie continued. "I have to pick up the tree and garlands from Turnage's Tree Farm by Wednesday." She rubbed her forehead. "And I've got to survive Granny's constant errands and sorting more of her stuff. The last round of unpacking went on for days. I thought Aunt Adale was going to lose her mind."

"Good luck with that." Serena wiped the counter. "Speaking of surviving, how's working with Paul?"

Mattie shot her a look. "No comment." She finished her coffee and tossed the cup into the trash bin, humming along with a jazzy version of her favorite Christmas carol playing in the background.

Her friend leaned against the counter with a conspiratorial look. "Oh, just admit you're still mad at him for beating you out of being valedictorian."

Mattie sighed. "That was ages ago."

"Ten years isn't that long."

The bell dinged, and Mattie glanced at the door. She nearly groaned. It was Paul.

She didn't dare look at Serena, who likely wore a smug expression as if she had conjured Paul Ammons out of thin air.

He ran a hand over his scruffy beard as he surveyed the menu above the counter. The beard and shoulder-length dark hair were such a contrast to his polished mayor father in a sleek suit.

Every time she saw Paul after hours on a workday, his wrinkled dress shirt was partially untucked—his appearance a cross between a haphazard professor and a uniformed kid glad to get out of private school. The ever-present messenger bag with its torn front was at his side.

He looked so different from the boy in high school who wore polos tucked into slacks every day, not a hair out of place. The boy who was a shoo-in for Most Likely to Succeed and Most Likely to Become President of the United States. The boy she still saw, despite the ten-year-older version before her now.

Paul greeted Serena and ordered an Americano, then leaned over the counter and said something to her that Mattie couldn't hear. Her friend smiled and turned to prepare his drink. He shifted to face Mattie, their eyes meeting.

Heat rose to her cheeks. She had been staring.

He didn't seem to realize, though. He greeted her, which she returned without equal gusto, and then he asked, "Are we still meeting at the market at five?"

"Same as I texted you this morning." She started to gather her items. She had just enough time to pop by the newspaper office to finish a story and run Granny's errand before the commitee meeting.

The espresso machine whirred, and when Mattie made the mistake of looking up, Serena raised her eyebrows and nodded toward Paul, who rummaged through his bag. With widened eyes, Mattie shook her head, silently urging her to not interfere.

When the noise faded, Serena handed over Paul's drink and said, "I was just asking Mattie about the market."

Mattie would have kicked her if she weren't on the other side of the counter. What was she playing at?

Paul looked her way. "Oh, and what did she say?"

Mattie shouldered her bag and stepped toward the counter. "Not much."

He smiled. "That doesn't sound like you."

"Ouch, Paul." She crossed her arms. "I do happen to talk to people for a living, but then again, so do you."

He sipped his coffee. "True. Well, I'll see you at the meeting."

"See you." Mattie waited until she heard the door close before leveling a glare at Serena. "Stop meddling."

"Sounds like flirtatious banter if I've ever heard it."

Mattie scoffed. "You've had too much caffeine. Your brain's muddled." She opened her mouth to say more, but a yawn escaped.

"Let me make you a drink for the road."

Mattie waved her hand. "I'll be fine."

Serena glared at her over the machine. "Not if you're gonna live on coffee forever instead of sleep."

Mattie ignored her while the machine whirred again. When it stopped, she offered an imploring look at her friend. "I have deadlines. I have things to do. When do I have time for sleep?"

Serena thrust a latte toward Mattie, who accepted the steaming cup with a smile. "Thanks. You keep me going. And don't worry. . .I'll sleep after Christmas."

"Sure you will. By then you'll say after Valentine's Day."

Mattie sighed. Serena knew her far too well. "See you later."

On Mattie's way out the door, she heard Serena's laughing voice behind her. "And thank Paul for the latte. It was on him."

Mattie almost crushed the to-go cup in her hand. Of course Paul would buy her a latte. *Perfect* Paul.

The man had been back less than a year after being gone from Moreau since they graduated. Why did he care about the market? And did he even care about the town?

The bell jingled as she closed the door of the Press and faced the brick sidewalk now coated in white. She grinned, the chill kissing her cheeks. She couldn't have planned it better herself.

A Louisiana snow, indeed. Just in time for the market's opening. And despite Paul, she would make the market successful.

Mattie inhaled deeply, and with coffee in hand and flurries settling onto her blue coat, she strode down Rue de la Chapelle toward the *Gazette*.

If the snow was any sign—and Mattie held to the belief that God showed his children signs from time to time—maybe the chapel could be saved after all. The market had to be a success. It was their only hope.

* * *

Paul wasn't a block from the Press when he heard the crunch of icy footsteps behind him. He glanced over his shoulder to see Mattie headed in his direction, and then she ducked behind a parked truck.

He groaned. What was her problem? Ever since he moved back, she had done her best to avoid him, even after his father selected them to work together on the market committee.

"Mattie, did you fall?" he called out, not able to keep from teasing her, as he retraced his steps.

She crouched awkwardly behind the truck and clutched a pair of gloves. "Got them!"

Paul narrowed his eyes. She had *not* dropped her gloves. She was avoiding him.

Mattie raised her latte. "Thanks for the coffee." She brushed past him and went on her way—full speed ahead.

His long-legged stride easily caught up to her shorter one. Though, she was only about five inches from his six feet two inches. She quickened her pace. "Paul, we're not supposed to meet for another hour."

"We're not meeting. We're walking. Is there some convoluted town ordinance where we can't walk in the same direction? I happen to know all the most absurd town ordinances, including the one that says black-striped pigs can't run down the street on Fridays."

She narrowed her eyes, forehead creasing. "*Black-striped* pigs?"

He smiled. "Yes. It's in the ordinances. I made a game of it when I was a kid. Find the worst ordinances and memorize them. Would you like to know about the ordinance to never wear purple socks on a Monday while standing in the river?"

A corner of Mattie's mouth rose, but she quickly stifled her amusement. "That's okay."

Paul focused ahead and thought of those lonely afternoons at the town hall. He made up the game to pass the time, not because he particularly enjoyed it. He was not that lonely kid anymore. It was just being back in this town that brought the memories with it.

The damaged La Petit Chapelle lay ahead, blue tarps peeking from the roof. He knew nothing about restoration work or construction, but Cameron had told him the damage was extensive and the materials alone would cost a small fortune.

From what Paul had seen of the inside, a corner of the sanctuary would likely have to be completely rebuilt from where the old oak fell through that section of the roof. The steeple had taken a thrashing as well.

Despite the tarps, the chapel's exterior looked much the same as it had all his life. A tall, steep roof rose in an upside-down V, and the pale brick spread from it toward the ground.

Mattie slowed until she stopped in front of it, her gaze roaming its facade as if looking at a prized possession. Snowflakes coated her blue coat, black hat, and long strands of blond hair at her shoulders. He saw in the way her green eyes lit up how much she cared about this place linked to her heritage and the town.

In his opinion, she cared too much—to the point that her every thought seemed connected to restoring the chapel. It was noble of her, for sure, but the woman was borderline obsessed. What did she do for fun? When did she not work?

Mattie approached the banner stretched over the front doors advertising the market as a fundraiser to restore the chapel. A corner had come loose, and with her gloved hands, she fumbled to retie it.

"Here, let me help." He moved behind her, and at first he didn't think she would let him, but after another moment of fumbling, she turned to the side, except he was too close.

She nearly ran into him. Her hand pressed against his chest in an attempt to steady herself, her eyes meeting his, a trace of surprise in them.

His hand went to her shoulder to settle her, and he didn't want to move away. She did, of course, and he chided himself for letting the moment put his thoughts back to the crush he had on her in high school. He'd never told her, and it was all in the past now. He quickly fixed the banner and rejoined her on the sidewalk, keeping his distance.

Looking at the chapel a final time, Paul noted its simplicity and beauty. "They don't make buildings like this anymore, do they?"

"No, they don't," she whispered into the snowy afternoon. "We'll restore you, beauty." Then she was on her way once again, and he caught up with her.

Mattie glanced at her phone, and Paul looked with her at a lengthy document. She scrolled through the many items.

"You've got a lot to do there. Anything I can help with?"

She shrugged. "Yeah, you can help. We both have a lot to do." She moved on. "We'll meet at five to mark the stall locations."

He added, "Cameron and I are finishing the stalls tonight."

"Good." She gave a curt nod. "Those will be delivered tomorrow, and your students are coming to help decorate on Wednesday, right?"

"Yep." He felt like he was in the meeting already.

She rattled off a few other items, which Paul answered with a quick "Done," and then she frowned. For some reason, she always seemed annoyed and on guard in his presence. It had been like that ever since his father put them on the same committee. But honestly, it really went back to high school, though that was over a decade earlier.

Outside the *Gazette*, Mattie stopped, staring at her phone. "Granny and her texting," she muttered before offering a brisk "Bye" and disappearing through the door with a ding of the bell.

Paul looked after her for a moment before he trudged onward through the snow toward Moreau Town Hall.

He was just a part of Mattie's to-do list. Nothing more.

Entering the office, he greeted Jeanette Walker, the secretary who had worked with his father since Paul was a kid.

"Is Dad busy right now?"

She gave a familiar sympathetic smile and nodded. "Yes, he has a call, but I can let you know when he's free."

Paul didn't let his shoulders sag, but inside, something deflated—just as it had for the little boy that Mrs. Walker had told the same thing to time and time again.

His father was the mayor and always busy, too busy for him. He held up his hand. "It's okay. I'll see him in the meeting." He turned and headed down the hall.

He almost went to the ordinance books to play the game. But that was all part of his childhood, not his present. His hand rested on his messenger bag full of students' papers and tests, and he took a seat in the meeting room and started to grade.

Some things never changed.

Chapter Two

When Mattie entered the *Moreau Gazette*, she answered Granny's text about an errand and turned back to watch Paul out the window. He trudged through the snow, shoulders slumped and head down. He looked so dejected. She almost wished to rush after him, but of course she didn't.

Paul was a grown man. He would be fine. She had a job to do.

She strode to her cubicle, passing the office of editor Frank Miller, who called out to her.

"Got that story yet, Mattie?"

She threw him a look and leaned against the doorframe. "Not yet. But have I missed a deadline in six years?"

He shook his head with a grin.

She pointed at him. "Exactly, and I'm not starting now."

Frank leaned back in his rolling chair. "Tell your aunt I said hello. And if she's ever free for dinner, I'm available."

Mattie laughed and hurried to her desk. He asked about Aunt Adale every chance he got. They had gone to school together, and it seemed like his crush had translated into a forty-year one.

Aunt Adale hadn't dated much since Uncle Pierre died seven years ago. The past decade had been hard for their family. When Mattie started high school, her father left her and her mother, and the summer Mattie graduated high school, her mother died after suffering a second stroke. She'd taken care of her, but it hadn't been enough to save her.

Tears welled in Mattie's eyes. She pushed them back. No, she could not get emotional. She had too much to do.

After her parents were gone, Aunt Adale, along with Granny, had stepped in to support her, and she would always be grateful to them. She and her cousin Jolene, who was two years older, shared a room while Jolene worked at a local restaurant and Mattie finished school, then went to college. She thought of Jolene and how she felt more like an older sister than a cousin. Two people could not be more different than the two of them—oil and water.

Jolene's artsy, carefree lifestyle clashed with Mattie's need for order and schedules and lists. She'd even put up a curtain in the middle of the room when she grew tired of looking at the clothes and art supplies strewn around the other side.

Her cousin hadn't been home in five years, and Mattie was more than capable of stepping in to care for her aunt in Jolene's stead. After her uncle died, she had tried to repay the care that was shown to her any way she could, and now the repayment would continue with Granny moving in with her and her aunt. Mattie had moved in after the hurricane damaged her apartment that summer, destroying most of her furniture and belongings.

Now Jolene was coming home—or at least she was supposed to. Mattie would believe it when she saw it.

The reminder of the homecoming prompted Mattie into action. She settled at her desk and focused on work for the next half hour.

"Done. Print." She grabbed the article from the printer and plopped it onto Frank's desk. "There you go." She glanced at the clock on the opposite wall. "Look at that. Five minutes before deadline."

"So it would seem." He picked up the pages. "Cutting it close as always."

Mattie blew out a breath. "Coming in on two wheels, my aunt always says." She moved toward the door. "I'm going to the meeting. See you in the morning."

Frank called out behind her. "And don't forget your interview. Good luck with Eloise."

She scoffed. "Yeah, I'll certainly need it." But she smiled as she left his office. Squaring her shoulders, she pulled her coat closer before heading into the cold.

Yes, Eloise Lavigne-Marchand would be a tough interview indeed, especially since she was her grandmother. And nobody got information out of Granny unless she wanted them to.

The snow continued its frigid dance to coat the streets of Moreau, the town resembling the inside of a snow globe.

She grabbed her phone and jotted a note. *Look into selling Moreau snow globes at market.*

Any idea might be the one to provide the funds they needed to restore the little chapel—*her family's* chapel. And Mattie refused to be the Lavigne who let the family down.

———◆———

Paul looked up from grading papers in the meeting room as his father strode in.

"Hi, Paul. Sorry. I was on the phone."

"It's okay," he said as he had a thousand times before.

Paul looked at his watch—ten minutes until the meeting started. He was about to speak when Cameron Armand and Nate Lewis entered the room. He shook their hands. "Cameron, we're still on for finishing the stalls tonight, right?"

Cameron nodded. "If you can be at the house by six, I'll grill some burgers."

Nate chimed in. "Wish I was free! But I gotta pack. Julie and I are going out of town tomorrow, but we'll be back Friday for the market opening." He looked at Cameron. "Send me the list, and I'll pick up the supplies we need for next week to start the courtyard mural."

Paul's father took his seat at the head of the table. "Save the receipts, Nate. The town will reimburse you."

"Thanks, Mayor. You know how we starving artist types are. Not a cent to our names."

Paul's father laughed. "I hear you. We small-town politicians don't exactly make the big bucks either." He opened a folder. "Let's get this meeting started."

Paul noted Mattie's empty seat beside his. It was two minutes to four. She was going to be late, or likely slide in right on time, which was typical. He sat, and not one minute later, Mattie slipped into the room.

She didn't apologize but opened her folder and started arranging papers in front of her like she'd been there for the past ten minutes and was only double-checking her setup. She scanned the list on her phone, then looked up as if the meeting should have already started.

His father greeted her and promptly began, asking about Cameron and Nate's progress. After a few minutes, he faced Paul and Mattie for their report. Mattie jumped in as usual to offer the same updates they had discussed on the way from the coffee shop that afternoon. He let her go on, even though his dad likely disapproved of his lack of engagement.

Mattie paused, then launched into another spiel. "I thought of another way to utilize the market stalls. We could use them for seasonal markets too—spring, summer, and harvest maybe—to continue interest in Moreau and the Christmas market each year. Artisans from other towns could come as well to offer variety and provide more revenue from booth fees."

Paul stared at her. The idea was great, brilliant even, but when did she let her brain rest? Every time he saw her, she was either working or on her way to work at something—the *Gazette*, planning an event, fundraising, volunteering. What did she do for fun, to relax?

Mattie didn't miss a beat as she shifted a few papers on the table. "I've lined up the carriage rides and started planning the children's day at the market as activities during the week before Christmas. We also received the final new lighting display for the river that was on back order, which will be installed tomorrow, and all is set to light it along the river when we officially open the market."

She undid a packet of papers held together by a large binder clip and started passing smaller stapled versions around to each committee member. "I've contacted the National Register of Historic Places about registering the chapel as a historic landmark. The paperwork is extensive, but I've already started on it. To have it on the register would be a tourist draw for our town. Some groups hold special tours of properties on the register. Ours could be added to the mix."

Mattie studied another paper. "Also, I spoke to the town clerk at Clintonville, and she said the old theater they renovated a few years ago as an event space is doing really well. We could do something similar with the chapel to host weddings, bridal showers, reunions, and other events. But we must get it restored first."

"I think I found something that could help us in that area." Cameron lifted a printed article.

Paul almost groaned. Cameron was as bad as Mattie when it came to organization and preparedness. Paul didn't even have a notebook open to take notes.

Cameron glanced at the article. "I came across a retired architect in New Orleans named Rémy Vachon. He specializes in historic restoration and is helping communities affected by the recent hurricane. He's offering his services at a discounted rate for restoration of damaged historic properties. We could try to get him to come here."

Paul nodded. "That's great, and I think—"

"Perfect!" Mattie interjected at the same time. "That's just what we need to get the chapel work going. We would need a restoration expert like this retired architect for the historic register too."

Paul slumped a little in his chair. He didn't have a chance to offer anything helpful. Mattie and Cameron had it covered.

His dad offered Cameron a smile. "Good work. Please contact Mr. Vachon to see if he would be interested in coming to Moreau. If he has questions, ask him to call me."

After the meeting, his dad, Mattie, Cameron, and Nate were locked in conversation about the mural, so Paul grabbed his bag and quietly slipped out the door, the exact opposite of Mattie's entrance. The two of them were nothing alike—why did that bother him?

When he and Mattie were chosen for the committee, he tried to find some common ground between them, some level to connect on, as he tried to do with all his students. But besides sharing a hometown and graduating with honors from Moreau High School the same year, he could not think of one single thing they had in common.

That didn't mean Paul was going to give up on Mattie yet.

Chapter Three

Mattie approached the Lavigne House, her aunt's white two-story wood home only a few blocks from town hall. Fragrant fir garlands intertwined with red ribbon, berries, and ornaments wrapped every column on the long porch. Granny had insisted they add bows and the large red ornaments dangling like crimson icicles.

The look was festive yet tasteful.

She and her aunt had decorated the week after Thanksgiving. They were the first ones at Turnage's Tree Farm when it opened for the season to choose the perfect tree and garlands. Their other additions to the exterior were old-fashioned lanterns set at the sides of the steps and strands of white lights draped over the bushes flanking the entrance. They had also wrapped lights around the few trees in the front yard.

Approaching the house at the end of her day was a treat this time of year for Mattie. A million memories and stories were woven into the place. The house had been in the Lavigne family for nearly two hundred years. Mattie's mom and Aunt Adale had grown up there and Granny too. After Jolene was born, Granny and Grandpa Oliver moved to a nearby cottage to allow Aunt Adale's family to move in. Mattie and her parents had lived in a small brick house a block away, the whole family close by.

Now Granny had returned home.

Mattie entered through the red front door, a crisp, woodsy scent filling her senses and mingling with cinnamon as she stepped into the foyer, its hardwood floors gleaming in the wintry sunlight. A staircase carpeted in burgundy rose ahead to the left.

She hung her coat on a hook and peered into the sitting room, but Granny wasn't in her usual spot. She wasn't there painting or sipping a glass of sweet tea on the red velvet settee by the seven-foot Christmas tree nor in the armchair by the fireplace. And she wasn't seated at the antique desk with its small, shiny faux tree she'd added to the decor.

Mattie studied the larger tree, checking to see if the decorations still looked fresh. She and her aunt had opted for no lights but instead added a traditional garland of dried cranberries and popcorn with cinnamon sticks, dried oranges, sprigs of red berries, and pinecones adorning the branches. Burlap wrapped the base, and the wooden star carved by Mattie's great-grandfather, a family tradition going back at least a century, perched prominently at the top.

The room beckoned Mattie into its coziness to sit with a book in front of the fire, which she rarely did anymore.

Mattie found Granny in the dining room rummaging through a box at her feet while wearing a flamboyant red hat with a large black feather. Dozens of boxes surrounded her, their contents spilling across every surface of the room—a collection of eight decades.

"Hi, Granny," Mattie spoke into the chaos.

Granny jumped, a greeting card flying across the room like a wayward paper airplane. She clutched her chest. "Mattie Marie Hayes, don't you dare go about scaring women nearing eighty like that. I almost needed my smelling salts."

Mattie bit her lip in an attempt not to laugh. She knew she hadn't scared her grandmother as much as she let on. Granny was known for her theatrics. Aunt Adale always said she had been meant for the stage.

Between Granny's response, the hat, and the room's state of disarray, the whole scene seemed like something out of a movie.

"Sorry, Granny." Mattie edged in between boxes to enter the room.

Granny waved a hand toward Mattie. "Never mind that, child. I'm still kicking after this long. A little fright ain't gonna finish me."

Mattie moved a large hatbox lined with purple silk from a chair and sat beside her grandmother. She handed over the book of stamps Granny had requested by text message.

"Thank you kindly." Granny tucked them into her shirt pocket. "I'll have the Christmas cards ready for you to drop by the post office in the morning."

Mattie nodded, surveying the sea of boxes and their varying state of unpacking, and dared to ask, "How's it going?"

Her grandmother shot her a sharp look from under the hat's wide brim. "It ain't going nowhere, as you can see, and your aunt is in a tizzy."

Mattie could imagine Aunt Adale was, in fact, borderline distraught at the upheaval, though she knew her aunt was more than happy to have Granny move in. Mattie and Aunt Adale were alike with their routines and organization. Granny was, well, she was much more like free-spirited Jolene.

Looking at the many painted canvases scattered around the room, Mattie also noted her cousin had certainly received Granny's artistic abilities. She leaned and retrieved a particularly captivating one.

The scene featured one of the famous bridges of Paris over the Seine at sunset. A young couple stood at the bridge's edge, arms around each other, their backs to the artist.

How romantic Paris would be with someone you loved. She thought of how she should have been in France the summer after graduation, and that made her think of Paul, so she pushed those thoughts away.

"Granny, this is stunning!" She held the small framed canvas toward her grandmother. "Why haven't I seen this one? You showed me your others from that summer you all were in Paris."

Granny offered a halfhearted shrug, but in her dark eyes, Mattie saw something there—a story perhaps.

Setting the painting aside, she looked over the others. "We need to display your art at the party. Make a mini gallery. This is all amazing."

Granny kept rummaging through the box. "Didn't you need to ask me something about that?"

Party, right. Back to the task at hand. She pulled a pen and small notebook from her purse, then straightened and fixed Granny with her most professional reporter expression.

"Mrs. Eloise Lavigne-Marchand, I would like to ask you a few questions about your upcoming eightieth birthday celebration. I have, of course, been informed that the whole community is invited. So, what would you like to say about this most blessed occasion?"

Granny pinned her with a glare. "I have nothing to say. When you get this old, you can choose to say nothing."

Yeah, tough interview.

Mattie sighed. "Come on, Granny. I need something to work with here. I've got the facts, but the people want to hear from the honoree herself. Do you want me to put words in your mouth? Because I will if I must."

"I'm a bit busy, as you can clearly see. Give me time to think, and I will gladly offer some sort of golden words for that paper. Just not now."

Mattie took in the room. At this rate, she wouldn't finish her story until next month, maybe next year. She went to ask one more time, but Granny fired back one of her own questions with a frown.

"Why isn't a pretty girl like you dating? You could date my good-looking repairman. He's single. I'd put in a good word for you."

She had to stop from rolling her eyes. Her grandmother was known to play matchmaker from time to time. "Granny, I appreciate it, but Cameron and I are just friends."

"Well, what about Paul then? If I were fifty years younger, you'd best bet I'd be on that handsome French teacher's arm. He's been back a year, but is he dating anyone? You and he are spending all that time on the committee. Are sparks not flying?"

Sparks were flying all right, Mattie thought, except they were the kind more likely to kindle arson than romance.

Mattie deflected the question to a different matchmaking prospect. "We need to join forces to get Aunt Adale on a date with Frank Miller. He keeps asking about her every day."

Granny grinned, and Mattie saw the wheels turning in her grandmother's mind, relief surging through her to leave talk of her nonexistent love life behind. When did she have time to date anyone anyway?

At that moment, Aunt Adale came by with a mug in her hand. She stopped at the open doors and covered her eyes. "Oh goodness,

I don't want to see what she's done with this house. I'm giving you two more days to sort through all this, Mama, before I'm forced to intervene. Are you trying to drive me to the edge of insanity?"

Mattie and Granny exchanged looks. Her grandmother wasn't the only one who had a touch of the theatrics.

Granny patted Mattie's knee, and her challenging expression said, *Watch this.* "Adale, Mattie here was telling me that her charming editor has asked about you for the hundredth time. Why don't you just go out with him and see what happens?"

Her aunt opened her eyes long enough to glare at them and take a long sip from her mug. *No comment.*

Aunt Adale leaned against the doorframe. "Jolene texted that her flight arrives on Sunday. She didn't give many details, of course, so I'm assuming she'll find her own way home and not need airport pickup."

Mattie pursed her lips. Sounded like her cousin's typical laid-back approach, offering only sparse details of her travel plans and her life in general. When Mattie and her aunt visited her a few years ago in Tennessee, they hadn't met any of her friends, and she only focused on showing them around the tourist spots of Nashville like a tour guide.

Sometimes Mattie browsed Jolene's social media to piece together what her cousin was like now. She loved her. There was no question about that. She just didn't understand her.

Jolene didn't fit into Mattie's tidy world of order in chaos—and for that matter, neither did someone like Paul with his flighty ways, changing schools almost every year.

Noting the time sent Mattie scurrying from her chair and weaving her way through Granny's belongings. She threw out an apology for having to run, but she was needed at the market.

Mattie didn't have any place for uncertainty, or instability, in her life. After all she had been through, she made sure of it.

Paul fought to stop a groan. Mattie had combated every single suggestion he made for the placement of the market stalls.

"What if the crepe stall goes here?" He pointed to the spot. "Near the stage so those in line can hear the music and be enticed by the smell of chocolate."

His grin shifted to a frown when Mattie shook her head, not looking up from her clipboard.

"No, I have Serena's coffee and baked goods stall there. The crepes will go on the opposite side. A few food and drink stalls on each side of the crowd."

Paul nodded. It made perfect sense. Of course it did. It was Mattie. She had everything figured out—which was why he didn't feel as if he was contributing much to their committee.

Mattie tapped her clipboard. "How is prep going with your students for the school's French language booth?"

"*Ça va très bien,*" he answered in French, peering at her expectantly.

Her gaze lifted, eyebrows raising. "Hilarious, *monsieur.*"

Paul crossed his arms and leaned against a lamppost. "Your ancestors were from France. You should speak French. You were always good at it in high school."

Her focus was back on the clipboard as she muttered, "Apparently not good enough."

Not good enough? At least that's what he thought she said. Did he say something wrong?

Before he thought better of it, he blurted, "I could tutor you if you'd like. I'm sure you'd catch up in no time."

What was he thinking? She didn't want to spend any more time with him than she already had to. Did he want to spend more time with her? The answer surprised him—*yes*.

"*Non, merci*," she said flatly.

"I'm just trying to help."

Her jaw tightened, and she met his eyes, pain lacing her features. "You can't just swoop in and take care of everything, Paul." She swallowed hard. "I have to go." She rushed past him, hugging the clipboard.

What had he done? He recalled the pain in her eyes and nearly went after her but stopped himself. She probably wanted to be alone. He sighed, his breath white swirls before his face. His trying to help was what had likely set her off.

Paul surveyed the market, then headed for his car. Whether or not Mattie wanted his help, he wasn't going anywhere until he saw this market through. He was not a quitter.

He pulled up at Cameron's house—the old LaCroix place Cameron had renovated over the past year. Impressive for sure. He knew what he was doing.

Heading to the large shop, light shone from the partially open double doors. Paul stepped inside, warmth meeting him from a heater in the corner, and placed a six-pack of colas and a package of cookies on a worktable.

The space was the most organized shop he'd ever seen, not a speck of sawdust in sight. How was that possible? He half-expected there to be labels by every tool hanging on a giant pegboard. That was the kind of guy Cameron seemed to be—efficient, prepared, organized.

Three words Paul wouldn't use to describe himself.

Did Mattie want someone like that? He shook his head. What did it matter what kind of guy she liked? He wasn't it.

"Hey, Paul." Cameron entered from the far door, leading to the patio. "Come on back."

Outside, Cameron stood at the grill next to a table and chairs covered in snow. Burgers sizzled as the lid opened, white smoke releasing into the cold night.

Paul's stomach growled. "Smells good. Thanks for the invitation."

Cameron flipped a patty. "No problem. We'll need the energy to finish these stalls tonight."

With a sharp exhale, Paul ran a hand through his hair. "I needed that earlier at the market."

"Tough going with Mattie?" Cameron shot him a knowing look.

"Always. She doesn't consider a single one of my suggestions. Her ideas are great, of course. I'm trying to find a way to, I don't know. . .keep up with her. She's a force of nature."

Cameron faced him with a raised eyebrow. "Do you want to keep up with her?"

Paul raised his hands, palms out. "I didn't say that."

Cameron laughed. "You didn't have to." He scooped the burgers off the grill and onto a plate. "Let's eat and get to it."

Paul followed him inside, the conversation replaying in his mind. Maybe that was it—he *did* want to keep up with Mattie.

Chapter Four

Wielding her pen, Mattie slashed through another line in her notebook. She had tried to pry more words out of Granny that morning for the story, even bringing her coffee in bed, but it had backfired with her grandmother stating, "I'll not answer a thing before I'm up and dressed."

Mattie groaned. She *would* have to put words in Granny's mouth to finish this article.

"What's the matter, darling?" Aunt Adale breezed into the spacious kitchen and leaned against the counter across from where Mattie sat at the small table in the breakfast nook. She nodded toward the notebook. "I haven't seen that many crazy lines since Jolene went through her splatter paint phase."

With a smile, Mattie settled back in her chair. That phase had been the only time she and her cousin had done any art together. Dipping slim paintbrushes with long handles into paint of all colors and slinging it over a canvas had been cathartic, and they had ended up slinging paint on each other in the process.

"Granny isn't cooperating."

Her aunt scoffed. "Tell me something I don't know. The dining room is still in a right mess from her memorabilia explosion."

The image of Granny sitting among the boxes wearing a huge red hat brought a grin to Mattie's lips. Her grandmother was nothing but original. That was for sure. The question was, how was the "woman of the hour" supposed to be honored when she wouldn't talk about herself?

Mattie scanned the page. She had most of the facts down, but she needed a bit more. "Maybe you can help me. She won't answer my questions. Usually turns them back on me. She would have made a good reporter."

Aunt Adale sighed. "It's like bleeding a turnip unless she wants to talk about something. What else do you need?"

"Well, I had an idea yesterday. I think we should display some of Granny's art at the party. Arrange it gallery-style in the entrance hall when people come in. She had quite a few paintings in the parlor, including one I'd never seen before of a man and woman on a Paris bridge at sunset."

Her aunt straightened as if something startled her, her face pale. Before Mattie could ask what the matter was, she cleared her throat and busied herself fiddling with the napkin holder.

"I think the display is a good idea. I'll see if Mary Ann will help me set it up."

Mattie narrowed her eyes. What had the mention of that painting done to her aunt? Did it mean something?

She slid the notebook into her tote bag. "I've got to get to the office soon. Frank is standing on his head for this article, but I've got another day to work on it." An idea formed in her mind. "Aha! Maybe if I can't get Granny to talk, I can get others to talk about her."

Aunt Adale nodded. "That should do it. You show that turnip who's boss."

With a laugh, Mattie stood and pinned her aunt with a piercing stare. "Speaking of boss. . .could you please just go out with the man and be done with it?"

Her aunt threw out her hands. "If it's not you trying to set me up with a man, it's Mama. I don't need or want a matchmaking service, thank you very much." She shoved her hands on her hips. "But if it'll get Frank out of your hair, I suppose one little dinner won't hurt."

Mattie let out a whoop and hugged her aunt, then grabbed Granny's Christmas card bundle and scurried out the door before her aunt changed her mind. When she strode into the *Gazette* office and told Frank the news, he wasted not a moment, called her aunt, and set their date for Thursday night at the Riverbend Bistro.

After finishing other articles, Mattie made a few dozen copies of the market flyers that she and Cameron would distribute that evening in the neighboring town of Hawkins when they got the tree and garlands. She stopped by the post office and made her rounds to each of the market vendors who had brick-and-mortar shops in town to make sure they were all set for Friday.

Each stall's occupant had been carefully selected by the committee to ensure a wide variety of offerings would be available to the public, from Mrs. Henning's homemade ornaments to Mr. Connery's handcrafted musical instruments.

The town's best wares would be on display, with one booth even selling authentic paper star lanterns imported from Europe and another featuring roasted nuts. She could see it all unfold in her mind—each miniature house draped in lights and garlands, all collectively surrounding a massive tree at the town square center, with hundreds of people milling around to enjoy the festivities.

Her final stop was, of course, the coffee shop. She stomped her fleece-lined boots on the welcome mat and greeted Gretchen, who waved her behind the counter and through the open doorway.

Serena stood in the storage room unfurling a mass of glittery gold ribbon, clouds of sparkles forming around her.

"Don't inhale. You might get glitter dust poisoning." Mattie waved a hand, fanning the air.

She whirled around. "You're hilarious. Come breathe in the dust with me."

A large intricately looped gold bow sat on the nearby table. A dozen more would have to be made to put on the tree and each lamppost in the town square.

Mattie grimaced. "I still don't know how you do these so perfectly. I'm not going to be much help, but put me to work anyway."

Serena handed over a pair of scissors. "You can measure the ribbon and cut. I'll make the bows."

With a flourish, Mattie did so until Serena had enough ribbon for all the bows and a few more completed ones had appeared on the table. Mattie scratched her forehead. "I think I need coffee."

"That makes us both," Serena said, then laughed when she looked at Mattie.

"What?"

With mirth in her eyes, she pointed to Mattie's face. "You look like you stepped out of our junior high years with the roll-on glitter trend."

Mattie snorted and nearly wiped her cheeks with her hands but realized they were coated in glitter, which would only make it worse. "We don't need that fad back. Though, I do remember the glitter being scented, which was nice." She grinned and headed to the restroom to see about de-glittering herself.

When she rounded the counter, Paul sat at the corner table with a male student. He was likely tutoring French. He smiled at the teenager, then pointed to the open book on the table and annunciated a phrase. The student nodded and repeated it.

The way Paul spoke, encouraged the student, and focused on him rather than the task warmed her heart. He really did care about his students, and his passion for teaching and the French language were evident—a perfect pairing like coffee and a chocolate-filled croissant.

She thought of the day before, rushing off from the market. Why had she reacted that way? He always offered to help, this time with stall placement and French tutoring. She didn't need his assistance though, but did she want it?

Either way, Mattie knew she shouldn't have run off—a childish move.

She studied the glass display case, an idea taking shape, a peace offering.

———◆———

Paul repeated the phrase, and Cory copied it, nearly perfectly. He smiled at the student and directed him to a brief exercise to further practice the verb tense.

Movement toward their table caught his eye. He looked up to see Mattie approach him holding a coffee cup and a croissant on a plate. He hadn't ordered anything. He also hadn't known she was there.

She held out the coffee and plate toward him. "I thought you could use this."

A slight determination held within her green eyes but maybe also a question too. Why was she doing this?

Paul didn't ask, thanking her instead. He noted a streak of gold glitter across her cheek and sprinkled across her navy blouse.

"The glitter is a nice touch." A corner of his mouth rose, then he peered at her curiously. "Wasn't that a thing when we were in school? Girls smearing themselves with glitter."

Mattie laughed and turned to Serena at the counter, who grinned at him. "See, even Paul remembers." Then she met his gaze, held it for the slightest moment, revealing a hint of uncertainty, before she remarked she'd see him at the market in an hour, and headed for the bathroom.

He sipped the coffee—an Americano. Just as he liked it. She had paid attention. Then he tried to shift Mattie from his thoughts and finish Cory's session.

Paul still thought about the gesture while he and Cameron unloaded market stalls with a small tractor and Mattie snapped photos with her phone for the market's social media. Her gaze had lingered on him, or had it? Was he reading everything wrong?

The snow had started again, and the flakes swirled around her, coating her not unlike the glitter earlier. She met his eyes and smiled, and he nearly forgot to keep his hands firmly on the stall while Cameron operated the tractor, sliding the stall to the ground and in its designated space.

When the stall was in place, he glanced at Cameron, who glared at him, then looked over at Mattie and back again. "What about that lack of love life now?"

Cameron apparently hadn't forgotten their talk about Mattie the night before, and he *was* reading too much into it.

"A love life?" Paul cleared his throat. If only he could clear his feelings toward Mattie as easily. "I don't think I'll be here long enough for that."

Mattie had moved closer to them. "Leaving so soon?" Her voice was tinged with surprise and a hint of disapproval, her face void of emotion.

Paul shrugged. Maybe it was best to tell the truth. Be open about it. "I'm not sure yet, but I have a few job offers in New Orleans, Baton Rouge, and in other states. I want to keep my options open."

He needed to stop talking. He didn't have to defend his decision or gain her approval. He'd given it almost a year in Moreau, and nothing had changed, no breakthroughs at home, and he wasn't sure there would ever be.

"Oh, I see," she stated, focusing on her phone again.

Paul shrugged. "Yeah."

The word sounded lame, and for a moment, the thought of leaving seemed like a mistake, but being back in this town resurfaced all the old hurts of not measuring up. If he left again, he could go somewhere new and start over. He could go where no one knew his past or his father.

He could be someone else.

"I forgot to tell you I heard from Mr. Vachon's office," Cameron said, looking between Paul and Mattie. "He's interested in our proposal and will be in touch soon."

"What great news," Mattie said with a smile at Cameron that sent a pang of longing through Paul, wishing to be the recipient.

Cameron was efficient and loyal like Mattie. He wasn't from their community, but he had woven into its seams in no time. The two of them together would be a force to be reckoned with for sure—the power couple of Moreau.

Paul let that thought die and turned back to the matter at hand. He helped Cameron finish unloading the stalls.

Cameron's phone beeped. He checked it, then looked at Mattie. "Sorry, but I've got a job. Sounds like it can't wait until tomorrow." He turned to Paul. "Would you mind taking Mattie to pick up the tree and garlands in Hawkins?"

Mattie frowned.

Paul hesitated. It was clear Mattie didn't like the change of plans. But they didn't have much choice. He nodded. "Yeah, I can do that. And you can borrow my car." He tossed the keys to Cameron, who caught them in one hand.

"Thanks, man. Appreciate it." Cameron grabbed a toolbox and a few other things from his truck and headed for the car.

Paul swallowed hard. This chance was what he needed to spend one-on-one time with Mattie, get her away from their hometown and its stifling familiarity and reminders. He needed to know if he was imagining something between them, and just maybe he could get to know *her* a little better.

Not just her checklist.

Chapter Five

Mattie glared at Cameron's retreating form. He'd been quick to abandon her to Perfect Paul, and Paul hadn't hesitated.

It wasn't that she needed Cameron to pick up the tree and garlands, but she was comfortable with him. A half hour drive with Paul was about the last thing she cared to do.

Paul cleared his throat, and she realized he held the passenger door open. "Care to make like a tree and leaf?"

Her frown deepening, Mattie strode toward him. "Is that what you call a joke? Because I can see why your career in comedy didn't take off."

He laughed, full and deep, the sound surprising her and more so that she enjoyed it. "No, if I'd told a joke, it'd likely be worse and probably involve an alligator crossing the road."

She scooted onto the truck seat and turned to him. "An alligator? Don't you mean a chicken?"

The side of his mouth lifted, his eyes full of mirth. "No, the alligator ate the chicken," he said and shut the door.

Mattie bit back a smile.

Paul clambered inside and started the truck, a hint of amusement still on his face.

As he maneuvered the truck and trailer from the square and through town, she checked the stack of flyers in her bag. "We'll go to Turnage's first and then pass out flyers in Hawkins. Okay?"

He nodded and kept his eyes on the road. The hum of the engine and gusts of wind beating the truck were the only sounds.

No more jokes? Mattie almost asked, but she kept the thought to herself. Instead, she scrolled her list and nearly rattled off the next day's to-do items, yet she hesitated.

Silence followed as the town's houses and shops shifted to darker countryside backlit by a sky full of stars. After realizing she sat board straight in her seat as if anticipating something, Mattie relaxed her shoulders, leaning back a bit.

She longed to break the quiet but couldn't think of a thing to say. Paul seemed content to focus on the road.

Music would work. "Mind if I play a few Christmas songs?"

"Sure" was his reply, so she hooked her phone up to the sound system and clicked on her favorite carol, "O Come All Ye Faithful." The rendition featured an old-time "crooner" as Granny would say, and Mattie thought of listening to the record with her grandpa this time of year. He always said the song was simple but profound with its message for the faithful to come and adore Christ.

She allowed the words to wash over her mind and heart. Could something as deep as faith be gained by simply coming and adoring? The song made it seem so.

A more upbeat version blasted through the speakers next, and after a moment, Paul glanced her way. "Is this the same song?"

Mattie looked at the phone, and indeed it was, this time in powerhouse ballad–style. She offered a half smile. "It's my favorite."

"It's a good one," he added and returned to ignoring her.

When the song ended, Mattie tapped her phone and an a cappella group sang next.

Paul peered sideways at her through narrowed eyes. "A third version? Really?"

With a smirk, she tapped SHUFFLE on the playlist and a completely different song started. "Okay. I admit the last one was on purpose."

His eyes took on that air of amusement again. "Good, because for a minute there it felt like I was caught in between *The Twilight Zone* and *Groundhog Day*."

A light laugh escaped Mattie, lessening the awkward atmosphere and bringing a memory to the forefront of her mind. "Remember hayride caroling every year with our church youth group?"

"Yeah, but I haven't thought about that in a long time. Do they still do it?"

"They do. Not much changes in Moreau."

"I'm aware," he said, his forehead creasing, a hint of sarcasm in his voice.

What did Paul mean? Did he want the town to change? Because Mattie sure didn't. She hoped its charm and simple beauty would help welcome more visitors to its streets and shops and to the market.

Paul broke through her thoughts. "Do you remember when Jared fell backward off the trailer during the hayride? We must have been about thirteen."

She did remember, and also that her mom was alive and her parents were still together.

He continued, "Jared was sitting on the edge, and when Mr. Bordelon took off a little too fast, he flipped right off—thankfully into a pile of hay."

"I remember! We had to yell for Mr. Bordelon to stop the truck so we could get Jared back on."

The memory stirred many others of Christmastime in their hometown. "What do you like most about Christmas? I think one thing for me has always been the community events and my family's gatherings."

Paul's hands gripped the steering wheel tighter, his knuckles white. "I don't really get into Christmas. Usually."

Mattie studied him. What was going on between Paul and his family?

Mayor Ammons seemed like the ideal dad, doing so much for others, doting on his family, and leading the town. He was everything her dad hadn't been, namely, there when she needed him the most. But she had always sensed something was off between Paul and his dad. Though she couldn't place what it was or why.

She didn't plan to bring it up—or voice her opinion that with his family so connected to Moreau, he should care more about it. Clearly, he didn't since he was planning to leave.

Then again, he *did* care about his students and teaching, as proven at the Press. Not to mention, he seemed awfully good at it.

The sign for Turnage's Tree Farm appeared ahead, and Paul slowed to turn into the large lot. Mattie wrapped her scarf tighter around her neck, slipped on her gloves, and pulled her knit hat farther down to prepare for the blast of icy air that met her outside.

Joe came forward with a smile. She introduced Paul to the older man, who had taken over the tree lot five years earlier. "Here for the Moreau Christmas Market, I gather? I've got the garlands ready."

"Thank you," Mattie said, consulting her phone. "What should we do first? Load the garlands or pick out the tree?"

He looked from Paul to her with a gleam in his eyes. "Why don't you two choose a tree while I get the garlands ready to load?"

"Sure" was Mattie's reply as she tried not to peer at him curiously. What was that look for?

Paul gestured toward the long rows of shaggy trees dusted with snow like some enchanted forest lit by white stringed lights zigzagging overhead. "After you," he said with a subtle smile.

Mattie strolled forward, glancing at the full boughs of each towering fir. Reaching out, she touched the nearest one with her gloved fingers and surveyed dozens of others standing at attention. Memories flooded her of being a young child and her dad carrying her on his shoulders while they walked through the trees as a family. She blinked back tears.

Paul's voice broke through her recollections of Christmases past. "What exactly are we looking for?" He glanced around him. "They all look the same to me."

Mattie peered at the next one, inspecting it. "Not up on your tree appraisal skills?"

He shook his head. "We've never had a real tree. My mom is allergic."

"That's too bad." Mattie met his gaze. "It was always a fun tradition coming to choose one to bring home and decorate."

She brushed aside those moments from the past, what had been for what was, and charged down the row, pointing out a few trees she liked and why with Paul following along.

Mattie paused at the base of a fuller tree that was one of the tallest on the lot, her gaze trailing to its top, where she envisioned a gold metallic star. She turned to Paul to ask what he thought of it when a gust of freezing wind swept through, knocking a clump of snow off the tree onto her head and down her neck.

She yelped from the shock and sting of the bitter cold. In a fury, she dusted it off.

When a burst of male laughter sounded, she whirled to glare at Paul, who to his credit was trying to stifle his amusement, but it clearly wasn't working.

Mattie thrust her hands on her hips, frustration mounting; then she pushed the emotion to action, scooping snow into her gloved hands.

"Let's see how you like snow in your face, Paul Ammons!" She hurled a snowball with precision at his chest. It exploded on target, icy powder spraying his face.

Paul jumped back with a stunned expression as he cleared the snow away. But a split second later, he ducked, gathered a fistful of snow, and threw it at Mattie, who sidestepped so it hit her arm. She scooped up more and flung it at him before ducking around the tree.

He rounded the other side with snowballs in each hand, but she was ready for him with her own. He laughed when she pegged him on the shoulder and leg, and she grinned after dodging one and being hit in the side with the other.

The fight ensued as Mattie sneaked behind him and crushed a snowball onto his neck. He danced around a moment to remove it and retaliated with a huge powdery heap of snow thrown her way.

A voice stopped their next move. It was Joe. "Hold your fire, if you will," he said with hands raised in surrender. He grinned, looking between her and Paul as if noting something important. "Is this the tree you want?"

She looked from Paul to the tree with a broad smile, the cold kissing her cheeks, anticipation thrumming through her. "Yes, I think it's perfect."

Mattie could imagine its place of prominence in the town square, lit up and sparkling, a finishing touch to all the details she'd meticulously planned for months.

The market would be a success. She just knew it.

———◆———

The scene was as picture perfect as Paul had ever seen, with Mattie grinning at the tree as snow whirled around her.

He couldn't look away even after Joe asked him to back up the trailer.

Mattie met Paul's eyes, her smile lessening. "We'd better get this one loaded and move on to Hawkins." She followed Joe while Paul went for the truck.

Whatever magic happened during the snowball fight, he wanted it back. He couldn't think of a moment he'd enjoyed more. He also couldn't think of a time when Mattie had let her composure slip. She was not one for spontaneity—or dare he say *fun*. This glimpse of a warmer side of her toward him suggested maybe the icy barrier between them had started to thaw. He could only hope.

With only a little difficulty, he backed the trailer to where Joe motioned. It had been a long time since he had driven a truck, much less backed up a trailer, probably the summer job helping Mr. Bordelon on his farm. He'd been out of his element, preferring academics to manual labor, but doing the physical work had been good.

When he got out of the truck, Mattie was speaking to Joe, who listened intently, while two teenage boys carried garlands to the front of the trailer. He joined them, and they tied them down with string.

A man and two more teenage boys brought the tree, and Paul helped secure it on the trailer. He thanked them and shook Joe's hand as Mattie climbed into the truck, her focus on her phone and that absurd list.

"I hope the market helps the town," Joe said, surveying the trailer load and nodding toward Mattie. "She drives a hard bargain. If she's the one heading it up, I think it'll go just fine."

With a nod, Paul said, "I have no doubts."

"You two been together long?"

Paul sputtered, "Uh, well, we're not together."

The man's eyes held a knowing gleam. "My mistake." But he seemed to see something between them. *Was* there something?

Mattie was acting very *Mattie*, besides the fleeting moment choosing the tree. He shook his head, snow falling from his hair, and trudged to the truck.

No, he wouldn't read into it.

And on the short drive to Hawkins, Mattie acted like nothing had happened at the tree lot other than a business transaction.

He didn't say much, still thinking about what Joe said despite his determination not to think about it. Maybe if he bought some more time with Mattie, he could figure out where they stood, but first they'd take care of her next task of the evening.

Paul parked the truck and trailer in an empty lot at the edge of Hawkins. Mattie handed him a stack of flyers from her tote bag and pulled on her gloves. They rounded the corner of a brick building, their boots crunching in the thin layer of snow still on the sidewalks.

The town was slightly larger than Moreau but only by a few hundred people. The setup was completely different. He hadn't been to Hawkins in years, and the town had made some improvements to their downtown with empty storefronts now housing new businesses.

Where Moreau's downtown shops formed more of a straight line facing the river with the market square nearer the water, Hawkins' downtown clustered around a small town square with a gazebo and the blocks of shops spread out from it.

Ahead, the gazebo was wrapped in white lights, and more strands spread in different directions from the roof, connecting with ornate wrought-iron, vintage-style lampposts that edged the area.

Paul glanced at Mattie, who stared ahead, her focus not on her phone for once but on the square. "Whoa. We need another gazebo." She met his eyes. "Think you and Cameron could build one by Friday?"

He raised his eyebrows. "Certainly. One of those can simply be thrown together. The real matter, though, is where would we put it? He's already rebuilding the one in the chapel courtyard."

Mattie's eyes hinted at her amusement along with the ghost of a smile on her lips. "Oh, I would toss it somewhere." She returned to the scene before them. "No, the gazebo in town square is Hawkins' thing. They've done a fantastic job revitalizing this area. I've watched the progress over the past five years. I want this for Moreau, Paul. I want to see it thrive again."

He nodded, and she continued, "Granny used to tell me the most wonderful stories of growing up in Moreau in the 1950s—of community dances and church picnics and talent shows. It sounded straight out of Mayberry. She told me about the time a pig got loose in the community center."

The excitement in her voice and the way her green eyes lit while telling the story drew him in.

"The doors were all open back then, trying to catch a breeze, and a squealing pig ran inside and started weaving through the dancers' legs. 'Causing quite a ruckus' were Granny's exact words." She shot a look in his direction. "It reminded me of the town ordinance about the pig you told me about."

Paul grinned. "Maybe something like that happening is why there is an ordinance. I haven't come across any about pigs being banned from dances, but I bet it's in there somewhere."

Mattie paused in front of the gazebo and turned to him. "It might be." She held his gaze, and he held hers, clinging to the camaraderie between them, but then she was back to business. "I think we should start passing out flyers on the opposite end of this street and work our way back. You take one side, and I'll take the other. We'll meet at the gazebo in half an hour."

"That's fine," Paul said, and what else was he supposed to say? He started on his side of the street and Mattie on hers until they finished. During the task, he had come up with a plan to buy more time if only she would go for it.

He looked at his watch, then at her. "The Italian place smelled really good when I dropped off their flyer. I didn't eat much for lunch, and I thought since we finished fairly quickly that you might want to get something to eat. While we're here and all."

He mangled the suggestion, but it was out, and Mattie would do with it what she would. She peeked at her phone and shrugged. "That's fine."

Paul hadn't been to this restaurant in years, but it still likely held the most date night potential in town. Did he want it to be a date?

If he was being honest, he did.

Mattie wouldn't consider it as such. For one, it was with him, and two, it hadn't been on her schedule for at least two weeks prior. Even veering slightly off her curated to-do list seemed to irritate her—or maybe it was only him.

Here was his chance to get to know her better. They were away from Moreau and alone. She wasn't in her element, so maybe her guard would come down.

The Italian House Restaurant's street-facing windows cast a welcoming glow on their path, and more white lights formed a canopy overhead, guiding them to the front door, which Paul opened.

A rush of warmth mingled with the tantalizing scents of garlic bread and marinara washed over him. His stomach growled as he helped Mattie out of her coat.

She peeked back at him. "You *are* hungry. I am too, honestly. The food smells wonderful."

He smiled, and so did she, their gazes holding until the hostess welcomed them, and they were shown to a table for two tucked in the corner with a full view of the snow-covered street. A single candle in a glass jar flickered in the middle of the small round table with a red-checkered tablecloth, and Paul noticed several couples holding hands.

Totally a date place even for a Tuesday night. Mattie had to notice.

He snuck a glance at her as they took their seats. She smoothed her cream-colored sweater, cast a quick look around the room, and straightened in her chair.

Their eyes met, the dim lighting casting her face half in shadow, an unmistakable intimate feel to the ambience. Her green eyes sparked with a hint of surprise; then she focused on her phone.

"I'll email flyers to all the area towns tomorrow and ask them to post on their social media. I may go to Nesmith to pass out flyers."

Resigned, Paul settled back in his chair with a sigh. "Mattie, can we have a conversation that doesn't revolve around a list, a plan, or an event?"

She dropped her phone into her purse and gave him a pointed look. "Well, since you're such a great conversationalist, what would *you* like to talk about?"

He chuckled, thinking of a topic to discuss, but after a few seconds, he threw up his hands. "I don't know."

Mattie laughed. "See? Neither of us is good at this."

"True." He leaned slightly forward. "But there must be something we can talk about besides taking care of the town."

Any trace of mirth left her face. "Well, someone has to take care of it."

He couldn't help but press her. She was not the only person in Moreau. "But why does that have to be you, Mattie?"

"I don't know. It just does." She waved at the menu, a bite to her words. "We need to order and get back."

But Paul wasn't finished. He knew what he wanted to talk about now. "Why do you care so much about Moreau? Truly. Beyond your family's legacy."

She hesitated, perhaps not used to being interviewed. She clearly liked to be the one asking the questions, steering the conversation.

"Why would I not care about my home?" She deflected his question in classic reporter-style.

The waitress arrived, the tension lessening slightly, as she poured water and took their orders, which he noted were the same chicken parmigiana special.

So they had two things in common: hometown and love of that dish. Not exactly encouraging, and Mattie seemed to be more on edge than ever.

But seriously, why did she care so much? He got it that Moreau was her hometown, but no one else in Moreau was working as hard.

Even his father didn't quite reach her level of devotion, and Paul knew firsthand how strong his father's devotion was to the town.

Mattie's motivation intimidated him, if he were honest. She pushed to excel and exceed expectation. But why? No one was pressuring her to do so. Were they?

Their food arrived, and he felt he had one more chance to connect with her. He had always felt the town's eyes on him because of his father being the mayor, and he thought maybe the pressure that had driven him away from Moreau was what also drove her being part of the founding family of the town.

"I just thought you might understand."

Her response was swift. "Understand what? Why you left and want to leave again?"

Her wall was up once more. He had lost his window. "Never mind. It doesn't matter."

That wasn't the truth. It *did* matter, and Paul wanted Mattie to understand, longed for her to. But how could he expect to help break down a wall when he didn't know why it was there in the first place?

Chapter Six

With the crunch of her boots on the snow-covered concrete, Mattie strode to the back door of the Press. She'd risen earlier than usual, and the shop wasn't open yet. She was restless and wasn't sure why.

Okay, that wasn't exactly true. She had an inkling of an idea, but she didn't want to admit it had anything to do with the night before and a certain someone.

The door was unlocked, so Mattie slipped inside the back storage room. Warmth and the delicious aromas of fresh baked goods met her, and she slipped out of her coat and hat, tossing them over a chair.

She walked into the kitchen to see Serena stirring a huge bowl of icing.

Her friend looked up, startled, and raised the spatula like a weapon before relaxing when she saw it was Mattie.

"You're as stealthy as a ninja." Serena shot her an exaggerated glare. "I need to put a bell on the back door."

Mattie plopped onto a stool at the end of the long silver industrial table. "Sorry. I wasn't trying to be stealthy."

Serena glanced at the wall clock and back at Mattie with concern. "It's barely six thirty. What's going on? You're never up this early."

Mattie shrugged. "I don't know. Just couldn't sleep, and I've got so much to do, I thought I might as well get going."

Serena set down the spatula and took the stool next to Mattie. "Yeah, something's definitely up." A look of recognition passed over her features. "This is about Paul and your outing last night, isn't it?"

How could Serena read her like a book? Mattie bit back a groan. She hadn't told her about their dinner. She'd only texted her the change in plans with Paul stepping in for Cameron.

Serena wasn't letting her off the hook. She fixed her with a stern look. "What happened? Spill it."

"Well. . ." Mattie considered her next words carefully. "We went to the tree lot and found the perfect tree, had a snowball fight, passed out flyers in Hawkins, ate at the Italian House, and came back. That was all." The last bit came out rather quickly.

"You and Paul had dinner at that romantic Italian restaurant in Hawkins?" Serena's jaw dropped. "You had a date with Paul Ammons!"

"It was *not* a date!" Mattie clarified. Though, her voice wasn't very convincing. "We were running town errands."

"That ended in dinner?" Her friend narrowed her eyes. "Yeah, right."

Mattie shrugged and grabbed a small spatula, rolling it around in her hands. "Well, it was nothing."

Serena looked at her as if she had caught her about to confess something. "Nothing, huh? You're up before seven and sitting in my kitchen fiddling with cooking utensils. Definitely not nothing."

Mattie dropped the spatula onto the table and stood, pacing, then faced Serena. "Okay, maybe it is something. I don't know." She sat again. "At dinner, Paul turned the conversation in a more serious direction and seemed about to discuss an important subject when I responded a little harshly, and maybe I'm regretting it."

Serena folded her arms on the table. "I see. Go on."

Mattie swallowed hard. "The snowball fight was unexpected. Going to dinner even more so. We were just supposed to do errands. Not any extra stuff. I was off guard, unbalanced."

"You clearly still are."

Mattie ignored the comment. "These past months we've had to work together—well, it hasn't been quite as difficult as I thought it would be. And maybe he's growing on me."

Serena's face brightened. "I knew it! You like him."

Mattie held up her hands. "I can't like him, though. He's *Paul*. There's a lot of water under the bridge between us."

"That was ten years ago, Mattie. I think the water is dry by now."

"Yeah, I guess. But maybe I'm afraid to like him. He doesn't plan to stick around. I overheard him tell Cameron he has job options out of state."

Serena offered a small smile. "Maybe he'll change his mind."

Mattie shook her head. "I doubt it. He left once already, remember? I don't know what would keep him here. Water under the bridge or not. He's leaving."

She couldn't keep the others there either. Would everyone leave her? Her dad. . .her mom. . .her uncle. Even Jolene had been gone for years.

Serena nodded as she stood. "Let's get you a latte so you can go on with your busy day."

Mattie thanked her friend, and within a few minutes, she was on her way down Chapel Street with a coffee in hand, their conversation replaying in her mind.

She couldn't *like* Paul. It made no sense, and he didn't fit into her ordered world.

Mattie unlocked the *Gazette* and busied herself with work in the quiet office. At eight she headed to town hall on her first official errand of the day. Granny texted her with another to add to the list—stopping by the grocery store.

She entered town hall and greeted Mrs. Walker, who waved her to the back of the building.

Mayor Ammons was there surveying the huge wooden letters propped against the storage room's walls. He greeted her and waved his hand toward the display. "I think Robby has outdone himself. These are fantastic."

Mattie smiled and studied the intricately carved letters that spelled out M-O-R-E-A-U. "They're wonderful."

The idea had come from seeing online photos of tourists posing with giant letter displays set up in European cities. Robby Pickett, the town's resident woodworker with Robby's Rustic Creations, had agreed to take on the project. He also had a market stall to sell his hand-carved toys and other items.

"The town crew will install them in the square this afternoon," the mayor said with a nod. "They'll put in two spotlights as well."

"Thank you. That'll be great. Cameron and Paul will unload the tree and garlands too. And the elementary students will decorate ornaments this afternoon in the square."

"I'll have the crew set out tables and standing heaters after lunch tomorrow. Is there anything else you need?" Mayor Ammons asked with a smile.

"Let me see." Mattie scanned the list on her phone. "Oh yeah, I need to check with Chief Manning to see if he would have an officer patrol the market throughout the day but especially at night. Don't want anyone getting into trouble there."

"We certainly don't. I'll take care of it."

"I appreciate it. That's another thing off my list."

The mayor was efficient and didn't spare any detail when accomplishing something. She related to him. But he was very different from his son.

She wondered about their relationship. Paul never seemed quite comfortable in his dad's presence. She'd noticed that over the months of committee meetings. Was it because they were so different?

Maybe she could find out.

She focused on the mayor. "Paul has been a great help with the market."

Mayor Ammons nodded. "I'm glad to hear it. I wasn't sure at first about putting him on the committee, but I'm glad he's proven useful."

Interesting admission. She pressed on, watching for any change in his demeanor as if she were reading someone for an interview. She dropped the bait.

"Yes, and he seems to be great at teaching. I saw him in a tutoring session at the Press. He really cares about his students. It's a shame he's planning to leave. We need more teachers like him here."

Mayor Ammons' eyebrows rose. "Leaving? What do you mean?"

Mattie frowned, taken aback at the mayor's surprised reaction. Paul hadn't told his dad about looking for another job? She sputtered, "I, uh, he mentioned having a few job options." She shrugged, trying to soften the situation. "It may not be anything serious."

She could have kicked herself. She'd spilled the beans and hadn't known it. Paul would not be happy when he found out. But on the other hand, why was he keeping his dad in the dark on such important decisions?

Mayor Ammons still looked troubled when she hastily said she had to get going and left the town hall as quickly as she could.

After a trip to the grocery store for Granny, Mattie was relieved to step into the cozy, inviting hallway of the Lavigne House. She hung her coat on a hook by the door and headed for the kitchen with the groceries. She stopped when she heard a rustling noise coming from the sitting room.

She peeked around the wide opening to see Granny fluffing and tucking the garland on the fireplace mantel.

"Granny," Mattie whispered, a slight tone of reprimand in her voice, "Aunt Adale is going to come unglued if you're messing with her decorations."

Granny whirled, hands raised like she was caught at a crime scene. "I'm done. A few things needed fixin,' that's all." She glanced around the room with satisfaction.

Mattie could tell she had rearranged several items. Aunt Adale would not be pleased.

Holding up the grocery bags, Mattie met Granny's eyes. "I got the items you wanted."

Granny clapped her hands together. "Good. To the kitchen, then. I'll get the crawfish étouffée going."

"Sounds good, Granny. You know it's my favorite."

With a nod, she marched past Mattie and led the way to the back of the house.

Mattie set the bags on the counter and started unloading. She had one more chance to get something out of Granny for the story.

She might as well throw out a question and try to catch her off guard. "The party's coming up quick, isn't it? What do you think about that?"

Granny waved a hand. "I'm not too bothered. Though the town making such a big deal out of me turning eighty doesn't seem right. I'm just living my life. I don't need celebrating, but it's nice of everyone just the same."

"Aha!" Mattie typed away into her phone. "A direct quote from the honoree herself. Check!"

Granny frowned. "You think you're a clever little fox. Well, you got some words for the story. That's all it's going to be, though." She placed a cutting board on the counter with a sly smile. "I'm forgetting. How was your date last night?"

It was Mattie's turn to frown. "What date?"

Her grandmother tilted her head, a false air of innocence in her expression. "I bought you and that handsome teacher some alone time. You were out late too, so I assume he took you to dinner."

Mattie's jaw dropped, the pieces falling into place. "Granny! You were the one who texted Cameron?"

She shrugged, but the ghost of a smile on her lips told the truth. She had a hand in all of it. "I heard some strange noises coming from the plumbing in my bathroom and thought he might need to take a look."

The sigh that escaped Mattie's lips was long and loud. "Granny, would you please stop playing matchmaker?"

Granny said nothing and turned back to her cooking.

Mattie pressed her lips together. She couldn't believe her grandmother was ultimately behind her and Paul's dinner, which had absolutely, positively not been a date.

———◆———

The bell sounded, and Paul reminded his final-hour French students not to forget meeting at the Christmas market the next two afternoons.

He followed the students out and headed down the hall toward the teachers' lounge, sidestepping two students carrying a large bass drum toward the music room. A framed photograph caught his eye in the display case—a photo of the senior officers from his graduating class. He as the vice president stood beside Mattie, the president.

The set in her shoulders and determination in her eyes were the same. Ten years hadn't changed that in her.

He'd had such a crush on her, but she had seemed barely able to stand him, especially after he beat her out of the scholarship for the summer in France. He had to admit he had been borderline arrogant after the announcement.

Paul sighed. He remembered the day well. He had mustered all his courage to ask her to the prom, but it had backfired. If he could take some things back, he would. He wasn't that arrogant teen anymore. He had grown up. Couldn't Mattie see that? But maybe she only saw him how he was then.

Should he apologize?

No, on second thought, it was better to leave the past alone. It could make things worse.

An idea came to him, a gesture that might break down a brick or two from her protective wall.

Paul found Julie in the choir room prepping for her next lesson. He knocked on the open door, and she looked up from her laptop and smiled.

"Hi, Paul. What brings you to my door?"

"Just checking in. Are you all set for choir rehearsal this afternoon?"

She rose and met him at the door. "Yeah, we'll practice here before heading over."

"Sounds good." Paul rubbed his neck. He didn't want to set Julie or the choir back by his request, but he had to try. "I was thinking about the songs we picked out for the choir to perform. Would it be okay to add one back in? If it's no trouble."

"Sure," Julie said a little too eager. "Which one?"

Paul relaxed his shoulders. "I thought it might be nice to add 'O Come All Ye Faithful' into the mix. It's a classic."

He didn't, of course, mention that the reason for the change was a certain person.

Julie nodded. "No problem. It's a simpler song, and it will already be in our school performance." She rushed to her desk and jotted a note. "I've got it down."

He thanked her and grinned, relief filling him. Mattie had to notice the song. He would make sure she did.

Suddenly he felt ridiculous, as if calling in a song request to a radio DJ for a special someone. Would it make a difference?

He shook the thought away, told Julie he'd see her later, and headed to the market.

Mattie was already there, sorting through supplies in cardboard boxes to prepare for the ornament making. She greeted him but continued working. "I've got four stations set up—one for each ornament. The kids will rotate every fifteen minutes." She lifted a pine cone coated in gold glitter. "They'll make one like this and paint a wooden snowflake, decorate a plastic candy cane, and string jingle bells together in the shape of a wreath."

Paul nodded. "I'll assign a few of my students to each station, and the school choir will be here to rehearse at five."

"Great." She studied her phone. "I haven't heard from Cameron about unloading the tree. Have you—"

"I checked with him earlier," Paul cut in. "He'll be here any moment."

Mattie looked up, a hint of surprise in her green eyes. "Good."

"I'll turn on the heaters too. They may take a while to warm up, and I'll be ready when Cameron arrives. A few of my students will help us unload and secure the tree."

"That would be great." She pointed to several cardboard boxes in the middle of the square where the tree would go. "The strands of lights and the extension cords are in those boxes."

Paul nodded. "Cameron is bringing the concrete base we made for the tree. We'll anchor a few branches beneath it with weights as a safety measure."

"That's a good idea. We certainly don't want it to topple over." She surveyed the table. "The kids will secure their ornaments to the branches with thin wire looped through the string hanger on each one and wrapped around the branch. It was the best thing I could think of to secure ornaments on an outdoor tree in the elements."

Paul moved across from her, noticing how her fingers gripped the clipboard. He could nearly read her mind as she agonized over what could go wrong. It took all his restraint not to reach across the table and place reassuring hands on hers.

Instead, he shoved his hands into his coat pockets and chided himself for having the thought. She would not react positively if he did anything of the sort.

Mattie met his eyes, and he held her gaze for a long moment. Then Cameron arrived and backed up the trailer, the moment lost. Paul headed to help him, and a dozen of his students showed up in the next few minutes. The square was a hive of activity as he and

Cameron directed the removal and securing of the tree and unloading of the garlands, storing them in nearby market stalls. He and Cameron straightened the extension cords and carried out the extra security measures for the tree.

When he finally returned, Mattie was showing the students each of the ornament stations for later that afternoon. He organized them to unpack the boxes and sort the strands of lights.

His student Jacey asked if they could have music, so he started his usual music streaming app and browsed the playlists. He nudged Mattie with his elbow. "Here's a playlist for popular songs from high school."

Jacey cringed and stated matter-of-factly, "That's *old* music."

Paul met Mattie's amused expression. "Old, huh? Yeah, I forgot when you're out of high school a decade you're practically ancient."

Mattie laughed. "Certainly."

Paul clicked SHUFFLE on the playlist, and the first song that played returned him to high school—a popular love ballad.

Mattie stopped rummaging in a box and looked up. "I remember this being the big song at senior prom. The DJ probably got a dozen requests for it."

Paul frowned, reflecting on that night. He barely remembered who he went with—a girl from their youth group who wanted to go but hadn't been asked. He had no trouble remembering Mattie in a one-shouldered, floor-length navy sequined dress, her long hair hanging in curls, dancing with a guy he didn't know.

"Oh yeah. I remember prom." He paused from untangling lights. Under his breath, he muttered, "I wanted to ask *you*."

Had that been out loud?

Mattie stilled, then turned toward him.

Paul acted as if the group needed his help, striding across the square so he could put a little distance between himself and Mattie.

Obviously, working so closely with her those past days was affecting him more than he cared to admit, because he hadn't thought of senior prom since he was in high school. And why in the world had he said anything now? He could only hope she hadn't heard his admission.

Chapter Seven

Mattie stared at Paul's retreating back as he strode across the square toward another group of students. Had he said what she thought he did?

Paul Ammons had wanted to ask *her* to prom. She'd been convinced he couldn't stand her in high school.

Mattie rushed after him before she thought better of it. "Hey, wait a minute. You can't say something like that and just walk away."

She grabbed his arm. He turned to face her beside the tree, his expression unreadable.

"You wanted to ask *me* to prom? Did I hear you correctly?"

He shrugged and smiled sheepishly. "Maybe you did."

She hadn't heard him wrong. The song played on as they stood looking at each other, something in his eyes holding her to the spot. In a quiet voice, she asked, "Why didn't you?"

Paul ran a hand through his hair and glanced off a moment before his gaze was back on her. "You're not leaving that confession alone, are you?"

She shook her head. "You know I can't. Curiosity."

He laughed, and she found herself smiling. "I guess I opened the can of worms." He touched the edge of a tree branch, his expression sobering. "The day I was going to ask you, we found out who got the France scholarship."

"Oh," Mattie said flatly, the day coming back to her. She had been gutted when he was announced as the recipient. She'd overheard teachers discuss how they thought the selection was likely rigged since he was the mayor's son and two council members were judges.

Mattie realized she was staring, and he looked just as intently at her. He tilted his head. "Would you have said yes?"

She sighed. The answer was no, but for a moment, with him looking at her the way he was, she wished her answer would have been yes. Instead, she said, "That was a long time ago, Paul."

He smiled, but his eyes held a trace of disappointment. "Yes, it was." He resumed his route toward the students and tapped his phone.

The love song stopped without its final verse, the end hanging there like the unraveled threads of time between them.

Paul looked at his students. "I think it's time for something different." He started a Christmas song. "Enough of the past."

Mattie bit back a sigh and finished prepping supplies. She only had to work with Paul a little longer and they could return to acting like they didn't know each other.

Deep down, she knew she should want that—to return to the status quo—but she could only muster a halfhearted smile, trying to shake her own feelings of disappointment.

She turned aside to assist Paul and his students as they draped the large Christmas tree in strands of white lights. She envisioned how everything would look on Friday night for the tree-lighting ceremony that would also light up the displays along the river. She hoped a festive and fun atmosphere would be enjoyed by all.

Serena arrived with the hot chocolate, and Mattie arranged a table with cups, plates, and cookies to serve the children. She could tell Serena wanted to inquire why she wasn't acting a hundred percent herself, but she didn't have time to get into it.

Honestly, it was probably better that she didn't get into it at all.

The elementary students and their families showed up in droves over the next two hours, a welcome distraction. Mattie snapped photos for social media and the newspaper, including pictures of parents wearing more glitter than the pinecones.

The joy the children had making and hanging the ornaments pushed aside Mattie's gloom, and the tree was nothing short of magical with white twinkling lights and the array of wonderful handmade ornaments. She handed out a flyer to each family about the lighting ceremony and other town events in the coming weeks.

The choir came a few minutes later, and she watched Paul greet their former classmate Julie with a grin. Her smile was warm, and Mattie noted how she was pretty, petite, and newly single.

Mattie frowned. Why was she concerned about Paul or Julie? It didn't matter to her what he said or did as long as he fulfilled his part of the committee duties.

The choir was arranged on stage and started with "Silent Night" in French. Mattie paused a moment, listening to the beautiful music and blending of voices. Paul had the idea of involving the choir, and it was a great addition to the market's opening night.

Her phone alerted her to a message. Aunt Adale asked when she was coming by the community center.

Mattie groaned. She had forgotten her aunt wanted to go over the table layout for Granny's party. She'd been so focused on ornament making with the kids and distracted after Paul's confession that she hadn't noted the time.

She should probably tell Paul she would be back in a little while, but when she looked his way, he was locked in conversation with Julie, who tilted her head and laughed at something he said.

Mattie whirled, trying to ignore the negative emotions twisting her insides at the sight of Paul and Julie acting so familiar with each other. It was none of her business. She shot him a text telling him she would be back in an hour and left the square without a backward glance.

The community center was only two blocks away on Rue du Jardin, so the walk wasn't far. She pushed through the double doors and strode down the entrance hall into the main room where her aunt consulted a clipboard, not unlike Mattie herself must look like at the market. They were similar, she and her aunt, with their organization and planning, their high standards and efficiency.

She approached her aunt, who surveyed a sample table setting in Granny's festive party colors of purple, green, and gold, borrowing from the state's Mardi Gras tradition.

Aunt Adale greeted her with a smile before glancing again at the clipboard. "I think purple should be the featured color with green and gold as accents like we discussed last week. What do you think about this setup?"

A long table draped in dark purple cloth held place settings of green plates on gold chargers with matching green linen napkins, gold utensils, and a clear stemmed glass.

"It's perfect. You got the details just right. Granny will love it."

Her aunt put her arm around Mattie with a squeeze. "I think the queen will indeed be pleased."

Mattie returned the squeeze. Yes, Aunt Adale was certainly more likely to be her mother than Jolene's. Her cousin was Granny through and through, which her aunt liked to mention from time to time.

Mattie's mom, Claudia, had fallen somewhere in between the tendencies of her older sister and their mother. She had a creative side like Granny, though hers had leaned toward photography. Mattie's bedroom walls were covered in framed photographs from landscapes to family portraits her mom had taken over the years.

Their family was a unique one, to be sure, with only the women remaining to carry on the town founder's legacy—an honor both daunting and special to Mattie. She would make their town proud and do all she could to save their iconic chapel, the place she hoped to one day walk down the aisle for her very own wedding as so many Lavignes had before her.

First, she had to focus on the market and the celebration of the year honoring their matriarch. For if there was another thing the Lavignes were known for—it was throwing a good party.

———◆———

When the choir started singing "O Come All Ye Faithful," Paul glanced around the square for Mattie. He saw her not long before, cleaning up the ornament-making aftermath along with Serena. He'd helped with the sound system and final pronunciation tweaks, and Julie locked him in conversation over the schedule for Friday night.

He then remembered his phone alerting him to a text message. He checked it, and sure enough, he had one from Mattie. She had probably left on her errand not long after rehearsal began.

He'd hoped she would hear the song and somehow know he arranged it for her, but it was wishful thinking at best. It figured she would go off chasing more of her to-do list when he tried to do something special for her. He'd apparently have to try harder.

The choir finished their rehearsal, and a few vendors came to stock their stalls. He assisted them and made sure everything was locked.

When Mattie returned, she seemed distant, distracted, and he wasn't sure why. She flitted around checking everything twice and rushed off again, saying she had to stop by the house for Granny's famous étouffée before going to her office Christmas party.

Paul took his time going home and trudged upstairs to his garage apartment attached to his parents' house. Their nightly dinners he was expected to attend were at seven thirty sharp, so he had about half an hour. He plopped onto the couch and closed his eyes, his mind going over the day's events, his focus straying to Mattie and his mistake in admitting he wanted to ask her to the prom.

What had made him say it? He rubbed his forehead. All this time with Mattie was messing with his head, dredging up the old feelings and dreams from years before. The whole summer in France he thought of her and wished she could have been there too. But why was he kidding himself? She had probably been thinking about how mad she was that he was in France instead of her.

On second thought, she likely hadn't been thinking of him at all because her mom died that summer.

During a call with his parents, they'd told him the sad news, and he instinctively wanted to rush home to be there for Mattie. But he couldn't explain to his parents why he was wasting his scholarship to return to Moreau, and he was nothing to Mattie except an annoyance. He still felt the same way ten years later.

Mattie had followed him all those years wherever he went whether she wanted to or not. Every woman he dated couldn't compare. His trips home were few, his parents traveling to see him. They joked that it was a package deal—see their son and explore a new place each year, but the thinly veiled criticism still stung. They questioned his unsettled lifestyle and lack of commitment to a school, a state, and a girlfriend.

But he wanted to commit—just not on their terms and not when he couldn't stop thinking about Mattie.

Paul forced himself off the couch and straightened his appearance before going next door. He showed up to dinner with no time to spare and had his usual excuse ready that he had work to do so he could leave right after it ended. His mother hugged him before she settled at the table. His father barely looked at him, which was typical.

The meal was more elaborate than necessary for a simple family dinner, but that was how his father preferred it. There were no casual pizza nights in front of the television for the Ammons household.

The conversation was as stilted as the meal, with his parents chatting about their day and asking Paul the odd question or bringing up his sister and her many achievements.

His mother dabbed her mouth with a linen napkin. "I heard from Katherine. She, Jared, and the kids can't come until the day after Christmas. Obviously, it's disappointing, but the reason is she and Jared have been invited to a Christmas soirée at the governor's mansion." Her face brightened. "Imagine that. Our girl dining with the governor."

With a grin, his father leaned back in his chair. "Katherine is certainly on her way. She'll be working for the governor's office in no time, and this event will provide key connections for Jared's campaign."

Paul stopped eating, his fork hovering over the mashed potatoes, and looked straight at his father. "Meanwhile, your son helped a kid go from straight Ds to an A and led a school-wide assembly on cyberbullying."

His father grunted but went back to eating.

His mother offered him a smile. "That's nice, dear."

There was no use arguing or standing up for himself or his chosen career any further. His accomplishments paled in comparison to Katherine's.

His sister and her family lived a few hours south in the state capital of Baton Rouge, where Katherine worked for the Speaker of the House, and Jared worked as a lawyer and planned to run for the state senate.

Paul hadn't seen them much in the past few years. He would like to get to know his five-year-old niece and two-year-old nephew better, but their parents' fast-paced, tightly scheduled life meant his path didn't cross theirs very often. He would only get in their way, which is why he kept his distance.

He was also convinced nothing would make his father happier than for him to follow in his and Katherine's footsteps to work in politics—the "family business" they'd called it on more than one occasion. Another reason he'd stayed away from Baton Rouge and Moreau, another reminder of his shortcomings.

His sister was a chip off the old block—career driven yet also with a family. His father liked to point out that Paul could have both too. But that's not how Paul saw it. His father's career left him feeling neglected when he was growing up. He didn't want that for his life.

His father turned his attention to Paul with a pointed look. "Is everything going well for the market? Mattie seemed flustered when she came by the office today. But she said you've been a great help."

Paul froze with his fork halfway to his mouth. Mattie had complimented him to his father. "Oh, well, I think it's going fine."

Before he could think further into the matter, his father's demeanor suddenly grew rigid, and it didn't take Paul long to find out the reason.

"Mattie also said you've been looking at jobs in other states."

Paul's stomach dropped. He hadn't wanted to tell his parents yet. Why would Mattie bring it up?

His mother frowned. "I thought you'd finally come home to stay. You've been away a long time."

In an attempt to diffuse the situation, he tempered his response. "I'm just keeping my options open, Mom. I wouldn't want to miss out on a better opportunity."

His father's jaw clenched. It was his mistake to have said that last part. He tensed for the forthcoming lecture.

"A *better* opportunity? What's better than working in your home-town?" His father scoffed. "You haven't stayed anywhere longer than a year, Paul. You've got to put down roots eventually. You should have taken the internship at the French embassy in New Orleans after you came back from France. It would have been a good fit, and you could be on your way to becoming an ambassador."

Paul frowned. Teaching *was* a good fit for him, and it wasn't simply a job but a way he could make a difference. He'd tried to explain to his father, but he didn't understand. *Mayor Ammons* only saw what he thought Paul should have done.

Weariness settled over him, and he wanted to leave the table and the scrutiny. "I'm keeping my options open. I have work to do, so I'll excuse myself. Good night."

He exited the room before either of his parents could say anything.

The urge to leave more than their house welled inside him—leave Moreau, run away to France, put distance between himself and the past. For now he could do what he did most nights when he felt this way. He walked.

As he headed the few blocks toward the river, his father's words kept running through his mind.

No matter what he did, it would never be enough.

Chapter Eight

Laughter ricocheted around the office, and Mattie joined in as Frank danced around the room after beating her and her coworkers at *Trivial Pursuit* for the fifth year in a row.

She'd gone home after the market to eat étouffée and then went to the office for games and snacks for their annual office Christmas party.

"Okay, Frank. I think that's enough of lording over us that you won again." Mattie grinned. "How about we take a break and play *Pictionary?*"

He groaned. The game was his least favorite, which is why, after he beat them at the trivia game, she always suggested it. "Fine. I'll let you rain on my parade. But first I need snacks." He moved to the table of junk food.

Mattie strode to the front of the *Gazette* and turned toward the hallway to the restroom when movement outside the large front window caught her eye.

A tall figure with hunched shoulders and head down strode past. Something about him seemed familiar. She peered out to get a better look at the man. It was Paul.

She frowned. What was Paul doing walking around after nine o'clock? Nothing was open.

Mattie turned back toward her route to the restroom, but she was struck by his posture, the almost dejected way he carried himself.

Something was wrong.

Without a second thought, she rushed to the front door and out into the cold, calling to him.

Paul stopped and turned around. She shivered and waved for him to come. He did so, and it was hard to ignore the determined set of his jaw and the conflict in his expression.

He paused before her, his breath forming a white cloud before his lips.

"What are you doing out here? It's freezing." She shivered again.

A ghost of a smile played on Paul's lips. "You better get back inside before *you* freeze, Mattie."

She grinned, breathing in the biting air, and nodded toward the door, the urge to invite him in and not be alone pressing on her. "Would you like to come in for a bit? We're on the last game of the night, and I could use a new teammate. Frank needs to be kicked from his high horse. What do you say?"

Paul hesitated, glanced at the well-lit office, and met her eyes. "I don't want to intrude on—"

She opened the door. "You're not intruding."

His expression shifted from reluctance to appreciation, and he followed her inside.

Everyone welcomed him without question, and Paul seemed to relax as they played Pictionary amid more laughter.

The genuine warmth Mattie felt toward him surprised her. In that moment, she realized they weren't taking care of a to-do list or prepping for the market. She and Paul weren't committee members taking care of assignments.

They were two people having a good time.

After the game, Paul offered to walk her home, and she accepted, which surprised her again. The boundaries she had created between them were blurring, and she wasn't sure if she should intervene or not.

He held the door open for her, and this time she was bundled in her scarf, hat, and coat when she stepped into the chilly night. Even so, she shivered and walked closer beside Paul.

They crossed the street and turned away from the market square with its stalls standing sentinel over the large Christmas tree at the center. She smiled, imagining it lit and festive with people milling around and the choir singing, which reminded her of Paul and Julie's earlier camaraderie. They obviously saw each other every day since they worked together and had worked closely for the choir performance. Had it brought them closer in a more-than-friends way?

"Don't worry. The market will be a success."

Paul's statement derailed her train of thought. She met his eyes, reassurance in their depths. Her face heated since she hadn't been focused on the market's outcome but him and Julie. She was glad her cheeks were already red from the cold.

She cleared her throat. "Thanks. It'll be what it is."

He laughed. "Yes, it will, but I've never seen you make a wrong move. It'll be fine."

Mattie buried the lower half of her face in her scarf to hide a frown. His faith in her was unmerited. She had certainly made mistakes. Ones she could never make up for no matter how hard she worked or cared for others and the town.

Tears stung her eyes. She blinked them back. No, she couldn't go there. Not back to that summer.

Pushing through the pain, she distracted herself by focusing on Paul as they walked along the quiet, snowy street past storefronts and houses edged in twinkling lights.

She thought about her conversation that morning with Mayor Ammons. Paul didn't seem mad at her, so maybe his dad hadn't mentioned what she'd said. Thinking of her slipup, a lingering question she'd wondered about since he returned to Moreau came to mind.

"Paul, why did you become a teacher? I remember you being set on a political career."

He shoved his hands farther into his pockets, his brow furrowed. "That summer in France, I was there to take classes, but I also volunteered with a group that taught English to immigrant children and their parents. I'd never done something with a profession that truly excited me like teaching did. I knew then it was what I'm supposed to do."

"I'm glad you found your calling in France," Mattie said, and she meant it. Only a trace of bitterness lingered now when thinking of losing out on the scholarship.

"What is it you like most about your job?" She chided herself for playing the reporter, but she genuinely wanted to know.

Paul glanced ahead at the row of homes leading to the Lavigne House. "I want kids to have an adult in their lives who truly cares about them, who sees them."

Mattie admired that. She couldn't help but wonder, did *he* feel that way when he was a teen?

She focused again on his relationship with his dad.

Mayor Ammons was such a nice and caring man. But she felt like the truth of Paul's answer connected to something from his past. She just didn't know what that something was.

"That's a good reason to be a teacher, to do more than teach, and to support the kids," she added when she realized she hadn't responded to his statement. "They're lucky to have you."

Paul offered a small smile, but gratitude shone in his eyes. "Thanks, Mattie."

She glimpsed the Lavigne House and its Christmas tree sparkling through the front window. The house never failed to lift her spirits and bring a sense of belonging every time she returned. Her pace picked up, and Paul matched it as they turned onto the path leading to the porch and approached the red door.

Being walked home felt nice, but what did she do now? Say good night and go inside? Invite him in for hot chocolate?

Thankfully, Paul saved her from having to decide. "Thanks for allowing me to crash the office party. It was quite memorable, especially Frank's dancing."

She laughed. "Frank's something else when on a winning high. Though, we showed him in the end, didn't we?"

Paul nodded. "Yes, we make a good team."

Mattie's smile slipped. She had been thinking the same thing but didn't dare voice it. It was true. They *did* make a good team.

She shifted nervously on the welcome mat. "I'm glad you came." Could the moment get any more awkward?

No sooner had the thought crossed her mind than the door swung open, and she jumped.

Granny took them in with a curious expression and pursed lips. "Why are y'all freezing on the porch? You can ask the man inside, Mattie Marie. We don't bite."

Mattie cringed, but Paul grinned. He held up a hand. "Thank you, Mrs. Marchand, but I've got to get home."

Granny clicked her tongue. "None of this, Mrs. Marchand. Call me Eloise. We're all adults here, Paul Ammons."

His eyes briefly met Mattie's, amusement shining in them. "You're right, Eloise. Though, if my mother hears me address you by your first name, it might get me in trouble."

Granny chuckled. "Your mama will do nothing of the sort. Tell your folks I said hi, won't you? You have a good night." She threw a pointed look at Mattie. "I'll leave y'all to it now."

Leave them to what? Mattie didn't like that conspiratorial look in her grandmother's eyes. It was a meddling one.

Paul rocked back on his heels, hands shoved in his coat pockets. Their eyes met. "She's certainly a character."

"You don't know the half of it." Mattie glanced at the closed door and lowered her voice. "Her belongings are strewn all over the place, and Aunt Adale is having a fit. I'm supposed to be the mediator of sorts. I won't survive it."

Paul laughed. "Do what you can, but let them fight their own battle."

Mattie scoffed. "Easy for you to say. You're not in the war zone."

"True." His grin faltered, a hint of solemnity in his features.

Did he have his own war zone? She nearly asked him, but he stepped backward onto the top step of the porch stairs. "Thanks again for tonight, Mattie. See you tomorrow."

"Good night, Paul," she said as he left. She stood on the porch with her hand on the doorknob watching him walk away and fighting the urge to call him back and ask him—what was the matter?

The question lingered on her mind the next morning while trying to concentrate on finishing Granny's story at the *Gazette*. After she'd reread the first paragraph three times, she nearly gave up but pressed on until she clicked to print.

Mattie grabbed the papers and handed them over to Frank in his office.

"Just in time." He glanced at them a moment, then looked at her. "Your aunt hasn't changed her mind about our date tonight, right?"

"Not that she's said. I think it's still a go. I hope y'all have a good time."

Frank leaned back in his chair and crossed his arms. "Maybe we should make it a double date."

She frowned. "A double date with whom?"

He gave a pointed look to rival Granny. "You and Paul looked awful chummy last night."

"*Frank.* It's not like that with Paul and me." She began to say they were only friends but stopped—because they weren't even that, were they?

Frank shrugged but didn't look convinced in the least.

She had better get out of there before he saw through her thinly veiled defense. "Have fun on your date. Gotta run."

Mattie returned to her desk and emailed the flyers about the Moreau Christmas Market to media outlets across their part of the state, asking them to share the graphic on their social media and attend if possible. She posted on the town's social media page with a countdown leading to tomorrow night's lighting ceremony.

With those tasks complete, Frank's comment once again claimed her focus. *Was* there something between her and Paul that she hadn't seen? She thought about their "non-date." Had he wanted it to be a date? Had he intended for it to be before her mouth got the best of her?

She sighed. There were way more important things to consider at the moment than if Paul liked her in any romantic way.

Besides, there was absolutely *nothing* between herself and Perfect Paul.

———◆———

Paul couldn't shake the night before from his mind as he went through his workday. Mattie was the last person in Moreau he'd expected to step out in the cold and invite him to join a holiday gathering.

But she had, and he'd enjoyed it. She was more relaxed without her clipboard in hand, without a task to accomplish. He hadn't glimpsed that side of her since their impromptu snowball fight at the tree lot.

This morning she was back to clipboard wielding and seemed more focused than ever on their preparation to be ready for tomorrow night's market opening.

He had assembled some of his students to help decorate the market stalls with garlands, ribbon, and lights, and they'd been hard at work for the past hour.

He watched Cory take a twig from a garland and hold it over Alyssa's head. "Oh, what's this? I found mistletoe."

She looked up and darted around the table, then glared at him. "Cory Tanner, don't think you're getting a kiss from me! Besides, that's not real mistletoe."

He simply shrugged and left with a piece of red ribbon and the twig toward a group of girls across the square.

Paul and Mattie stopped working when the episode started and now shared an amused look. Then she started climbing the ladder.

"Careful, Mattie," Paul cautioned. "It's slick."

She proceeded with her climb and straightened the ribbon and lights on the garland edging the stall's roofline. When she took a step down, her foot slipped, and she fell.

Paul lunged and caught her midfall, the impact knocking them both into a pile of greenery.

"*Oof!*" Mattie exclaimed, slamming into him.

Paul groaned, his arms tightening around her.

She twisted to look at him, her hands on his chest. "Paul, are you okay?"

He nodded, drawing in a deep breath. "Someone knocked the air out of me. That's all."

A smile lifted a corner of Mattie's lips. "A consequence of saving me. Thanks."

Paul grinned up at her, enjoying their nearness, the feel of her in his arms.

Mattie stilled, a curious glint in her eyes; then it was gone as fast as it appeared. She edged back and flopped a garland onto his chest. "Paul Ammons, let me go! This rescue is over."

With a laugh, he released her, and they scrambled to their feet. As he turned away toward the nearest group of students, he could have sworn her face held a tender expression, and when he glanced back at her, she swiftly looked away as if she had been watching him.

No doubt, she was affected, but what that meant was a mystery. He hadn't wanted to let her go. *He* was certainly affected.

Another half hour passed with no mishaps, and after his students left, he pulled his car around to pick up Mattie for their final supply run to Nesmith.

Mattie settled in the passenger seat and consulted the list. "I've already called in part of our order, so we'll save some time there. I need a few items for Granny's party too." She didn't look at him but kept scrolling the list on her phone. "And there won't be any time for dinner."

Paul masked his reaction. After their earlier moment in the garland pile, she was back to business; except he now saw through it. He saw it for what it was—caution.

In an attempt to lighten the mood as they headed out of Moreau, he stated, "So, we're on *official* party business."

Mattie glanced at him with a frown. "Isn't that something from the *Lord of the Rings*?"

She let little get past her, and he had her attention.

His grin broadened. "I recall a freshman year English Honors team project that was quite spectacular. I think it got an A++ if I'm remembering correctly."

She scoffed. "Only because I stayed up until midnight two nights in a row finishing the impressive trifold display board for the presentation."

Paul chuckled, thinking of their elaborate project, complete with Aragorn and Arwen costumes. "Not fair! I was involved and actually read the trilogy while you watched the movies. Besides, you wouldn't let me near the glue and scissors to help you. All because of that one time in first grade when my collage art got stuck in your hair and I tried to cut it out. You were so mad, I think you'd have cut a chunk out of my hair too if the teacher hadn't stepped in."

Mattie burst into laughter, covering her mouth with her hand. "Paul, I'd forgotten about that—the project *and* the first-grade incident." She leaned back against the seat. "I was so mad at you. I went on a tirade at the Lavigne House for a solid week about how you were the worst boy in the world."

He'd known it too when she refused to talk to him for the rest of the school year.

When Mattie Hayes set her mind to something, it didn't change. He glanced her way, and she met his gaze, amusement dancing in her green eyes.

Clearing her throat, she straightened. "Hopefully, Granny's party will be much less eventful than Bilbo's."

He couldn't help himself when he added, "You mean no dragon fireworks from Gandalf or disappearing hobbits?"

"You're such a nerd," she said, but he heard the warmth in her voice. "Just get us to Nesmith and back in one piece, please." She shook her head and scrolled through her list as a more comfortable silence settled over them.

Having Mattie beside him was familiar, natural even. As far back as he could remember, she was there—whether with blond braids and a Minnie Mouse T-shirt, the numerous class projects, church youth group, or giving a salutatorian speech that blew his valedictorian speech out of the water.

She excelled in whatever she did, was committed to seeing things through, and genuinely cared about those in her life. He'd always admired her for the latter most of all. It's what he most admired about her still.

But could she care about him?

Their time in Nesmith went quickly, with stops at two stores and Mattie closely watching the clock. The talk on the way back was strictly business, going over the next day's tasks. They had taken off work to focus on the market and the lighting ceremony, and from the size of their to-do list, they would need most of the day to finish everything.

After Paul dropped Mattie and the party supplies at her car, he once again didn't feel like going home, so he texted his parents that he wouldn't make it for dinner and headed for the river, alone with his thoughts.

Time with Mattie was akin to emotional whiplash. No matter how many times they danced around each other, he didn't think she truly saw him any differently. Deep down, how she saw him in high school was how she still saw him.

Honestly, it shouldn't matter what she thought. Wasn't he leaving anyway?

That afternoon he'd received an email about being considered for at least two jobs he'd applied for, and his friend Taylor texted that he was pulling some strings to get him an interview at his school in Colorado and would call soon with details.

Paul felt like he'd been spinning his wheels since coming back, not getting anywhere with reconciliation or further understanding with his father. No breakthroughs had happened, and they weren't likely to happen when his father saw nothing had gone wrong on his side.

The temperature had dropped with the sunset, and he hadn't grabbed his hat or scarf before embarking on the hour-long wander. He walked in the direction of the market and his car, thinking he could probably grab food from a drive-through and sneak into his apartment.

Movement around the market stalls drew his attention. He squinted and could just make out a figure in the shadows moving around the back of a stall.

With a sigh of frustration, he strode that way to investigate in case someone was causing trouble. The market had to go off without a hitch. If he did anything for Mattie, it would be that.

Chapter Nine

Mattie peered at the Riverbend Bistro's front window from across the street. She wished she had binoculars, but this distance was the best she could do to see how her aunt and Frank were getting along on their date. Thankfully, they were seated near the window, so Mattie had a full view of them.

Front row center was not her aunt's style, so Mattie could only imagine what Aunt Adale was thinking, namely, why Mattie had encouraged Frank to persist in asking her out.

Frank laughed, and Mattie shifted in her position to better see her aunt's face. She wasn't laughing, but at least she smiled. Was that her nervous smile or the one she used when she'd rather be anywhere else? They were similar.

If only she had those binoculars.

Her phone chimed. It was a text from Granny asking how the date was going. Granny would be out here herself if Mattie hadn't promised to spy and offer a full report. She was not letting her grandmother sit in the freezing weather.

Mattie huddled farther into her coat. She had to stay in the shadows, unseen. She scooted closer to the wall.

Swift footsteps sounded behind her, and before she could react, a hand touched her shoulder, and a man's voice whispered, "Causing trouble?"

She jumped with a yell and whirled, arms up to defend herself. Then she saw it was Paul.

A grin broke out on his face, which was half in shadow.

Mattie slapped his chest. "Hey! What were you thinking, scaring me to death!"

His smile widened.

She glanced behind her and saw people across the street look their way. "Oh no, has Aunt Adale seen me?"

Mattie didn't waste time to find out but grabbed Paul's arm and pulled him into the dark market.

"Hey! Easy there." He didn't go willingly and squinted as he stared behind her. "Is that your aunt and Frank having dinner?"

"Shhh." She gave him a shove around the stall until they were out of view of Chapel Street.

Paul stopped suddenly, and she ran into his chest, bracing herself with her palm on his jacket. His arm came around her in reaction, reminding her of their earlier tumble into the garlands.

A slice of light from the street illuminated his face, hazel eyes dancing. The press of his arm lessened, but he didn't release her. "Where are your binoculars if you're in spy mode?"

Mattie glared at him. "Look. If Aunt Adale knew I was doing this, she'd have a cow. I'm only doing Granny's bidding."

Paul's grin returned. "You make her sound like a crime boss."

She pictured Granny in a *Godfather* movie setting, seated at a large desk with henchmen kissing her rings, and mirth bubbled up within her until laughter escaped.

When she shared the thought with Paul, he started laughing too.

A gust of freezing wind whipped around them. Mattie shivered and felt the urge to snuggle closer to Paul, but she made herself do the opposite, stepping back until they no longer touched.

Paul's amused demeanor dimmed a bit, but his gaze still held hers. His eyebrows rose. "Are you sure you don't want to go wave at your aunt and Frank? It'd be pretty funny."

She scoffed. "For you maybe. You don't have to live or work with them."

He nodded. "I understand."

At his words, Mattie returned to their dinner and how she'd met his heartfelt statement with a biting remark.

She studied him, his gaze direct, focused on her in the moment. Did she dare bring it up? "Paul. . ."

"Yes?"

Mattie slid her gloved hands in her coat pockets, more out of nerves than seeking warmth. *Just spit it out*, she urged herself. She wasn't accustomed to not knowing what to say.

"When we were at dinner in Hawkins, you said you thought I might understand something." She pressed on, mustering her courage. "I didn't exactly hear you out, and I'm sorry. What did you mean?"

He rocked back on his heels with a sigh. "It's okay. It doesn't matter."

The same thing he'd said before. But in the depths of his eyes, she saw the truth. It *did* matter, and she wanted to know. She waved her hand toward the nearest bench. "Why don't we sit?"

Paul nodded, and they settled on it, Mattie facing him and giving him her full attention.

He didn't speak but surveyed the empty market, and for once she didn't fill the silence, allowing him the space to collect his thoughts.

After a few minutes, Paul leaned back and met her gaze in that straightforward way of his. "You intimidate me."

Mattie's mouth dropped. The words were the last thing she expected to hear. "Me? Why?"

The spark returned in his expression; then it sobered. "Your drive and motivation to excel intimidate me. Always have. You're a force to be reckoned with, Mattie, and everyone admires you for it."

She straightened. "I guess that's a compliment. Though, I sounded like a hurricane for a minute."

A corner of Paul's mouth lifted. "I meant it as a compliment."

"Thank you." She forced herself not to say another word to see if he'd explain further.

Paul rubbed his bare hands together before tucking them into his jacket. "I couldn't face the pressure of staying in Moreau where it seemed everyone's eyes were on every move of their beloved mayor's son. Living in my father's shadow has been hard enough."

Mattie stared at him, his confession settling over her. "I had no idea. In high school, you seemed able to conquer the world if you wanted to. Every *t* crossed and *i* dotted kind of perfect."

He smiled, but it didn't reach his eyes. "Well, looks can be deceiving."

She thought of her own situation. "How about living up to the expectations of the town's founding family? That's three hundred years of pressure."

Paul chuckled. "I think we finally understand each other—on at least one thing. The expectations of family legacy."

She offered a subtle smile, thinking of all she tried to live up to. She pushed herself because she had to. She couldn't let anyone down again.

"Why did you come back now? After what you've said."

"I didn't intend to, but I had a sudden layoff from my job in Virginia, and the one in Moreau came at just the right time." He shrugged. "I don't know, maybe it was a sign from God for me to come back and face the past."

He said the last part with a heaviness beyond what Mattie thought would concern the town's scrutiny of him—but maybe someone else's? His father's? It would explain the strain she glimpsed between them. Her heart ached for him and the weight he carried. If only she could help.

With a shake of his head, Paul stood. "I'm freezing, and we have a busy day tomorrow. Maybe we should call it a night."

Mattie rose from the bench, but she wasn't in a rush to go just yet.

"Paul, thank you for sharing. You didn't have to. But you're right. I do understand."

He began to speak but was stopped by a barrage of white flurries falling.

Mattie held up her gloved palm to catch a few snowflakes. A fresh dusting of snow was just what they needed for a European-style Christmas market. Her gaze shifted skyward, specks of white sparkling in the darkness—but also something else?

Frowning, she asked. "Is that Cory's twig hanging there?"

Paul shifted beside her, his focus above them now. He let out a laugh. "Yes, it sure is. His *mistletoe*."

And it was. She could make out the red ribbon he'd tied on the end.

"He thinks he's funny." Paul angled his gaze down at her with a smile; then it faltered.

They were close again, barely a foot apart. He edged nearer still until only a breath separated them.

Mattie froze, a thrill of anticipation coursing through her that she couldn't ignore as his intentions grew clear.

He was going to kiss her!

What should she do? As she thought it, she found herself leaning forward enough to encourage him.

His eyes drew her in with warmth and longing. What would it be like to kiss him?

Paul's hand rose to her cheek, caressing it ever so gently, holding her to the moment. He leaned in, his lips nearing hers.

Suddenly, a bright light shone on them, and they jumped, separating, both shielding their eyes.

The beam of a flashlight moved, and Chief Manning stared at them with raised eyebrows. "I got a call about the market. Heard someone yell and thought they might be up to no good." He shined the light above them, spotlighting the twig.

"I see the only mischief happening is under the mistletoe." He chuckled.

Despite the cold, Mattie felt her face heat. The incident would be all over town by morning.

"Tom! We were not—" But she couldn't finish the statement. They *were* going to kiss, weren't they?

She, Mattie Hayes, was going to let Paul Ammons kiss her. And part of her was disappointed at the interruption.

She moved another step away from him. "Thanks for checking on the market, but everything is fine here."

Chief Manning nodded, but his eyes twinkled. Yeah, they would be the next day's top story.

———◆———

Paul surveyed the scene between Mattie and Chief Manning, the former trying to explain away the intimate moment he'd almost witnessed.

If Paul was honest, he wished the chief *had* witnessed it because it would mean he'd kissed Mattie.

Even now, with her likely regretting what almost happened, Paul wanted to take her into his arms.

Why was he kidding himself—he wasn't likely to have another chance, especially with her encouraging him. She had leaned toward him. He was sure of it.

The conversation cleared the tension between them, their connection palpable, but the conflict resumed as Mattie told him and the chief good night and rushed from the market.

She'd barely looked at him.

The chief told Paul to have a good night and left. In his expression, Paul read much of what Joe at the tree lot had hinted at.

Paul wasn't the only one seeing something between him and Mattie. But did she truly see it?

Mattie had practically run from the market. She was affected. He didn't know if it was the almost kiss or Chief Manning spreading it all over town.

Probably the town.

Paul kicked a pebble on the concrete, and it skidded across the square and under the Christmas tree. He remembered their snowball fight around it, how Mattie smiling at him with snow all around her had shifted something for him.

The shift had continued when seeing her help the kids make ornaments, interact with her family, and laugh with him that night after he scared her.

Every day he looked forward to seeing her, thought about something to tell her, and wished their dinner in Hawkins could be a redo except as an actual date. He'd kiss her in front of that gazebo she admired.

He opened his car door with a groan. He was kidding himself. It would never happen.

Maybe returning to Moreau hadn't been such a good idea.

Family dinners grew more unbearable with each passing night, and Mattie wouldn't see how much he cared for her.

His head fell against the car seat headrest. *Whoa. . .*he was in deep. Forget high school crush. It went beyond that.

He was falling in love.

And she had gone from tolerating him to acting as if they were friends to nearly kissing him.

He couldn't take a chance and tell her how he felt, could he? It was a setup for heartbreak if he'd ever seen one.

His cell phone vibrated in his pocket. Was it Mattie?

It was a text from Cameron.

GRILLING STEAK. HAVE EXTRA. COME OVER IF YOU WANT.

As if on cue, Paul's stomach growled. It was nearly eight, and he hadn't eaten. He texted back.

SURE. ON MY WAY.

Paul drove down the street and past the chapel shining in the moonlight.

Had God brought him here to fail? Because it sure felt like it. He'd come back to face the hurt of the past, to try to reconcile with his father, start over, but he wasn't any closer now than when he showed up.

He focused on the headlights illuminating the road. He didn't doubt God wanted him back in Moreau for the past year, but he had to wonder, what was the point?

Paul was barely in the door and seated on a barstool in Cameron's kitchen when he took one look at him and said, "You look like your hind end is about to drag through the door. What's going on? Is it Mattie?"

Paul met his eyes, his brow furrowing.

His friend grunted. "Yeah, it's Mattie." He slid a plate in front of Paul with a large, juicy steak and fries.

Paul picked up his fork. The meal looked excellent, but he didn't feel like eating. "We almost kissed tonight."

Cameron took a seat beside him with his own plate, a look of confusion on his face. "Why didn't you? Did she brush you off?"

"Sort of," Paul said with a frown, reliving her reaction. "But not until after we got interrupted by Chief Manning."

Cameron raised an eyebrow. "The man will tell everyone by breakfast."

Paul put down the fork. "Yeah. That's the problem. That's why she brushed me off. She was freaking out and tried to explain away what almost happened. The chief wasn't buying it, though."

A minute passed as Paul started cutting his steak to give him something to do, and with a furrowed brow, Cameron ate a few bites of his.

Cameron held up his fork, pointing it at Paul. "You said she wasn't running from the kiss. She must be feeling something, then. It's not just in your head." He lowered the utensil. "But you also can't assume she knows how you feel. Have you told her?"

Paul's shoulders fell. "I've tried. Well, I've wanted to try, but it never feels right. I can't get a clear read on her."

Cameron nodded. "I understand that. But you've got to take a risk, or you'll regret it." He cleared his throat. "Mattie doesn't stop. It's like she's running for her life or something. Maybe she needed to stop tonight to face what's going on between you two. She had to slow down to see it. That could be why she's freaking out too."

Paul considered it. Maybe Cameron was right. Should he take the risk?

Cameron sat back with hands raised. "That's all I've got, man. Love is a risk and a risky business."

Paul smiled. "Yeah, it is that. Thanks for the advice. She's going to be stressed enough between the market and the gossip. I'll see how tomorrow goes."

But could Paul risk his heart to tell Mattie the truth? What if he was being too hasty and it derailed any chance he had?

Chapter Ten

The almost kiss kept resurfacing in Mattie's mind as she busied herself with the market. She had been out of her senses thinking she should let Paul kiss her.

Something monumental like that between them would only lead to regret—on her part at least.

As much as she admitted to liking Paul as a person, she couldn't *like* him romantically. He couldn't be trusted. He wasn't staying. She would only serve as a temporary distraction, and then he'd be gone.

Mattie pushed the sinking feeling away and got back to work. It didn't matter what she felt or didn't feel. The truth was he wasn't someone to be in one place for long.

But their conversation, like the almost kiss, remained with her.

Paul was right about her understanding the pressure. After the market, maybe they could go for coffee and talk. She could figure out more about his relationship with his dad. She had always looked up to Mayor Ammons and even wished he were her dad instead of the one who abandoned her.

There was no time to think about the past when the future of the chapel was at stake.

Mattie surveyed the empty market in the morning sunshine, snow glistening and clinging to the tree and the stall roofs like icing on a gingerbread house.

She wanted to—*had to*—believe she had done enough to raise the money.

Footsteps sounded on concrete, and she stilled. Was it Paul?

Coming around Robby's Rustic Creations stall was Serena holding to-go cups and harboring amusement in her eyes.

Oh no, that look couldn't be good.

Her best friend greeted her with a latte and steered her to a nearby bench, thankfully not the one with the twig, which Mattie had removed as soon as she arrived at the market.

"I heard about your *mistletoe* moment."

Mattie scoffed. "It *wasn't* a mistletoe moment."

Serena shot her a look. "Not according to Chief Manning, who grabs his morning coffee at seven and shares the town gossip."

"Great," Mattie muttered and blew out a breath, the air swirling white in front of her. "That's just what I need today."

Serena draped an arm around Mattie's shoulders and gently squeezed. "It's going to be fine, Mattie. No matter what happens."

Mattie wanted to believe her friend, but so much was riding on this idea, *her* idea, for the market. "You're right," she finally said, as all the things she had to do rushed through her mind.

She helped Serena organize her stall and was glad to be occupied when Paul arrived, leaning in the window and greeting them.

Mattie offered a quick "hi" in return but didn't look up from stacking cups. How could she face him after what almost happened? What did the town now think about the two of them?

"I'm going to work at the school booth. If you need anything, let me know," he said, then left.

"She needs a mistletoe moment," Serena whispered from behind Mattie.

"Serena!" Mattie hissed, whirling around with mouth agape, relief flooding her that Paul was already out of earshot. She glared at her friend. "What *are* you thinking?"

Serena folded her arms across her chest. "I think deep down you wanted to kiss him."

Mattie frowned. "There's too much to do around here to worry about kissing anybody." She resumed organizing supplies.

"Sure there is" was the reply, and Mattie didn't care for her friend's smug tone, the I'm-not-buying-it one. The same one she used on an eight-year-old Mattie who tried to sneak her new kitten home and said it was an accident it climbed inside her backpack.

Serena could read her like a book, but she wouldn't admit it.

For the next half hour, Mattie made quick work of helping Serena set up her booth before she headed back to the Press. She assisted a few other vendors and avoided Paul at all costs.

She saw her aunt helping Mary Ann Drake decorate small Christmas trees on each side of the Cajun Cooking booth. She met Mattie's eyes and smiled before speaking to Mary Ann, who also looked her way, curly red bob swinging and offering her usual friendly smile and a wave.

Mattie waved back as her aunt approached with arms open wide for a hug. She didn't let Mattie go but slipped an arm around her shoulders and gave a motherly squeeze.

"Mattie, darling, you've outdone yourself. It's going to look spectacular. Your mama would be so proud. Just like Granny and I are."

At the mention of her mom, Mattie swallowed hard, fighting back tears. She had tried not to think about her. But her mom would have loved every second of the market and every single event the town would host over the next two weeks. She would have been right in the middle of helping with it all.

She wrapped an arm around her aunt. "Thanks, Aunt Adale. I appreciate you saying that." Changing the subject, she asked, "What are you doing up here so early?"

Her aunt released her and nodded toward the stall. "I'm helping Mary Ann for a bit. Chef Perot will be beside himself. He likes to hide away in his kitchen, not be out among the public." She waved a hand in an exaggerated fashion.

Mattie smiled. "He certainly needs to overcome that preference today. It has to go well."

"It's going to be fine."

Why was everyone telling her that? They didn't know the future. She bit back a sigh. She had to get going again, but she needed updates first.

Mattie hadn't laid eyes on her aunt or Frank since Paul scared her. She hadn't dared look at the restaurant as she fled the market and holed up in her bedroom, seeking solace under her covers, trying not to think about how the evening transpired. Maybe the night went better for her aunt.

"How did the date go?"

Her aunt blew out a sharp breath. "It was fine. . . ."

"But?" Mattie added, when her aunt's words trailed off. The response didn't sound promising.

"It was nice, but honestly, I'm not good at dating. Frank is a sweet man, and I don't mind a dinner here and there as friends." She grimaced. "Please don't tell him anything, though. We've known each other so long, and I don't want to hurt his feelings."

Mattie completely understood, but she wondered about what she would tell Frank at the office. The conversation would come up. She couldn't not say anything.

Time for a subject change again. "What's Granny doing? I haven't gotten any texts with errand requests."

Aunt Adale scoffed. "I told Mama over and over that she does not need to keep bothering you at all hours with those messages. You don't need anyone pestering you."

"Thanks, but you know I don't mind helping Granny. What's she doing today?"

With a shake of her head, her aunt said, "I hope staying out of trouble. She's fine. Don't worry. She's at her society meeting, and the group will come to the lighting ceremony. She's likely bragging about your article. Since I wouldn't let her text you, she asked me to inform you she wants ten copies of this week's newspaper."

"I can do that. I'm glad she liked it." Mattie's phone rang. Nate. She apologized to her aunt, who motioned for her to take the call.

Mattie answered. "Hi, Nate. What's up? I left those art supplies you needed at town hall."

The line was silent for a moment before he said, "I need to tell you something." His voice was hesitant, pained.

She stilled. "What's wrong?"

He released a deep sigh. "I'm sorry to tell you this, Mattie. But when we were hiking, I tripped over our dog and sprained my wrist. It's my painting hand."

Mattie gasped. "Oh no, that's awful, Nate. I'm so sorry you're hurt. Don't worry. We'll figure something out. You just focus on getting better—and be careful." She said the words calmly, but inside she felt anything but.

The mural had to be finished. It was on the town event schedule she sent everywhere, and *he* was the artist.

The artist who now couldn't paint.

He thanked her, and they got off the phone. Mattie stared at it a few seconds before her aunt touched her arm.

"It's about the mural?" she asked with a grimace.

Mattie closed her eyes. "Yes. Nate hurt his wrist, and I feel bad for him, but the mural is part of Moreau's two weeks of holiday events. He's supposed to start on Monday. The supplies are paid for and everything."

She sank onto a picnic table bench. "What are we going to do? There's no time to line up another artist on such short notice. I've been advertising all the events for weeks now."

Aunt Adale sat next to Mattie, her blue eyes sobering, then brightening. "I've got it. You can ask Jolene."

Mattie bit back a groan, because her cousin was talented, but the issue was would she stick around long enough to finish the project? She was coming for the party, and they weren't sure yet if she would stay for Christmas.

There was no planning with Jolene. She did what she wanted, and that was that, which reminded her of Granny.

The only reply she dared to give was "Maybe, Aunt Adale."

She had no doubt of Jolene's skill. She'd witnessed many of her cousin's and grandmother's art lessons over the years. But could she trust her to see the job to completion?

Mattie could only dream of being so carefree. She was the efficient one of the pair. Jolene was unreliable. Mattie was loyal. Jolene lived on her next whim. Mattie wanted others to depend on her, and she would not let them down, especially today.

Paul watched Mattie from across the market square as she spoke to his father, likely about the order of events for the lighting ceremony. She had avoided him all morning.

Even after his chat with Cameron, Paul still hadn't determined if Mattie avoiding him meant it embarrassed her that they nearly kissed *or* that she had wanted to. Cameron's words came back to him about love being a risk. That was the truth.

Paul only had to convince himself to take the chance. He shook his head and returned to arranging the French language booth. He also ran through Mattie's to-do list for the day in his head. He should have it memorized after the number of times she'd spouted the items off to him over the past week.

Maybe if he helped take care of as many items as he could, remove more of the load off her, then she could relax. He'd overheard her phone call with Nate, which was not a good way to start the day.

He should approach her somewhere she couldn't avoid him, assure her everything was going to be fine, and encourage her to have a little faith.

Paul wished she had more faith in him, wished she believed he could help her instead of trying to do everything herself. She was only one person.

He finished setting up the sound booth and tried out Christmas music he'd play before and after the choir's performance. He purposely chose yet another rendition of "O Come All Ye Faithful" and glanced Mattie's way, where she still chatted with his father.

As the song picked up in tempo, she briefly met his eyes, recognition dawning, and he smiled. When she heard the choir perform that night, he would look at her again, and perhaps she would think more of the gesture.

He left the music playing to add a festive mood to the commotion and walked the perimeter, the stalls facing inward. He saw Mattie's vision from many months ago becoming a reality. It would all come together once the lights were on.

The thought reminded him of another item on her list—double-check all the lights. He stopped by each booth, plugging them in one strand at a time to be sure everything was in order. After nearly an hour of testing, he could assure Mattie they worked.

The tree and overhead strands he had yet to check, though.

Mattie stood at the Rustic Creations stall talking to Robby when Paul walked over and glanced at the display of wooden toys, miniature versions of the town letters in front of the stage, and other hand-carved items.

Robby greeted him with a hearty handshake, which Paul returned. Mattie kept her eyes on the items.

"The talent runs deep in your family," Paul said, thinking of the wooden train set Robby's father carved for one of Paul's fifth birthday presents. He still had it in a box in the top of his closet and hoped to pass it on to his own kids one day.

"Thank you," the middle-aged man said with a grin. "A family trade for sure. My grandpa taught me to whittle at age seven, and I haven't stopped since."

Mattie smiled at the man. "These are perfect. Please save me a sign if you don't mind."

With a nod, he removed one and tucked it inside a box on a small table. "Taken care of."

Mattie thanked him, and he looked from Mattie to Paul, a curious glint in his eyes.

Nope. Paul couldn't let him mention the gossip from last night. Mattie would be sure to avoid him the rest of the day.

"Thanks, Robby." He faced Mattie. "May I borrow you for a minute?"

She met his gaze, her expression guarded, and stepped away from the stall. "Sure. What's up?"

The words were stilted at best, but he pressed on anyway. "I checked all the booth lights, and they're good. Will you check the others with me?"

Mattie nodded, glancing at her clipboard to an unchecked item that she now checked off. "Okay. I'll take this end." She left him on her mission, and he started his until he plugged them all in.

Every strand lit just as they should. He offered a thumbs-up to Mattie across the square, and then her mouth dropped.

One strand flickered a few times before shutting off.

"I got it," he called to her and went to unplug and replug it without success. He strode toward her, panic showing in her eyes, and racked his brain for a solution. One came swiftly, his memory serving him well.

"Didn't we use one less than you planned?" He pointed overhead. "The ladder is still under the stage. I'll switch it."

Mattie nodded, handing over the keys to her SUV. Her shoulders fell a little. "The extra strand is in the plastic tub on the left."

Paul jumped into action and retrieved the light strand, which was exactly where Mattie said it would be. Robby offered to help, and together they replaced the lights.

When he found Mattie again, she was in crisis mode at the Cajun Cooking stall. Chef Perot wasn't around, but Mary Ann's face matched her red hair as she and Mattie frowned over a generator.

"Generator giving you trouble?"

Mary Ann looked up. "Yes, and I'm not sure why. Chef will have a fit if his fryers aren't working. Most of the menu is fried."

Paul knew little about generators, but he stooped to look and carefully unhooked and rehooked a few things. When he tried it again, the machine roared to life.

Mary Ann clapped her hands together and threw a side glance at Mattie. "What a help you are, Paul. Someone needs to snatch you off the market."

Mattie coughed and recovered enough to mumble a thank-you and mention she needed to run across the street to the *Gazette* for a few minutes.

After Mattie walked away, he told Mary Ann goodbye and got out of there. The more he stood by Mattie, the more people would talk—but they were literally running this market together. He couldn't win.

With a sigh of resignation, he surveyed the scene for any sign of trouble. The market was on his watch, and he would be vigilant.

When he spotted Mattie's aunt Adale at the crepe-making stall, he grimaced. She was fluffing and rearranging the garland.

Despite the fact her actions would improve the decorations, Mattie would likely stress out if she saw it. Paul needed to steer her away before Mattie came back. He recalled that Mattie's aunt spoke French and had spent a summer in France like he had. He could *borrow* her.

"Mrs. Broussard, would you mind helping me at the French language booth?"

"I'd be honored, Paul," she said in flawless French.

At the booth, he lifted a box of assorted Christmas decorations, a few items he snagged from his parents' attic, and continued the conversation in French.

"I know for a fact you're a good decorator, and I'm not. Please tell me what to do."

Mrs. Broussard offered a curt nod—though her blue eyes shone, and it seemed she debated what to say next before stating, "Let's begin." She pointed for him to set the box down, which he did, and she rummaged through the contents.

Withdrawing two small matching wreaths, she instructed him to hang one on each side of the booth sign at the back of the tent. The French language and heritage booths were tents set side by side near the stage. He and his students would man one and Mattie the other featuring the chapel restoration information and a donation box.

She caught him staring at the other booth and suggested they add the little fiber-optic Christmas tree on the table. After he did so, he looked up and noticed her studying him intently.

Mrs. Broussard sighed. "Can I be frank with you, Paul?" she asked in French.

The question surprised him, but he was also curious. "Of course."

"You told me to tell you what to do." She gave him an amused look, something about it reminding him of Mattie. "You didn't mean about my niece, but I'd like to offer some advice just the same."

Paul stilled, his hand on the next item, a fake poinsettia plant. He certainly hadn't expected this turn of events. He swallowed hard, glad anyone in listening range would not likely understand the conversation.

"I'd appreciate that."

"It didn't take Tom Manning's gossip to put this on my radar," she said, propping a gloved hand on her hip.

The mention of the gossip should have put him on edge, but it didn't. He respected Mrs. Broussard, and if anyone had good insight to offer about Mattie, it would be her or Serena, who likely wouldn't say a word.

"And this is certainly not a 'stay away from Mattie' talk. On the contrary. Mattie has lost so much—not by choice. She has almost gotten used to loss, if anyone can say such a thing. I understand it, and we all grieve in different ways, but she works so hard to keep as much of her home and the memories along with it from changing. I love her for it, but no one should attempt to shoulder that sort of responsibility."

Paul listened intently, the words falling into place like a puzzle, the parts of Mattie he couldn't figure out on his own.

Mrs. Broussard's expression grew solemn, a faraway look in her eyes. "If you care about Mattie, you have to prove to her you have staying power, Paul. Women need men who will stand by them no matter what, who will *stay*."

A hint of moisture filled her eyes, and he wondered if she'd been hurt before, if she spoke from experience.

"Mattie doesn't need a perfect man, but the one from God who is worthy of her very caring heart." She gave a gentle smile. "She needs someone she can depend on and who will be in Moreau for her. Please consider that before you pursue anything."

Paul nodded and thanked her, the only response he could muster after her charge to him regarding her niece.

Was he willing to stay in Moreau and continue to face the pain of his own past for Mattie?

Chapter Eleven

Mattie hadn't needed to go to the *Gazette* for anything except space away from Paul and the gossip. She'd done her best to avoid him all morning, but he kept showing up where she was.

She groaned, the sound echoing through the empty newspaper office. Frank closed the *Gazette* early since half of Mattie's coworkers were helping family members with stalls at the market.

Relief flooded her that Frank wasn't there. He'd already texted her about what he called *her* "breaking news story." She'd sent back the annoyed emoji.

Mattie was thankful he hadn't mentioned the date with her aunt. She didn't want to have to dodge that subject too. She scrolled through her to-do list, organizing the tasks by importance, and took a few steadying breaths before returning to the market.

She couldn't hide any longer.

The whole undertaking was happening for better or worse, and she would either sink or swim. Swimming was preferable, so she'd best get to it and make her rounds with the vendors.

The market activity hadn't ceased with her absence. She glimpsed Paul and her aunt decorating and chatting at the language booth, and traveled the opposite way around to the stage.

All seemed well with vendors at their stalls. The sound booth looked ready, and the Christmas music still wafted from the speakers. She hummed along with a song.

The lighting ceremony would start in two hours, the kickoff to everything she and Paul had set into motion. She glanced his way again as the song stopped and overheard their conversation. Were they speaking French?

Mattie shook her head with a smile. Appropriate for the booth.

Her phone rang, and a glance at the screen showed it was Wyatt with the crepe-making stall. She answered on the second ring.

"Hey, Wyatt. What's up?"

"Hey. I, uh, have had a change of plans." An edge of panic laced his voice, and she thought of Nate's injury. "Haley's water broke. She's not due for another two weeks. We're heading for the hospital."

Mattie's heart thrilled at the news of their baby girl's impending arrival but also sank at the absence of a key stall for the market. She'd looked forward to eating a crepe.

"Wyatt, you and Haley get to the hospital safely. I'll be praying for you. And I'll take care of things here. Don't worry."

"Thanks, Mattie."

She told him goodbye and sank onto the edge of the stage, the development surging through her thoughts. What was she going to do?

Mattie didn't know anyone but Chef Perot who may be able to make crepes. He had his own stall, which was likely to keep him too busy.

Movement caught her attention. Her aunt and Paul approached wearing worried expressions.

"Darling, what's the matter?" Aunt Adale's reassuring voice soothed a little of her worry. "And don't you dare say 'it's nothing.' You won't be fooling me."

Paul nodded but said nothing, so Mattie explained the situation.

A slow smile spread across his face. "I might have a solution. When I was in France, one of our classes was for crepe making, and I think I still remember what to do."

Her aunt patted his shoulder. "Look at you coming to the rescue."

Mattie blew out a breath of relief and also annoyance. That instance was the second in mere hours that someone mentioned Paul coming to the rescue. She could handle things too if he'd give her a moment.

"What about the language booth, Paul?"

Her aunt jumped in. "I can help with it, and the crepe stall too. Mary Ann shouldn't really need me. I'll just be in the way."

"Okay." Her answer was hesitant, but they had to do something.

Paul looked at her aunt. "If you wouldn't mind, I think we should go check out the crepe stall, and you can supervise while I practice."

Aunt Adale laughed. "Oh boy, sounds like an adventure. I'd be glad to."

Paul met Mattie's eyes again, the mirth in his sobering. "You okay with this, Mattie?"

"It'll be fine. Thanks."

He offered a slight smile. "I may need a crepe tester. You up for that?"

Mattie smiled. "Chocolate and strawberries—and you have a deal."

"You got it." He left with her aunt for the crepe stall.

Mattie expelled a sharp breath. It would all be fine. She double-checked the chapel project and language booths and reorganized her table until she was satisfied. She should be able to man both with the help of his students as long as there were no more mistletoe shenanigans.

Her phone dinged. A text message from her aunt.

Crepe tester needed.

Her gaze lifted across the square where she spotted her aunt and Paul laughing as he operated the electric griddle.

Paul grinned when her aunt added the chocolate. Seeing the pair having such a good time together warmed her heart. He cared about people. She saw it in his actions, and he was genuine.

The man was truly different from the self-centered teen she once knew. Although admitting that observation wasn't easy—especially when it was simpler to hold him at arm's length by viewing him through the lens of the past.

Last night had been a warning for her. She'd let her guard down and couldn't make that mistake again.

Her aunt waved her over and presented her with a beautiful crepe folded into a triangle filled with melted chocolate and strawberries. The first bite was perfection with warmth and sweetness.

Mattie grabbed a napkin to wipe chocolate off her chin. "Wow, Paul. This is wonderful. I don't think Wyatt could do better, but don't dare tell him I said that." She glanced at Paul, who seemed pleased. "I think you must have aced that crepe-making class. I would likely burn—"

Aunt Adale gasped, stopping Mattie midsentence, her focus across the square toward the Cajun Cooking booth. "Oh my word. Is that Mama?"

Mattie followed her gaze to the stall, where Chef Perot was locked in an animated discussion with a white-haired woman in a long peach coat.

Definitely Granny with arms flailing as her voice rose across the space, fury in her tone. The man, only a few years younger, matched her with waving hands, as if proving a point. Mattie met her aunt's wide eyes. "I'll go see what's going on."

Another bite of crepe pushed her toward the bickering pair, who had drawn every eye in the place. Chef Perot was out of his element, meaning the privacy of his kitchen. He didn't need any provoking, and Granny could push buttons with the best of them.

"Ernie Perot, you're not gonna call that a roux for gumbo. It looks like dirty river water."

Oh no, she'd gone for the jugular—*the roux*.

How in the world did this start? Better question: How was Mattie going to put out the fire?

"Eloise, I've seen your gumbo. It's like you dipped a pot in the bayou. Old murky swamp water."

Granny scoffed. "Swamp water? My gumbo is a favorite in this town. Been that way long before you came to Moreau."

It was Chef Perot's turn to scoff. "Oh, then why does my Wednesday gumbo special sell out every week? Tell me." He crossed his arms.

"Because people can't get my gumbo, so they have to settle for second best." She jutted out her chin. "Better than nothing, I suppose."

"I'd like to see whose gumbo is on top in this town. I'll even make a little wager if you're up for the challenge."

Granny's dark eyes flashed fire. "Oh, I'm up for the challenge. You name the time and place."

Mattie needed to interrupt before things escalated any further, but she would have to throw herself into the line of fire.

Before she could take a step closer, Paul approached the dueling pair holding two crepes. "Would you mind giving me your opinion on these? I haven't made them in years, and Wyatt needs me to man his stall."

Mattie's mouth dropped when both Granny and Chef Perot completely switched gears. The bickering stopped cold as their attention turned to Paul and the crepes.

"I adore crepes. I must have eaten one every day that summer we spent in France." Granny took a bite, appeared thoughtful, and looked at Paul. "Young man, I think you got it spot-on. What's your assessment, Ernie?"

Chef Perot bit into the crepe, eyes narrowing, probably letting the flavors settle in. "I think Eloise is right. Good work." He tapped the crepe in the air. "Eloise, did I tell you I've been to France? When did you go? You must have told me years ago."

"We haven't talked about that in ages. Why don't you tell me about it now?" She looped her arm through the chef's and led him back toward the stall as if nothing had happened. "I loved visiting this little café near Notre Dame. Maybe you saw it."

Paul swiveled, his eyes meeting hers, a satisfaction in them that usually set her on edge. But he wasn't Perfect Paul, saving the day and leaving her feeling second best once again; she was relieved he'd stepped in.

And realization dawned. Maybe he'd been doing the right thing all along, not to best her but to help her.

———◆———

Paul barely had the gall to interrupt Chef Perot and Eloise Lavigne-Marchand in midargument over gumbo. He apparently didn't value his life enough, but he'd put it on the line for Mattie.

When he faced her, her expression somehow held a mix of awe and confusion. He moved closer, intent on figuring out what the look meant.

Her expression softened to one of gratitude, and she nodded toward her grandmother and Chef Perot. "Thanks for that. Diffusing a food argument with food was brilliant. I didn't dare intervene."

He grinned. "Well, teachers have to think quick on their feet and have tough skin, you know. Kids will walk all over you if you don't stand up for yourself."

Mattie looked at him as if she wanted to say more, but he heard his name called from the stage area.

Julie waved to him with a smile, and out of his peripheral, he could have sworn Mattie frowned before heading to another stall.

Paul sighed and made his way to Julie and the choir. The market would kick off in less than an hour.

Maybe when Mattie saw the market was a success, which he didn't doubt it would be from all her hard work, and heard the song he'd planned for her, she would relax and enjoy everything. He'd glimpsed joy when she tasted the crepe before she sprinted toward the Ernie-Eloise fire, which he thankfully put out.

He greeted Julie and Cameron, who would run the sound booth, and went over the order of events and did a sound check.

By the time they finished and his attention returned to the rest of the market, a crowd had gathered, and a group of his students stood near the language booth, ready to share with visitors about French culture and language.

Paul excused himself and explained to the group that, after the lighting ceremony, he would have to man the crepe stall, but Mattie would be at the neighboring booth if they needed anything.

Jacey, one of his top students, whose determination and drive reminded him of high school–age Mattie, assured him they'd be fine and would make him proud. The fact she said it in French made him prouder. He had outstanding students, and he would miss them if he left Moreau.

He searched for Mattie and found her by the tree talking to his father.

The square had swiftly become flooded with people, some faces he recognized and many more he didn't. He sidled up beside Mattie.

"See. You had nothing to worry about. It'll be fine."

Mattie didn't look at him but bit her bottom lip and surveyed the crowd. He fought the urge to take her hand or slip his arm around her shoulders, something to comfort her.

Instead, he turned to his father and saw his mother on his other side. He offered a small smile. "Ready?"

"Ready," his father said, and Paul handed him a microphone and waved to Cameron at the sound booth as a signal.

The afternoon sunlight faded to early evening, the lampposts lighting around the square. Paul glanced at Mattie again. "Are *you* ready?"

She nodded, and for the briefest moment, she held his gaze and smiled. "Ready as we'll ever be. Go ahead, Mayor Ammons."

Right on cue, his father introduced himself and welcomed everyone to Moreau and the first-ever Christmas market, followed by applause. He introduced Mattie and Paul and explained about the committee's efforts to restore the chapel, pointing out the booth to donate and learn more about the project.

Passion and charisma came through his father's speech. He truly cared about the town and wanted others to as well. Seeing his father in his element as mayor made Paul proud, and at the same time, Paul wished his father could be as proud of him as he was of his father.

Paul swallowed hard. He wasn't going there, not this evening. He must stay focused.

His father gestured toward the tree. "I invite everyone to count down from ten so we can light up the night and kick off the festivities." He started the count.

Paul and Mattie joined in along with the crowd until they reached "one" and his father plugged in the cord to the tree and all the overhead lights burst to life. The river displays followed, blinking on one by one from the dark riverbank, a sparkling Christmas trail leading Santa Claus to Moreau.

The crowd cheered, and his father told everyone to have a great time and to come back the next day with their friends.

"It's Beginning to Look a Lot Like Christmas" wafted from the speakers as everyone began milling around. Paul didn't move because Mattie didn't either, her gaze roaming the entire scene. He should be at the crepe booth, but it could wait a few more minutes. He wanted to stay with her longer.

"You deserve to enjoy this moment, Mattie. You've done a great job with everything."

She faced him, her expression softening, appreciation in her eyes. "We both have."

As if on schedule, snow fell in dancing flurries, glistening in the light. Paul laughed. "Would you look at that?"

Mattie grinned. "Couldn't have planned it any better." She breathed in deeply. "Time to get to our stations. I'll keep an eye on your kids."

"Thanks," he said and couldn't keep from adding, "When the choir begins, I think the third song may spark your interest."

She slanted a curious look at him. "Okay. I'll be sure to pay attention."

Paul watched her go, wishing she'd pay attention to him, wishing he could walk hand in hand with her around this amazing market she'd envisioned and brought to life.

He glimpsed a line in front of the crepe stall and Mattie's aunt waving at him with a look of panic, and he got to work.

The choir began not long afterward, and Paul made crepes as fast as he could while listening in anticipation for "O Come All Ye Faithful."

As soon as it started, his gaze sought her on the other side of the square. She looked his way, recognition dawning, and a broad smile spread across her face.

He grinned back and hoped she realized it had been for her. It seemed she might, her eyes not leaving his. The talk with Cameron over steaks came back to him about how love is a risk.

With the snow falling, choir singing, and lights sparkling, he couldn't think of a better atmosphere for a romantic gesture, even if the idea put his nerves on edge.

"Watch it. You're about to burn a crepe," Mrs. Broussard said, pushing him from his thoughts. He quickly flipped the crepe before disaster struck.

The line had thinned to two customers. Even so, he hated to abandon his post but also needed to act while inspired. "Think you could manage without me for a bit?"

She narrowed her eyes. "Does it have anything to do with my niece?"

Paul grinned. "You don't miss a thing."

Mrs. Broussard patted his arm. "Not much, darling. Get on, then. I'll handle this."

He didn't wait a moment longer but left the stall, skirting the congested crowd in front of the stage.

As Paul neared the tree, his phone vibrated in his pocket, and he saw it was Taylor calling from Colorado, the call he'd been expecting all week. He groaned, not wanting to take it but needing to. He'd answer and tell Taylor he was no longer interested in the job.

"Hey, Taylor."

"Hey, Paul. I just heard from the principal about the opening. He said it's yours if you want it. We can talk more next week."

Taylor had indeed gone out on a limb for him, and he couldn't flat-out refuse right away. Maybe he should ask questions and agree to talk next week, figure out exactly how to break it to him.

"When does the job start again? January?"

"Yeah, we'd need you here by the third."

"The third. Got it. Well, like you said, let's talk more about the job next week. I appreciate it, man."

"No problem. Talk to you then."

Paul hung up. He hated stringing his friend along, but he felt bad turning it down right away after all the trouble he'd gone through to help Paul.

With a deep breath, he shoved his phone back into his pocket and returned to his mission, more like his confession. Though cold, his palms were sweating. He wiped them on his jacket and rubbed them together, walking around the tree toward Mattie's booth. He would ask her to step away from the crowd and share his heart. Easy, right?

When he rounded the tree, he nearly ran straight into Mattie, the anger and hurt on her face slamming him in the chest.

Chapter Twelve

Mattie couldn't believe her ears. After the song Paul had arranged for her and their mistletoe moment, she hadn't read the signs wrong, had she? He *was* interested in her.

But she'd heard enough of the phone call, and it confirmed the truth. He was still leaving. How could he lead her on, only to be gone by next month?

Anger welled inside of her. He made her believe in him. He planned a song just for her, and now he was leaving. When she saw him, something within her cracked, tears burning her eyes.

"I was such a fool. I thought you'd changed from the self-centered boy always staying ahead in high school. But you haven't. You're leaving again—just when I thought something was happening. . . ."

She didn't finish with "between us," but the look in his hazel eyes told her he knew what she had planned to say. He opened his mouth, but she didn't want to hear the excuses.

"I don't need Perfect Paul coming to my rescue. I don't need saving. I can manage just fine without you. I have everything under control and—"

Paul jumped in. "Mattie, I'm not perfect, and I'm not trying to save anyone. I only want to help. You could just say thank you and let someone help you sometime instead of trying to take on everything by yourself. The world isn't going to spin off its axis if you don't hold it. You do understand that, right?"

She froze, stunned at the bluntness of his words and the fact he thought she believed she was so self-important that she could single-handedly save the town. The past weighed on her, old feelings dredging up that she must force down, because the more she thought on his words, the more she found truth in them that she couldn't face.

"Thank you for speaking so plainly, Paul. And I wish you well on your new job."

His hard expression softened, a hint of regret flickering in his eyes as Mattie turned and rushed from him through the crowd and past the woodworking stall into the shadows.

"*Hey*," Paul called. "Mattie, wait!"

But she didn't wait. She rushed across the street, fumbling for her keys, then quickly unlocked the *Gazette*'s door and slipped inside as the tears started falling.

Mattie sank into her desk chair and pressed her fingers to her temples, head throbbing as the exchange with Paul played in her mind.

A long, loud sigh escaped. She shouldn't have lashed out at him, and why had she?

Paul had only been back a year after being gone for a decade. What did it truly matter if he left again? She'd get along without him just as she had before, wouldn't she?

The truth was she didn't know. She didn't know why she cared so much about what Paul did or didn't do.

A loud tap on the glass sounded at the front, startling Mattie. She leaped from her chair and grabbed her chest. She forced herself to look, hoping it wasn't Paul.

To her surprise, it was Granny.

Mattie rushed to unlock the door and usher her grandmother inside and into an armchair in the small seating area.

"Granny, what are you doing here?" Mattie swiped at her tear-streaked cheeks. "And how did you know where I was?"

Her grandmother leaned back in the plush green armchair and steepled her fingers before her chest, fixing Mattie with a pointed stare.

"More than one person saw the heated exchange by the tree. I wasn't quite sure what was lit up most—the tree or *you*."

Mattie groaned and sank into the twin armchair opposite Granny. "Like I needed to fuel any more gossip."

Granny was silent a moment before she reached to place a comforting hand on top of Mattie's. "Why are you upset with Paul, Mattie? What did the boy do? He looked completely gutted when you ran off."

Fresh tears fell unbidden down Mattie's face, and her voice shook as she fumbled for the words. "I don't know, Granny—except, *well*, he's leaving."

"And why does that concern you, Mattie Marie?" Granny asked in a straightforward tone. "I thought Paul Ammons was nothing more than a 'thorn in your side' as you put it the day you burst into my cottage when he got the France scholarship."

The scholarship again. . .

The day flashed back to Mattie with stunning clarity. She hadn't wanted to go home so mad. Her mom hadn't taken well to stress or emotional outbursts after her stroke, so Mattie had come to Granny's cottage to fume.

When Mattie didn't answer the initial question, Granny persisted. "Do you remember what I told you that day? Because I do. I said, 'Some opportunities come, and some go. It's a way of life. Don't doubt your place because one has passed you by. There's always a reason. And God is always orchestrating things in the background.'"

Mattie remembered. At the time, she hadn't understood. But her thoughts went to losing her mom that same summer. If she'd gotten the scholarship, would she have gone? She hadn't thought about it, hadn't allowed herself to think about it.

All those years later, the truth was clear. She wouldn't have left her mom, and she was glad for the time with her over the summer.

The tears had stopped with the realization, but Mattie's confusion hadn't. She studied her grandmother, who studied her.

"Why does Paul leaving concern you?"

Mattie thought about their recent months on the committee and the past week they'd been forced to spend together. Why *did* she care he was leaving?

Because she cared about *him*.

Her eyes widened, and she swallowed hard, the confession sinking in.

Granny only nodded as if Mattie had spoken aloud. How had her grandmother known before she did? Was it obvious to everyone but her?

Another wave of emotion assailed her, the words coming out this time in a whisper, "I want him to stay."

Granny shrugged. "Have you told him? How's he gonna know he *should* stay? He can't read your mind. You gotta tell the boy. Give him a reason to stay."

A reason to stay was the one thing Mattie didn't believe she could give, the past bearing down on her as it hadn't in over a decade.

———

Paul stood in the shadows behind Robby's stall longer than he cared to admit, perplexed about how the moment he was finally going to tell Mattie he was in love with her had ended so terribly.

He scoffed, berating himself for taking the phone call. He should have let it go to voice mail. But he hadn't, and Mattie had overheard and misunderstood. How would he set things straight?

Mattie latched on tight to what she believed was truth, and she was not swayed. He didn't stand a chance to explain or apologize. What he'd said was true, but he hadn't said it in a loving way, more like an accusation. No wonder she acted on the defensive.

Paul had messed up, the truth seeping into him. When it came to Mattie, he'd always made a mess of things, trying so hard to win her over, but he'd never tried standing up to her before.

He glanced at the time. He'd been gone too long. Mattie's aunt was likely ready to ring his neck. He tried to wipe the frustration from his face when he stepped back into the stall and regained the crepe-making helm.

It only took a few customers for Mrs. Broussard to hit his sore spot. "What happened with Mattie?"

He tried to play it off. "What do you mean?"

She stared at him with narrowed eyes. She was not buying it, and before he realized, he'd told her everything.

"So, you're not leaving?" she ventured, adding strawberries to the crepe.

Paul shook his head, relieved the music was loud enough outside the stall to muffle their conversation. The town already knew too much about him and Mattie.

"You've got to explain what happened and tell her how you feel. She's already building that wall higher than ever," Mrs. Broussard said with a sigh. "She's trying her hardest to control everything, to ensure her world doesn't upend again whether by hurricane or the death of a loved one. This all started for her in high school. Loss does a number on a person, especially one so young."

She surveyed the crowd with the same faraway expression as earlier, then it cleared, and she met his eyes again.

"You're wrapped up in all of this too, you know, whether you or she realizes it."

"Me?" Paul asked with a frown. "How do I from back in high school factor into it?"

Mrs. Broussard nodded, her expression solemn. "You got the scholarship she really wanted. You got valedictorian. She was in a competition with you to prove she could work harder, do better, control what she couldn't. Paul, it's really about losing her parents and there being nothing she could do about it. No matter how hard she worked, how much she cared, they still left her, and there was nothing else she could do to make either of them stay."

The realization washed over Paul like light from a light bulb coming on in a dark place. It all made sense—Mattie's focusing on the past, fighting to preserve it, save the town, best him still.

How could he break through to her, show her that nothing she did would be enough to outrun the hurt of the past? He knew that firsthand. How could he show her she was enough just as she was, not for what she could accomplish?

Paul spotted his father walking through the crowd, shaking hands and smiling at each person in his wake—the perfect dedicated mayor.

The challenge he wanted to give to Mattie turned the mirror to his own reflection. How could he show *himself* that nothing he did would be enough to outrun the hurt of his past? Could he, just as he was, be enough—for his father, for Mattie, for God?

"O, Come All Ye Faithful" started playing over the speakers, and he truly listened to the lyrics this time while he made more crepes. The song was about a simple but strong faith, coming into God's presence, finding joy, and trusting Him to be faithful even when life is hard.

And through the song, Paul heard truth spoken within him. *It's time to stop running and come home.*

Tears stung his eyes. God had been the one to call him back to Moreau, back to Him.

It was time to stop running.

When he turned to Mrs. Broussard, he didn't have to say anything. "Go do what you need to do, Paul. I'm fine here."

He smiled and left, rushing into the crowd, searching for his father, who was headed across the street. He called out, and his father stopped on the sidewalk.

"Hey, Dad. Where you heading?"

His father nodded toward town hall. "Just popping into the office real quick."

Of course. He shook the thought away and breathed a silent prayer as he plunged forward into unknown territory. "Mind if I come with you? I have something I want to talk to you about."

His father's eyebrows rose slightly, but he nodded, and they walked the block to the municipal building.

Paul followed his father to his office, where he opened a desk drawer and the filing cabinet before coming around the desk, leaning against it, and giving Paul his full attention.

The gesture took Paul aback. It had never happened before in this place.

"What is it you'd like to talk about, Paul?"

With a sharp inhale, he ran through how to start such a conversation—over twenty years in the making. "Well, I, uh," he started, then mustered the courage to come out with it. "I've always felt less important to you than the town, your job, even this building. I can never measure up, Dad."

His father's face fell, confusion in his eyes. "That's not true, Paul."

Paul dropped into a chair. "It's felt true my whole life."

"I didn't realize," his father said, the truth evident in his shocked expression. "I just wanted you to be the best you could be. I thought I was setting the example—working hard, caring for a worthy cause, sacrificing."

With a frown, his father sank onto the edge of his desk. "I guess I overdid it."

Paul sighed. "That's an understatement. You're an incredible mayor, but I needed an incredible dad more." He couldn't help the anguish in his face, fighting back the pressing emotion. His father seemed in the same boat, moisture rimming his eyes.

"I'm sorry, Paul. I never meant for you to feel this way. I thought I was doing the right thing, but I can see now I've failed you."

For his father to admit a fraction of what he just had left Paul speechless and also lighter, this burden of the past falling away—not gone but lessened in the span of minutes.

"I got so wrapped up in a cause, a good one, that I let down the most important one. Can you forgive me?"

Paul didn't hesitate, because this peace offering was more than he had hoped for a year ago. "Yeah, Dad. I can."

His father had tears falling as he opened his arms to embrace Paul, and the years fell away to the little boy playing the ordinance game, longing for his father to choose him instead of his job.

The hurt of the past was still there, but forgiving his father had already dulled Paul's pain. He dared to hope that they could truly reconcile.

Paul thought of another reconciliation he longed for—with Mattie. God would certainly have to intervene there too.

———◆———

Mattie returned to the market long enough to close the booth, avoid Paul, and leave as soon as possible.

She'd spent a fitful night, alternating feelings of regret for what she'd said and justifying it to protect her heart. She had admitted to herself she cared about Paul, but she was clearly out of her senses. He obviously didn't feel the same way if he still planned to go away.

The best thing to do was keep avoiding him until she could get a better grip on her emotions and put this first weekend of the market behind her. She had plenty to distract her since it was a full market day, and he would be occupied in the crepe stall again.

The day passed in a blur with Mattie tending to more tasks and speaking to dozens of visitors about saving the chapel. The crowd had doubled in size from the night before, and she still needed to pinch herself that her idea was working.

She passed out flyers about the following days for the market and the town's other events leading up to Christmas, including that evening's candlelight caroling service in the chapel courtyard.

Before Mattie knew it, the market was closed, and she had just enough time to run home, thaw out, and go with her aunt and grandmother to the chapel. The two women were uncharacteristically quiet on the walk, and Mattie prayed they would hold their peace for now.

What Granny had said at the *Gazette* gave Mattie plenty to occupy her thoughts, along with her admission that she cared about Paul and wanted him to stay. Could she tell him, give him a reason to stay, as Granny had encouraged?

She wasn't sure. It was a risk. She would be vulnerable. And if she told him, would it matter? What if he said no, said that he was still leaving?

Mattie couldn't bear it. Another person leaving her by choice like her dad.

Her aunt had spent most of the day with Paul, and if she was planning to try to mend things between them, Mattie couldn't give her the chance. She needed distance from Paul, space to clear her head and her heart.

The chapel rose in a dark silhouette against the night, a beacon of light temporarily extinguished, but Mattie would see it come back to life. She would see to its restoration. They stepped into the old brick courtyard directly behind the church as snow fell, and Mary Ann handed each of them a lit white candle with a clear cup around it.

Aunt Adale led them to stand behind Robby and his wife, Margie, and Mattie stood between her aunt and grandmother and didn't dare look around, knowing Paul and his parents were present.

Instead, she focused her attention on the back of the chapel, the blue tarp covering a corner. She imagined the old oak tree that used to stand sentinel near the building, only a rough patch of ground marking where it once stood.

The service began with voices raising in unison to sing "Silent Night," but Mattie didn't join in.

She studied the chapel, thinking of all the services the old stone had witnessed over its many years, those of heartache and of joy, as well as the whispered and penitent prayers of the faithful who gathered there over the centuries, her own ancestors praising God within its walls.

Mattie's breath caught at the memories of her mom praising God beyond her circumstances, beyond the limitations of her body, encased in a pure, steadfast faith.

The next song was called, and Mattie's heart squeezed, eyes filling with tears, the words drifting through her mind and heart like a whisper of truth.

O come all ye faithful, joyful and triumphant.

Like Grandpa Oliver said, simple but profound with its message for the faithful to come and adore Christ the Lord, the light of the world. She bowed her head, eyes watching the flicker of the candle, as everyone sang about the simplicity of coming and adoring the one who saved them.

Conviction washed over Mattie, not heavy and condemning, but like the dusting of snow, cleansing and new, coating the world in white as if to welcome a new start, another chance.

She had been so focused on restoring the chapel, a physical place of wood and stone, but what about the restoration of her own life, of the past?

Maybe God wanted to restore *her* as much as she wanted to restore the church and town.

Was restoration as simple as coming and adoring the one who held her, had held her through it all? Could she be restored and truly live again?

Paul's words returned to her about how she tried to take on everything by herself as if she could take care of it all. He had been right. She spent years of her life with that exact aim, pushing herself to do more and care more and take care of everything she could, holding on too tightly to what she couldn't control, as if she could change the past and regain those she had lost.

But the truth was she didn't have to do everything right or take care of everyone or work to deserve something. She simply had to come as she was, stepping out in faith and surrender, and praise Him who had given all for her.

Tears flowed freely, the realization seeping into her, and she slipped past her aunt and out of the courtyard. She didn't stop until she reached the market, the tree, and the overhead lights still brightening the space.

Mattie sank onto a bench, the same one she and Paul had sat on, and grappled with further truth. She couldn't save the town because she couldn't save herself.

No one could be perfect, not even Paul.

She inhaled deeply of the cool air, this new perspective opening her eyes to what she hadn't seen because she was too busy, too concerned with tasks and accomplishments, besting a high school rival. But for what purpose? To prove she could handle things.

Paul had proved to her she couldn't.

Hurried footsteps falling hard on concrete met her ears, and in a rush, Paul ran into the market, twisting in frantic search until his gaze met hers.

"*Mattie*," he said, catching his breath and striding toward her, a look of determination on his handsome face, concern in his eyes. "I need to apologize. I shouldn't have said what I did last night. It wasn't fair."

She stood, arms wrapped around herself, tears still falling. "But it was true." She offered a sad smile. "And what I needed to hear."

Paul moved closer until he stood a few feet in front of her. "You don't have to go through life with the world on your shoulders, Mattie. You don't need to try to save anything or anyone. That's what God is trying to do, and sometimes He brings us together as a way of getting our attention, to show us we're not alone." He closed the space between them and took her hand. "I'm not taking the job. I'm staying in Moreau."

Relief flooded Mattie, a smile breaking through the tears as she gazed up at him. Despite how she'd treated him, he had supported her, believed in her, in all the moments since he had come home. And in all those years before when she thought he had stolen something from her, she had been wrong.

She raised a hand to touch his cheek, drawing nearer to him, reminiscent of the last time they'd stood so close in that exact spot. She stopped herself from looking to see if the twig had reappeared.

Paul smiled, arm slipping around her waist, his admiration for her, and dare she imagine love, reflected in his eyes.

It was time for restoration, and she would start here, white flurries swirling around them.

Mattie drew Paul toward her, their lips meeting in a promise of second chances and a restoration of faith beneath the Louisiana snow.

Morgan Tarpley Smith is a world traveler who weaves stories of history and heart. She loves to write inspirational fiction that transports readers to faraway places and intertwines past and present to explore questions of truth and faith. She has coauthored a split-time fiction writing book with award-winning author Melanie Dobson and is the founder of A Split in Time Fiction Group on Facebook for lovers of novels where the past and present collide. Morgan is an award-winning journalist who works as a freelance writer and author assistant and lives in Louisiana with her family. For more information, visit www.morgantarpleysmith.com.

Restoring Christmas

Betsy St. Amant

DEDICATION

To Megan
Who would have thought Twitter could be so life changing?

Acknowledgments

Every book requires a village, and I'm so happy that my tribe for this novella included my coauthors, Lenora Worth and Morgan Tarpley Smith. I've never had so much fun in an endless Facebook Messenger chat! I'm grateful for you ladies and your encouragement as we created this Christmas town! I keep forgetting the Lavigne family isn't actually real.

As always, I'm grateful for my wonderful agent these past fifteen years, Tamela Hancock Murray, and for the talented team at Barbour for providing their editing, marketing, and cover art skills to make this set truly shine!

Special thanks to Megan for her fast turnaround when critiquing my hastily written pages, and to my other dear friends who prayed me through this deadline—Georgiana, Anne, Nicole, and Ashley, to name a few. (And my mama!)

I'm also grateful to my sweet hubby, who endured my sporadic "on deadline" freak-outs, and who kept my Starbucks app loaded with plenty of coffee funds. Love you!

And praise be to God for gifting me with yet another opportunity to write fiction that offers hope to readers. *Soli Deo gloria.*

Chapter One

Two weeks till Christmas

S he was being stalked by Christmas.

Jolene Broussard shoved her hands in the pockets of her orange peacoat as she strolled the all-too-familiar streets of Moreau, Louisiana, decorated in full color for the coming holiday. The twinkling lights strung between lampposts and the sun glistening off the Petit River should have shot thrills of yuletide joy through her weary spirit, but as it were, those shots felt more like shrapnel.

Moreau hadn't changed much in the five years since she'd last been back, though the effects of the hurricane this past August lingered. Despite that storm—maybe even *because of* that storm—the heart of the community still pulsed rapidly all around her, evident in the carefully tied bows on the wreaths mounted on each streetlight, in the ornaments piled upon every branch of the Christmas tree gracing the center of town square, and in the way the shops along Rue de la Chapelle offered free hot chocolate to everyone who strolled by.

Moreau had always possessed a good heart, but the people didn't usually have to deal with someone walking away and not coming back.

As her mom and cousin pointed out, she always had "marched to her own drum."

Jolene lifted her chin into the wind. She'd flown in from Nashville roughly an hour ago, took an Uber to her childhood home, left her bags in the corner of the spare bedroom, and decided a walk was in order. Not only to stretch her legs after the flight but to emotionally prepare for the onslaught of her family once they realized she'd made it to town. She'd intentionally left her arrival time vague.

Thankfully, her mother still had the bad habit of not locking doors during the day, so Jolene had been able to slip in and out before confirming if anyone had been home. As a child, it had been fun to get lost in the Lavigne House, with its sprawling layout and echoing hallways.

Now, as an adult, she just felt lost in a different way.

Jolene shoved back her hair as she strolled, her stack of multicolored bracelets jangling on her arm. Coming home should be a good thing. After all, her mom and cousin and grandmother had been requesting she return for the holidays for the last five years. They'd be happy to see her.

So why the knot in her stomach the size of a lump of coal?

Jolene kept walking, having no real destination in mind except procrastination—and maybe scoring one of those free hot chocolates. Shopkeepers and patrons passed her on their way home for the evening, beanies pulled low and shoulders hunched against the wind. No one seemed to recognize her yet, though time—and her winter cap—might be helping.

Hammering sounded, then a familiar voice rang over the pounding.

"Jolene Broussard. As I live and breathe!"

So much for not being recognized. Jolene forced herself to stop and turn. She might not have been home for years, but she'd recognize Kimberly's southern drawl anywhere. The middle-aged woman owned Moreau's most popular hair salon—Kimberly's Kurls—and wore her gossip-queen badge with pride. That is, when the police chief wasn't threatening to take over the throne. "Hey, Kimberly."

"Is that really you, darling?" Her bottle-red hair screamed Christmas, especially when paired with her emerald-green sweater.

"Guilty." Jolene shrugged, raising her voice over the incessant hammering, which she now realized was coming from a man in a gray long-sleeved T-shirt standing on the end of the porch.

"Cameron—looky here. It's Moreau's very own long-lost daughter." Kimberly gestured grandly, as if Jolene might start swallowing fire or juggling balls. "Jolene Broussard."

He lowered his hammer and strode toward her, a tool belt slung low on his hips. "So, you're Eloise's girl." His blue gaze lasered into hers. Not accusing, but not welcoming either.

Jolene stiffened. "Her granddaughter. I'm Adale's daughter."

"*Long-lost* daughter," Kimberly corrected with a peal of laughter.

Long-lost was a bit of a stretch, but leave it to Kimberly to treat the truth like Laffy Taffy. Jolene forced a smile. "So it seems."

As usual, Kimberly didn't take a hint. "Goodness, it's been years! How's Nashville treating you? Have you gotten settled in yet? You should come by and let me give you a quick shape-up." She reached forward and touched strands of Jolene's dark brown hair. "On the house, of course."

Had anyone ever mastered the art of being insulting under the guise of being nice like Kimberly? Jolene eased out of the woman's grasp. "I'll keep that in mind." She glanced at Cameron—was that a flicker of a smile on his lips?

"Cameron here was helping me hang my new salon sign." Kimberly let out a loud puff of air. "He's a regular handyman."

Cameron shifted his weight on the porch deck. "Contractor, actually. I—"

Kimberly waved one hand in the air dismissively. "Po-tay-to, po-tah-to. . . He can fix anything."

"How do you know Granny—I mean, Eloise?" Jolene asked. Then winced. Stupid question—it was Moreau. Everyone knew everyone, and if they'd been around Kimberly for long enough, they probably knew what they each had for dinner too.

"I did some repair work on her cottage this past summer, immediately after the storm." Cameron belted his hammer, then crossed his arms over his chest. "But I guess you wouldn't know anything about that, would you?"

Kimberly's overly plucked eyebrows shot toward her hairline.

Jolene's heart stammered. "Excuse me?"

"Like everyone says—you've been gone." He shrugged, his gaze steady on hers. "You missed it."

She checked her watch. Since leaving for her walk, it had taken exactly thirteen minutes for someone to point out her unforgivable sin of leaving town after community college. Well, less time than that, if she counted Kimberly's digs, but she'd learned years back not to let the village busybody affect her.

But receiving instant judgment from a total stranger—an unfortunately handsome stranger—was setting a new record.

An argument rose in her chest, splotchy and loud and begging release. "And where exactly did *you* come from? I was born here."

"Maybe I'm not a native, but Moreau has been my home for years now." Cameron shot her a pointed glance. "I'm loyal to it—*and* its people."

She bristled. "Well, that obviously means you left somewhere else to come to Moreau, so if we're done here, Mr. Kettle. . . Or do you prefer Mr. Pot?"

Kimberly threw back her red head and guffawed. "I didn't know I was going to need popcorn!"

Cameron ignored her, holding Jolene's gaze. "My family were Katrina survivors. We moved to Shreveport when I was younger, but I've always wanted to plug back into a southern community like Moreau. It reminds me of my old neighborhood. So I came here."

"And we're so glad you did." Kimberly patted Cameron's arm, and Jolene noticed his slight wince as he eased away.

Kimberly, unfazed, gestured toward Jolene. "On the contrary, this one couldn't wait to skip town."

Jolene opened her mouth to defend herself, simultaneously wondering why she bothered but unable to stop the explanation from coming. "I've been building a career in Nashville."

Following her dreams, making her path outside of the family name and legacy—and as she'd learned two weeks ago via one life-changing letter—she'd done it all for nothing.

"She's an *artist*." Kimberly pursed her lips, somehow making the term sound scandalous.

Jolene started to reply, then clamped her lips together, her fire extinguishing. Finally, the good ol' gossip queen had gotten something wrong.

Jolene shook her head slowly. "Actually, I'm not anymore."

———◆———

Cameron opened the door of his truck and tossed his tool belt inside, wiping a bead of sweat from his forehead despite the cold night air. He'd finally finished hanging the sign, which he'd done as a favor for Kimberly before realizing exactly what it would cost him. He'd never heard anyone talk so much in his life. And she'd had plenty to say about Jolene, even after the woman continued down the street.

Somehow, in all the stories he'd heard about Jolene Broussard over the past few years, he'd not been told how strikingly beautiful she was. Her orange jacket set off her long dark hair, and a white beanie made her green eyes blaze with fire—especially when she looked at him. Which he deserved. He hadn't been very welcoming. But this was *Jolene Broussard*—the one who ran away and hurt the family he'd come to adore since joining the town of Moreau.

One thing was certain—the framed pictures Granny had on her piano didn't do the woman justice.

He hoisted himself inside his truck and slammed the door shut. Not that it mattered. Jolene's beauty was irrelevant, because anyone who hurt Granny made it on his list. And his list might not be neatly divided into Naughty or Nice like Santa's, but he kept records all the same. His organized, structured, detail-minded brain couldn't help it. He formed a first impression after meeting anyone and filed the information away for the future.

Those lists of his had come in handy over the years of becoming a business owner and discerning who to trust. He'd saved himself—and his bank account—a lot of grief by learning to trust his gut.

He cranked the engine and adjusted the heat blowing through the vents. Right now his gut—as evidenced by the poorly veiled hurt in Granny's eyes every time she spoke of Jolene—said that Jolene was only out for herself. Why she'd chosen to come home this Christmas instead of the last several, he didn't know, but he could bet it was for a selfish reason.

Granny—and Adale, though he knew Jolene's mom less well— didn't deserve to ride Jolene's whims again. Why would anyone want to leave a picturesque, ideal community like Moreau for the flash of Nashville lights? In Moreau, everyone was family. And with her own mother a widow, even Jolene's cousin Mattie helped Adale out more than Jolene did.

He'd nearly married the Jolene type once before, back when he lived in Shreveport, and that had been more than enough. He'd sworn he'd never fall for that scam again.

He drove down the block, lifting one hand in a wave to his buddy Paul Ammons coming out of the town hall—probably running a last-minute errand for the town revitalization committee and Mattie, as the two of them had seemed cozier the past few days.

And there she was. Jolene and her orange coat, standing in front of the historic chapel that he'd been hired to help renovate. Of course, they were attempting to bring in a professional—Rémy Vachon, an architect who specialized in historic restoration—but thanks to Mattie, Cameron had secured a place on the committee to help redo the interior courtyard. Local artist Nate Lewis had been working with him on the big mural on the north wall while Cameron tackled the gazebo, but Nate had recently hurt his wrist. He wasn't sure who was going to take his place, but he planned to meet with Mattie tomorrow and figure it out.

Of course, Mattie being Mattie meant that she'd prearranged for a big publicity event to reveal the mural a week before Christmas. The woman was marketing savvy and had been a great help with securing the funds the town needed to repair Moreau to its pre-hurricane status.

The tight reveal schedule meant he and Nate's replacement wouldn't have much time to finish, but thankfully Nate had already gotten the initial outline nearly completed, featuring a mossy bayou surrounded by cypress trees and a pelican. They had planned to replicate the original design as closely as possible.

Cameron's foot eased off the gas as he passed Jolene. Something about the vulnerable expression on her face as she stared up at the storm-affected church didn't exactly scream manipulator.

He slowed further. The wind chill was downright frigid. In fact, last week it had snowed for the first time in forever—and near the holidays. A Louisiana miracle, if he'd ever seen one. Maybe she needed a ride.

Before he could change his mind, he jerked the wheel and pulled his truck to the side of the road. The street was deserted, as it was officially suppertime in Moreau. He got out, shrugged into his thick work jacket, then shut his door. Jolene spun around, wariness etched across her face. Once again, he couldn't help but notice how beautiful she was.

But then, his ex-fiancée, Samantha, had been a looker too.

He cleared his throat, resting his hip against his door. "I was driving home and thought I'd make sure you were okay."

"*Okay* because I'm standing out in the cold?" She shoved her hands into her pockets, her slight frame shivering. "Or *okay* because you know how rude you were back there?"

Yikes. He winced. "Both?"

Something that might have been a grin tugged at her lips, but it vanished before he could tell for sure. "I'm okay, trust me. I expected it."

"Expected the weather? Or me?" He tilted his head, unable to take his gaze away from the strong curve of her jaw, her petite nose, her flashing green eyes.

"Judgment." She glanced down at the sidewalk before turning her gaze back to the church. "I always expect that around here."

He swallowed as conviction pinched. He attended church inside that very chapel every Sunday—minus the time it had been out of commission from the hurricane—and he wasn't exactly living what he believed when it came to how he'd treated Jolene.

"I'm not judging you." Well, that was a lie. He tried again. "I mean, I don't. . .know you."

"Exactly."

Point taken. He gestured toward his truck. He couldn't undo his first impression, but he could at least be a gentleman. "Do you need a ride to the Lavigne House?"

She hesitated, and he had the sense it wasn't so much that she was debating his offer as it was that she didn't want to go at all. She shifted in her boots. "I don't know *you*, either."

"Worried about stranger danger?" He couldn't help but release a smile at the absurdity that he could be dangerous to anyone. "Your cousin can vouch for me. We're on the town revitalization committee together." He held up both hands. "I promise I'm not a serial killer."

Jolene squinted at him, and now he was the one who felt like he was being judged.

Then a gust of wind lifted her dark hair off her collar and sent a cold rush down the neck of his own jacket. She shivered and edged toward his truck. "Okay, thanks. I didn't mean to go quite this far."

He opened the passenger door for her, trying not to inhale the scent of her coconut shampoo as she squeezed past him and hoisted herself into the tall seat. He rounded the truck and climbed into the driver's side, pausing to adjust the heater vents to aim in her direction.

And as he shifted the vehicle into Drive and became increasingly aware of her proximity, he realized that he too hadn't meant to go quite this far.

Chapter Two

Silverware clanked against her mother's beautiful red and gold Christmas dishes—the ones she'd set out every December since Jolene could recall—mixing with the animated chatter between Jolene's mom and cousin.

"The market is a hit so far." Mattie dabbed her mouth with her napkin. "We're already raising a lot for the chapel, and we've still got several events coming up! Like the ugly sweater cookie party, Santa's appearance at the market, and the big mural reveal."

Mom shot Mattie a look from across the table, one Jolene couldn't interpret. Mattie, clearly ignoring it, nodded at her cousin. "Jolene, are you staying long enough for the ball?"

"Of course she is." Granny, sitting to her right, tapped Jolene on the arm. "No way she came all this way for only a week."

It wasn't so much a hopeful suggestion but a command. Coming from Granny, though, that type of statement was a lot easier to swallow. No one told Granny no. The woman was a mastermind at urging people to do what she wanted but making them think it was their own idea. It seemed in recent years, however, she'd skipped the manipulation tactics and gone straight to bossy.

"I'll see." Jolene smiled and hoped it didn't look as awkward as it felt. It was good her family wanted her around—right? Her greeting upon arriving back at Lavigne House—after Cameron dropped her off at the foot of their long driveway—had been nothing like Jolene expected. No subtle digs on how long she'd been away. No "Kimberly" comments. No judgment. Only open arms, big hugs, ear-piercing squeals from Mattie, and a command from Granny to set the table for gumbo.

As usual in the Lavigne House, first things first.

"Well, what do you have to get back to?" Granny pressed. Unlike Kimberly, Granny *could* take a hint but brazenly chose not to.

And the answer was nothing. Thanks to one singular letter containing a form rejection, Jolene now had nothing to get back to except her longtime job doing graphic design that technically she could do from anywhere that offered a power source for her laptop. But that didn't mean she wanted to do it from Moreau.

Stalling, Jolene pointed to the remaining gumbo in her bowl. "Is this a new recipe?"

"You're kidding, right?" Mattie scoffed. "Granny? Change a recipe?"

Granny looked as offended as if Jolene had suggested it had been made with mud. "Of course not. Have you lost your faculties? First Chef Perot and now this."

Mom sighed around the amused smirk she was failing to hide. "Jolene, you could just answer your grandmother's question, you know."

Busted. Jolene ran her spoon over a mound of rice and released her own sigh of surrender. "I don't have anything to rush back to, Granny."

"Perfect!" Granny slammed one manicured hand down on the table so hard their tea glasses shook. "Then it's official. You're here through Christmas."

She should have seen this coming. Jolene smiled around her glass, but inside she fought back panic. She'd only planned to stay through Granny's big eightieth birthday reunion that upcoming Saturday night. Wasn't six days in Moreau after five years away plenty of penance?

No one knew her secret. . .and she wasn't sure she could hide it the two full weeks until Christmas. She needed to humor her grandmother, though. It wasn't every day someone turned the big 8–0. She owed it to Granny—after all, she was the one who taught Jolene to paint and had encouraged her during her teen years to pick up a paintbrush instead of her cell phone. The memory twisted the knife in Jolene's heart. Yet another regret to add to the list.

Another way she'd failed.

The gumbo—one of the few things she'd grudgingly admit she missed the most about Moreau—sat in her stomach like a rock, and Jolene nudged her bowl away. "I'm really tired from my flight. I think I'll crash early if that's okay."

Mattie's lips pursed in disappointment. "I was hoping to catch up."

"We will. I promise." Thanks to Granny, they'd have two weeks to do so now.

Just not tonight, when the tears pressed and Kimberly's—and Cameron's—comments about her absence weighed heavily on her heart. She wouldn't cry in front of any of them. In fact, the last official tear she'd shed had been at her father's funeral seven years ago, and she'd cried enough then to last a lifetime. She pushed back her chair.

Mom stood and gestured for Mattie to start clearing the dishes. "We'll clean up. Why don't you get some rest?" She came around the table and gave Jolene a hug, one that pressed the lump in Jolene's throat into an even tighter ball. "I'm glad you're home."

Home. Where was that anymore?

She couldn't help the pinch of jealousy as she eased out of the room, watching as her mother and Mattie slipped into a rhythm they'd obviously performed hundreds of times since Jolene had been away. Working together as a team, clearing the dining room, chuckling at inside jokes. Mattie had moved back in with Adale after the recent hurricane, and it seemed like they hadn't missed a beat. Mattie, her mom, and Granny—a full family. They didn't need her, so why on earth pretend they wanted her?

Especially after what she'd done.

Granny, who still sat at the table, stirred her remaining tea with her spoon and let out a delicate cough, jerking Jolene back to the present. "Before you go upstairs, be a dear and grab me some more sugar, will you?"

"Of course, Granny." Jolene changed course and headed toward the walk-through pantry that connected the dining room to the kitchen. She hesitated outside the open door at the terse whispers sounding from around the corner.

"You've got to ask her." The shutting of the refrigerator door punctuated Mom's whisper. "You really don't have a choice."

Mattie's voice was quiet, resigned. "I know. You're right."

Jolene started to step through the doorway, then stopped at her mother's urgent response.

"Then do it, sweetie. You're running out of time. The reveal is in a week!"

"I just. . ." Mattie's voice trailed off as water ran in the sink. Then it shut off. ". . .don't want her to. You know I love Jolene, but she's not exactly reliable."

Jolene reared back. The comment, on top of those from Cameron and Kimberly tonight, was too much for her first night back. What happened to the warm welcome she'd received an hour earlier? She pushed around the corner. "Ask me to do what?"

Mattie spun around, hands clutching a red dish towel. Her face blanched white. "I didn't mean. . ."

"Yes, you did." Jolene crossed her arms over her chest. "And just because I chose to move away and do something for myself outside of this town doesn't mean I'm not reliable."

She'd shown up repeatedly in the face of rejection to art gallery after art gallery. She'd submitted work after work, design after design, to numerous contests. That fateful letter—the rejection of her application to the prestigious art school she'd dreamed of since she was a freshman, painting with Granny in the parlor—had been the nail in the coffin of her dreams.

Her dream might have died, but not because she wasn't *reliable.*

"That's not what she meant." Mom lifted both hands in a gesture of peace. "Hear her out."

Of course her mother would take Mattie's side—the good kid. Jolene fought back the emotion pressing against her throat. She hated feeling that way. Once upon a time, she and Mattie had been best friends. But that was before they'd grown up and life became so complicated. Mattie had found her place in the world. . .in their family.

While Jolene felt like a dusty, lost puzzle piece.

Mattie dropped the towel and crossed the kitchen to Jolene. "I shouldn't have said that. But I have a big favor to ask, and I know you're probably not going to want to do it."

"Because I can't be trusted with it?"

"You tell me." Mattie inhaled a deep breath. "One of the events the town revitalization committee is planning to draw tourists is the big reveal of the repainted mural at the church courtyard."

Jolene's heart skipped a beat. Oh no.

Mattie continued. "Cameron has been working on the courtyard gazebo, fixing it up after the storm, and we're still waiting on the chapel roof to be patched and to hear whether or not the architect will accept the project. . . ."

"The point, Mattie," Mom gently urged.

Mattie flapped her hands. "Anyway, Nate, our artist, sprained his wrist. He has the initial outline, a replica of the original, but hasn't started painting yet. And. . .the entire thing has to be finished in a week."

Jolene's throat tightened. Surely her cousin wasn't going to. . .

"And you're—you know. An artist." Mattie offered a hopeful smile. "And you're here."

She was, indeed. She was also a last resort. Her mom's words to Mattie rang in her head. *You really don't have a choice.*

Jolene swallowed. "No thanks."

"See!" Mattie turned to Adale, shaking her head with frustration. "I told you."

"I'm not an artist anymore." Jolene forced the words from her dry mouth. "I'm sorry." They didn't know about the art school rejection. And the dozens of contest losses and the galleries ghosting her attempts at shows. Right now she couldn't find the words to tell them.

"Of course you are." Mattie frowned in confusion. "I follow you on social media."

Mom moved toward Jolene, taking her hand. "Now, darling. Your cousin needs you. Your *town* needs you."

The gentle dig, however intended or unintended, found its spot in Jolene's heart. Was Moreau still her town? At this point, it seemed it depended on who one asked. Cameron? He'd say no. Kimberly? Big no. But her family still wanted her involvement, and Jolene had to admit, it was nice to feel needed.

But the pressure—not so nice.

"I've never done a mural, and that's a tight time frame." To put it mildly. Not to mention that mural had been a town favorite. The spot where all the high school kids snapped their selfies and tourists gathered for pictures. Annual photo scavenger hunts in the town had always involved capturing an aspect of the detailed painting on camera. She'd never do it justice, even if it was essentially coloring between the lines Nate had already drawn.

Jolene tugged her hand free from her mom's. "I'm sorry." She kept repeating the apologies, and her family kept ignoring them.

Granny bustled into the kitchen holding her tea glass, oblivious to the tension. "I suppose being the eighty-year-old matriarch of a family isn't reason enough to have sugar brought to a woman." She opened the spice cabinet door, then stopped as she took in the tense silence. "What's all this?"

"Mattie asked Jolene to finish the courtyard mural since Nate hurt his wrist." Adale leaned one slim hip against the kitchen island. "And Jolene said she's not an artist anymore and turned her down."

"Pishposh!" Granny declared as she grabbed the canister of sugar. She had to stretch on her toes to do so, but it didn't deter her. Nothing did. She set the canister on the counter and pointed at Jolene. "Once an artist, always an artist."

Not according to the art school, but Granny always did live in a world of her own rules. Jolene sighed. "You don't understand, Granny."

"I don't need to." She lifted her delicate chin as she dumped a generous spoonful of sugar into her tea. "The town needs a mural painted. You're a painter. There's nothing to understand except why I'm getting my own sugar when there's three able-bodied women in this same room."

Mattie rushed to Granny's side and replaced the canister in the cabinet. "Sorry, Granny."

"I'm kidding. I'm turning eighty—not exactly Methuselah. And I can still touch my toes." She bent over and did exactly that before straightening upright and adjusting her elastic-waisted pants. "Now, that's that."

She took her glass and left the room, leaving Adale and Mattie staring hopefully at Jolene with raised eyebrows.

"Fine. I'll do it." How could she argue with. . .whatever it was Granny had just done.

Mattie wrapped Jolene in a hug. "Thank you! And to make up for my careless comment, I'll make it my personal mission to help you find something awesome to wear to the ball."

Oh joy. Jolene hid her wince before Mattie pulled away and could see her face.

Her cousin rambled on as she went back to the sink full of dishes. "There's a revitalization committee meeting in the morning, so I can officially propose the idea to Mayor Ammons. I'm sure he'll go for it, but for protocol's sake, you'll have to go with me, of course."

Her mother's smile of approval kept Jolene from arguing.

Jolene nodded, too tired from her trip and the emotional roller coaster of the evening to argue any further. "Whatever. Wake me up in time for coffee."

"I'll set my alarm to Christmas music. You'll hear it across the hall." Mattie beamed. "Paul will be so excited when I tell him!"

Her cousin, back now turned, was still talking as Jolene mouthed, *Good night*, to her chuckling mother and slipped silently from the room to go to bed.

One thing to look forward to—even exhausted, post-travel dreams would have to be better than this nightmare she'd agreed to.

Chapter Three

H e needed coffee.

Cameron poured the remaining bit of the dark brew into his mug, casting a quick glance around the nearly empty conference room. Mayor Richard Ammons, Paul's father, was already there, sitting in his typical seat at the head of the large round table and scrolling on his iPad. Mattie was supposed to be there any minute for their weekly update meeting, though Paul wouldn't be able to make this one because of work.

Speaking of, he needed to be working on the gazebo. The courtyard wasn't going to be ready for the big reveal if he didn't get a move on. The tight timeline had been a little optimistic, even for Mattie, but he admired her ambition and passion for restoring Moreau. Hopefully, he wouldn't let anyone down.

Unfortunately, with Nate's recent injury, the courtyard would be even further behind schedule.

Cameron took a seat near Richard and inhaled his steaming coffee. He'd been up too late last night, repeatedly reliving his brief interaction with Jolene and then berating himself for doing so. Had he learned nothing from his last breakup? The woman was trouble. He'd be polite to her while she was here, but in his experience, zebras didn't change their stripes.

He wouldn't be fooled by a pretty face again.

"How's the gazebo coming along?" The mayor replaced the stylus on his iPad and leaned back in the swivel chair, the faux leather squeaking under his weight.

"Slowly but surely." As soon as the meeting was over, he'd get back to it. He took a long sip of the bitter liquid to fortify himself, then dared to ask the looming question. "Do you know if Mattie has found anyone to replace Nate on the mural yet?"

Richard braced both arms behind his head as he nodded. "I think she's going to update us today. There's no time to waste, that's for sure."

The door opened, and Mattie breezed inside, unwinding a scarf from around her neck. Her long blond hair shook loose. "Sorry I'm late!" Clearly flustered—had Mattie ever been late a day in her life?—she cast an annoyed glance behind her. "This way, Jolene!"

Jolene?

Cameron's eyes widened. Kimberly's words from yesterday tapped at his memory. *"She's an artist."*

No. Surely Mattie hadn't asked her cousin to—

Jolene strolled into the room next, carrying a canvas bag and covering a yawn with her hand as she headed straight to the coffee pot. Then she noted the empty carafe and sighed loudly enough to wake the rest of Moreau.

"Jolene." Mattie hissed as she took a seat on the other side of Richard. "We're starting."

"Sorry." Blinking rapidly, as if trying to wake herself up, Jolene hurried to the empty chair beside Mattie and slung her bag into her lap as she sat. Her gaze dropped to Cameron's coffee mug; then she raised her eyes to meet his. She squinted at him. "You."

He turned up his mug and swallowed the last lukewarm sip, then toasted her with it. "Me." And speaking of pronouns, he had a sneaking suspicion this courtyard project was unfortunately heading toward "they."

She opened her mouth to reply, but Mayor Ammons interrupted by calling the meeting to order.

And sure enough, Mattie got right down to business. She sat up straight in her chair, squaring her shoulders. "I'd like to propose that my cousin Jolene fill Nate's shoes for the mural so the reveal doesn't have to be rescheduled."

"Wait. Rescheduling is an option?" Jolene half-raised her hand like a kid in school. "Why don't you just wait for him, then?"

Sounded good to Cameron. It certainly beat having to work with Jolene in that courtyard all week. But Mattie would never go for it—as evidenced by her tight-lipped expression and narrowed eyes.

"It's his right wrist," Richard offered to Jolene, patiently, as if she was new in town. And technically, she was. "It'll take weeks to heal, and even then, I'm sure he'd have to work slowly once he started to use it."

"A spring reveal could be nice. Good weather." Jolene shrugged. "There are plenty of other events between now and Christmas, right, Mattie? You were mentioning them last night."

"That's a good point." Richard nodded as his chair creaked again.

If it were possible for steam to literally come from one's ears, Cameron was certain Mattie could have fueled an entire locomotive.

Mattie braced her forearms on the table. "Even so, this *has* to be done by next week's scheduled reveal. I've already sent out press releases, and we're depending on this publicity. Every little bit helps rebuild Moreau." Her clipped words left little room for argument.

But that didn't stop Jolene from trying. She leaned forward, matching Mattie's energy. "If Nate is that good of an artist, isn't he worth waiting for?"

"That's also a good point." Richard's eyes darted back and forth between the two cousins, like watching a June bug hop between blades of grass.

Cameron remembered Kimberly's comment last night about bringing popcorn and stifled a laugh. He could see now what she meant. At least this time he wasn't the one in Jolene's line of verbal fire.

"Maybe so, but you said you would do this." Mattie cleared her throat, her cheeks pink as she held Jolene's gaze. "You said you were *reliable*."

A thick tension filled the conference room. All eyes focused on Jolene.

She let out a slow sigh. "I know." Then she looked down, tracing the grain in the tabletop with one finger as if thinking. The jumble of brightly colored bracelets on her arm clacked together over the sleeve of her dark sweater. She lifted her chin, her expression resolved. "I'll do it."

"Great." Mattie clapped her hands together and smiled, crisis averted. "If that sounds good to you, Mayor, then Jolene can start this afternoon."

"Today?" Jolene's eyes widened.

"There's no time to waste." Mattie began typing a note on her phone even as she continued rattling off instructions. "Cameron, she'll be on your team like Nate was. You'll have to show her the ropes."

He fought to hide his own sigh. Perfect. The woman he most wanted to avoid this Christmas had just been assigned as his direct responsibility. And judging by the slight challenge in Jolene's eyes, she wasn't going to be nearly as amiable to work with as Nate had been.

He forced a smile anyway. "Welcome to the team." What was the adage about if you can't beat 'em, join 'em? Or was "Keep your enemies close" more appropriate here?

"What about supplies?"

Jolene's question was directed at Mattie, not him. Subordination already. This was going to be fun.

Cameron cleared his throat, determining to answer anyway. "Nate already purchased everything he needed, and it's locked in the chapel's supply closet. I can show you."

"Cameron has a key," Mattie explained. "He's the team leader for the entire church project. He's even working on getting Mr. Vachon to restore the roof."

Jolene raised her eyebrows. "Who's he?"

Mattie tapped the tabletop. "Rémy Vachon. He's an architect out of New Orleans who has expertise in historic renovations. Him agreeing to help us out would be a huge coup."

To put it mildly. The renowned architect was supposed to arrive that week—possibly as soon as Wednesday—to view the property and give a final verdict on his decision. With Mattie's eagerness to get the chapel on the historic register, they needed Rémy's expertise. But he'd have to heavily discount his work in order for them to afford it, so a bit of a Christmas miracle was still needed.

"All of this sounds great to me. Let's carry on as usual this week, and Cameron, keep me posted on Rémy's arrival." Mayor Ammons picked up his iPad, clearly in a hurry to end the meeting. "Mattie, I trust you'll update Paul on today's meeting? Or should I?"

The knowing twinkle in his eye belied the man's professional exterior, confirming Cameron's suspicions that something had recently shifted between Mattie and Paul.

A slight blush tinged Mattie's cheeks as she stood and gathered her things. "Yes, sir. I'll tell him."

Jolene stood a bit more slowly, nodding at Mayor Ammons as she shouldered her canvas tote bag. Apparently, she was about as excited to work on this mural as Cameron was to have her do it. Of all the weeks for Nate to sprain his wrist.

But it wasn't like the guy wanted an injured hand for the holidays. At least Cameron was able to work and do his part for Moreau. He was certain Nate would trade places in a heartbeat. Cameron needed to adjust his attitude.

Of course, Jolene did too, but he could only control himself.

He rounded the table to stand beside his new partner. "Ready to get to work?"

"I guess we have to." She shook back her dark hair, and her giant wooden earrings, the same variety of colors as her bracelets, swung wildly by her jaw.

The woman wasn't afraid of color, he'd give her that. Would she be content to follow the mural's muted, pastel design? The last thing he needed was her trying to change a town staple at the last minute. Cameron swallowed hard as he thought once again about Nate. Weren't there people out there who learned to paint with their feet?

"I rode here with my cousin, so I can walk to the church." Jolene's stiff posture spoke volumes of her lack of interest in working with him.

Cameron frowned. "It's cold out. Ride with me."

"If you insist."

Mattie and the mayor had paused to talk over by the coffee station, so Cameron pulled the door open for Jolene, nodding at her hastily murmured thanks. It was time for a peace treaty—for Moreau, if for nothing else. He could be civil and not get pulled into her charade, which he was sure existed. Jolene obviously wasn't back in town for her family, and she clearly hadn't come to paint the mural and help her hometown, so a question remained. Why *was* she here when she didn't want to be?

He touched her arm before she neared the main entrance of the building, slowing her hasty departure. "You don't have to do this, you know."

She frowned. "Ride with you?"

"No. Paint." Cameron crossed his arms over his chest, lowering his voice in case Mattie or Richard was close behind. "I realize we didn't exactly get off on the best foot yesterday, but this isn't an actual gunpoint situation, you know. No one is forcing you to do this."

"You don't understand." Jolene shook her head, clutching her bag strap. "There's more to it than that." She hesitated. "But it's my problem, not yours."

A cloud of emotion filled her eyes, and he tilted his head, hating the surge of sympathy that rushed through him. That was exactly what Samantha had resorted to—using tears to get her way. It had always worked, and he was left the sucker.

He drew in a defensive breath. "Let's just work together and get this project done—the sooner the better." For multiple reasons.

She shrugged, looking away. "Works for me."

Her guard was still up, and a piece of him desperately wanted to see what she was like when it came down. But that would mean lowering his too, and well—fool him once. . .

He pushed open the door and held it for her against the cold wind rushing inside. Jolene shivered, and he remembered how her face had fallen at the sight of the empty carafe.

He sighed. "Coffee first?"

That solid guard softened, and she nodded with a grateful smile as she edged past him, her coconut scent wafting in his face.

Fool him twice.

———◆———

The chapel before them stretched far above their heads, its steeple jutting toward the azure sky like a regal, slightly crooked spike of a tiara. The blue tarp covering the roof in various patches offered another sad testimony to the damage done months ago—giant, spotty blemishes on an otherwise beautiful canvas.

Jolene clutched her still-warm coffee against her chest as a sudden gust of wind ruffled her hair. This environment for painting was a far cry from the designated corner space in her studio apartment in Nashville. Or from Granny's cozy old cottage, where they had painted together on the weekends every summer throughout high school and into college.

Until Jolene's dad died.

She shuffled her boots against the dry, brittle leaves underfoot, kicking away the memories. "Any chance of getting heat lamps out here while we work?"

"The committee actually owns a few heaters that we pass around from site to site as needed." Cameron shoved his hands into his pockets as he tilted his head back, surveying the church roof. "I think they're being used at the market most nights, but I'll see what I can do. Thankfully, the snow seems to have stopped, or this would have been nearly impossible to get done."

Jolene shivered. "I still can't believe it snowed in Moreau at all—especially in December."

"No one can."

"I'm assuming the mural is going back on the north wall?" Her hands shook around her to-go cup, and it wasn't from the chill seeping through her jacket and scarf. Cameron's proximity in the quiet courtyard rattled her, which was ridiculous. Also ridiculous that his kindness in securing her coffee had rattled her, as well as his judgment and obvious reluctance to work with her.

All of it. Ridiculous.

Especially the rogue butterflies in her stomach when she caught sight of his strong profile as he faced the church.

"Yep." Cameron gestured toward the newly rebuilt wall in the courtyard, and Jolene slowly followed his pointed finger with her gaze. "Everything is going back like it was."

Standing here brought back so many childhood memories—some nostalgic, some painful. Scavenger hunts. Photo ops on field trips with her art class in school. Goofy selfies with Mattie to cheer her up that first birthday after her father, Uncle Barry, left her and Aunt Claudia high and dry. That had been when Mattie first moved into the Lavigne House and they'd become more like sisters than cousins, fighting over borrowed clothes and who was hogging the bathroom.

At the time, Jolene couldn't imagine how it would feel to lose a father like Mattie had. But then several years later, she'd learned exactly what it was like.

"Just like it was, huh?" Jolene echoed. Funny. Nothing felt like it used to, and not only because of the lingering storm damage.

"Exactly the same—including the bayou and pelican design." Cameron assessed her with a suspicious gaze. "I'm assuming Mattie told you it's already been sketched out and the wall primed and sealed. You'll only need to paint what's there, maybe shore up some lines."

"Color by number, at your service." Jolene offered a mock salute.

Cameron's eyes narrowed, but he didn't comment. "Ready to see what you're working with? Nate left everything inside." He chose a specific key from his ring and, without waiting for an answer, headed for the back door of the community hall set opposite the chapel across the courtyard.

Jolene followed, brown leaves crunching under their shoes. The chapel might qualify for the historic register, but the other building was much newer, built to provide restrooms, reception space for weddings, and a place for parishioners to host fellowships or youth nights. She had memories there too but none as poignant.

They passed the gazebo that was still a work in progress, and her stomach clenched. Her father had brought her to this courtyard to sit on the gazebo bench with snow cones after fifth-grade graduation.

To cry with her after her heart was broken in seventh grade when Kyle Sinclair asked Gabby to the dance instead of her.

To make business calls in the sun while she sketched the mural a dozen times over, practicing getting the pelican's eyes right. Eyes had always been tricky—they were the windows to the soul, after all.

Lost in her thoughts, Jolene trailed after Cameron down the hall to a supply closet. She stopped short, nearly running into him as he paused to unlock the closet door. Her hands provided a quick barrier that kept her from ricocheting off his broad back. But the taut muscles under his flannel work shirt surprised her and the impression felt permanently engraved on her palms.

She quickly stepped aside. "Sorry about that. Daydreaming." An annoying flush of heat crept up her neck, and she chastised herself. Cameron might be handsome enough, but she knew better than to fall for anyone who already had made up his mind about her.

Or for anyone in Moreau, for that matter. Come the day after Christmas, she'd be back in Nashville, figuring out her next life move.

He raised his eyebrows but didn't comment as he gestured inside the closet. Multiple shelves held folded plastic tarps and a variety of acrylic paint cans. Sage green, buttercup, periwinkle. . .all muted pastels.

Just like before.

"Everything you need should be in here." Cameron pointed to the obvious. "Brushes, drop cloths to protect the grass, and of course, paint. If you realize you need something else, let me know."

What she *needed* was an excuse not to do this, but thanks to Granny and Jolene's sweet but slightly bulldog cousin, that didn't seem to be an option.

"I guess you should keep this for now." He wiggled the closet key off his ring and dropped it in her hand. "Don't lose it."

The metal was cool against her palm. "I won't." She tucked the key into her jacket pocket.

Cameron opened his mouth, as if about to argue over her choice of safekeeping, but settled for shaking his head. "I'll help you tote all this stuff out there. Are those painting clothes?" His gaze ran down the length of her, and she found herself straightening a little under his scrutiny.

"All my clothes are painting clothes." Or at least they had been. "If you look hard enough, you'll probably see flecks of color on my sleeve on any given day."

"About that. . ." Cameron hefted two paint bottles from the shelf and handed her one before grabbing a third. "I thought you said you quit."

She rolled in her lower lip. "I did."

"But you're here, about to paint." His brow furrowed.

"Trust me, I'm as confused as you are." She shook back her hair and reached for another gallon. "Welcome home, right?"

Chapter Four

S he was up to something.

Cameron tried not to watch as Jolene painted, dabbed off what she'd done with paint remover, and started over—four times. Okay, so maybe he was watching a little too intently, but she *was* in his direct line of vision from his stance in the gazebo. . .where he had just nailed a board upside down.

He grimaced as he pried the board free. If he didn't focus, the mural would be completed on time but not the gazebo, and Mattie would have his head. He reached for another screw from his toolbox, then picked up the drill. He and Jolene had yet to speak after that awkward encounter in the supply closet. She'd said twice now that she was no longer an artist, yet there she was, committing to this project anyway. And doubting herself, if her frequent broad strokes and immediate removal of them were any indication. At the rate she was erasing, she'd have to redraw Nate's redrawing.

He couldn't figure Jolene out, and if he were a smart man, he'd stop trying.

Yet he couldn't keep his eyes off the way she tilted her head as she studied the wall, then looked at her phone—hopefully analyzing the photo of the original mural that he'd texted her before she'd begun. The colors needed to be as close to the "before" as possible, though obviously the original had faded with sunshine and time. The fresh image would be invigorating for the town—a reminder that not everything good was lost in that fateful storm.

Memories of Katrina still lingered in the back of his mind—along with a spike of adrenaline every time he saw the red warning banner flash on his weather app. He'd been in middle school when notorious Katrina demanded he and his family leave his childhood home in New Orleans, all of them assuming they'd be back. But there had been nothing left to go back to. Even though they'd settled in Shreveport and he'd attended good schools, he'd never felt truly at home in north Louisiana.

Finding Moreau had been like an answer to a prayer he hadn't realized he'd prayed. His hand tightened on the drill.

Which was why he needed to talk to Granny Eloise ASAP.

———◆———

"I'd offer you a glass of tea, but they keep putting the sugar where I can barely reach it." Granny Eloise greeted Cameron on the front porch of the Lavigne House like she'd known he was coming. "Apparently when you get older, you shrink."

"Don't worry, Granny. You'll always be larger than life." He shut the truck door, the slam echoing across the sprawling front yard of the property as he smiled at one of his favorite people in all of Louisiana. Maybe in all the country.

Granny Eloise reminded him a lot of his own high-spirited grandmother who had passed away from breast cancer not long before Katrina. It had been a blessing getting to know Granny Eloise better this year while fixing up her cottage before she moved back into the Lavigne House.

And it was also how he'd learned so much about Jolene, which was why he was here. He began the trek to the porch stairs.

"What have I done to deserve the pleasure of your company, my boy?" Granny gestured toward one of the porch's rocking chairs, where a thick blanket lie draped across the one on the left. A space heater was plugged into the outlet near the chair. "I came outside for some fresh air. It's easier to avoid unpacking the rest of my boxes when I'm not in the same room with them." She shot him a wink. "Would you like water instead of tea?"

He was thirsty after working on the gazebo, but he didn't want to put her out. She might seem larger than life, but she *was* turning eighty this weekend, and it was evident in the slight turning of her knuckles, blue-veined hands, and thin stature. But her eyes—they'd never lost their spark for a minute. And her mind was as sharp as ever.

Granny cuffed him on the shoulder. "Quit looking at me all sappy like that. I'm turning eighty, not about to drop dead."

Apparently her tongue was still perfectly sharp too.

Cameron hid his smile as he took the chair she'd indicated. "I'm fine, Granny. Just needed to ask a question while you were alone."

Her dark eyebrows rose as she sank into the rocker next to him. "Adale is in the house, I believe. Unless she's working the Christmas market. I can barely keep up with her social calendar these days."

"No, I meant alone as in"—he coughed—"Jolene."

Granny's chin lifted. "I see."

She hadn't seen that he'd grabbed his tools and hastily left the jobsite at sundown, well before Jolene had time to clean up her paint supplies, in hopes he'd beat her to the Lavigne House. Not to mention be able to say his piece and leave before Jolene realized he'd ever been there at all. The last thing his and Jolene's fragile partnership needed was for her to bust him with her own family.

Which meant he needed to hurry.

"Is she giving you grief over that mural already?" Granny chuckled as she slowly rocked, her short, cropped hair refusing to budge despite the wind wafting across the porch. The front yard trees rustled in its wake, offering their remaining leaves to the sky in a swirling dance. "I wouldn't be surprised."

"Not yet." Cameron wouldn't be either, truth be told. He matched the rhythm of Granny's chair with his own as he worked to figure out the best way to voice his suspicion. "But I'm worried about her."

"That's sweet of you." Granny cast him a sidelong glance. "Or are you sweet on her?"

His boots shot hard onto the porch, abruptly stopping his easy rocking. "No. Neither." This wasn't coming out right. He needed to get to the point, which is how Granny always talked. He ran one hand over his hair and let out a breath. "I'm worried she's only in Moreau to try to get back into your will."

Granny stopped rocking then too, staring at him with such a blank, unreadable expression his heart skipped a beat.

He swallowed. "She's in town for the first time in so long, and from what you've alluded to in the past, that's a big deal. It seems a significant coincidence that it's right during your big milestone birthday."

She finally spoke, her tone low and even as she held his gaze. "My will is my business."

"Of course, Granny Eloise." He ducked his head, regretting bringing up his concern but still worried he might be right. He'd seen manipulative family members take advantage before—and he'd been on the receiving end of such manipulation from his own ex-fiancée. The idea wasn't out of reach.

Her steady gaze bored a hole into him. "I realize my Jolene has been gone for some time, but she's not like that. You'll see for yourself soon enough."

He offered a noncommittal grunt. Sure, Jolene had revealed a brief vulnerable side earlier that day, but it could have been an act. All he'd really seen so far was that she was painting a mural against her will and got cranky without coffee. "Sorry, Granny. I shouldn't have said anything."

"And, for your information, your harebrained idea is impossible anyway." She sniffed as she resumed her rocking. "Because I plan to never die."

Cameron let out a half laugh, half snort. Of course.

"But if the good Lord doesn't agree with my plan for immortality, then we'll see where those chips fall." Granny nodded briskly, as if that was that. "Now, be a good boy and hush. I'd hate to have to write you out of it. Those wills are such a hassle to amend." She shot him a wink.

"Yes ma'am."

"And go bring me the sugar."

———◆———

Mattie dropped Jolene off at the chapel early the next morning before heading to work. With a honk and a wave, she drove away, tires catching the loose gravel of the parking lot. Jolene waved back, then shoved her hands into her pockets as she strolled toward the church, already resenting the cold weather assaulting her cheeks. How in the world was she going to paint with gloves on today?

She did, however, have a fire burning in her gut that would likely keep her warm for at least a few hours. Her jaw tightened as she caught sight of Cameron rummaging through the back seat of his truck.

"How dare you?" She came up behind him, snorting in amusement as he jerked and nearly bumped his head against the frame of the open door.

"How dare I what?" He backed away from the truck, a tape measure in one hand as he regarded her warily.

"Don't play dumb." She crossed her arms over her orange jacket. "I had an interesting conversation with Granny over breakfast."

"Before you get too mad. . ." Cameron held up one finger and leaned back into the cab.

She tapped her foot. He wasn't getting out of this. She couldn't believe he'd had the nerve to suggest to her own grandmother that she—

He emerged from the cab and handed her a coffee, still warm beneath the cardboard sleeve.

The roaring fire in her stomach tempered to a smaller blaze. Less dragon, more matchstick. Still. . .

She gripped the cup and shifted her weight. "Thank you, but how dare you—"

He held up both hands in surrender. "I was wrong. I had an assumption that wasn't true, and I'm sorry. Now, before you throw that coffee in my face, I have one more surprise."

She snapped her mouth shut, then narrowed her eyes. "I'm listening."

"This way." He shut the truck door and led her around the chapel to the courtyard. "Not that I figure you'd waste a good coffee on scalding me, but it had to be said."

"Valid." She took a sip of the warm brew as she followed him around the low brick wall, then gasped. A tall blue tent covered the in-progress portion of the north wall, and a propane space heater filled the middle of the cozy space, evident via the tent flap that was pulled open and tied back on one side, awaiting her entry.

Relief flooded her body, all the way through to her cold fingers. It was the ideal setup—she might not even need her gloves. And now the paint would dry so much faster being out of the elements and this unseasonably cold weather. But how had he—

"I got here a little early today." Cameron shrugged, his expression sheepish. He gestured toward the tent. "So. . .truce?"

She peered up at him, having forgotten how tall he was. Standing this close, she had an easy view of the permanent shadow on his jawline, the hint of a dimple on his right cheek. She narrowed her eyes. "You did this to get on my good side."

The dimple widened a little. "Mostly. Also because the mural needs to be protected in case it snows again."

Right. "And because you felt bad about accusing me of manipulating my elderly grandmother out of her money."

He winced. "Precisely."

Conviction gnawed at her heart. It might not entirely be Cameron's fault—after all, hadn't she come back to Moreau with a defensive position any middle linebacker would be proud of?

"So. . ." He inched a step closer, close enough now that she could faintly detect his spicy aftershave, and held out his hand in an offering. "Truce?"

She studied the way his blue eyes held hers, genuine in their apology, and rolled in her lower lip. She'd expected judgment upon her arrival home and had probably created a bit of a self-fulfilling prophecy where Cameron was concerned. She'd been cold toward him, even when he drove her home that one night.

He might have thought the worst about her, assuming she had ill intentions toward Granny, but how much of that had been accelerated by her own attitude?

She took his hand and shook it. "Truce."

A shadow of relief flickered across his face as he continued pumping her hand. "I'm really not a bad guy, you know."

"And I'm not a bad granddaughter." She shook his hand harder, matching his energy.

"Fair." He laughed as he let go. "I'll be at the gazebo if you need me."

His gaze lingered a little longer than necessary, and she appreciated it, though she most definitely did not need him.

So why couldn't she look away?

———◆———

Between the space heater and her own frustration, Jolene had no trouble staying warm. After two hours of painting, tweaking Nate's sketched lines, and starting over, the only thing progressing was her bad mood.

She didn't want to risk taking it out on Cameron, who had thankfully left her alone in her tent most of the morning. She could hear him in the courtyard, hammering, drilling, and occasionally singing under his breath as he worked, and the thought of him out there was both comforting and unsettling. Apparently it was safer for them to be enemies, but that didn't lend to a decent work environment. If she had to do this mural, she wanted it to be as painless as possible.

And she wanted to do a good job. Maybe that was why she kept doubting every stroke she made.

"Just paint," she murmured to herself as she picked up the brush dripping with sage green. She was working on the cypress tree currently, having abandoned her multiple attempts on the pelican an hour ago.

She glanced over at the open photo on her phone, set on the top rung of the ladder Cameron had also provided, along with a secondhand bistro table for her supplies. She knew the original mural design by heart, but something about it felt off—and not because of Nate's sketch. He'd recreated the original impeccably, adding a few more ripples to the water in the bayou, a few more details on the bird. He'd given her a great canvas to work with.

So why did the thought of filling in those cypress branches leave her with such dread?

She touched the brush to the tree, gritting her teeth as she carefully trailed the paint over the brick. Talent-wise, this wasn't that hard. Nate had tackled the much harder job in drawing the design in the first place. She only needed to match the colors to the original, pay attention to shadows and blending, and essentially simply work to stay inside the lines.

But every time she extended her hand toward the wall, paintbrush at the ready, something seized up in her heart.

She dropped the brush back onto her palette. She needed a break.

She needed to figure out this paralyzing feeling when it came to the mural.

And mostly, she needed to *stop* feeling whatever it was that welled up in her chest every time she heard Cameron singing his slightly off-key rendition of "I'm Dreaming of a White Christmas."

The singing stopped, and a few moments later, Cameron's unmistakable presence lurked outside the tent flap. "Knock, knock."

She opened the flap and slipped outside, hating to leave her cocoon but unwilling to let him see how little progress she'd made that day. Once again, the scent of his aftershave greeted her before his smile did.

"How's it going?" He tried to peer over her shoulder.

She quickly dropped the flap behind her and stood between him and the opening. "Are you asking as a friend or as my boss?"

"Wait." The dimple was back in full force. "We're friends now?"

Drat. "Of course not." She squared her shoulders. "It was an easier word than trying to figure out whatever you call people in forced proximity under a temporary truce."

He nodded with mock seriousness. "You're right. That's obnoxiously long."

At least she'd successfully avoided his progress question. Her stomach growled again—the perfect excuse. "I was actually about to grab some lunch."

Except. . .she didn't have a car. Drat again.

He eyed the parking lot, empty save for his work truck. "I can drive you. How does pizza sound? I know a great place over near the Christmas market."

"Moreau Pizza Café." They spoke simultaneously.

Jolene tried to mask her frown with a quick nod as she retrieved her phone and followed him to his truck. Cameron had only lived in Moreau a few years, yet he was the one telling *her* about the café? She had practically grown up in that establishment, had skinned her knee in the parking lot when she was six years old, and had spent most of her childhood allowance between the ages of eight and eleven on the arcade games in the back.

The moment he said the café's name, that feeling had returned— the one crowding her heart. The one that made her so unsettled trying to paint. The one that felt like indigestion roiling in her stomach, creeping up her chest with bitterness.

She desperately tried to analyze it as she climbed into the passenger seat and buckled her seat belt, but it slipped away like Peter Pan's shadow, laughing and mocking as it darted out of reach.

They drove slowly toward the café, Cameron finding someone to wave to at every stop sign. He even rolled down his window to holler an inside joke at Wyatt walking his Labradoodle down Rue de la Chapelle.

As Cameron pulled into the parking lot of the Pizza Café, rambling on about their updated menu offering specialty pizzas, it hit her, the shadow now finally clutched in her eager fists yet still managing to get the last laugh.

This was *her* hometown. . .but she was the outsider.

Chapter Five

Now full of pepperoni and more small talk than she'd anticipated, Jolene stared once more at the mural in her heated cave, imagining the pelican's outlined eyes to be staring right back. Maybe the propane was getting to her, but she could have sworn that bird knew something she didn't.

Namely, why it was so hard to simply apply paint to a wall.

Over lunch she'd talked Cameron out of viewing her progress twice, asking for a little more time before he peeked. At this point, she'd settle for completing a tree branch or pelican feather, much less a whole section.

Of course, they'd talked about other things over their pizza too. Like how Granny had been the one to teach Jolene to paint, and how her cousin and aunt had moved in with her family when she was a teenager. They talked about Cameron's childhood in New Orleans and how he chose to become a contractor because he couldn't escape the images of those dilapidated, storm-damaged homes from his past and wanted to do something to help.

In other words, he had a good side, and it was most unfortunate she'd discovered it. She already reluctantly found the man attractive, which was dangerous enough, considering he'd insulted her twice in the two days she'd been in Moreau. Though to be fair, he'd also apologized twice and gone out of his way to help make her workstation comfortable in the courtyard.

And he'd given her the last slice of pepperoni, even though she'd have bet her designer brush set he'd wanted it for himself.

Her cell buzzed. Mattie's contact photo lit the screen, and Jolene swiped to accept it, welcoming the interruption from her runaway train of thought—and the opportunity to procrastinate a bit longer from the wall. "Hey."

"How's it going?" her cousin chirped. "I was going to see if you needed a lunch break. I can come pick you up."

Jolene peered around the edge of the tent flap where Cameron worked in the gazebo, then ducked back inside. "Actually, Cameron and I already ate. We grabbed a pizza."

Mattie paused. "You and Cameron?" Her voice held two parts suspicion, one part surprise.

"He eats too, believe it or not." Jolene shifted the phone to her other hand, lowering her voice in case Cameron came near the tent.

"I meant that's nice you went together, is all." Mattie's voice now had taken on a distinct cat-who-ate-the-canary purr.

Jolene winced. "I'm hanging up now."

"I'm kidding." Mattie laughed, even though they both knew she wasn't. "How's the mural coming? Nate did a great job drawing it, didn't he?"

Jolene hesitated, not wanting to share her fears. Especially not to Mattie, who apparently had everything together as always—even a boyfriend now in her long-ago rival Paul, if Cameron's update at lunch held any validity. Once upon a time, Jolene would have been the first person Mattie told about a new crush. But clearly those days were over.

"He did a good job. It's just. . ." Jolene squinted at the pelican. Had he glared back?

"What? Did he mess something up on the design?" Mattie sounded confused.

Jolene sighed. "No. It's exactly like it was before." Then her eyes widened. That was it. It was the same.

Saying it out loud had connected the dots.

Jolene's pulse quickened and her mind whirred. "Uh, Mattie? I gotta go."

"Why? Is someone there?"

Yes, finally—her muse. "I'll explain later. See you at home."

She ended the call and tossed her phone on the bistro table, barely registering the fact she'd called the Lavigne House home. One revelation at a time. Finally, she knew exactly what to do.

With a grin, she bypassed the paintbrush and grabbed her sketch-book from her tote bag.

Now for a few adjustments.

———◆———

Rémy Vachon arrived in Moreau much like Christmas arrived in Whoville—silently, unexpected, and without fanfare.

Cameron's boot caught one of the legs of Jolene's tent as he rushed by, eager to meet the famous architect in the parking lot in front of the chapel. The man was early by a day, but when one had the experience of Rémy Vachon, one did what they chose. It was sort of a miracle he'd even agreed to come.

Cameron paused, finished composing his quick text to Mayor Ammons, alerting him to Rémy's sudden appearance, and hit SEND as Jolene poked her head out of the tent flap. "Hey! Got a second?"

"Someone's waiting on me, actually." He pointed to the parking lot.

"It'll only take a minute." She grabbed his arm and tugged him into the space before he could protest further. Her cheeks flushed pink, whether from the cold, the space heater, or excitement, he couldn't be sure.

Her coconut shampoo nearly assaulted him with her proximity, and he took a deep breath before inching back a step. He'd sat next to Jolene in his truck and across from her in the café booth, but this cozy little space had him realizing several things. Namely, how she was the perfect height for his six-foot, one-inch frame and how her eyes lit when she was happy—something he hadn't seen a lot of from her yet—and how much he *really* liked the scent of coconuts.

Maybe one more step back. Just in case.

"I've been working on something." She flipped through pages of a sketchbook, and it was only then he realized the brick wall beside them was completely void of paint.

Panic lit his chest. He knew she'd gotten a slow start, but Jolene hadn't made any progress at *all?* Mattie was going to flip out—along with the mayor if this event got canceled last minute or made the town look bad. It had been obvious Jolene hadn't wanted the task in the first place, but to have not even started yet. . .

He swallowed hard, his jaw clenching. "Something that is clearly *not* the mural."

"I know, I know." She held up one finger, struggling to find a particular page in her book. "Wait."

He blew out his breath. "That's just it, Jolene. We can't wait." The warmth emanating from the heater suddenly felt hot and oppressive. "I thought you realized this project is on a major timeline."

"I do." She looked up at him then and blinked, clearly taken aback, but of the two of them, he had a lot more reason to be surprised. She was a mural artist with no mural.

"Then explain this." He gestured to the wall, which contained Nate's outline and nothing more.

"I know it looks bad. But I had an idea." She clutched the notebook to her chest, then slowly turned it around to show him a hastily rendered sketch. "What do you think?"

He shook his head at the random artwork she revealed, his frustration building. "I think you've been in here drawing instead of painting."

Her brow furrowed. "You don't understand."

"Maybe not. But I understand this mural has to be done by Sunday and that I have a famous architect waiting for me in the parking lot right now." Cameron shoved his hand through his hair, hating his frustration but unable to rein it back in. This whole courtyard project—not only the gazebo—reflected on him. Mattie and Mayor Ammons had put Jolene under his charge, and if this mural didn't happen on time, it would be his responsibility. He didn't want to look irresponsible. . .or a fool, as Samantha had seen to so many times.

Jolene's lips flattened into a thin line. "It'll be done."

He couldn't deal with this any further, though, not with Mr. Vachon waiting in the cold. He already felt pressured to impress the guy. "I want to believe you, but this isn't looking good." He let out a long exhale, regretting his aggravated tone. "Look, there's a lot going on right now. Let's talk about it in a little while, okay?"

"No need." She shut the sketchbook with a snap. "I've got it covered."

Guilt pressed but so did the clock. "Jolene—" He glanced at his watch.

"Go." She opened the tent for him, and he had no choice but to hurry through the opening. He had barely emerged into the brisk air before the material flapped back down behind him.

Message received.

He felt bad he'd upset her, but if an argument was what finally motivated Jolene to get to work, maybe it was for the best. Though he hated to undo all the progress they'd made that day—especially at lunch, where conversation had flowed as easily as the soda fountain where he'd had way too many root beers and learned Jolene had never even tried one. He'd dared her, and the puckered face she'd made upon first sip had him laughing well after he'd dropped her back off at her workstation.

He'd messed up their fragile camaraderie now, but the mural had to come first. Jolene clearly still wasn't taking the project seriously. And why should she? She was only back for Granny's party. If she really cared about Moreau, she wouldn't have stayed away so long. Obviously, her loyalties were elsewhere. Didn't she at least care enough about the *people* who cared about Moreau to do a good job on something this important?

Cameron tried to push the exchange from his mind as he strode toward the parking lot, catching sight of a tall, slim figure in a pullover sweater and jeans standing before the chapel. "Mr. Vachon. Cameron Armand." He held out his hand on his approach.

"Please, call me Rémy. And I apologize for being early." Rémy smiled as he shook Cameron's hand. A hint of a French accent highlighted his voice. "I finished a project sooner than expected, and Moreau was on my way back home to New Orleans. Seemed like destiny."

Cameron certainly hoped so. "It's no problem. Mayor Ammons should be arriving any minute, but I'd love to show you the full property and answer any questions you might have."

"Sounds good." Rémy tilted his head back and gazed up at the damaged chapel, much like Cameron often did. "She's a beauty, isn't she?"

"She was—and certainly can be again." Cameron resisted the urge to add any more obvious nudging to that statement and hoped Rémy could take a hint.

He shot Cameron a sidelong glance. "I gather this is an important part of your town's heritage."

"It is. The chapel was hit hard, and the whole town felt that. We haven't had services here for a long while. Meanwhile, I've been repairing the gazebo in the courtyard, and we have an artist redoing the much-loved town mural as we speak." Cameron pointed toward Jolene's tent. *Hopefully* as they spoke, anyway.

"Looks like the roof took on significant damage. You were fortunate, though." Rémy shook his head, his features pinched. "You should see Magnolia Bay."

"I bet." Cameron had seen the news clips of the island city off the coast of Louisiana. It had taken the brunt of the recent hurricane before it made its way inland. "Are you doing some work down there too?"

Rémy nodded. "It's only an hour south of New Orleans, so I've been lending as much time as I can spare to their cause. They're practically starting over from scratch."

"I hate to hear that." Cameron turned back to the church, trying to imagine what it would be like if the entire structure had been demolished. "My friend Mattie is on the Town Revitalization Committee with me and Mayor Ammons and a few others. She's hoping to get the chapel further protected by having it placed on the historic register. . .which is where you'd come in."

"I see."

A sudden quiet fell over them as Rémy continued studying the property, the silence growing longer and thicker until Cameron was no longer sure how to interpret the man's stoic face. Was he leaning toward taking on the project or trying to find the right words to turn Cameron down gently?

Cameron finally cleared his throat, needing at least a hint. "I'd love to hear your first impressions."

"Of course." Rémy crossed his arms over his chest. "First, though, let me ask you this. What does this chapel mean to you?"

Cameron rocked back on his heels, feeling like he'd been given a sudden test he hadn't studied for. "Well. . .this church and courtyard have seen a lot of weddings. Vow renewals. Anniversary parties and church services. Funerals. It's a staple of the town for generations back."

"I imagined as much. I've always been interested in this little town myself." Rémy turned and clapped his hand on Cameron's shoulder, his arresting gaze holding Cameron's hostage. "But what does it mean to *you*, son?"

Cameron shifted his attention to the damaged building, opening his mouth to reply, then realizing he had no answer. He'd attended church here over the last few years he'd lived in Moreau, but that didn't seem to be the kind of answer Rémy was looking for. He snapped his mouth shut. "I—"

Gravel crunched. They both turned to see Mayor Ammons pulling into the parking lot in his sports car, parking next to Rémy's white two-seater. Cameron sighed as relief and regret warred for top bidding. Saved by the mayor?

Or had Cameron's lack of answer hammered the final coffin nail in their dreams of getting the chapel repairs completed?

———◆———

"This whole town smells like Christmas." Jolene shoved yet another slinky dress she wouldn't be caught dead in across the rack, the hanger squealing against the metal rod.

After her altercation with Cameron, she'd called Mattie to come pick her up from the jobsite early, needing space to regroup and revisit her new sketch away from judgment. She wanted to hide in her room at the Lavigne House and figure out her next steps—which meant either bailing on the project or going rogue with her new idea. She still couldn't decide which.

She discarded another dress, sniffing the Christmas-scented air. "How does Moreau do that, anyway?"

"Mary Ann likes her cinnamon-apple candle warmers." Mattie chuckled as she pulled a sparkly gown from the rack and considered it. "Is it that bad?"

"What? The scent or that dress?" Jolene raised her eyebrows.

Mattie scrunched up her nose. "Either."

"In that case, both."

Mattie rehung the dress. "This was supposed to be fun, you know."

"I know. I'm sorry." Jolene let out a huff of tension, wishing a portion of it would remove itself from her shoulders, where it seemed permanently attached. Fun for Mattie, maybe. Her cousin had made good on her threat—er, promise—to take Jolene shopping for a dress to wear to the Christmas Eve ball next week. Apparently, Mattie had had her own dress for almost two months now, which made Jolene feel even more behind in everything she was supposed to be accomplishing.

She'd never been an organized person. Go with the flow, impulsive, and easygoing described her best. But since being back in Moreau, it was as if all her old insecurities had morphed with her new ones, and now she was just one giant identity crisis.

A month ago, she never imagined she'd be standing in a clothing shop in her hometown, picking out a dress for a ball and painting someone else's art. Her life felt like it was moving backward. Her stomach clenched.

She wanted—needed—to go forward.

"Granny's birthday party is Mardi Gras themed, but the ball is black and white. Not sure if anyone mentioned that yet." Clearly oblivious to her cousin's internal agony, Mattie's brow furrowed as she pawed through the dresses. "Would you rather wear black or white? Maybe that'll help us narrow this down."

A pinch of guilt tugged. Her cousin was making a peace offering—she knew Mattie still felt bad about the *reliable* comment the other night in the kitchen—so the least Jolene could do was go with it. Especially since she had, as of the past hour, considered proving Mattie right and ditching the entire project.

Jolene moved to the next rack over, another waft of cinnamon-apple attacking her senses. "Black, I guess. I can always accessorize with red." She attempted to extend an olive branch. "What does your dress look like?"

"It's black, vintage-style, and formal length." Mattie's eyes lit up as she joined Jolene at the next group of dresses. "I'm so excited. I still need to pick out my shoes, but I can get some neutral pumps later."

Jolene hesitated over a knee-length cocktail dress, then dismissed it. "You should go for a color. Red heels, or gold. Something festive."

"You think?" Doubt clouded Mattie's face. "I can't really pull that stuff off like you can. My style has always been more neutral."

"It's a party though, right? And besides, Paul will like it." Jolene nudged her cousin in the side, and for a moment, it was like they were in high school again, gossiping over who was cuter in the youth group. Despite being two years apart, they'd shared a lot of the same interests—and the same shoe size, for that matter—growing up.

The same blush Mattie had worn at the committee meeting yesterday hovered over her cheeks again. "Maybe so. I'll see what they have."

"You know what? I brought a pair of red heels with me that would look great on you. Are you still a size seven?"

Relief flooded Mattie's face. "That would be so perfect."

Her guilt slightly assuaged, Jolene pulled a strapless black gown from the rack. "I'll try this one on."

Mattie grinned and grabbed for another dress. "Yes! And this one."

Jolene considered the halter-style garment in a dark gray and immediately didn't like it. But her cousin was having so much fun. . .she took it and draped it over her arm. "Worth a shot."

Another olive branch extended. Mattie deserved it after the way Jolene had been acting the past few days. She really wanted to get her attitude together, but with Christmas assaulting her at every turn, and with every landmark serving as another reminder of her father's absence—not to mention this unsettling feeling of being the odd man out in her own hometown—it felt increasingly hard to accomplish.

Why did it bother her so much when she was the one who moved away? She'd intentionally chosen to put space between her and Moreau, so it didn't make sense why being back now would make her feel anything other than eager to leave.

But she didn't feel that way at all.

They continued browsing, pausing by the jewelry counter as Mattie held a pair of gold hoops to her ear in the display mirror. "Can I ask you something?" Her tone lowered, and she turned to face Jolene, her expression serious.

Oh boy. Jolene took a deep breath. All those olive branches might be about to smack her in the face. "Shoot."

"Why do you hate Christmas?" Mattie's gentle question, more curious than judgmental, tugged at her heart.

Jolene shifted her weight. "I don't hate Christmas."

"Come on." Mattie shot her a knowing glance as she returned the earrings to the basket. "You're even complaining about how Christmas smells."

She had her there. "I don't know." Jolene lightly ran her finger over a rose gold bracelet. "Ever since Dad. . ." She cleared her throat. "Ever since moving to Nashville, it didn't feel the same. I guess not being here for the traditions was part of it. Picking out the tree at Turnage's Tree Farm, decorating cookies with Mom, making cinnamon rolls Christmas morning. . . ."

"You could have come home, you know." Mattie kept her gaze riveted on the jewelry display.

"I know." A fresh wave of guilt washed over her. "And I really appreciate the year you and Mom came to see me."

It had been awkward, but they'd made it work, bringing old traditions to Tennessee, such as Christmas breakfast. Though it hadn't been the same without Granny there, barking her instructions everyone pretended not to hear and ignoring her as she scooped her finger into the tub of leftover icing.

Mattie looked directly at her, clearly waiting for more. And for once, the old guard against vulnerability that Jolene always carried fell to the wayside.

"Christmas just became another day." Jolene hugged the dresses to her chest. "I would sit on the couch and watch *It's a Wonderful Life* and eat ramen noodles."

It had become her own pathetic tradition—an attempt at an anti-tradition, really. A way to fight back against the emotion that slid down the chimney every Christmas Eve and refused to leave until after New Year's.

"Aunt Adale wished you had come home more." Mattie's lips twisted to one side. "And for that matter, *I* wished you had too."

Jolene didn't know how to offer a believable "why" without giving away her secret. She paused. "I'm here now, though."

"You're right. You're here now." Mattie straightened her shoulders. "And you know what? Forget black and white."

"Huh?"

"For the ball. You've never been a neutral kind of person. You deserve to wear color."

"And be the only one?" Jolene's eyes widened.

Mattie snorted. "Like you've ever had a problem standing out."

True. But this year felt different—in every way. She squinted suspiciously at her cousin. "That's breaking the rules, you know. You never break the rules."

"Technically, I'm not breaking them—I'm encouraging you to." Mattie laughed. "Which was a lot of our high school experience, if I remember correctly. Besides, if I can wear red shoes, you can wear a colorful dress. So, come on. What color makes you happy?"

Jolene hemmed and hawed, but the truth was, she knew immediately. She acquiesced to Mattie's prodding. "Green."

"Got it. You go try those on, and I'll see if I can find a green dress you like." Mattie rushed away before Jolene could argue.

She headed to the dressing room and slipped off her jeans, a realization tugging on her even as she tugged at the zipper of the black dress. She *had* to complete the mural—Mattie would take it personally if she backed out now, and she couldn't do that to her. Not when their friendship was finding solid ground again. Which meant there was now only one other option.

And Cameron would have to get over it.

A few minutes later, Jolene emerged from the dressing room in the black strapless dress, tugging at the scratchy fabric. She stood in front of the trifold mirror and winced.

Mattie tilted her head. "It's pretty. But you don't look comfortable."

"I'm not." Jolene pulled up the sides of the loose-fitting top. "It's not. . .me." She wore black sometimes, when she had colorful accessories to have her outfit serve more as a blank canvas for something fun. But this felt like dressing more for a funeral.

In fact, the last time she'd worn all black was to—

"It's official. You need color." Mattie held out a rich green dress she'd found, formal length with a glittering black net overlay covering the sweetheart bust. "Here."

"If you say so." Jolene turned an about-face into the dressing room.

"And hey. . ." Mattie called over the closed door, a happy lilt to her voice. "Don't tell your mom I'm encouraging you to break the rules. I have a reputation to protect."

Jolene wiggled into the green gown and thought about the mural. If Mattie knew exactly which rules Jolene was preparing to break, she wouldn't be worried about dress colors at all.

She grinned. Cameron, however, would find out soon enough.

Chapter Six

Cameron's phone blared from his nightstand, and he slapped at it with eyes still half shut. He hadn't been fully asleep but groggy enough to be confused. He rolled over in bed and grabbed for his cell as it rang a third time, squinting at the contact name on the display.

Police Chief Tom Manning.

He cleared his throat. "Hey, Tom. What's up?"

In any other town, such a late-night call from the local police chief would have warranted a full-blown adrenaline attack, but in Moreau it could mean anything from an arson fire blazing on Rue de la Chapelle to a forgotten invitation to a church potluck.

"Sorry to bother you, but we got a call that there's some lights on over at the construction site at the church." The chief's deep voice was slightly muffled by road noise. "I'm on my way there now to check it out and thought you might like to know. Probably nothing, but the last thing this town needs right now is vandalism."

No kidding. Not after all the work everyone had done. Cameron grabbed for his T-shirt at the foot of the bed. "I'll be right there."

Ten minutes later, dressed in sweatpants, T-shirt, and his work jacket, Cameron pulled into the parking lot of the church. Only two cars sat in the nearly abandoned lot—Tom's police cruiser and. . .Mattie's SUV.

Oh boy.

Cameron shut his door softly and headed toward the courtyard, where a voice already sounded through the darkness. Namely, Jolene's.

"Isn't checking out a spotlight in a courtyard a little under your pay grade, Chief?"

Cameron stifled a snort as he approached the scene. Jolene stood in front of the tent's open flap, arms crossed over her coat as she squared off with Tom, who rested his hands loosely on his hips. No uniform tonight, but he'd bet the chief was still packing. Of course, that fact didn't affect Jolene's offended tone in the slightest.

"I haven't committed a crime."

"That depends." The chief crossed his arms, mimicking her stance. "Does Ms. Hayes know you've borrowed her car?"

"Mattie is family. Besides, I'm *painting*." Her eyes cut pointedly to Cameron before staring the chief back down. "Not cooking meth."

"Well, now, I see Nashville hasn't softened your edges any." Tom shook his head, a smirk barely visible beneath his thick mustache. "What would your grandmother say?"

"She'd say I have Lavigne blood." Jolene lifted her chin, a slight grin turning up the corners of her mouth. "And probably throw in a 'good girl.'"

"Fair. That does sound like Eloise." Tom snorted. "Look, it's late, and this was suspicious, you must admit. Most people don't work on art projects this close to midnight."

Jolene visibly bristled at the phrase "art projects," her eyes narrowing.

Tom held up both hands, as if sensing the pending torrent. "I don't know if it's safe for you to be out here alone this late—anyone could walk up on you."

The glare on her expression practically dared them to try. Cameron coughed, taking a step closer before they fed off each other further. "I'll take it from here, Chief."

"I thought you might." Tom chuckled as he backed away. "Good luck." He cast Cameron a knowing, side-eyed glance as he strode out of the courtyard toward the parking lot.

And then there were two.

Cameron cautiously edged toward the tent entrance. No telling what the chief would generate on the gossip mill after this late-night encounter. Hopefully, Kimberly at the hair salon didn't catch wind of it, or there'd be a full-blown town scandal by sunrise. "May I come in?"

Jolene didn't agree but didn't protest either as he followed her inside the warm space.

"Before you tell me I shouldn't be here this time of night too, remember how you freaked out earlier that I hadn't made any progress yet." Jolene brushed her hands briskly together as she held them up under the heat lamp. "So consider this me going for extra credit."

He looked doubtfully at the wall, which was still blank, but at least she had the supplies out and the heat turned all the way up. She shed her jacket and draped it over the bistro table, then tugged on a pair of thin gloves before grabbing a stick of chalk.

He shoved his hands into his coat pockets, missing the hand warmers that he usually kept nearby during winter projects. Jolene, however, had already flipped open her sketchbook and turned her back, ready to start drawing as if it wasn't thirty degrees—and as if he wasn't even there.

He didn't like her ire, but somehow he disliked being ignored more. He shifted his weight. "You're still mad, aren't you?"

"Not mad." The stiff line of her shoulders confirmed that wasn't the whole truth, but he let it go. At least she didn't want to fight.

"I'm sorry I was harsh this afternoon. Rémy was waiting, but I should have handled my stress better. You just surprised me with the. . .you know. Blank wall."

To put it mildly. Even now, standing in front of the barely started mural, he felt panic rise. But she'd said it would be done by Sunday, and she was out here at midnight trying to make it happen, so he had to have a little faith.

"Apology accepted. Again." She shot him a glance he couldn't quite read as she knelt beside the wall. "And, for that matter, I'm sorry too. I should have been more open about my rough start and not caught you off guard."

"I think I was worried you weren't taking it seriously."

"I am. I promise. That was sort of the whole problem." Jolene brushed her hair out of her eyes with the back of one hand, then drew a steady sloping line across the bricks. "So is he going to do it?"

"Mr. Vachon?" Cameron thought back to the afternoon spent with the architect and Mayor Ammons. They'd taken Rémy for a brief tour of Moreau and ended with coffee at Le Petit French Press, where they'd pitched their full vision for the restoration. "He said he'd let us know. He drove back home tonight, but he'll be back this weekend for your grandmother's party."

Jolene paused, her hand hovering over the brick. "He knows Granny?"

"I don't think so. The mayor just invited him to come see the bulk of our community gathered." Cameron smiled. "I think that's part of Mr. Vachon's decision process—seeing the heart of a town before he decides to invest his time and money. Since we're requesting a heavy discount from his usual quotes, it's understandably a big decision."

"I suppose." Jolene moved into a cross-legged position as she focused on her sketching.

Cameron frowned. Why was she sketching? Hadn't Nate already drawn the bulk of the mural? He squinted to see what she was drawing, but the light in the tent was limited, and he couldn't get closer without casting a shadow over her workspace. He hovered a minute, hoping to get a better grasp of what she was doing.

"I don't need a bodyguard, you know." Jolene twisted to peer up at him, her green eyes wide. "In other words, I work better without an audience."

Fair. But. . .he didn't want to leave. Cameron moved closer to the heat lamp. "Is that why you came up here in the middle of the night?"

"Partly."

He rubbed his hands together. "Always marching to your own beat, aren't you?"

She drew another line. "According to my mom and cousin, yes."

"And what about Granny? What does she think?"

Jolene paused, chalk in hand, as she considered. "Granny probably understands me more than anyone else."

For a moment, he wondered what it would be like to be in that inner circle around Jolene. To be the one she came to with secrets and problems and frustrations. Well, he was already privy to hearing her frustrations, since he was causing most of them.

He watched as she drew. "I didn't mean to imply that was a bad thing, by the way."

"It is what it is." Jolene lifted one shoulder in a shrug, as if it didn't matter. But the pinch of her brows suggested otherwise. "Like

I told the chief—I'm a Lavigne. But I'm also a Broussard, and maybe that particular mix didn't turn out so well for me."

Cameron tried to stifle his surprise. "What do you mean?"

"You don't have to spend much time around me and Mattie to know we're opposites. She and my mom are cut more from the same cloth, even though Mattie is her niece."

"You two were raised like sisters, though, right? That's what you told me at lunch." Which seemed like a lifetime ago. It had been a long day, and judging by the dark smudges under Jolene's eyes, she felt it too.

"We were. And all the arguing and bathroom hogging that went with it." A ghost of a smile flickered across her face. "But those days are over. Everything changed when. . ."

"When you went to Nashville?"

"Something like that." Jolene's back stiffened.

And that was when it hit him. His assumptions about Jolene—the prodigal daughter vibe, the hard shell to crack—were just that. Assumptions. Maybe she'd left town and hurt Granny and her family with her abrupt departure and lingering absence, but this wasn't an overtly selfish woman before him.

This was a wounded one.

Maybe it wasn't that she hadn't wanted to come home all these years—maybe she'd been afraid no one wanted her to come home.

The silence stretched, but he couldn't leave it at that—even if her body language suggested he should. He was a sucker for repairing damage, after all. "You're too hard on yourself."

"You're right." She rubbed at the chalk line on the wall with one finger. "I really shouldn't be so hard on myself. . .especially since you're doing such a good job of that for me."

Ha. Cameron cleared his throat. "Listen, I know we said we had a truce earlier, and I really would like to enforce it." Good grief, she was pretty under all this lamplight.

Then his eyes registered the sketchbook she had pulled into her lap, open to the same drawing she'd tried to show him earlier that day. The one he'd been in too big of a hurry to fully absorb.

His chest tightened. "Is that a new sketch?"

Jolene's jaw clenched, but she kept drawing. "Remember what you said about a truce."

Cameron briefly closed his eyes, but when he opened them again, the design in her lap had yet to change back into Nate's. "Please tell me that's for an art class back in Nashville."

She brandished the chalk stick with a smile. "You said you wanted progress, right?"

A tension headache crept up his neck and into his forehead. He briefly massaged his temples. "Jolene, you just said you were taking this project seriously."

Maybe he'd unjudged her too quickly. But no, everything she'd shared—that had been genuine. Her wall had cracked.

Too bad it wasn't this physical one she was drawing on. Then he could stop this redesign nightmare.

"I am taking it seriously." She stood, moving to stand next to him under the heater. The sketchbook hung limply at her side, and her coconut scent wafted toward him. "Maybe more so than anyone else in this town."

"How do you figure?" He wouldn't explode again. It wasn't right to raise his voice, and besides, he had reiterated their truce. Still... He swallowed hard. Jolene pushed his limits like no one had in a long time. No one since Samantha, honestly.

And that train of thought certainly didn't ease his headache.

"Because everyone is so focused on the future, they're ignoring the past. They're pretending the hurricane this past summer didn't even happen." Frustration clipped her words.

"I don't think that's fair." Cameron gestured broadly around them. "You don't have to walk very far in Moreau to see lingering storm damage. We're obviously aware. That's why we're trying to get Rémy to come fix the chapel."

"Right—*fix* it. Forget the past and move forward like it was all a bad dream." She held up her sketchbook, but he couldn't make out the design in the shadows. "My new mural will be a reminder of the past. One this town needs, in my opinion."

She wasn't making sense. He inhaled a sharp breath. "Why would anyone *want* to remember something horrible?"

"Because maybe some storm damage isn't reparable!" The words exploded from her small frame, bursting into the space between them. There they hovered, lingering, like tiny crystals of snow before crashing to the ground and taking Cameron's fight with them.

They apparently took Jolene's too.

"You need to go." Her tense request emerged as a defeated whisper, and she turned pleading eyes on him. "Please. I can't work like this."

"Jolene. . ." He ran a hand through his hair, wishing there was a better solution. But she couldn't ramrod the entire project on an emotional whim.

He sighed. "This is bigger than me. I can't sign off on a new idea without committee approval." Nor did he want to. The whole point in restoring was to bring something back. Revive what *was*. Not create something new.

She waved the sketchbook in agitation. "Can't anyone around here just trust me?"

Not when she'd been gone for so long. Not when she'd burned up her merit in Moreau.

"I'm sure they'd like to." He held her gaze, resonating with the regret and sadness in her eyes. "But you've got to give them a reason to first."

———•———

Stupid logic.

Stupid rules.

Stupid chivalry. Jolene peered out the tent flap. Cameron had left at her request but had stayed in the parking lot with his car running and headlights on. Waiting. To make sure she was safe.

Despite the fact she was ruining his life.

Blatantly ignoring his authority would be a lot easier if he was a horrible person. But he wasn't, and he kept showing that to her, despite every effort to convince herself otherwise. He was a man who messed up but who apologized, who spoke his opinion boldly but with gentleness. Then hung around to ensure her safety. That was Cameron.

Which left the nagging question. . .who was *she?*

Jolene clutched her sketchbook, staring blindly at the design swirling on the page before her tired, bleary eyes. Now she had a choice. She could be a bullheaded jerk, directly defy orders, and finish painting the mural her way. Or she could stifle her own voice and go back to Nate's design.

Neither seemed doable.

Neither felt right.

She sank down on the cold tarp that provided little shelter from the cold concrete beneath the tent. The warmth from the heater didn't reach this low, and she shivered, but not completely from the cold. This cold seemed to come from deep inside, from a heart that had partially frozen over years ago—the moment that late-night call about her father came from the hospital.

She was terrified at what she'd find if it ever thawed.

Jolene let the sketchbook slip through her limp fingers, bringing her knees up to her chest and cradling them as she stared at the brick wall before her. Walls couldn't talk, couldn't tell her what she should paint.

But she couldn't shake Cameron's words, like they were a hint of some kind. *"This is bigger than me."* It was bigger than her too. Bigger than the one wall. Bigger even than committee regulations and tradition.

Or maybe she'd been sitting out in the cold too long.

"Jo?" A sudden presence filled the tent. "Are you okay?"

Jolene looked up. "Mattie?"

"What are you doing out here?" Her cousin's long blond hair draped across her face as she reached down for Jolene's hand.

She allowed her cousin to pull her up. "What are *you* doing here?"

"It's the middle of the night. I came to get you." Mattie shoved a thermos toward her. "Here. You must be freezing."

Jolene grasped the warm container and inhaled. Hot chocolate. "No, I mean literally, how did you get here? I took your car." She unscrewed the lid and took a careful sip.

"I saw that, so I took Aunt Adale's car." Mattie twisted her lips. "You used to only steal my sweaters, you know." Her expression softened. "Cameron called me."

"He did?" Jolene took another gulp, the hot beverage and the care in her cousin's eyes threatening to thaw all that was cold inside. She screwed the lid back on. "Why?"

Mattie tossed the end of her scarf over her shoulder. "He's worried about you. Said you guys fought over the mural and you refused to come in out of the cold."

"I'm not refusing. I wanted to make progress."

Mattie's eyes cut to the wall. "Did you?"

"We're at a bit of a stalemate." To put it mildly.

"You and Cameron?"

More like her and the world. "It's a long story."

"Look"—Mattie held up both of her gloved hands—"I don't know what's going on, but Cameron is in charge of the courtyard project, so I'd rather leave this between you and him."

Jolene blinked. Her control-freak cousin, backing off? She squinted at Mattie. "But aren't you running, like, everything else?"

"Basically. But this. . ." She gestured around them. "This is Cameron's gig. I'm not going to butt in. Nate had the mural handled, but when he got injured, I just wanted to help Cameron out by finding a replacement." She touched Jolene's arm. "I recommended the artist I did because I believed in her."

Another piece of ice began to crack. Jolene's throat tightened. "I thought you were worried about her being unreliable."

"I was." Mattie met her eyes, her gaze genuine. "But the Jolene I know loves to prove people wrong. Seems like a prime opportunity, don't you think?"

"This has become sort of a mess." Jolene scooped up her sketchbook from the tarped floor. "I'm not sure what to do next." Not when all her creative effort was constantly engaged in holding herself in one piece.

"Why don't you and Cameron fix it together, then? Give him a chance. He's a good guy, Jo."

Jolene inched closer to the heat lamp, tucking the book under her arm. *Jo.* "You haven't called me that in years." Not since they were teenagers at least.

"It slipped out." Mattie grinned. "But I think we all need a reminder of better times now and then. Right?"

"Right." Better times. Was that what everyone was so focused on with this mural? Remembering how good things were before? Yet. . .guilt surged at her cousin's grace. At Cameron's compassion. She was the issue here, not their mindset. Jolene needed to figure this out, and fast.

She tugged off her gloves and rubbed her hands together under the heater. "I really do want to do this project well." She meant that. So why did she keep getting paralyzed?

Mattie cupped her hand to her mouth as she dramatically stage-whispered. "That means you have to start."

Jolene drew in a breath. "I think I'm. . .intimidated." Maybe if she told someone—anyone—about the art school rejection, it would free up whatever was keeping her blocked from this design.

Or better yet, maybe it would finally allow her to share the same vision that Cameron and Mattie and everyone else had. Then she could stop being the black sheep of her hometown.

But could she share her intimidation theory without telling the reason behind it?

Mattie crossed her arms over her jacket. "You're good at what you do. I mean, we all doubt ourselves sometimes, but if I believe in you, then you should too. You've always been an artist."

"I got rejected from my first-choice art school." The words slipped out into the chilly space, finally free. "My next big career move—gone."

"It's only one school." Mattie's brow furrowed. "And clearly their loss. Can't you try for another one?"

"You don't understand. It's not just this school." Which was one of the top five in the country, one she'd dreamed about since first starting classes at community college years ago. It was also their second rejection of her work. She'd applied too soon out of college, had been overeager and prideful. She always thought if she matured a little, got a bit more experience on her résumé, her next attempt would be a sure thing.

But she'd failed. Again.

"This rejection came on the heels of being ghosted by art galleries, dismissed for shows. . .I don't think I have what it takes anymore." Jolene swallowed. She was getting dangerously close to her "why," and that couldn't happen.

"That's got to be disappointing." Mattie hesitated. "I don't know why they rejected you, but I do believe that everything happens for a reason. And you're not at the school right now—you're here, in Moreau. With *this* task in front of you to complete." She waved toward the wall. "That has to count for something."

Jolene considered her words. Her cousin was right. This project was what had been put on her plate—however hard she'd tried to avoid it at first. But something in her still couldn't conform to the original design.

As if reading her mind, Mattie prodded one more time. "Talk to Cameron."

"You're right. I will."

"Good." Mattie bounced a little on the balls of her feet, rubbing her arms with her gloved hands. "Now, can we please go home and get warm? Tomorrow is a new day." She checked her watch. "Make that, *today* is a new day."

"Sure. I'll follow you home in Mom's car. Thanks for the loan." Jolene handed her cousin the keys to her SUV, then reached up to power off the heat lamp. "And for the pep talk."

"That's what cousins are for." Mattie looped her arm through Jolene's. "I'm glad you're back."

Jolene squeezed Mattie's hand as they exited the tent. "I am too." But the knot in her stomach didn't fully release as they strode toward the parking lot. Maybe her secret about art school was out in the open, but another secret still lingered.

One she was pretty sure would have her cousin taking back those kind words.

Chapter Seven

He was almost ready to stain.

Cameron stepped back to admire his gazebo progress, sweat trickling down his temples despite the December chill in the air. The sun was out in full force this morning, melting what remained of the ice from last week's snow, and making the outdoor work much more tolerable. Snow was back in the forecast for next week, though he'd be shocked if it happened twice in the same December—a true Christmas miracle.

Much like what it was going to take for Jolene to finish that mural.

He draped his tool belt over a sawhorse, trying not to look toward the makeshift tent that had been unoccupied all morning. Jolene and Mattie had driven away from the church—allowing him to finally do the same—around one o'clock in the morning. He'd slept fitfully at home before getting up at dawn to come back and work. If he was going to toss and turn and mentally relive his encounter with Jolene, he might as well be productive.

So he'd hammered and sanded while convincing himself that Jolene hadn't weaseled into his heart with her brief display of vulnerability last night, that he wasn't making the same mistake he'd made falling for Samantha, that everything was going to be completed on time, and his reputation in town would remain solid, and Rémy would commit to restoring the chapel, and. . .

And if wishes were snowflakes.

Gravel crunched in the lot. Probably Mayor Ammons coming to check on their work. His chest constricted at the thought of anyone else finding out how far behind Jolene was in her task. Hoping to head him off, Cameron quickly covered the distance to the parking lot.

But it wasn't Richard's sports car parked by the entrance to the chapel—it was Mattie's SUV. And Jolene sat behind the wheel, wearing her trademark orange coat and a white beanie that set off her dark hair. She rolled down the window, gesturing him over with an arm loaded with colorful bracelets.

Cameron approached cautiously, unsure which Jolene he was going to get. "Morning." He leaned down and braced his arms on either side of the window opening.

"Get in." She pushed the button to unlock the passenger door, a smile softening her abrupt command. "I'm buying you coffee."

He checked his watch. It was almost nine o'clock, and the coffee he'd brought from home had grown cold about two hours ago. But he really needed to finish the gazebo, not to mention get busy on his other regular contracted projects he'd been putting off for the courtyard repair.

"I promise I won't bite this time. Plus, I owe you." She ducked her head to better see him through the window opening. "Pretty sure I'm responsible for those bags under your eyes."

He snorted. "First insult of the day, and it's not even noon."

"I didn't mean it like that." She tossed her long hair over her shoulder. "That was my backhanded apology for keeping you up so late last night." She rolled in her lower lip. "Thanks for waiting around, by the way."

"No problem." After he'd called Mattie to let her know Jolene could use some help—and common sense—he'd sat in his truck with the heat blasting, wondering exactly how stubborn she'd be for how long. The two women had finally emerged arm in arm, so hopefully their friendship was strengthening.

Scary how he wished his own friendship with Jolene would strengthen too.

"So. . .coffee?" Jolene's gaze looked downright hopeful. "I'll throw in breakfast."

He drummed his fingers on the frame of the car as he weighed his options. He could use some caffeine to get this project finished today. Not to mention something about Jolene's presence pulled him like a magnet.

Or, more accurately and detrimentally, like a moth to flame.

He got in the car.

Immediately, her coconut scent surrounded him. "I have a proposal for you." She handed him a bright red folder before shifting into DRIVE and steering them onto Rue des Iris. "You can review it at the Press."

He resisted the urge to flip through the pages as they drove the few blocks to the town's best coffee and pastry shop. Once they greeted Serena and were settled at a table by the window, a plate of beignets nestled between them, Cameron wielded the folder. "Now?"

"Now." Jolene folded her hands together, then unclasped them, her fingers drumming an anxious rhythm on the table.

He took a fortifying sip of his chicory coffee first, which he'd refused to let Jolene pay for. Granny—not to mention his own late grandmother—would have his hide if he'd let a woman pay for his food. Old-fashioned, maybe, but he liked to think chivalry wasn't dead.

Besides, he didn't like the idea of Jolene feeling like she owed him. She clearly had enough on her mind and heart without adding another burden. He opened the mystery folder.

"No. Wait!"

He snapped it closed before he registered the contents.

"First, let me say I realized last night that part of the issue with my new idea was my faulty presentation." Jolene reached across and tapped the file in his hand. "So this is the official proposal to change the mural design, with my"—she cleared her throat—"*rationally* explained reasoning this time."

Fair. He opened the folder, the new design leaping off the page. He forced his eyes to the corresponding typed page tucked into the pocket, skimming where she'd written a professional—almost painfully formal—proposal of why she thought the new idea was superior. The words bled together before his eyes.

> *Doesn't hide from the past.*
> *Doesn't forget history.*
> *Acknowledges change.*

He allowed himself to study the design next. The art itself, a chaotic whirlwind of a storm, all dark shadows and bending trees except for the vivid splashes of neon whipping through the hurricane's inner circle as it drove across Moreau, practically burned his eyes. She'd even included a few details of Moreau itself under the relentless torrent—he recognized the shape of the chapel steeple, the gazebo, the line of restaurants over by the river.

It was intense. Heavy. And draining.

He slowly closed the folder, drawing a deep breath.

"What do you think?" Nervous energy radiated off Jolene in waves.

He didn't want to tell her the truth. He could state one fact honestly, though. "I think you drew it well. If I attempted to draw a hurricane, it'd be a big, spiraled circle." He smiled.

She pressed her lips together. "Not quite the answer I was going for."

"Jolene, look." He slid the folder across the table to her, wishing he could tell her what she wanted to hear. "You're going for a vision that's darker than the one the town has. The original mural was a staple around Moreau. It's lighthearted and elegant. It reflects the beauty of Louisiana and our heritage. That's what we want."

If there was more time, he could suggest Jolene come up with a different idea, one that would still bring the easygoing, bayou feel that the original design brought. But there wasn't any time.

A fact that churned the beignet in his stomach.

"I hear you. But do you *know* for a fact the town feels that way?" She reached up and tucked her hair behind her ear, bracelets jangling. "Are you truly speaking for them, or are you assuming based solely on your committee meetings?"

He opened his mouth, then shut it. She had him there. They hadn't polled the town, they'd simply made a plan to put everything back the way it was—fresh and updated, of course, but the same. No one had complained or suggested otherwise.

Until Jolene.

He had a feeling this wasn't the first time she'd challenged the status quo, and he couldn't help but admire that trait, even while arguing against the specifics of what it looked like.

221

Jolene's gaze lowered, and she slowly tugged a beignet off the plate between them and onto her napkin. Powdered sugar coated her fingers as she pinched off a bite. "Granny tells me I'm stubborn."

"I might have heard that adjective once or twice while fixing up her house." Cameron leaned back in his chair, the wooden back digging into his shirt. "From Granny, though—that's a compliment."

"It can be. She used to tell me to use my powers for good and not evil." Jolene smirked. "I think that's why my dad always wanted me to go to law school. He knew I'd be good at it." Her smile faded, and she quickly ate the bite of beignet in her grasp.

She'd triggered herself somewhat with that statement. He didn't want to push, but he also really wanted to know why she had lit up that way before she'd caught herself. Had she and her dad been close? He knew her father had passed away years ago, before Cameron had moved to Moreau and met Adale or Granny. Knew the loss had been sudden and hard on the whole family.

He picked up his coffee cup, trying to keep his tone casual. "I take it you didn't agree with your father?"

"The point is, I haven't been using my so-called powers for good since I've been home." Jolene neatly dodged his attempt for information, leaving him with an eager ache to understand her better. Unlike Samantha's, Jolene's moments of vulnerability and transparency were genuine. He might have been duped by Samantha's beauty and faux charm at first, but he'd been lying to himself after about their third date. That part was on him.

While Jolene was unpredictable, she was also very honest. Raw. What you saw was what you got. He could appreciate that, even while not always agreeing.

"Is this your effort toward powers for good?" He glanced at the folder on the table.

"Contrary to what my family might suggest, I'm not trying to be difficult." She wiped powdered sugar off her mouth with a napkin. "But I don't think the original design is what this town needs."

"The problem is, we don't have a lot of time to figure it out."

"I believe in this design. Maybe I can tone back some of the colors, compromise in a different way?" Her eyes beseeched him.

"Why is this so important to you?" Cameron leaned forward, lowering his voice. She'd missed a spot of sugar by her lip, and in a moment he couldn't take back, he reached over and gently rubbed it clean with his knuckle.

Instant electricity snapped through his finger. Her eyes widened, and she quickly grabbed for her napkin to wipe her face again.

"Sorry. Instinct." He shook his head quickly, flexing his hand under the table. It wasn't usually in his instincts to be that forward, but that whole moth-to-flame thing had kicked in. . . .

He cleared his throat. "I was saying, you haven't been back in town in years. Why are you so passionate about this project?"

He immediately regretted using the word passionate so soon after touching her, but if she felt uncomfortable, she didn't show it. Instead, she tilted her head and took a deep breath. "I don't see the wisdom in playing pretend."

"And why is redoing the original mural pretending?"

"This town isn't the same as it was before the hurricane last summer—even if people want to pretend it is." Shadows clouded her eyes.

"But how do you know?" He tossed her logic back at her. "Are you speaking for them, or are you assuming?"

She picked up her unused fork, spinning it between her fingers. "I don't know, I guess."

"And neither do I."

"So we're at an impasse. We both think the mural should look a certain way, and we're both convinced it's for the good of the town, but neither of us can prove it."

"Sounds about right." What were they going to do? Cameron went for another sip of coffee, but it was gone. He set his empty mug down with a clatter.

"Look, we've got to get a mural on that wall by Sunday, one way or another—or it's your head and my reputation." He ran a hand through his hair as he tried to picture the ramifications of each choice. "I don't feel right trying to enforce something you feel this strongly against."

Hope lit her eyes.

"But I still don't agree with you."

The light flickered.

"I think. . ." His voice trailed off as he glanced out the shop window at the adorned lampposts, at the garland draped over storefronts, at the bustle of people in winter coats striding down the sidewalks with shopping bags and strollers. Those people needed hope in the power of restoration. Needed light after a dark season. Expected a mural reveal on Sunday afternoon.

He drew a breath. Mattie and Mayor Ammons might kill him, but they had put him in charge of this portion of the restoration project. He had to make an executive decision. And he could only imagine Mattie's face if Sunday afternoon rolled around and the media crews were staring at a blank wall.

Decision made. "I think at this point, any mural is better than nothing. If the community doesn't like it, maybe they can redo it again in a few years."

"Deal!" Jolene reached out and grabbed his hand across the table. "I promise I'll use all my stubborn powers to prove this is a good idea. You'll see." She squeezed his palm before releasing her grip.

He returned her smile. "I hope so." Mostly he hoped he wasn't making a big mistake.

And he really hoped his hand would stop tingling.

———◆———

"Better than nothing."

Sort of summed up her art career, didn't it?

Jolene cleaned her paintbrushes in the bathroom of the community hall as Cameron's words echoed, puddling in her mind like the swirls of black and gray puddling in the sink. She knew he hadn't meant anything harsh by it. It was the facts. He didn't believe in her new design, but still she'd won.

She could officially paint the mural that she wanted to without pushback—and had started to do so. Made significant progress during the afternoon, even.

So why did she feel far from victorious?

And why couldn't she think of a single thing to buy Granny for her birthday?

Her mom's reminder text about Granny's upcoming party and "Don't forget to grab her a gift" had buzzed in her pocket an hour ago, while she'd been lost in chalk drawing the outline of the mural on the wall. Nate's original design was completely removed now. Erasing it had brought more trepidation than elation, but she was committed now.

No going back.

She wrapped up the brushes in paper towels, then returned everything to the supply closet. The next few days would be full of nonstop painting, but meeting Sunday's deadline finally seemed attainable. At least with her new hurricane design, she didn't feel so paralyzed when lifting a paintbrush. But she still had to work in a few other things before then—like shopping for Granny.

She shot off a quick text to Mattie as she turned off the heat lamps in the tent.

WHAT ARE YOU GETTING GRANNY FOR HER BIRTHDAY?

Dots appeared as Mattie wrote back. I MADE HER A PHOTO SCRAPBOOK WEEKS AGO.

Jolene shook her head. Looked like she was behind in that as well. PROBABLY ALREADY WRAPPED IT TOO.

More dots. OF COURSE.

Of course. Jolene was running out of time in every way, and since painting at night wasn't ideal, she could at least shop for Granny this evening and knock that out. Besides, her fingers were cramping from clutching her tools in cold hands. She needed the break, mentally and physically.

Jolene hesitated, knowing she might be walking into a minefield with her next text, but it seemed inevitable. She quickly typed her invitation.

WANT TO HELP ME PICK SOMETHING OUT AT THE MARKET TONIGHT?

The response was immediate. ABSOLUTELY! 6:30. WE CAN EAT DINNER THERE TOO.

Jolene could practically hear her cousin's squeal through the typed letters. Mattie loved to shop, but more than that, Jolene suspected Mattie was glad *she* had initiated hanging out. Mattie had obviously missed her cousin over the years—and the feeling was surprisingly, genuinely mutual. That had been one silver lining to coming home—reconciling with Mattie. Now if only Jolene and her mom could reach a similar place of connection.

But that would require telling the whole truth, and, well. . .

Jolene quickly pocketed her phone, then secured the tent flap and headed for her mom's car. She'd returned Mattie's SUV after her coffee meeting with Cameron earlier that day and picked up her mom's sedan instead for the afternoon so Mattie could go to work. If she'd known she'd have so much driving to do when she came home, she'd have driven from Nashville instead of flying. Though, to be fair, no one could have predicted the turn of events that had occurred since Sunday.

Had she really only been back in Moreau for three days?

The church parking lot was empty, save for her mom's borrowed sedan. Cameron had finished painting the gazebo with a first coat of stain after they'd returned from the Press and had gone home for the day. He'd offered to give her a ride back to the Lavigne House, but she didn't want him waiting around on her.

Or watching her progress.

Jolene slid into the driver's seat and cranked the ignition, taking a moment to hold her hands in front of the vents and let the warm air thaw her fingers.

All afternoon she'd pondered that moment at the pastry shop when Cameron had brushed sugar off her face. At the time, she'd jerked back in surprise, but now that gentle touch felt imprinted on her cheek. Along with the obvious struggle in his eyes when he'd shot down her idea, then reluctantly gave her the green light. He might not believe in her vision, but he clearly believed in her—at least enough to trust her to move forward.

Nerves wrecked her stomach. What if the directors of the art school were right in rejecting her application? What if she wasn't good enough? What if she proved to be unreliable?

What if her father had been right?

She didn't doubt her design. She'd just fought so hard for it, she was surprised she'd gotten it. Sort of like a dog chasing a car and never actually expecting to catch it. But Cameron, not to mention Mattie, was trusting her to get this done. The mayor. Her family. The entire town.

So she'd better figure out exactly what to do with it, and quick.

Chapter Eight

The Christmas market was hopping. Mattie would be ecstatic. Cameron strode past the wooden stall selling homemade ornaments, inhaled the cinnamon-scented air wafting from the roasted pecans booth, and headed toward the woodworking booth. Now that the gazebo was finished and the mural was underway, he could take a breath. Maybe even find a Christmas gift to send his mom. When she'd visited last summer, she'd liked those hand-carved signs of Robby's that were selling like crazy over at Rustic Creations.

He dodged the string of clamoring kids lined up to see Santa, who had yet to take his seat by the giant Christmas tree. According to Mattie's schedule, tonight was the big guy's first appearance at the market, and already the line stretched all the way to the crepe stall.

Cameron dodged a mom pushing a double stroller and two teens strolling hand in hand. He tried not to wonder what it would be like to attend the market with Jolene—shopping together, trying out the food trucks, sharing a bag of roasted pecans. In a different time and place, it would have been a very entertaining thought.

But he lived in reality—one in which he totally cramped Jolene's style. One where she lived two states away and clearly was still dealing with things she refused to share.

Not exactly "let's make Christmas memories together" material.

"Ho, ho, ho!" The sudden exclamation grabbed everyone's attention, as a full-bearded Santa in a red suit finally took his seat in the high-backed golden chair set in the center of the square. The kids cheered, and Cameron paused to watch, smiling as the first boy in line scrambled up the makeshift platform to talk to Santa. Nothing like being a child again at Christmas, where your biggest stress was wondering if that much-desired present would show up under the tree.

His own memory of whispering wishes to Santa stretched way back to holiday outings with his grandmother and mom in New Orleans, pre-hurricane. He remembered how his grandmother, so much like Granny Eloise, would tease the elves while they waited in line, then demand Cameron be given the biggest candy cane in their treat bucket. He would flush red and turn around when she wasn't looking to hand it off to the kid in line behind him. How Mom laughed while she watched that unofficial yearly tradition, the creases in her brow not nearly as pronounced then as they were after Katrina.

That last Christmas before Katrina, he'd been in sixth grade, too old for Santa visits but still enjoying those traditional outings with his family. No one had any idea what was coming that fateful August. Or, for that matter, what was coming the very next month, when his grandmother's cancer returned with a vengeance.

He sobered, his smile fading. Maybe Jolene had a point—nothing could ever be the same as it was before a storm.

"Cameron!"

He turned at the female voice calling his name, scanning the weeknight crowd until he spotted Mattie and Jolene occupying the picnic table near Robby's stall. Mattie waved big, her smile bigger, while Jolene hesitantly raised one hand, her expression pinched. He let out a dry chuckle. Eager to see him, as usual.

Even still, he changed course to head their way. . .because he was still a winged creature and Jolene was still a candle. "Evening, ladies."

"You're here just in time." Mattie stood and began to gather their dinner trash. "Paul texted that he needs me to help him at the language booth, but I promised Jolene I'd go with her to find a birthday gift for Granny."

Jolene widened her eyes at Mattie, who clearly pretended not to see.

"You can help her instead, right?" Mattie continued, brushing crumbs off her jacket. "You know Granny pretty well." She nodded briskly before either of them could respond. "So it's settled. Jo, I'll meet you back at the Christmas tree in about an hour."

Jo? He raised his eyebrows at Jolene, unable to stop his grin, and she narrowed her eyes at him. "Don't even think about it."

"Have fun!" Mattie fluttered her fingers in goodbye, then made a beeline for the front of the market.

"Based on that conversation, I'm not exactly sure who is babysitting who here." He snagged one of the empty soda cans to help clean up as Jolene finished clearing their picnic table.

"Sorry about that. Mattie is. . .well, Mattie." She cast him a sidelong glance as she dumped the wad of napkins and burger wrappers in a trash can. "Pretty sure she's playing matchmaker, so watch your back for Cupid's arrows."

"Wrong holiday." He snorted, as if the entire idea was ridiculous, but his neck warmed, and he tugged at the collar of his sweater. Hadn't he been thinking along those exact lines a moment ago, watching the passing couples? And now here he was with Jolene, about to walk and shop and admire the market's Christmas lights.

Not hand in hand, obviously. But bonus—she didn't look nearly as annoyed with the whole concept as her apology made it sound.

"So what are we looking for?" Cameron kept his hands in his jacket pockets—just in case—as they began to walk. "What is this perfect birthday gift?"

"I'm not sure. Granny is harder to shop for than I am." Jolene also shoved her hands into her coat pockets. But their ambling gait didn't stop their shoulders from occasionally brushing as they navigated the crowd. He didn't move away, and she didn't either. "Mattie made her a scrapbook, a collection of memories from Granny's whole life. Hard to top that!"

"I sure wish I had known Eloise sooner." Cameron chuckled. "I'll never forget the first thing she said to me when I showed up at the cottage to begin that long list of repairs."

Jolene tilted her head back and groaned. "I can only imagine."

He raised his voice a few notches to imitate Eloise's. "You're three minutes late. That means you only get unsweet tea."

Jolene laughed. "And I bet by the end of the day, she was pouring on the sugar."

"Literally and figuratively. She followed me around that little house, alternating between pointing out everything she thought I should be doing instead of what I was doing and telling tales from her past. Then when I finally left, she hugged me and left a red lipstick stain on my shirt collar that was hard to explain." He shook his head and grinned. "She's considered me her adopted grandson ever since."

Jolene had quieted, though her smile remained in place. "I didn't realize you two had gotten that close."

"Granny gets what Granny wants." Cameron laughed. "But seriously, I'm the one who benefited from her taking me in. And not only because she pays well."

"How so?" Jolene looked directly at him for the first time that night, the wind sweeping a lock of dark hair in front of her face.

Like at the Press, his hand reacted with a mind of its own. He carefully tucked the errant strand behind her ear, letting his fingers linger against her cheek for a moment before shoving his hand back into his pocket. "She filled a gap." He studied Jolene's upturned face. "One I didn't know I had."

Jolene didn't look away, much to his surprise, and the myriad of emotions flickering through her eyes was nothing less than a hurricane itself. "You never have to wonder with Granny, do you?"

"Nope. What you see is what you get."

"I've wondered about other members of my family over the years." Jolene resumed walking, and he matched the rhythm of her slow steps. "How they felt about me, what they thought about me. But never Granny. She made it clear."

"I think we're all guilty of assuming things to our own detriment." Cameron fought the urge to take her hand, even though he knew she'd probably slap him away. He hated seeing her so down, especially this close to Christmas. But how did you help carry a burden when the other person refused to share the load?

A hearty "ho, ho, ho" echoed once more through the market, giving him an idea. Cameron paused, tugging at Jolene's arm. "Let's get in line."

"What?" Her eyes widened, and she laughed. "Don't be silly."

"Come on. When was the last time you saw Santa?"

She rolled in her lower lip, thinking. "I was probably in elementary school."

"Same. I think we're due." He led her to the line before she could protest.

Fifteen minutes later, it was finally their turn. Cameron gestured for Jolene to go first, and she did, hesitantly, perching on the side of the stool set beside Santa's chair. He couldn't hear what she said over the din of children around him, but he watched Santa respond to her comment and then offer her a high five.

He was next.

"Merry Christmas." Santa dipped his head in acknowledgment. "I take it you don't want a wagon or a football?" His wise blue eyes twinkled.

"You're right." Cameron sat on the stool vacated by Jolene, who now stood off to the side, pawing through the bucket of Christmas candy. "Can I ask for something on behalf of someone else?"

"Well, certainly," Santa boomed. "That's not a request I get a lot of."

He subtly nodded toward Jolene. "My friend there needs to find her Christmas spirit again. She's been kind of down since coming back home."

"Friend, hmm?" Santa rubbed his beard, following Cameron's gaze. "I can't deliver relationships down the chimney, you know."

"No, no, that's not what I'm asking for."

"Those hearts pulsing out of your eyes say otherwise." Santa chuckled.

Great. Now his growing attraction to Jolene was obvious to complete strangers. Cameron shifted his weight, wishing his grandmother were here to distract everyone with her peppermint demands. "That might be more in the Christmas miracle department."

"Seems to me your friend needs a reminder of the real meaning of the season, then." Santa lowered his voice, leaning sideways in his painted throne. "I might invoke some Christmas spirit, but there's only one who can bring real joy. Real peace."

"I agree." Cameron swallowed hard as memories of past Christmases flooded his heart. His grandmother might have been playfully sassy with the mall employees at Christmas, but she also made sure he'd been sitting right next to her in the third pew of his hometown church every Sunday morning. Christmas Eve services were always special—she'd let him hold the real candle instead of the fake bulb kind the younger kids typically held, and told him to always remember that real men loved God and went to church on more than just holidays.

And those moments spent on those pews were where he always found his deepest measure of joy and peace.

He cleared his throat. "I think my friend needs both of those. She's carrying some heavy stuff."

Santa tilted his head as he considered Jolene, who hugged her arms tight to her body. Her hair lifted in the cold evening breeze. "How about I pray for her? Will that suffice?"

Cameron's throat burned. "That'd be great. Thank you, Santa." He quickly stood before the sudden emotion overtook him.

"And, son?" Santa called after him as he started off the platform.

Cameron turned.

Santa smiled. "Don't be afraid to pray for Christmas miracles."

———◆———

Jolene hadn't had that much fun with a guy in. . .well, a very long time. Maybe ever.

She pulled a piece of funnel cake free from the shared plate on the table between her and Cameron, where they sat waiting for Mattie. After visiting Santa, they'd toured every stall at the market, ending at the art booth, where she found a leather brush roll for storing paintbrushes, which the shop owner customized with Granny's name and the commemorative year. The perfect sentimental nod to their shared love.

Cameron had been the one to suggest they check out the booth, and at first Jolene had balked. She didn't even want to think about art, not when they'd been having so much fun people watching and browsing the homemade gifts available at each stall—and more importantly, not stressing over her deadline. She hadn't even minded the incessant blare of Christmas music streaming from the overhead speakers. Thankfully, she'd acquiesced to his suggestion and found the perfect gift for Granny.

For the first time, the truce with Cameron felt like it was fully in action. And somewhere around the homemade ornament booth, where they'd cracked up over a hand-painted crawfish wearing a Santa hat, she realized she liked laughing with Cameron a lot more than arguing with him. When he grinned wide, his dimples appeared and sort of made her forget what they'd even argued about in the first place. That grin made her want him to be proud of the mural.

Proud of her.

"Granny is going to love it." Cameron pointed to the present, tucked carefully inside a paper bag stamped with the store's logo. "It was a good choice."

"I think so too. Thanks for your help." Jolene rubbed her fingers on a napkin. "I'd probably still be wandering around if not for your recommendation. I wanted this gift for Granny to be perfect."

"You're not trying to earn her favor back, now, are you?" Cameron tore off a bite of cake for himself.

Jolene shifted a little on the picnic bench. "No." I mean, it had crossed her mind but only for a minute. Granny wasn't like that. Maybe her mom was, but not Granny.

She hoped.

Cameron raised his eyebrows as if sensing her hesitation, and her defenses crumbled. How did he keep doing that?

Jolene went for a piece of funnel cake at the same time he did, and their fingers brushed. He took her hand instead of the dessert and held on. "Promise?"

She should tug free, but she didn't want to. Why didn't she want to? She stared at their joined hands, simultaneously loving and hating how protective he'd become of her. "How do you do that?"

"Do what?" He didn't let go, either.

"Cut through all my walls." She glared at him. "I've worked really hard to build those, you know."

He grinned, his blue eyes sparking something deep inside to life. "Maybe it's *my* superpower."

She let out a huff. "Use it for good."

"I'd like to think I am." He finally released her hand, then offered her the last piece of the powdered cake. "I've got to know. . .what did you tell Santa you wanted for Christmas?"

Heat flushed her chest under her jacket, despite the cold night air surrounding them. She drew a circle in the spilled sugar on the tabletop with her finger. "I told him the truth."

"Which is?"

"That I hadn't been all that great the past few years." Jolene snorted. "And to feel free to leave coal in my stocking."

He smirked. "You did not."

"I did too." Jolene laughed, remembering the initial surprise on Santa's face. Then the way his eyes had grown serious and pierced right through her surface-level joke. *"Sounds like you might need to give yourself the gift of forgiveness this year."*

No reason for Cameron to know that part, though.

His voice lowered an octave. "You're not coal-worthy, don't worry."

"Never can tell." She kept her own tone light, despite her desperate desire to believe him.

"Even if you are. . ." He put his hand over hers, stilling her powdered-sugar design attempts and forcing her gaze up. "I have a question."

His hand, warm on top of hers, trembled slightly. Was he nervous? Now she was too. "What is it?"

He took a slight breath. "The big Christmas Eve ball is next week. I know you'll still be in town, and, well. . .what do you say? About going with me."

"With you?" She didn't mean to parrot, didn't mean to inflict that slight frown now lingering between his brows. "That came out wrong. I'm just surprised you're asking. I mean, this whole week, we've been sort of. . ."

"Enemies?" His dimple was back in full force. "Don't worry. The truce is still in full effect. I refuse to cancel it until at least New Year's."

New Year's. She'd be gone by then. Back to Nashville, to a cold studio apartment and a handful of rejection letters. To frozen microwave meals for one.

To the reminder of dead dreams.

She tensed, and his hand, still on hers, rubbed the top of her knuckles, as if sensing her temptation to bolt.

"Think about it?"

As Granny would say, "Bless his heart." He'd given her an out. But in that same breath, she realized she didn't want it. She squared her shoulders. "I'd like to go."

His eyes widened.

She smirked. "As long as you don't mind escorting a woman wearing green to a black-and-white ball."

"I'd be more shocked if you followed a theme." He grinned. "Seriously though. . .I'm looking forward to it."

She smiled back and nodded, even as tension radiated into her shoulders. Easy for him to say right now. He didn't know her secrets.

He didn't know her father's death was her fault.

Chapter Nine

Jolene couldn't sleep—not with her evening with Cameron fresh on her mind and the burden of the unfinished mural returning now that the distraction of the market was over. She knew better than to try to take Mattie's car back up to the church this late, but she needed something to occupy her thoughts.

"This will be fun." Mattie had handed Jolene a mug of hot chocolate before she shuffled through the dining room in her fuzzy house shoes.

Jolene cupped the warm mug with both hands. Mattie to the rescue, as usual. They'd stacked all of Granny's unpacked boxes of her old art onto the dining room table to sort through and were ready to dive in. "Remember, we're only picking out the best ones to display at her party."

"That's going to be hard to determine." Jolene took a sip before setting her drink out of the way of the boxed canvases. "Granny's really good."

She'd taught Jolene everything she knew about art. At least when Jolene decided to move to Nashville, Granny had understood and been the most supportive of anyone else in the family. Of course, she never would have expected Jolene to stay away as long as she did.

Jolene hadn't intended to, either.

"Maybe focus on finding the ones that will mean the most to her, then." Mattie flipped through the stack of framed pieces in the carton closest to her, the protective packaging crinkling with each movement. "Speaking of things meaning the most. . ." She looked up and grinned. "I heard Cameron is taking you to the ball?"

Jolene's stomach flipped a little. She kept her face as stoic as possible, not wanting to feed her cousin's matchmaking fever. "That's the plan."

Mattie clapped her hands together. "We'll have to get a lot of pictures together at the dance. Me and Paul, you and Cameron. . .and they're already friends, so this is perfect."

Jolene pointed a finger in warning at her cousin. "Before you start planning our double wedding, you should know we're still in a kind of weird place with the mural stuff." Though all of that had faded to the wayside while shopping the market together.

"Can't be that weird, or he wouldn't have asked you." Mattie shrugged as if that was that.

Maybe she was right. Maybe Jolene was overthinking it in her stress. "I guess Granny's party will be a good test run. See if tonight was a fluke or if our truce really exists."

"I saw the way he looked at you." Mattie shot her a knowing glance before taking a sip of her cocoa. "It exists, trust me."

She wanted her cousin to be right, but that would also stir up a heap of drama she didn't want to deal with. Her life felt completely up in the air. Throwing dating into the mix seemed risky—maybe even foolish.

But the other part of her, the part that had worked very hard not to melt into a puddle when Cameron had tucked her hair behind her ear earlier, thought it worth the attempt.

"Oh, here's this one again." Mattie lifted a small canvas featuring a Parisian scene by the river. A couple stood poised against the sunset backdrop, arms wrapped around each other in a loving embrace. "Maybe we should include it for her party. From what I understand, she painted this one in France decades ago."

"That's beautiful." Jolene moved to stand by her cousin to see the framed work up close. Shades of marigold and crimson and cobalt leaped off the page, rich and inviting. Granny had outdone herself. "But what do you mean by again?"

Mattie handed the canvas to Jolene for further inspection. "Granny saw me with it last week, before you came into town, and was odd about it."

Jolene looked up from the scene with a frown. "Odd how?"

"She got. . .quiet."

Hmm. That *was* odd for Granny.

Mattie shrugged. "It's almost like this painting has a story. Or a secret."

Jolene had too many of those herself to worry about ones buried in acrylic. "Well, either way, let's display it. It's lovely, and a tribute to her life of world travels."

"Perfect." Mattie added it to the designated party pile.

A shuffling sound came from the kitchen; then Jolene's mom walked into the dining room, covering a yawn with her hand. "What are you girls doing up so late?" She wrapped her black-and-white robe tighter around her thin frame.

"We're finally sorting the art to display at Granny's party. I meant to do this earlier in the week." Mattie scooted the stack over to make room for her to join them at the table. "I hope we didn't wake you. We'll keep it down."

"Yeah, sorry." Jolene chimed in. "Want some cocoa?"

"No, it's okay. I was coming down for a glass of water—" Her face blanched. "What is that?"

"Granny's art." Jolene watched as her mother fixated on the Parisian scene at the top of the pile. She shot Mattie a questioning look.

Mattie shrugged.

"You can't display this one." Mom plucked the canvas from the stack, her knuckles white against the dark frame.

Jolene frowned. "Why not?"

"It's not suitable." Mom glanced down at the French scene once more before handing it over to Mattie. "I'm sure there are plenty of others to choose from."

"Does Granny not like it? We think it's one of her best ones." Mattie tucked the frame back into the *no* box.

"I wouldn't know. But let's not bother her with it. She's got a lot going on this weekend to have to deal with all of this." Mom flitted her hand in the general direction of the table. "I'm going back to bed. Good night, girls."

"Good night," they chimed in unison.

"Was that strange to you?" Jolene asked once her mom was out of earshot. She hadn't spent much time around her mom in person the past several years, but that felt off. Had she even gotten that glass of water she'd come down for?

"A little. But I think we're all stressed. Maybe she's just worked up over the party details." Mattie pulled another piece of art free from a nearby box—this one featuring an elegant fleur-de-lis. "What do you think?"

"Sure. Let's do it." But Jolene wasn't ready to change the subject. "Doesn't it make you curious that Granny and Mom have both acted odd about the same painting?"

"It does." Mattie chewed on her lower lip. "But like she said, she doesn't want us bothering Granny about any party-related stuff."

They resumed their work of sorting Granny's lifetime of masterpieces, and eventually the conversation changed back to guys. But even as Jolene listened to Mattie list all of Paul's amazing qualities, she pondered the best way to find out the truth about that painting.

And why no one in the family seemed to want one of Granny's best pieces displayed at her party.

"Scoot over."

Jolene jerked in surprise from her position on the ground as the tent flap lifted, letting in both Granny and a rush of cold air despite the warm afternoon sun. "Granny?"

"I thought I'd come help. For old times' sake." Granny dropped a bulging tote bag on the floor of the tent. A package of peanut butter crackers and a Twinkie fell out, and she promptly scooped them back up before snagging a set of paintbrushes from the bag's depths. "I brought my own gear, don't worry."

"I can share." Jolene scooted over as instructed, where she'd been painting the eye of the hurricane. She wasn't happy with it yet, but that might have been partly due to the fact that Cameron kept checking on her—bringing her coffee, making sure the heat lamp was still working, asking if she wanted lunch brought back. Those parts she liked.

It was the deep concern in his eyes every time his gaze flitted to the mural that she didn't enjoy. He still wasn't convinced, and it bothered her more than she wanted to admit.

"What do you think?" Jolene asked as Granny positioned a portable folding stool in front of the mural and plopped onto it. She half-feared the answer, but Granny would be honest.

Granny couldn't help be anything but.

Her grandmother took a breath, turning her white head to view the full scope of the wall and the halfway completed storm. "You sure know how to paint sadness."

Jolene winced as she looked up at her. "It's not supposed to be sad."

"Hurricanes sure aren't happy, honey." Granny pushed up her sleeves, then seemed to realize how cold it was and tugged them back down.

"The original mural wasn't happy either."

Granny raised her penciled brows. "How so?"

"It was the same." Jolene dabbed emphatically on the new design with her brush, as if painting faster would make everyone see what she saw. "It wasn't giving any honor to the fact that nothing after a storm can be like it was. No matter how many famous architects you bring in or how many fundraisers are held to pay for updates, it's not the same town as it was before."

"Why not?"

"Because the *people* aren't the same." Jolene held up her book to show Granny the full design. "They need to be reminded that this happened. And that it's okay that it happened."

Granny looked down at the drawing, then at Jolene, her eyes darkening with emotion. She opened her mouth, but Jolene didn't want to hear what she was about to say.

Somehow, she knew it would wreck her.

"I really appreciate you coming, but can we please talk about something else? It's too late to change anything now, and I finally got Cameron on board." Out of desperation from a ticking clock, but it counted.

"Of course. You're the artist, and I respect that." Granny settled in with her two-inch brush. "I'll add highlights to this part of the storm here, if that's okay."

"Please do. Sunday is coming." Cameron's frequent check-ins kept reminding her of the deadline—and reminding her how much she was looking forward to the ball. Just a little over a week and she'd be dancing with Cameron, wearing her new green dress, the mural a memory behind them.

Of course the day after the ball was Christmas, and the day after that was her return to Nashville, which meant any potential relationship with Cameron would turn into a pumpkin.

But for one night, she'd wear glass slippers.

"So what would you like to talk about?" Granny wiped her brush with the damp cloth lying between them, then applied a shade of mahogany paint to the tip.

"What's the deal with the Parisian painting from your collection?" Jolene cocked her head to one side as she filled in the outline of one of the storm's clouds. "Mom acted weird last night when she saw it. Said she didn't want it at your party this weekend."

Granny, either avoiding eye contact or truly focusing that hard on the mural, shrugged a little as she leaned back on her stool and evaluated the wall. "Well, what did she say when you asked her?"

"I didn't want to push, but this morning at breakfast I mentioned it again, and she said it just reminded her of her time in Paris." But it hadn't been the words her mom said that raised suspicion so much as her tone. Guarded. The tone Jolene defaulted to herself when asked about certain subjects best left avoided—like her dad.

"Then maybe that's it." Granny kept her gaze on the mural. "Sometimes all there is to a story is all the person wants to share."

Jolene snorted. "Your wise-old-owl cryptic answers aren't exactly easing my curiosity, Granny."

"Hoot, hoot."

Jolene shook her head. "Well, if there's more to it than that, Mattie will get it out of Mom eventually. Seems like they talk about everything." And did everything together. And went everywhere together.

"Is that a bit of jealousy I detect, Jolene Broussard?" Granny pointed her brush at Jolene, and a drip of brown paint landed on the tarp between them.

"No. Yes." Jolene rinsed her brush in the cup of water by her knee, watching the water turn murky. "A little."

"No one forced you out of the house, my girl." Granny's voice lowered. "Especially not your mother."

"I know. I chose Nashville." Jolene swallowed against the lump lodging in her throat. She'd had so many reasons at the time. Being back in Moreau, all those reasons felt shallow. "It's so complicated now."

"Doesn't have to be." Granny went back to painting. "Besides, I happen to know a certain blond cousin that is a mite jealous of *you*."

"Me?" Jolene reared back, looking up at Granny with her mouth open. "Mattie isn't jealous of anyone. She's like Mary Poppins—practically perfect in every way."

"She's told me before that she envies our bond and time together painting over the years. She never had that connection with anyone." Granny sighed. "And she's lost a lot too, you know."

"I know." Which was part of why, despite their arguments and vast differences over the years, she never could stay upset with her cousin for too long. Jolene had only lost one parent. Mattie had lost two, for different reasons. Though to be fair, Mattie didn't understand the burden Jolene carried.

No one did. Which was why it was so much easier to live two states away.

"Maybe Mattie envies us, and maybe you envy her and Adale. But you know what? We're all family." Granny's lips pursed. "You need to speak with your mother. After all, she's much less likely to bite than I am, and you have no trouble talking with me."

Jolene sighed. "That's different. You understand me."

Granny might be all bark and no bite, but Mom didn't even bark. Hers was more of a mild, passive aggressive response, one that had always left Jolene wondering if she was disappointed in her. Until Jolene became disappointed in herself enough for the both of them.

"You two don't know each other as adults." Granny squinted at the mural, then reached over and dabbed a bit of white into the black cloud to create a gray shadow. "I'm only saying there could be a lot of assumptions from both directions."

Maybe she was right. Jolene had been gone a long time—there was no telling what her mother assumed about Jolene's motivations for staying away. Jolene had been the one to hold her secret close, like a wall she needed and a burden she hated, all at once. That wasn't her family's fault.

Jolene took a shuddering breath. "How'd you get to be such a wise owl anyway?"

"A lot of life lived. Eighty years this weekend, remember?" Granny sat up straighter on her stool. "Though I know it's confusing since I don't look a day over sixty-five."

"Very confusing indeed." Jolene stood, stretching out the ache in her lower back, then moved to the other side of the tent to view the mural progress in full. She'd painted half the storm so far, the colors toned down from her original pitch to Cameron—her attempt at a compromise. From a skill level, she wasn't displeased. It looked better from a slight distance, as she'd hoped.

But something felt off.

"What do you see?" Granny joined Jolene on the other side of the enclosed space, planting her hands on her hips.

"I see. . .a storm. A life-changing event." Her voice caught, and she cleared her throat. "What do you see, Granny?"

"I see your design." Granny wrapped one arm around Jolene's shoulder. "And you've done very well with it."

She could practically hear the looming conjunction in Granny's voice. "But?"

"It's a well-drawn mural." Her grandmother squeezed her shoulder. "But is it for *you*? Is it what *you* need? Or is it what Moreau needs?"

Chapter Ten

Cameron handed his end of the string of lights to Paul Ammons, who perched midway up a ladder in the community center. "Is school out for the holidays already?" He'd have assumed his friend would be teaching today as usual.

"Not yet. I got a sub so I could help Mattie." Paul secured the string lights to the top of the tall windows lining the back wall, then scurried down the ladder before moving it a few feet to the left.

Cameron trailed behind, the rest of the lights wound around his arm, as Paul climbed back up. "Nice brownie points."

"Well, I'm not sure I need them anymore, partially thanks to your good advice last week." Paul laughed. "She had to turn in an article this morning at the paper, but she should be here soon." He cast a look around the in-progress party room, and Cameron followed his gaze.

Adale had covered two long tables in purple cloths while Kimberly alternated between hanging purple and gold ornaments on a Christmas tree and shooting Cameron smiles. He quickly looked away, not wanting to engage with the overeager hair stylist this morning. Even if she did remind him of his first meeting with Jolene. He smiled.

Paul positioned the ladder for his next climb. "I hope Granny likes all this—for Mattie's sake especially. She'd be crushed if she thought Eloise was disappointed over anything."

He knew that feeling—no one in Moreau wanted to see Eloise upset, which was part of his initial reservations toward Jolene. She'd hurt her grandmother, however indirectly. But the more he got to know Granny—and Jolene—the more he realized he'd read the situation completely wrong.

She wasn't Samantha, and he wasn't repeating history. Jolene hadn't used him or Granny. She wasn't manipulative and self-serving. She was raw, honest. . .and still hurting from old wounds. Sort of like the chapel—a bit damaged but beautiful inside and out.

He wanted so badly to see them both restored to their full potential.

"You think it's too much?" Paul asked, gesturing around the room.

"I can honestly say I've never seen so much purple, green, and gold, and I used to live in New Orleans." Cameron braced one foot on the ladder as Paul climbed back to the top. "But Granny has always been colorful. I bet she'll love it."

Part of why he'd volunteered to help today was in hopes he'd catch Jolene and could talk to her away from the mural. But she was probably painting, as she should be. He'd just hoped by giving her free rein she'd stop fighting so hard and see what he saw in the design—that it wasn't right for Moreau. Cameron knew it. He was pretty sure the whole town would know it Sunday at the reveal.

Why didn't Jolene know it?

He lengthened the strand of lights to give his friend slack as Paul reached overhead. Cameron had second-guessed his decision to let Jolene make the final call on the mural a dozen times since Wednesday. The new design wasn't poorly done—the bit he'd seen yesterday while Granny was there looked amazing craft-wise. Jolene could deny her identity as an artist all she wanted, but the proof was on the wall.

She was talented.

But he worried about Mattie's reaction Sunday, along with Mayor Ammons' and the rest of the community. He needed to warn Jolene. The last thing he wanted was for her to be humiliated—she didn't seem like she could withstand another blow right now. It seemed her family ties were strengthening, she'd found her rhythm with the mural, and he'd even caught her humming along to Christmas music as they'd shopped the market booths the other night. It seemed like Santa's prayers—and his own—were taking effect. He didn't want to burst her fragile bubble, so he hadn't said anything about the design when he'd checked on her yesterday.

But was he doing her a disservice by withholding his true opinion? Was he setting her up for embarrassment? Though it would be much more embarrassing—for them both—to have nothing to present at all.

"Speaking of brownie points. . .I hear you asked Jolene to the ball next weekend." Paul climbed down.

Cameron stepped aside as Paul moved the ladder to the last window. "I did."

"And she said yes?"

"She did." Cameron handed Paul the last string of lights. "You sound surprised."

"Mattie is ecstatic."

"Nice dodge."

"I'm not surprised." Paul laughed. "I guess I'm more surprised that you asked. I thought you two got off on the wrong foot."

To put it mildly. Cameron nodded. "We did. But now. . ."

"Right foot?"

"Not quite, but maybe getting there." Assuming Jolene didn't take back her acceptance to be his date once he brought up the mural again.

If he did. Should he? Cameron sighed. He wanted to protect her. And to be honest, he wanted to protect his own reputation. If everyone hated the design and knew he'd signed off on it, he might lose his good standing with the people who had come to trust him. Like Mattie. Mayor Ammons. The local business chamber. And what would Rémy think if he took the job? He'd worked so hard to make a good impression in Moreau, this town that meant so much to him.

"Let's just say we're having creative differences." Cameron held the ladder for Paul. "There's something I need to tell her, but she's not going to want to hear it. It'll hurt her if I tell her, but it might also hurt her if I don't."

It was too late for Jolene to start over or make any big changes. So on the one hand, there was no point in saying anything negative about it. But he also didn't feel right in throwing her to the wolves and having the town's crestfallen faces be all she saw on Sunday afternoon. She'd quit art for sure, then.

It felt like a no-win.

Paul climbed to the top rung. "Love is a risk, as a wise man once told me."

"Whoa!" Cameron jerked back on instinct, the ladder shaking from the jolt. He steadied it. "Who said anything about love?" He cast a quick look at Adale, who thankfully was still across the room, out of earshot.

"You didn't have to." Paul shrugged. "Your face kind of looks like mine did when I came to you looking for answers with Mattie."

The community center suddenly felt hot. Cameron cracked the tension out of his neck. Love? He barely knew Jolene. He swallowed. But he wanted to know her better. Wasn't that all he'd thought about all week?

Paul chuckled, twisting slightly to peer down at Cameron. "Remember what you told me at your house that night?"

"*No*. And I also can't be responsible for what I said while grilling."

Paul snorted as he resumed hanging the lights. "You asked me if I wanted to keep up with Mattie. So now I'm asking you the same. Do you want to keep up with Jolene?"

Like that was possible. "She'll be moving back to Nashville after Christmas. It's kind of a moot point, isn't it?"

"Plans change, man." Paul shrugged as he joined Cameron on the floor. "I know mine did. And look where it got me." He gestured around the room.

Cameron tilted his head. "Hanging up lights for an eighty-year-old's birthday party?"

"That too." Paul grinned. "But I was going more for making the woman I care about happy."

Cameron took the end of the string of lights and headed for the nearest wall outlet. "So you're saying I should choose whatever would make Jolene happy?"

"Ha. See?" Paul pointed at him, a knowing grin covering his face. "You do care about her."

He couldn't deny that. Cameron plugged in the cord. Instantly the twinkle lights sprung to life, illuminating the community center with a soft glow. He wished an idea of how to solve this problem would come to him as swiftly. Unfortunately, he wasn't sure if Jolene even knew what she needed to be happy.

And that was the real problem.

———◆———

Granny was right.

Jolene turned the knob on the helium tank they'd rented earlier that morning for party preparation, filling her third green balloon of the hour. A dozen purple and gold ones floated above her now in the living room of the Lavigne House, tied to the strings dangling from the high ceiling.

Her mural design wasn't for the community—it was for her. The design she'd fought to reveal had only revealed her own selfishness, and the entire town was going to pay for it. She couldn't finish the design, seeing what she saw now. Which meant Mattie had also been right.

Jolene was unreliable.

Perched on the edge of the couch, she filled another balloon, tying it off as her mind raced. She should have told Cameron this turn of events earlier in the day rather than essentially hiding from him. Or at least Mattie. Cameron might be her official supervisor, but Mattie, being family, would likely be more understanding of the way this had snowballed.

Then again, Mattie had been the one to assume something like this would happen in the first place.

Jolene groaned, batting a dangling balloon string out of her face. Maybe she should have stayed in Nashville. No, she never should have left *for* Nashville.

Her dad had been right too.

Mom walked into the living room, dusting off the front of the apron she still wore from her earlier cookie baking session, and gazed appreciatively at the room full of balloons. "Look at all this!"

They'd ordered the elaborate Mardi Gras–themed cake for the big party tomorrow but decided to scale back the budget a little by providing the bulk of the side items themselves. Mom and Mattie had been baking the past few hours, having finally kicked Granny out of the house so she could have a few surprises tomorrow. Jolene wanted to help but knew she couldn't be around Mattie for long without blurting out the truth, so she'd assigned herself balloon duty—the least-vied-for chore on the task list.

It was the least she could do once they all found out there would be no mural Sunday.

"You're making great progress." Mom beamed, brushing back a lock of hair from her face and revealing the smile lines that had gotten slightly more defined since Jolene had last been home.

"On this, maybe." The words tumbled free before Jolene could censor. She quickly reached for another balloon, but Mom was faster.

"What do you mean?" Her smile turned into a slight frown. "Are you having trouble with the mural?"

"More like the mural *is* trouble." Or really, Jolene was the trouble at this point. She secured another balloon around the nozzle, then pressed it down, watching as the shiny green latex expanded. She knew how it felt. Filling up tighter and tighter. So much pressure. Just one more moment and—

POP.

The balloon exploded. Jolene fell backward against the couch pillows as her mother shrieked.

Jolene scrambled upright. "I'm so sorry." She grabbed for the broken balloon, tossing it to the side of the coffee table. "We have plenty, don't worry."

"I'm not worried about the balloons, honey." Mom sank down on the cushion next to Jolene, her stiff apron bunching around her waist. "I'm worried about *you*."

"What do you mean?" She couldn't look her mother in the face, not with tears pressing so close to the surface. Everything was falling apart, but that didn't mean she had to fall apart too. She scrambled for another balloon, scrambled to busy her hands so her emotions would stop threatening to explode.

"I *mean*, you're home but you're not really here." Mom plucked the shiny latex from her hand and tossed it aside, tilting her head until Jolene finally met her gaze. "Where are you?"

The tears filled Jolene's eyes until, like the green balloon, they burst free. Tears tracked down her cheeks in hot streams. "I don't know." She swiped the back of her palm over her face. "I think I'm lost." The dam had broken, and now the tears poured faster.

"Oh, sweetheart." Mom scooted closer, wrapping her arm around Jolene's shoulders and squeezing tight. "Just be here. With us. That's all we want." Her voice dropped to a hoarse whisper. "That's all I've ever wanted."

"Really? You didn't seem to mind when I left for Nashville." Jolene swiped her face again. "And then you and Mattie got so close."

Mom inched backward until she held Jolene's gaze again. "Don't you dare sit there and think for a minute you were replaced. You are my daughter." She gripped Jolene's hand. "I love Mattie too, but our relationship is our own. It's unique, and so is yours and mine."

Jolene let out a shuddering breath. "I'm sorry." Oh no. There it was—the truth, her big secret, hovering right behind her lips.

Mom frowned. "For what? I supported you chasing your dreams. We all did. You're a talented artist, and not everyone is meant to stay in their hometown forever."

"Tell that to our hometown." Jolene half-chuckled, half-hiccupped.

"Well, I've never been all that concerned with what people think, and I know you haven't been." Mom hesitated as she studied Jolene's face. "Or maybe you have, and I never realized. And for that I'm sorry. I should have noticed."

"It's not your fault. I haven't been honest with you about a lot of things." Jolene squeezed her mother's hands, their strength and warmth providing her with a little of both. "I never told you the real reason why I didn't come back often after Dad's funeral."

"I always thought you were busy." Her mother's brow pinched.

"I was. But that wasn't all." It was time. Now or never, and never didn't feel doable anymore. Jolene swallowed hard, even as fresh tears threatened. She had to do this. She owed it to her mom. And to herself.

"The night before Dad's heart attack, we argued. He didn't want me to move, said he was afraid of me trying to find a career in art. He wanted me to go to law school after community college or something that would give me a 'secure future.'"

Mom listened, emotion flickering through her eyes. "He wanted the best for you."

"I know. We didn't *fight* fight, but I was very adamant in my opinions and he in his."

A ghost of a smile lit Mom's face. "That is where you get it from, I suppose."

Jolene hung on to her mother's hand, lost back in the memory. "I told him it would be good. That I'd prove to him that I could do it, and he'd see. But he couldn't get on the same page. He was stressing over it, pacing like he always did when he was worked up. It seemed so important to him that I change my plans."

"It's *your* future," Mom gently reminded. "Not his. He knew that."

"You don't understand." Jolene tugged her hands free, raking them through her hair. "The conversation kept getting tenser after that. If I had just agreed or even asked to talk about it later, maybe. . ." Her words broke off, but she couldn't stop now. She sniffed. "Maybe he wouldn't have had the heart attack the next morning."

The burden rolled off her shoulders even as the words left her tongue. She'd finally admitted it. And for all the fresh grief it brought, it brought equal measures of relief.

"Oh, sweetheart." Mom's face fell. "*No.* That's not true."

Keeping the rest of her confession inside was like trying to stop another bursting balloon. "Even after he died, I went to Nashville anyway. I thought I could prove myself, that it was my chance to make it right. If I didn't stick to what I told him, then my stubbornness was all for nothing." Jolene wiped her eyes. "It would mean he'd be proud of me, but I didn't make it. I failed. Dad was right, and I failed."

Mom pulled her in close again, her own voice choking up. "I hadn't realized. He said you had talked about your Nashville plans but didn't mention an argument." She squinted, pulling away from Jolene to look directly at her. "I think about that last night a lot. And you know what he did say? Before we went to bed, he didn't talk about anything cross between you."

Mom smiled a little, as if the memory had once again become vivid. "He said he thought you were going to be great at whatever you chose. That he was proud of you."

Jolene's stomach flipped. Could that possibly be true? Was her guilt completely misplaced? A fresh wave of emotion lapped at her heart, this time offering refreshment instead of threatening to drown her. She dared to dip a toe in its potential, feeling it out. Testing the new waters.

"I don't know why I never told you. I guess I never thought to in the shock of it all, and then, well, life happened, as you know. I'm so sorry you've carried this burden alone." Mom took her hands again, her voice urgent. "Listen to me. I knew your father, and I know whether you'd become an artist or a lawyer or anything in between, he'd have been proud of you. And you have *not* failed."

"Maybe. But I'm failing right now. The mural. . .it's all wrong." Jolene shook her head. "Cameron tried to tell me, but once again, I was too stubborn to listen to anyone else."

"It can't be that bad."

Jolene shot her mom a pointed look. "It's a hurricane. Everyone around here is doing their best to forget the storm ever happened, and I planned to plaster it on a church courtyard for all eternity." She'd been so selfish. How could she not have seen it before now?

"What was your theme behind the hurricane design? Your reasoning?" Mom offered a gentle smile. "You've always marched to your own drum, but you've also always had good rhythm."

"I was triggered by the constant talk of everything going back to being the same." Jolene picked up a curl of balloon ribbon and wound it around her fingers. "I wanted to show that storms happen, and you can't go back to what you were before."

"Literal storm or figurative?"

Jolene met her mother's eyes as the truth ricocheted around her heart. "Both."

"That's understandable considering what you've been through." Mom took a deep breath. "None of us are the same after we experience grief and loss. So why should the town pretend?"

"Exactly." She wound the ribbon a little tighter. "It's all an illusion, and it doesn't seem healthy. We should recognize what's happened and remember it."

"I think you're on the right track." Mom patted her knee. "But I think you stopped too soon."

Jolene frowned, the ribbon going slack in her grip. "What do you mean?"

"What's after the storm?" Wisdom cloaked her mother's gaze, making her look a lot like Granny—minus the sass. "If nothing is the same, what's different?"

Everything.

Jolene rolled the question around, revisiting various griefs. Losing her dad, the shock of rejection from art school, the abrupt halt of all her future plans. *Everything* was different after a storm.

But it wasn't all bad, was it? Those storms had strengthened her, changed her, forced her to grow. They'd nudged her into the world and into a calling she'd happily pursued for years. They'd challenged her. Humbled her. Made her look at the world differently. And because of these storms, literal and figurative, she was back in Moreau. Mending old relationships and forming new ones. . .that is, if Cameron ever forgave her for presenting a blank wall to the media.

Plenty of good had followed those storms. She'd just been too lost in the dark lately to see the light.

Mom stood, tugging her apron back into place. "I need to get back to those cookies. But there's a solution hiding somewhere in all this." She reached down and touched Jolene's chin. "You'll find it. I believe in you."

Jolene smiled her gratitude, still deep in thought as she wound another ribbon around her finger. Hopefully, Cameron would be as supportive.

Chapter Eleven

T he fairy lights look wonderful, Cameron. You did a great job."
Cameron turned, punch glass in hand, and smiled at Adale's
compliment. "No problem. I was happy to help."

She patted his shoulder before moving through the crowd, greeting other guests who stood in groups chatting and laughing. Music
pulsed from the sound system in the corner, and a small dance floor
had been cleared near the speakers. Little kids hopped around on
the makeshift floor, while Kimberly danced by herself, wearing a
glittery green blazer that caught the overhead lights. Mayor Ammons
stood by the treat-laden food table, talking with Mattie's boss, Frank
Miller. It seemed the entire community had come out to celebrate
Eloise, as they should.

And the feisty birthday girl was eating it up, holding court in
a chair near the front of the room, next to a table piled high with
more presents than could fit in Santa's sleigh. A receiving line filed
past, ensuring everyone got to talk to the honored guest.

Everyone except Jolene, whom he'd yet to see. Cameron frowned. He hadn't seen her yesterday either. With all the party prep help he'd done with Mattie and Paul, on top of trying to finish up another work project that he'd put on the back burner because of the gazebo, he hadn't had a chance to swing by the courtyard. She must have been painting like crazy the past two days—hopefully. But no, he trusted her to see it through. She wouldn't humiliate either of them by leaving the wall unfinished for Sunday's reveal.

He just hoped, for her sake, the town liked the design more than he imagined they would.

"Thanks for all your help yesterday, Cameron." Mattie appeared at his elbow, holding a plate with two small cookies and a smattering of veggies and dip.

"All he did was hold the ladder." Paul winked as he joined her, holding both of their drink cups. "Just kidding, man. It took a village. And hey, it looks like Granny is having a blast."

"She's the center of attention, so of course she is." Mattie grinned. "She especially loved the gallery of her art we hung in the foyer. Some people even started making offers to buy pieces, which I figure Jolene will get a kick out of." Her gaze flitted around the room. "Speaking of. . .Jolene isn't here yet?"

"I haven't seen her." A pinch of worry knotted Cameron's stomach. "Do you think she's okay?"

"Aunt Adale mentioned she had something to finish up before she came, so I'm sure she'll be here soon. She wouldn't miss Granny's party." Mattie suddenly gestured with a carrot from her plate. "There she is!"

Cameron turned. Jolene slid through the crowd, smiling as she greeted people on her way into the room. She looked beautiful in a long purple sweater dress and black boots. Beautiful *and* happy—which meant she must have gotten the mural done. Thank goodness. He released a sigh of relief. Now they could enjoy the evening.

Hopefully, together.

Cameron dipped his head at Mattie and Paul. "If you'll excuse me."

Mattie's grin stretched wider. "Don't let us stand in your way." Paul dramatically sidestepped to clear Cameron a path.

Cameron was so glad to see Jolene, he didn't even mind the teasing. He quickly made his way to her, gauging her smile as she turned its full effect on him.

But it didn't waver—if anything, her look of joy grew bigger. "Hey."

"I've—" He stopped the admission of having missed her seconds before it left his lips, swallowing the words. No sense in scaring her off right when she got there. He settled for smiling back. "I've not seen you for a few days."

"Been swamped, between the mural and party planning." She gestured around the room, her trademark bracelets clanking together. "I need you to appreciate every balloon in this place, by the way. I personally blew them all up." She laughed.

He grinned. Something was different. There was a peace in her eyes, a lightness to her that hadn't existed all week. Finishing the mural had to take a massive weight off her shoulders—he knew his felt a whole lot lighter.

He gently took her hand, which was still pointing at the balloons. "You've accomplished a lot. It's impressive, really. I can't wait to see the mural tomorrow."

Her expression flickered, some of the light in her eyes shadowing, and she squeezed his hand. Then her gaze suddenly shifted to something behind him. "Hey, isn't that the architect you and Mayor Ammons invited?"

"Rémy came?" Cameron spun around, searching the crowd. Another weight off his shoulders. Surely the man wouldn't attend the party if his answer was no, right? Sure enough, there he stood by the back windows with Mattie and Paul and the mayor, holding a plate of food and nodding at something Mayor Ammons was saying.

"Come on, I'd like to introduce you." And get the official answer. He tugged Jolene along through the crowd until he reached the group.

"Good news!" The mayor clamped one hand on Cameron's shoulder. "Mr. Vachon has agreed to take on our project."

"Isn't that great?" Mattie bounced on the balls of her feet. "We're so blessed."

What a night. Everything was finally falling into place. Cameron enthusiastically shook Rémy's free hand. "Glad to hear it, sir." Understatement of the year, but he figured a giant hug wasn't appropriate. Mattie looked like she was barely containing her own excitement.

"Your community is pretty special." Rémy nodded toward the packed room. "To see an entire town come out for one woman's birthday party. . .well, that's rare. It says a lot."

"Moreau has always been special, but I believe that hurricane united us." Mayor Ammons dipped his head. "Despite all the damage along the way."

Rémy smiled. "And that's exactly why I want to offer my skills."

Jolene squeezed Cameron's arm. He quickly introduced her. "This is Mattie's cousin and another granddaughter of the birthday gal—Jolene Broussard."

"It's very nice to meet you." Rémy shook her hand. "I understand you're the artist behind the courtyard mural I've heard about."

A flush of red tinged Jolene's cheeks. "That's the word on the street."

He nodded encouragingly. "I'm sure it'll be lovely. I can't wait to see it."

Jolene darted a look at Cameron, one he couldn't quite read, and he smiled down at her in return. Probably just needed a confidence boost. He wrapped one arm around her shoulders. "She's worked hard."

Hopefully, Rémy would appreciate that even if he didn't love the mural design. It seemed like he was helping them out because of Moreau's heart and community, and the finished mural would still play a part in demonstrating that. Cameron could stop stressing over it—at least it was done, and that was what was most important.

"Cameron and Jolene have been a great team on the courtyard revitalization." Then Mattie gasped. "Oh, Mr. Vachon, you *must* meet my grandmother." Mattie stood on her toes and waved to the front of the room, where Granny had just vacated her birthday throne. "Granny! Over here!"

"And Mom too." Jolene cast a look around the crowded room. "I don't see her."

Cameron joined her search but didn't see Adale. He shrugged. "I'm sure she'll turn up soon."

"What's all this? Someone trying to steal my thunder?" Granny grinned as she made her way toward them, her gold skirt billowing around her legs. Then her gaze landed on Rémy, and her eyes widened slightly as if she recognized him. She hadn't met him yet, though, so that was impossible. But was that alarm on her face?

Cameron frowned. Maybe she recognized him from the internet—not that Granny was exactly web-surfing savvy. Jolene looked confused too, her gaze darting between Granny and Rémy.

Mattie performed the introductions, and Granny, composed again as usual, smiled politely. "It's nice to meet you."

Rémy regarded her carefully, then with a nod, took Granny's hand and bowed low. "It's a pleasure. Happy birthday."

"Rémy, I'd love for you to chat with our newspaper editor next." Mayor Ammons motioned toward Frank, standing by the punch bowl. "He'll be wanting a quote from you for an upcoming article, I'm sure. We'll grab you a drink while we're there."

"Sounds good. Cameron, I'm sure we will visit more soon." Rémy nodded at him, then at the group in general. "Nice to meet you all." His gaze lingered briefly on Granny before he followed the mayor across the community center.

Relieved the restoration expert's help was finally official, Cameron took Jolene's hand. But her smile had vanished, replaced by a cloud of worry in her eyes. "What's wrong? Isn't this great news? The chapel will make the register now."

"Absolutely." She bobbed her head, but her eyes didn't match the enthusiasm.

He wished he could press away the stress furrowing her brows. He settled for tugging lightly at her hand. "Come on, you need a break. Dance with me?"

That won a smile, so he led her toward the dance floor, where a dozen people were already performing the Electric Slide. Jolene jumped right in, her feet gracefully sliding across the floor. Cameron awkwardly joined her, not minding his lack of coordination nearly as much when that meant she tried to clap his arms for him.

Laughing as the song wrapped up, she stumbled into his chest as he misstepped a final time, and he caught her around the waist. The music shifted to a country ballad, a slow song about broken roads and blessings.

The line dance was over. He should let her go. But they were already standing so close together. . . . Taking a risk, he tightened his grip around her waist and slowly began to sway to the music.

Jolene's breath hitched, and she briefly tensed. She was going to leave the floor. Then, just as suddenly, she relaxed, wrapping her arms around his neck.

Cameron pressed his cheek to the top of her head, inhaling his new favorite scent—coconut. She fit so perfectly right here. Had it only been a week since she stormed into his life?

He held her a little tighter as the song continued, as if she might vanish if he let her go. But she would be vanishing soon, back to Nashville.

They weren't officially at the party together—it wasn't a true date like next weekend's ball, but he couldn't help but take the opportunity while he had it. There were things that needed to be said.

"I'm proud of you, you know." Cameron pulled back a little so he could see Jolene's face. "You've come a long way."

"What, with my attitude?" She grinned up at him, and it took everything in him not to move a few inches closer and kiss her.

"Hey, you specified, not me." He chuckled. "I mean with all your progress on the mural. But now that you mention it, you seem different today. Happier. I figure it's because the painting is done."

"I am happier. I had a breakthrough last night." She took a deep breath. "Mom and I had a big talk, and we worked through some things I've been carrying. It's not completely fixed, of course, but I'm feeling lighter."

So that was the difference. He tugged her a bit closer as they continued to sway. "I'd love to hear about it sometime—if you want to tell me."

"I will." She nodded, her slight smile a promise. Then that same shadow from earlier crossed her eyes. "But there's something you need to know first."

———————

Cameron's dimple had never been this close before.

Jolene wanted to kiss him, wanted to explore how his scruff would feel against her cheek—not tell him the truth. But she couldn't move forward with her new plan until she told him everything. The realization of her selfishness, the healing that started last night thanks to that conversation with her mom, and—her new idea for the mural. The final vision that she knew, deep in her soul, was perfect.

She just needed him on board with her idea for tomorrow.

"What's wrong?" Cameron peered down at her as they swayed, the first song having ended and a second slow number beginning. He hadn't missed a beat in the transition, as if he hoped maybe she wouldn't notice it was a new song. Not that she needed convincing to stay in his arms. Right now, there was nowhere else she'd rather be than dancing with him.

It was only a matter of whether he'd still feel that way after what she was about to tell him. Which was now or never—and unfortunately, never wasn't an option. She drew a breath. "There's something you need to know about the mural."

Cameron pulled back a little, searching her face. "It's finished, right? You've been working on it nonstop the last few days."

"Not exactly." Her stomach knotted.

He frowned in confusion as they spun in a slow circle. "How much is left?"

She rolled in her lower lip, unable to look directly in his eyes. "That's what I have to tell you. It's not going to be finished by tomorrow afternoon's reveal."

Cameron abruptly stopped dancing, bringing them to a standstill in the middle of the floor. "What do you mean?"

She pressed her fingers into his shirt collar, not wanting to let go. Not wanting to finish this conversation. Judging by the storm clouds gathering on his face, he wasn't going to take the news as well as her mom had.

"Do we need to go by there tonight? I can help you." Cameron looked at his watch, then toward the door, as if planning their imminent escape. "I'm not a great painter, but I'm sure I could help fill in some—"

She finally dared to meet his gaze. "You don't understand. It's not going to get done."

A tense silence stretched between them. Then. . .

"You're right. I don't understand." His arms dropped to his sides, and she reluctantly stepped back. "You heard your cousin tell Rémy a minute ago that we've been working on this *together*. My reputation is attached to this too."

"Rémy is part of why it's so important to get this right. It's not just about me." Jolene huffed, frustrated that the words she had practiced so carefully last night were not coming out in the right order. "Listen. . ."

She tugged at Cameron's sleeve, leading him off the dance floor to a nearby corner, away from the blaring speakers. "Isn't this what you wanted? I was being selfish before by insisting on that hurricane design. I see that now. I figured this would be good news."

"But how are you not being selfish still? There's going to be a half-finished wall tomorrow for the media!" He ran an agitated hand through his hair. "The whole town is expecting a mural. A restoration of a community trademark."

"I know."

"I appreciate you changing your mind away from the hurricane, but I told you any mural was better than none at all."

If he would just let her explain. She held up both hands. "I have a plan."

"What plan could you possibly have that would get the mural done in less than twenty-four hours? That's all that matters." Cameron looked across the community center, where Mattie and Paul stood by Granny's table full of gifts, restacking them to make room on the crowded table. "What about Mattie? Does she know?"

"Not yet." She took a deep breath. "I wanted to tell you first." Surely Mattie wouldn't have this same level of reaction. She didn't think she could take it twice. "This new idea is for the good of the whole community."

"Not keeping your word is for the good of the community?" Cameron pointed toward Rémy, who stood by the food table, unwrapping a cupcake as he talked to Granny. "What is Mr. Vachon going to think tomorrow when he shows up for an event that doesn't exist? What is *everyone* going to think?"

"Nothing negative about you." Jolene's cheeks heated. "This isn't about you. If anything, they'll think poorly of *me*." Nothing new there. But no, she was trying to break those negative patterns of thought. She was still part of Moreau, born and raised. Always would be.

Even after a storm.

"I'm in charge of the project overall. I'm still responsible." Cameron sighed in defeat. "Okay, look. I don't want to argue. If there's not a lot left to paint, maybe we can—"

"You can't fix this, Cameron." Jolene put her hand on his arm. "I need you to trust me. I told you—*I* have a plan."

"No. No more plans or ideas. It's too late. I *can't* trust you."

She flinched.

"How can I trust you after this? I had doubts about your new design, and I gave in to what you wanted. You were so confident, so sure about it. . .I wanted to believe you." Sadness cloaked his eyes. "You said the mural would be done tomorrow."

"Things changed. *I* changed." But he didn't want to hear it. Which meant he had never really believed in her or trusted her.

"I'm glad you're in a better place now, really. I've wanted that for you all week." Cameron took her hand and gave it a slight squeeze before letting go. "But maybe this is too much change, too fast."

He wasn't just talking about the mural anymore. It was obvious in his eyes.

"What are you saying?" Her entire body felt cold, missing the warmth of their dance and his hand on hers. She crossed her arms over her sweater dress, huddling into herself. "Are you uninviting me to the ball?"

"No. I don't know. I need some air." He wouldn't look at her, only at the doors across the room. "This is your grandmother's party, so you stay. I'll see you later."

Then he was gone, winding through the crowd toward the sign that read EXIT in big red letters.

Jolene hugged herself tighter as she stared after him. Leaving sure was a lot easier than being left.

Chapter Twelve

The crowd in the courtyard was even thicker than he'd imagined. Nervous energy far exceeded the caffeine in Cameron's system as he wound his way toward the gazebo, where several townspeople already stood under the newly repaired roof. One of them complimented the renovation to his friend, and the knot in Cameron's stomach eased a bit. Yet one question remained—why hadn't Mattie canceled the reveal? Surely Jolene had told her this wasn't happening.

But *something* was happening. The curtain Mattie had ordered for the mural wall weeks ago was in place, replacing the tent Jolene had used when painting. Had Jolene pulled off a miracle and finished the mural overnight?

Impossible. So why the platform, microphone stand, and extension cord?

Cameron offered a tense nod at Mayor Ammons and Rémy, who stood with coffees in hand in the middle of the courtyard next to the local news crew and their cameras. Granny and Adale hovered near the drawn curtains at the wall, talking to each other with serious expressions and standing guard over whatever was behind it, but Mattie was nowhere to be seen—neither was Jolene. She hadn't been at church that morning, nor had she answered the handful of calls and texts he'd sent her way.

Not that he could blame her, after the way he'd acted last night.

Cameron moved to a better vantage point beside the gazebo, near where the police chief talked with Kimberly and a few other shop owners. He'd messed up at the party. As soon as he'd gone outside for a breath of air and some clarity, he'd realized he was mixing things that didn't need to be mixed. This was Jolene's project, and she'd poured herself into it. Just because the results hadn't been what he had hoped or assumed didn't make it meaningless. She was dealing with bigger things than just a painting, and he'd gotten his priorities messed up.

He shoved his hands into his pockets, rocking back on his heels as the crowd mingled. He'd started out wanting to protect Jolene over the controversial design, but essentially he'd ended up putting his own pride and reputation in front of her needs. Just because Samantha had been manipulative and self-serving didn't mean Jolene was intentionally being so. And he hadn't been there for her while she sorted it out.

Now she might not ever let him.

Jolene had vanished from the party by the time he'd come back in, and judging by the Looks with a capital *L* being shot at him from Mattie, he figured he best not try to explain himself for the time being. He'd wished Granny a happy birthday, then quietly slipped home, trying to think of a way to make things right with Jolene.

"Good afternoon." Feedback squealed, and the crowd hushed. Jolene stood behind the mic, wearing a bright red winter cap, her long dark hair tucked behind her ears. She looked. . .nervous. And rightfully so. Was she about to confess there was no mural?

Suddenly, he didn't care a whit about his reputation. He just didn't want her to be humiliated. He wanted to protect her, even to his own detriment. Even Rémy's good opinion, while important for the town, wasn't the end all, be all.

Cameron flexed both hands, needing an outlet for his nerves. How could he have been so blind? He'd accused Jolene of ignoring the true needs of the town, but he'd been the one shuffling around in the dark.

He didn't want her to do this alone. This was his fault too.

He started to make his way toward the makeshift stage, but the crowd had thickened, blocking his attempt.

"Before I show you the renovated wall, I'd like to ask you to keep an open mind." Jolene gripped the microphone stand with a gloved hand, her own nervousness sketched across her face.

Cameron stopped and his heart raced. Maybe she'd finished the hurricane after all. But how?

"I know what you're all expecting, and this won't be it." She smiled, her voice trembling. "But I'm hoping you'll love it anyway. And now, without further ado, I'd like to present to you"—Jolene gestured like a game show host, and the curtains dropped on cue—"a message of hope."

He craned his neck to see the wall as cameras flashed around him. A murmur rippled through the crowd, part confusion, part complaint. He stretched on tiptoe, and there it was. Her partially completed hurricane covered one half, as he'd expected.

But the other half was nothing like he'd expected. The right portion of the wall was covered with long rolls of taped drawing paper. Colorful sketches covered the sheet in a collage-like format.

He couldn't make out all the details from here, but some appeared to be shop logos. Robby's Rustic Creations was on there. . .and was that the same sign that he'd just hung last week at Kimberly's Kurls? And there was the gazebo.

His eyes darted back and forth, taking in both halves and trying to process them together. Shades of gray and turquoise swirled into a violent tangle on the left, trimmed in shadows of navy and crimson. The painted image brought a storm surge of emotion from his childhood, triggering the memories he'd rather suppress from those fateful days in New Orleans.

But when he focused on the other half, when he imagined those light and colorful images representing Moreau completed in stark contrast, peace stirred. The turmoil of memories eased.

Jolene had been right. The town didn't need to turn a blind eye back to better days. They could look ahead and see them just as they were—right here, right now.

"Let me explain." Jolene held up both hands, and the animated whispering ceased. "When I was first commissioned to paint the mural, thanks to Nate over there"—she pointed to Nate in the crowd, who lifted his wrapped wrist in a good-natured salute—"I was intimidated. I had just gotten some bad news about my future career plans in Nashville, and I didn't think I could keep pursuing art. When I went to start painting the mural that Nate had so beautifully recreated, I just couldn't."

She drew a deep breath. "So I started thinking that if the mural were different, maybe then I could be different too."

Cameron risked a glance at the crowd. The murmuring had started again, but this time it was layered with compassion. Their gazes were riveted to Jolene, sympathy pulling their expressions.

"I couldn't bear the thought of everything simply going back to the way it was after the hurricane. Because nothing has been the same for me since the big storm that roared through my life seven years ago." She ducked her head for a moment.

Mattie, now standing near the front of the crowd, started to step forward, but Paul gently pulled her back, leaning down to whisper in her ear. Beside them, Granny and Adale linked arms and smiled proudly at Jolene.

When she lifted her head again, tears shone in her eyes. But her smile was genuine and full of peace. "I wanted to force you all to see things the way I did—that storms change us, and there's no going back. I thought if everyone here could admit that, maybe it would make my recovery easier." She snorted a little. "Misery loves company, and all that."

Cameron swallowed against the knot in his throat. He'd never seen Jolene this vulnerable. Or this beautiful. Her face shone with the very light she'd been afraid of losing.

"But when I started painting the hurricane, much to the dismay of my supervisor, I realized it wasn't quite right either. A wise woman told me I stopped too soon." She smiled at her mom, who nodded at her while clutching Granny's arm. "And then I could see it. The whole picture."

She gestured to the wall behind her. "My final vision came together too late to create it for you. But then I realized that was for the best. Because this mural is bigger than me." She met Cameron's gaze then for the first time since she'd started speaking, and visibly swallowed. "Another wise person reminded me of that fact, and I couldn't agree more."

Time seemed to pause as they stared at each other. Cameron's heart pounded unsteadily in his chest, and he hoped she could read the apology on his face. Was it possible she'd forgive him? He didn't dare hope, but he couldn't help but do so anyway.

"This mural is about *all* of us. The whole town of Moreau." She looked away from Cameron and let out a breath. "So I've drawn out the remaining portion, which is a collage of all the best things about our town. The shop logos, the storefronts, the gazebo. The church and courtyard. The river. I sincerely hope you'll all join me in finishing the mural. . .together."

Wow. That was. . .wow.

A stunned silence pulsed through the courtyard, and Cameron started to clap. Then suddenly all around him, the crowd erupted into applause and whistles. Jolene ducked her head, her hair swinging in front of her face. The clapping grew louder, along with shouts of "We love you, Jolene!" and "Welcome home!"

Mattie apparently couldn't contain herself any longer, for she rushed to hug her cousin. Cameron knew the feeling. He wanted to do the same but still wasn't sure if Jolene would want him to.

The din finally died down, and Jolene wrapped one arm around Mattie. "After I get the collage fully sketched out on the wall, Mattie will create a schedule for volunteer slots. Then you can all pick a portion to paint! We'll have this mural done in no time."

Granny and Adale met her on the platform then, and Jolene was enveloped in a giant family hug. Cameron started to move forward, but Rémy suddenly appeared at his elbow, a broad smile covering his face.

"That sure was something." He shook his head, awe in his eyes. "This town is even more special than I assumed."

"I agree. Especially it's favorite prodigal there." Cameron nodded toward the stage.

"The Lavignes are a special family." Rémy clapped Cameron on the shoulder with a knowing smile. "It's hard to feel worthy of them, isn't it?"

Very hard. But how would Rémy know that about them? Hadn't he only met them a few times? Cameron looked back at Jolene surrounded by her family and looking happier than he'd ever seen her, and his confusion transitioned into a desperate urge. *Was* he worthy?

He set his jaw, nodded a quick goodbye to Rémy, and started for the stage. Only one way to find out.

———◆———

She'd done it. It was over.

A Christmas miracle.

Relief poured off Jolene in waves as she turned off the mic and started to disassemble the stand. She needed something to do with her hands and all the adrenaline still flowing through her veins now that the bulk of the crowd had left.

"Here, let me." Paul took the stand from her, grinning as he began unplugging the cords. "Your fans await."

"Thank you." But she wasn't sure she could talk to anyone else, not after the rush of people that had swarmed her immediately after her speech, praising her idea and eager to volunteer for painting slots. It had been nice but a little exhausting. She needed to crash after the constant emotion of the last two days.

But when she turned around, it wasn't another random community member waiting to talk to her. It was Cameron.

"Hey." She startled, stepping back an inch. After the party last night, she was surprised he'd even shown up, and she had no idea what he was thinking. Did he hate the new mural idea? She couldn't tell from his face and was too afraid of the answer to guess.

But there was Mattie, nudging her forward.

"You two go talk. We've got this." Her cousin gestured toward the mic stand and the curtain. "I'll drive you home in a bit, Jolene. . .unless you get a better offer." Mattie smiled.

"Shall we?" Cameron extended his hand toward her, and Jolene hesitantly took it, allowing him to lead her to the now deserted gazebo.

"I've been a jerk. You thought you were being selfish, but it was me all along. I'm sorry." He shrugged, still holding her hand and looking way too handsome for his own good in a dark green pullover sweater. "I'm so proud of you. You did that so well."

She gripped his hand a little tighter. "You like the new plan?"

"I love it. It's perfect." Cameron shook his head, still looking surprised. "You amaze me. Despite all the obstacles, you managed to come up with something even better than any of us dared to hope. You saw what the town needed, not just what we asked for."

Relief filled her chest. But a wariness lingered, despite his apology. "I was trying to tell you about it last night." Jolene bit her lower lip as she looked up at him. "You didn't want to hear it."

"I know. I'm really sorry." Cameron let go of her hand and raked his fingers through his hair, mussing the dark strands. "I let some of my own past stuff get in my head, like you did. I misinterpreted everything."

He looked down, then back at her. "You threw me off when you said it wasn't going to be done, and I majorly overreacted. I should have let you finish explaining. But I was more worried about what Rémy or other people thought of me than I was about what was best, and. . ." His voice trailed off and he helplessly lifted a shoulder. "I completely understand if you don't want to go to the ball with me anymore."

Jolene nodded slowly, the apology seeping in deep. She couldn't really begrudge him for letting his own past lies skew his thinking—not when she'd been struggling with the same all week. Not to mention, it was the holidays—the perfect time for second chances. Forgiveness. Healing.

The kinds of Christmas miracles they all needed.

Decision made, she reached for his hand. "Truce?"

Surprise lit his face, followed by hope as his fingers laced with hers. "Really?"

"*At least* a truce." She edged another step closer, looking up at his stubbled jaw. There was that dimple. She smiled. "Hopefully more."

"You really still want to go to the ball?" Cameron locked his arms loosely around her.

"Might as well." She tilted her head in exaggeration. "I mean, I do have a new dress. It'd be a shame to waste it."

"I agree." Cameron tugged her an inch closer, and it was all she could do not to snuggle into his embrace. "So. . .truce. Again."

"Again." She repeated with a snort. "We'll see how long we can keep it this time."

His voice grew husky as he closed the remaining distance between them, his breath warm on her cheek. "I have a feeling this one will last."

"Me too," she whispered, their words mingling together in the final moment before his lips claimed hers. Her heart soared with hope and new beginnings as his gentle embrace locked her safely against his chest. She kissed him back, her hands buried in the hair at the nape of his neck. A kiss of joy and wonder and promise.

A kiss of restoration.

Betsy St. Amant Haddox is the award-winning author of more than twenty romance novels and novellas. She resides in north Louisiana with her hubby, two daughters, an impressive stash of coffee mugs, and one furry schnauzer toddler. Betsy has a BA in Communications and a deep-rooted passion for seeing women restored to truth. When she's not composing her next book or trying to prove unicorns are real, Betsy can be found somewhere in the vicinity of an iced coffee. She writes frequently for iBelieve, a devotional site for women. View her book list at www.betsystamant.com.

A Christmas Reunion

Lenora Worth

DEDICATION

To Mary Ann Draper—thank you for being my friend!

Acknowledgments

I want to thank Betsy St. Amant and Morgan Tarpley Smith for inviting me to join them in this fun, faithful novella collection. I really enjoyed every moment of the planning, the brainstorming, the discussions, and the final story of this family saga. I lived in Louisiana for thirty years, so these connected stories are like taking a trip back to a place that will forever be in my heart.

Working with these two young and amazingly smart women reminded me of the joy of writing and each phase that makes up a writing career. I've known Betsy for years because we lived close to each other and finally met at a conference (we love sharing shoe and purse stories). I've watched her career take off. And meeting Morgan for the first time through Zoom, emails, and messaging has been a joy. She is a wonderful writer and now a friend. These women make me feel young again. Thanks to all. I loved this project!

I also want to thank Barbour Publishing and Rebecca Germany for letting us write these stories to share with our readers and hopefully some new readers.

Find me here:
https://www.lenoraworth.com
https://www.facebook.com/lenoraworthbooks
https://www.bookbub.com/profile/lenora-worth
https://www.instagram.com/lenoraworth
@lenoraworth twitter

Chapter One

Adale Lavigne-Marchand Broussard stared at her laugh lines and wondered how she could avoid the man who'd returned to her life Saturday night at her mother's eightieth birthday party. After all this time and an ocean between them, Rémy Vachon had shown up here in Moreau, Louisiana, in *her* town, of all places. As a renowned architect at that? And he'd been living in New Orleans for years?

She had to discreetly find out how long he planned to be here. She'd spent hours on her laptop, learning more about him. He'd come to help with the chapel restoration, someone had mentioned. But then someone else said he'd be back and forth between here and New Orleans.

Maybe he'd left again already. She couldn't stop thinking about how she'd felt when she'd seen him across the room. Their eyes had met and that was that. She'd remembered being a lovesick sixteen-year-old standing on a Paris bridge with the most handsome young man she'd ever seen.

Now, all these years later, the boy who'd left her waiting heart-broken in a Paris café had walked into the party and found her right away. Found her, watched her, but had not approached her because Adale had stayed busy avoiding him. She'd wanted to ask her mother how he'd managed to be here. She'd kept blinking, thinking it couldn't be him.

But Rémy was here, and he wasn't a boy anymore.

She hadn't slept a wink since then. Now with bags under her eyes, she stared at the framed photo of her and Pierre, taken not long before he died of a heart attack. Seven years ago. Her life had changed that day. A widow with a daughter in college. Jolene had been floundering since her father's death, moving to Nashville, then returning to Moreau for a while, only to go back to the city again. Now, after five years, she'd come home, hopefully for good. With Cameron's help, she'd finally begun to heal after blaming herself for her father's death. After a few doubts, she'd become passionate about the new mural in the courtyard behind the chapel, but she'd brought in the whole community to help her finish it. A true homecoming.

Adale loved that. Which is why she hadn't ruined Jolene's big day with blasting everyone for finding the one man she didn't want in her town.

Adale had loved Pierre Broussard with all her heart. They'd had a grand life there on the Petit River. He'd never once resented his days being centered around her family's heritage or pride. Pierre had accepted being the family lawyer and accountant, because as he used to tell her, "The Lord put me where I need to be—with you, Adale. Always with you."

Their strong faith and the love between them had gotten them through good and bad. Pierre never had to doubt her love because it had become her life's work to be the best wife a man could ask for. She'd be forever glad that she had done her best to make him happy for twenty-eight years.

Now, finally, she'd thought she could be happy again. Her wayfaring daughter was home and happy. Adale had enjoyed a brief moment of pure contentment. Then, seeing the man she'd loved and lost so long ago standing in a corner at her mama's eightieth birthday party had stopped Adale cold.

Now she stood here, floundering like a river catfish caught on a line when she needed to finish getting ready for a Monday morning meeting.

She'd been meandering since Pierre died. Now her mama was getting on in years and had moved back into the main house so Adale could keep an eye on her. Mortality had hit Adale straight in the face. She had a plan to get out more, live her life to the fullest, be joyful. She'd already volunteered to work in one of the booths at the Christmas market, and she'd enjoyed helping Jolene finish the mural by painting one corner. Her committee work would continue, starting with the Christmas Eve ball, a Moreau tradition since the late 1800s. That should keep her mind off the man who'd appeared out of nowhere, reminding her of the past.

Turning from the mirror in her bedroom, she remembered when she and Pierre had moved into the Lavigne House. The stately two-story white house had been in her family for over a century, so it was her responsibility now. Her mother, Eloise Lavigne, and her father, Oliver Marchand, had two daughters. But her dear sweet sister, Claudia, had died not long after her no-good husband had left her and Mattie high and dry when Mattie was a teen.

This house had come full circle, with Eloise moving back in. Her cottage behind the house would stay in the family, of course.

Hurrying downstairs, Adale glanced at the paintings displayed. Watercolors and landscapes and a few portraits lined the walls along the curved stairway. Eloise, a well-respected artist, still painted. Some of these were hers; others had been passed down through the family. The paintings were cherished, but mercy, Mama had stacks of paintings, some of which had been displayed at her birthday party. Mama kept at it. She needed to stay active. But with all this stuff around, they'd stumbled on the one piece of art Adale had thought long gone.

One of Adale and Rémy Vachon standing on a bridge in Paris. A scene her mother had painted while sitting on a hotel balcony nearby, keeping a keen eye on them.

That discovery had generated questions from Mattie and later, Jolene, and a tight-lipped response of "You know, it wasn't his fault," from her aging mother.

And now, the man himself—here in Moreau.

She needed answers, but she didn't think her mother would give them to her. Because, yes, it had been his fault. He'd left Adale waiting at a sidewalk café, and she'd never heard a word from him since. Until now.

———◆———

Adale let out a hiss of frustration when she walked into the dainty sitting room with the Louis XV desk, which she often used to organize her various volunteer jobs. "Mother, we made you a studio out in the sunroom, but I can see that suggestion went right out the window."

Eloise pulled her brush away from the magnolia blossom she'd been working on and pushed the easel aside. "You called me Mother instead of Mama. Someone needs a strong cup of coffee this morning."

"I'm fine." Adale brushed a finger through her silvery-white long bob, thinking she might have been too hasty on going all gray. Then she glanced around. "Where are the girls?"

"Off to meet their fellows for breakfast," her mother said. "You know, full of energy, tapping away on their smartphones." Eloise chuckled. "Ah, to be young and in love again."

That statement had been thrown down like a challenge. One Adale couldn't take on yet. She'd corner Mattie and Jolene later to find out how a man from her past had shown up here looking so carefree and handsome. Why did she suddenly feel so old?

He hadn't had much gray. No, Rémy Vachon looked as young as he had the day they'd met as teenagers in a quaint café in Paris. Well, he had *some* gray, but he looked distinguished and confident. He'd aged well. Tall, in shape, distinguished, and debonair. Not fair at all.

Eloise stopped painting and now sat with her hands folded in her lap, her bright yellow and green floral caftan fluttering around her soft slippers, her hair short and sassy, groomed and puffed around her porcelain face. "We didn't get to talk much yesterday. Did you have a nice time at my party, *mon chéri*?"

Sitting near the small Christmas tree Adale had placed on a table, her mother blended right in with the holiday glitter. And looked so elegant and innocent, Adale couldn't be pouty. Adale hadn't brought up Rémy Vachon yesterday. They'd all been excited about the mural reveal. No one had offered her much of an explanation on the new man in town. Her mother had been too quiet, however.

She gave her mother a shrewd frown, wondering why she'd ask such a question. Eloise might be forgetful at times, but she still knew how to wield control when she needed to. "You saw me there. Didn't I look happy to you?"

"Happy *for me*, yes," Eloise said. "But you seemed distracted when that new man came in. Did he look familiar to you?"

Adale had to think carefully about her answer. On the one hand, Eloise could be as sharp as a tack. On the other, she could be as evasive as a gator hiding along the riverbank, waiting to strike. Or, she could actually have forgotten, given the tad of dementia she presented these days. Moving her back into the main house had been the best choice, but Adale had some attitude adjustments to make. Grace being a big part of things.

She shrugged. "I don't recall anybody like that."

"Like what?"

Adale smiled. "Whatever you said, Mama. I stayed busy with the food and gifts and. . .other things, so I don't recall."

Adale went straight to the kitchen to pour herself a strong coffee, thankful for the timer that started a pot every morning. Then she returned to the sitting room and managed another smile. She had insisted her mother move back after a few near falls and other complications. She wanted to make the best of it. But first, coffee.

Eloise's dark brows lifted. "I see. Well, I wish you'd stayed at the party. I didn't even know you'd left until Jolene went to look for you. Did you tell me you were leaving early? I don't remember. This is what happens when you turn eighty. Most of your cognitive thoughts just go *poof*." She gestured grandly with one hand.

Adale kissed Eloise on the cheek, thinking she should have said something to her mother before she left in a hurry. "I'm glad you had a nice party, and I'm glad you're here with me again. I hope you like how Cameron redid your suite to make it roomy and comfortable."

"Cameron has a gift for creating wonderful homes," Eloise said with a smile. "I love my sitting room near the sunroom, the cabinet he built for my supplies, and the little corner counter for my coffee and sweets. He's perfect for our Jolene. He'll keep her centered, I'm sure." She shrugged. "Same thing her *grandpère* Oliver did for me."

"Cameron is not like my daddy," Adale pointed out, her voice rising. When she received another eyebrow lift from her mama, she added in a softer voice, "Daddy liked to control things too much, including my sister and me."

She thought of that bridge in Paris. How she wished she had Claudia to talk to. Her sister was always the calm, sensible one.

"He loved us, Adale. Always. He tried so hard to be a good father to you and Claudia."

"On that we can agree," Adale replied, thinking of how much she missed her late sister. And her bullish father. "He did love me, I know." Even when he'd forced her to return home after. . .Paris.

She came back to the subject at hand. "I'm excited about Jolene being home, and I'm hoping Cameron will convince her to stay. They were so adorable together."

"Love is in the air," Eloise said. "It's Christmas, after all. Joy and cheer and family. Celebrating the Lord and our blessings. Good things can happen. Love can happen, no matter how long it takes."

Adale studied her mother with another pointed stare. What was Eloise hiding? Instead of asking her mother about this situation, she said, "I'm off to the Christmas ball meeting. After that, we need to have a talk."

———◆———

Rémy Vachon entered the conference room at the community center and glanced around. He'd seen some of the committee members at the birthday party, so he expected he'd know a few people here. Would Adale show up? Or would she evade him like she'd done at the party?

He'd arrived late to the birthday party for her mother, but he'd expected Adale to at least be civil when she spotted him. In her mind, his being delayed probably only reminded her of the last time he'd been late for their final dinner in Paris. The night he'd hoped to declare his love and ask her to wait for him. That had never happened.

Well, she couldn't avoid him now, could she? He'd been at the mural ceremony yesterday, but he'd stayed in the background. He'd find a way to talk to Adale. She couldn't exactly hide from him in such a small community.

He watched the doors now as people came in. Cameron Armand strolled by, his smile warming the chill of this functional room. Rémy waved, glad to see the person who'd asked him to come to Moreau. Soon the dozen or so volunteers entered and settled at the table. Rémy sat by the last available chair, sipping on the famous Moreau coffee someone had offered him.

"Where is our chairperson?" one woman asked, her nose in the air. "I have things to do."

"Christmas Eve weather is looking iffy," someone else asked, clearly prepared for the worst. "What if it snows even more that night?"

"Then we'll have a beautiful night to celebrate," came the sweet voice from across the room.

Everyone glanced up, including Rémy. He almost choked on his coffee.

Adale waltzed into the room, the scent of jasmine subtle around her. She wore a long open black sweater over a stark white blouse loaded with a strand of pearls, tan pants, and leather boots. She carried a big designer handbag.

She was beautiful.

"I'm glad everyone is here," she said as she turned to pour herself a cup of coffee. "We have a lot to decide this morning. The black-and-white decor will be stunning mixed in with a little gold to highlight it. The decorating committee has outdone themselves."

Then she pivoted, came to the empty seat, and stopped short, her gaze hitting Rémy like a swatter hitting a fly. "I. . .uh. . .excuse me, but what are you doing here?"

"I was invited to cochair the ball," he replied in a calm, controlled voice. "An honorary position. We're waiting for the chairperson."

Adale's skin blushed a becoming pink while she stared him down.

His heart pumped an alert as he realized Eloise had not mentioned any *names*. But now he knew.

He and Adale had been set up.

***

"That would be me," Adale said, her voice purposely sliding sweetly like honey on a biscuit. "And I'm afraid that won't work at all."

The whole room went silent.

She put her handbag down with a thump, her heart sputtering while she tried to think of something to say. "I'll admit I'm a bit confused. Who decided a perfect stranger should help me plan the Christmas Eve ball?"

Jolene sat at the other end of the table near Cameron, her expression fighting between a blank stare and a confused frown.

But Mattie raised her hand in a bold way. "Granny suggested it after she met Mr. Vachon at her party, Aunt Adale. We looked for you, but you'd already left the community center."

Jolene came out of her stupor. "I tried to find you that night, and yesterday we were so busy we couldn't really talk about this."

"Granny." Adale took a calming breath and checked her anger. "I see. My mother forgot to mention this to me when we talked earlier.

I'm sorry I didn't hear this from you, Jolene. It's been a morning." The one time she'd ignored her family, now this.

Rémy stood and pulled her chair back. "Allow me."

She didn't want to allow him anything, but it would be rude to refuse.

"Thank you," she said as she sank onto the chair, her knees a bit wobbly, her skin too warm. "Now would someone like to explain what's going on here?"

Mattie raised her hand. "Aunt Adale, Mr. Vachon is here to help us restore the chapel. He's an expert in restoring historic buildings. His work is known all over New Orleans and beyond since he grew up in France." She shrugged. "Another thing you missed when you left the party early."

No one had to tell her what she'd missed. She knew everything she needed to know about this interloper. "What do Mr. Vachon's amazing credentials have to do with the Christmas Eve ball?"

Mattie shot Jolene a helpless glance. "The theme? Yes, the theme is a black-and-white ball. Perfect for celebrating our heritage. Mr. Vachon would like to help with putting up the decorations and designing the last-minute props. That's right, isn't it, Jolene?"

"Well, yes. That's perfect," Jolene replied, clearly uncomfortable. "Another able body. Can't turn that down."

"I suppose you two and your *grandmère* decided this *after* I'd left her party, then conveniently forgot to inform me yesterday?"

Rémy cleared his throat. "If I may, it happened rather organically. I helped Cameron carry out gifts when the girls were chatting with Eloise. They introduced me to her, and later after we'd talked for a while, she insisted I needed to get involved in every aspect of Moreau's restoration project."

"I reckon she did," Adale murmured as she adjusted her reading glasses.

"She didn't really name names," he said to the room in general.

"I reckon she didn't."

"If it's a problem," he began but stopped. "I can see it's a problem."

Adale glanced around, smelling a setup. A very public setup. She'd deal with that—and her mama, daughter, and niece—later.

Right now, to save face, she gave the whole room a brilliant smile. Then she turned to Rémy and gave him her best bless-your-heart smile. "We are honored to have you. We appreciate your kindness in helping us with this event. But do you really want to stay in Moreau through Christmas? I'm sure you'd rather be with family."

Rémy's gaze held hers, and her heart did that silly dance again. He had the most beautiful deep blue eyes. And the salt-and-pepper still-thick hair on his head only complemented those eyes.

"I'd like to stay as long as I'm needed," he replied, his accent tickling at her senses. "I find everything about Moreau charming—and challenging."

Adale nodded, her fate sealed. "We'll see about that." Then she opened her notebook and slapped the pages back. "Let's start this meeting. We have a lot to get done here. The next time we meet we'll get down to business—finish the decorating and go through a final pass with the caterers, the orchestra, and the million other things that need to get done."

Before they reached the first list of to-dos, Jolene sent Adale an apologetic glance. "Oh, Mama, Granny also invited Mr. Vachon for dinner at our house tonight."

Chapter Two

"Cochair for the ball? Dinner tonight? Really, Mother, what were you thinking?" Adale took a breath then finished making the chicken salad she'd planned for lunch. She guessed what her mother had planned—Rémy and Adale together after all these years. Which made no sense, considering how, back then, her parents had been dead set against her seeing Rémy.

After the meeting this morning and the surprise of seeing Rémy there, she'd waylaid her niece and daughter. "Lunch, girls. At home, noon. Don't be late; don't make any excuses. We need to discuss this new development."

"Uh, okay," Jolene said, her eyes wide. "Mom, I don't know why Granny asked him to be your cochair. I thought she'd explain."

"Your grandmère is playing coy, as usual. I'll get the truth out of her."

"So is it that you don't want a cochair, or you just don't like Mr. Vachon?" Mattie asked, questions in her reporter eyes.

"Not here." Adale had gathered her things and tried to corral her nerves. Thankful Cameron had ushered Rémy out in a hurry, she said, "At the house. And don't cancel."

"We'll be there," Jolene had promised, her worried glance bouncing all around Adale.

Now her mother shot Adale a confused smile. "I was thinking since this man came from New Orleans to help us restore the town, we should repay his kindness with a good meal. He's single, in case you didn't know."

Adale knew this kind of talk. Her mama wanted to trip her up so she'd admit that seeing Rémy again had ruffled her feathers. Her mama knew *this man from New Orleans*, and also knew exactly what she was doing.

"I don't care if he's single," Adale said, her heart sighing with a little bit of relief that irritated her to no end. *Rémy single?* Why should that matter? "I do not want to work with Rémy Vachon."

She waited to see how her mother would react to that name.

Eloise picked up a wheat cracker and studied the seeds blended in it. "But why not? We had a good talk. He's a very accomplished man."

Adale put more pepper on her salad and tried a nonchalant shrug while she stirred the mix. "He'll make promises he can't keep."

"He's a perfect gentlemen to me," Eloise replied as she daintily nibbled on a grape. Adale knew her mother loved walnuts and grapes in her chicken salad. "And so familiar. You might like him if you get to know him. Or even if you already know him."

Should she call Mama's bluff and shout out why the man seemed so familiar? Or should she ignore the whole thing and focus on planning the Christmas Eve ball? Without his help. Somehow. Where were the girls? She needed them to explain this.

"He'll be such a great cochair. He knows our culture, Adale. His name alone will bring in more funding to restore Moreau. That is your goal, *oui*?"

"So you do know his name?"

"You said it out loud."

Adale couldn't argue with that or with his credentials. She'd looked him up. She wasn't proud of doing that, but desperate times called for desperate measures. Hoping she'd find something on him—a flaw, a failure, another broken promise—she'd been surprised to see the man had a spotless reputation. Rémy Vachon was a renowned history buff and a successful architect who specialized in restoring old buildings. Exquisitely, from what she'd seen on his website. He'd always wanted to be an architect. Well, good for him. No evidence of him being married, single, or with a significant other. However, that didn't mean he had to be in her life, restoring her town. And why now?

Maybe he didn't have anywhere else to be during Christmas.

"How did I not know these things?" she murmured after she got up to pour their mint-infused tea into goblets full of ice. Thinking she shouldn't be selfish, Adale brought out the decorated sugar cookies for dessert and tried to adjust her attitude.

"What, darling?" Mama asked, still sounding sweetly innocent as she admired the cookies with the shiny white, green, and red icing. "You know I'm a bit hard of hearing."

Only when she wanted to be, Adale thought. Then she silently fussed at herself. She couldn't take out her frustrations on her own mother. Especially now that they'd be living under the same roof again.

"Nothing," Adale replied as she sat back down then rubbed her hand against her eyes. "I think I'm still tired from your big party the other night."

"You *don't* party much," her ever-so-kind mama reminded her. "What's really wrong, sugar?"

Adale didn't want to talk about Rémy with her mother. What if Eloise really didn't know this was the same man who'd stood Adale up so long ago? He hadn't just stood her up; he'd broken her heart. She'd had no choice but to forget their brief time together then return home and start her life. She and Pierre had known each other all through school, and while her formidable father had practically handpicked him as her husband, they'd taken their time getting married, but they'd had a wonderful life until he died. She blamed his early death on the hard work he'd done on behalf of her family, no matter that the doctor had told her he'd been predisposed for heart troubles. Pierre had done everything in his power to make Jolene and her feel loved and cared for, and he'd tolerated her mama after Daddy had passed.

Thinking of Pierre and their daughter who'd come home at last, she put everything about Rémy out of her mind. She wanted to rebuild her relationship with Jolene, who'd doted on her daddy. Not work with the man whom Adale had once thought the love of her life. Pierre had filled that spot completely. Besides, Jolene had no idea about the past or that her mother had once loved another man. Jolene would be shocked and maybe a little hurt that Adale had held this secret for so long.

"Adale Melissa Lavigne-Marchand Broussard, are you listening to me?"

Mama meant business when she used all the names. But right now, Adale meant business herself. She wasn't sure how to handle this situation.

"Nothing is wrong. I don't like being ambushed. I looked like an ill-prepared leader, not even knowing a stranger had been invited to help me with a ball I've been putting on for what—twenty years now? It would have been nice to be forewarned."

"Just a spontaneous invitation, Adale." There might have been an eye roll with that declaration.

"No, an embarrassment, Mama. I only agreed to save face and be cooperative."

"You are always the lady. Those royals could take a lesson from you."

"I didn't want to be a lady. Now he's coming to dinner in a few hours. I don't even have a menu planned."

"I can cook," Mama offered, a cracker halfway to her mouth, her red lipstick still intact. How did she pull that off?

"No, ma'am. I can cook a dinner. You've already helped enough."

Her mother went quiet. Adale glanced up and, seeing the hurt in her mother's eyes, took Eloise's hand. "I'm sorry, Mama. Really. It's nice of you to offer, but I don't mind cooking. What should we plan?"

Her mother's eyes lit up. "How about a French-style dinner? But with Louisiana flair?"

Adale knew it then. Her mother was fibbing to beat the band. She remembered Rémy, all right. She'd never suggest French food for just anyone. Crawfish, maybe, or some good ol' gumbo, but French dinners were for special people because they required time, work, and the best of ingredients.

And her worn Julia Child cookbook.

"What do you have in mind?" Adale asked, deciding she'd have to be on her toes to keep up with her matchmaking mother.

Her mother's shrewd gaze missed nothing, making Adale feel as if she were sixteen again. But Mama played it cool and carried on. "How about your bouillabaisse with some fresh crusty bread? You do such a nice crème brûlée too. For an appetizer, you can never go wrong with some baked Camembert and crackers."

Mama had been planning this overnight, apparently.

Adale let out a sigh. Two could play that game. Maybe if she pretended interest, one of the conspirators would spill the details. "I suppose if he's determined to work with me, we do need to discuss a few things—such as boundaries and who is in charge."

"Oh, darling, I believe the man already knows who's in charge," Mama said with her sweet smile back in place.

Adale went along for now. "After lunch, I'll make a list then go by the seafood market for the shrimp and mussels. We want fresh, of course."

"Of course," Mama said, suddenly gathering dishes to use with lunch. "I'll clean up here once we're done so you can get busy."

"Thank you," Adale said. She kissed her mother's cheek. "It's nice to have you around."

"It's nice to still be around," her witty mama replied.

Adale finished preparing their salad while she said a few prayers for patience and guidance. She'd do what she'd always done. Get on with things. She wouldn't be distracted from her duties or her tasks.

She would not let Rémy Vachon back into her heart. But first, she had to figure out how her family had managed to get him back into her life.

———◆———

Jolene came in the back door, Mattie right behind her, a gust of cold air surrounding them, like the old days when they'd gotten into trouble.

When they hurried to get some tea, Adale said, "Have a seat, you two. We still need to establish a few boundaries."

Mattie looked sheepish, her green eyes bright. "If it's about us fussing over the bathroom, we'll work that out. We always do."

Jolene nodded as she dug through her aged leather tote. "We're keeping it clean and organized, Mom. I mean, Mattie's super organized and I'm—"

"—not at all organized," Mattie replied, grinning. "But we're learning to deal."

"Then learn to deal with this," Adale said, motioning to the breakfast table. "You both might be a few minutes late going back to work today."

They dropped their equipment bags on the floor with nervous thuds.

Granny clapped as she came back from her room. "A girls' lunch! What a delightful idea, Adale."

"It's not the fun kind," Jolene said, tossing her long hair back. "Not if Mom wants to discuss boundaries."

Granny made a face. "Oh, she did mention that earlier. I haven't been here long enough to annoy you that much, have I, Adale?"

Adale shook her head and brought over bowls and fruit. "We need to talk about Rémy Vachon."

"Oh, is that why you summoned the girls home?" Her mother looked confused and agitated at the same time. "If you insist."

"I do, Mother. Have a seat."

They all looked so sheepish, she almost laughed. But she couldn't muster up a chuckle. "So let me get this straight. Cameron did some digging to bring a restoration expert here, and he found Rémy Vachon, who is a renowned architect specializing in historical buildings. But no one knew who he was?"

"Mom, if this is about Granny asking him to be cochair, we were surprised too. But it's a good idea, publicity-wise."

"But did you know, Jolene? You and Mattie? Who he really is?"

Jolene glanced at Mattie then back to Adale. "What do you mean, who he is? Cameron knew him, but none of us did. You're not making any sense, Mom."

Adale gave her mother a moment to confess, but Granny played with a half grape sticking out of her chicken salad and refused to look at anyone in the room.

"Right," Adale said, gaining speed. "So none of you knew Rémy Vachon's background. Mama recognized him at her party and decided she'd mess with my life. But she somehow forgot to tell him who chairs the Christmas Eve ball committee, and she obviously forgot to mention *his* name or any of this to me. But how did you two discover he's the boy in the picture with me?"

Mattie sat shocked into silence. Jolene glanced from her grandmother back to Adale, her mouth falling open. "What are you talking about, Mom?"

"What? Wait!" Mattie jumped up, ran to Granny's studio, and came back with the portrait. "Are you saying the man Cameron found to help us renovate the town is the young man in this portrait? And the girl is you?"

Jolene grabbed it and stared at it, her gaze scanning it over and over, then looked back at Adale. "Mom, is this you with Rémy Vachon?"

Adale could see the genuine shock in their expressions. But she also saw the dash of triumph in her mother's eyes. "Oh my. Neither of you were aware of who he was before he came here?"

Her mother cleared her throat and took a long sip of tea but said nothing.

"We still don't," Jolene said, shaking her head. "I mean, we know his name and why he's here, but Mom, this about the portrait is news to me." She glanced at Mattie. "Did you know? Seeing it got us both wondering, but—"

"I didn't know," Mattie said, shaking her head. "I would have told you something this important."

"Oh, hush up," Eloise said in a loud voice, her salad fork clanking on her plate. "I knew. It was me."

"Took you long enough to admit that." Adale let out a sigh. "I figured as much, but I thought you had them in on your little surprise."

Her mother shook her head. "They are innocent. I recognized him before anyone introduced us." She shrugged. "Honestly, I don't know why I felt the need to suggest the things I did, except to say I felt a nudge. But I didn't say a word to these two about anything in the past."

"Well, we were curious after your reaction to the portrait," Jolene admitted. She looked at her grandmother. "Is this why you told us not to mention it to Mom?"

"Mother!" Adale stood up and stared out at the backyard that slanted down toward the river. "I knew you were bluffing, but what have you done?"

Mattie lifted her hand and waved it toward the portrait. "Granny, is this really the same man?"

Eloise shrugged. "Take the back of that old frame off the painting. I always document my art with names and dates—for this very reason. So others will know what's what."

"Oh, I know what's what, all right," Adale said while trying to keep her anger tamped down. "Mother." She shook her head, unable to speak.

Mattie helped Jolene carefully take the frame and heavy cardboard away from the portrait so they could look at the back of the canvas.

Jolene read aloud from the aged sticker on the back. "Adale Marchand with Rémy Vachon, Paris 1984."

Jolene and Mattie looked at each other, then back to Adale. "Wow," Jolene said, her expression hovering between shock and concern. "Just wow."

"You always did like to leave little details on your paintings," Adale said, glancing around then back to Eloise. "Now, isn't that an amazing coincidence?"

"It's not a coincidence, darling," her mother said. "It's a God wink."

"Excuse me?" Adale had heard it all now. "You think this is what the Lord wants for me? Are you sure you didn't tell them after Jolene got here?"

"She didn't tell us anything, Aunt Adale," Mattie insisted. "We're as surprised as you are right now. Cameron had already gotten in touch with him before we found this portrait."

Adale's heart jittered like a bird's fluttering wings. "You two really weren't in on this at all?"

"Of course they didn't know. I did it alone," Eloise said again. "I thought I recognized him, and then he introduced himself." She took a sip of her tea. "At first I thought about tell-ing him to leave. But then I realized what perfect timing. God always has perfect timing."

"But you neglected to clue me in on this perfect timing," Adale said. "Why didn't you warn me?"

"I might have if you hadn't run off to hide," her mother admitted. "Then I decided I'd take matters into my own hands. With a quick prayer to the Lord for courage."

Adale let that soak in. "Meddling is what broke us apart in the first place. But then, you know because you let Daddy do the meddling."

Her mother looked ashamed, her eyes misting over. "I didn't know until it was too late, darling."

Jolene pushed at her chair. "Mom, you need to tell us what happened with you and Rémy. He seems like a really nice man now—successful, distinguished—what could it hurt? He's alone, you're alone. It's romantic." Her eyebrows lifted. "Granny might have the right idea."

"No, it's not a good idea. It's interfering and assuming," Adale said. "Now I have to deal with him following me around. It's too much." She got up to make coffee to go with the cookies. "Besides, maybe I like being alone."

"It's not his fault," her mother said. She'd said that right after they'd found that picture too. "Sugar, for the sake of the holidays and for your tired old mother, can you be kind to Rémy? He's alone, and he's been nothing but a gentleman. He and I had a wonderful conversation. He told me he'd leave if you didn't want him here, but I'm the one who insisted he needed to stay, although I might have neglected telling him your rank around here. Humor me, please? Be polite to the man."

Adale drew back. "I've tried to be polite, and I will behave, Mother. But I needed to know the how and why of him being here." Tapping her polished fingernails on the table, she said, "Now I see how this happened. You made a decision that affects me—my life—again. You have no idea what you've stirred up. I don't know how to handle this."

"You always did need things to work in your mind," Eloise said, nodding toward her. "We've explained to the best of our abilities. You don't have to handle anything. Even if I hadn't asked him to stay or to be your cochair, you would have been surprised and angry either way. The rest is fate."

"Fate?" Adale wanted to shout out about the fate of her broken heart long ago, but that was water under the bridge now. "Okay, Mama. We'll go with fate."

"And we'll keep the *faith*," her daughter said, her pretty eyes full of a sweet sincerity. "You're the best at that, Mom." Jolene got up and came around the table to hug her. "You've taught both of us to keep the faith no matter what happens. To seek God's guidance through good and bad. Your strong faith is why I came home."

"Now you're just trying to butter me up," Adale said, her eyes growing misty. "But I did pray, waiting for you to return home. I prayed for you and Mattie to become close again, and yes, I even prayed for good men to love you both and appreciate you."

"Did you pray for me to move back into this house?" her mother asked, her eyes glistening a bit too.

Adale almost said *yes, but that now she regretted that*. Her mother looked contrite and sincere, so she replied, "I did, Mama. I prayed for the right way to handle this. I love having this house full of my favorite people." She wiped at her eyes. "Even when they meddle with misguided intentions in my business."

Eloise grabbed Adale's arm across the table. "Then can you forgive me for surprising you? I mean, I figured if I didn't make it a surprise, you'd shut down the whole idea."

"That I would have done," Adale admitted, patting her mother's hand. She took a deep breath, smiled at her daughter, and touched a wayward curl on Jolene's cheek. "You are all forgiven. I'll get through this. It is amazing how this happened, but y'all are right about some of it. Rémy is the best person for the job."

"God is in the details, you know," her mother said, satisfied now that she'd been proven somewhat right. "So may we please be allowed to finish eating? I'm famished."

Adale let out a laugh. "I think so. Eat up and take some sugar cookies to your fellows, girls. Mama, let's go sit in your new sunroom and have our cookies. You're not off the hook yet, but I can't send you packing, so there is that."

"Well, that's more like it," Eloise said before standing up to dance toward the tea pitcher. "We can gossip about everyone who walks along the path."

Adale smiled again and remembered Paris and the bridge over the Seine. She'd believed she found the right *path* then.

Now she wasn't sure what the right path would be from here on out.

Chapter Three

Rémy walked all around town with his camera. Moreau truly was a beautiful place. The main street followed the narrow Petit River and highlighted historical buildings that could rival those of New Orleans, their aged brick walls and wrought iron balconies as timeless as any he'd seen. He admired the aged magnolias and crape myrtles lining the avenues, the old-root camellias and thick azaleas thriving underneath the trees surrounding stately mansions and quaint cottages. The Cajun and Creole traditions had merged here to form a lovely little town. Moreau made for a beautiful Christmas backdrop. No wonder everyone here wanted it restored to its original glory. It bespoke of simpler times with deeply rooted traditions.

He wanted that too, now. He wanted to do something that might make Adale forgive him. Her mother had been encouraging the other night, but Adale had been shocked this morning. He didn't like starting off with her in that way, but he wouldn't speak badly of her mother either.

The same woman who'd helped her husband interfere all those years ago.

"I want to make amends," Eloise Marchand had told him last night. "Please let me handle my daughter. The more you're around, the better things can be. I need to know she'll be all right with this. You know, I'm not getting any younger."

Rémy couldn't help but smile, even while he worried about hurting Adale. Her mother seemed to have a need to help them along, but the woman looked as spry as a thirty-year-old. Who was he to argue with that?

He thought of Adale and stopped to stare at the Christmas decorations along the river. She'd mentioned this scene long ago.

"It's so pretty in Moreau, Rémy," she told him as they walked the streets of Paris. "The river is lit up with all sorts of shining decorations on each side. Stars, Santa, a manger scene—my favorite—huge bells and bows. You name it, they've made it into a light fixture. We have the big parade. People pour into our little town. You can't find a parking place if you're late. I was Christmas Princess once, and Mama was Christmas Queen when she was young."

Rémy let her go on, enthralled by her accent and her carefree attitude. "I imagine you were a beautiful princess, Adale."

"I almost froze to death. We had unusually cold weather that year. I had just turned fourteen, and I wore a furry white cape over my bright green dress." Then she giggled. "My first pair of kitten heels did not keep my feet warm."

He laughed as she danced around like a ballerina, then took her hand to hold her still. "I'm glad you didn't freeze."

Her smile had lit up the City of Lights. He'd fallen for her from the first moment he'd met her at some boring dignitary party his parents had forced him to attend. Her parents had forced her also, but she explained they were there for a few weeks visiting relatives. So she had plenty of time to make up for this not-so-fun dinner.

Maybe because they were both young and bored but mostly because she'd been the prettiest girl he'd ever seen, they spent the rest of the dinner getting to know each other. Then they'd snuck out for that first walk. She spoke fluent French, and he'd been taking English classes all through school. They'd become inseparable the next two weeks, despite her father's frowns and her mother's concern.

He'd tried to make everything fun for her in the time they'd had together.

A horse and carriage came by, jarring him out of his memories. A couple taking a ride through town waved to him. Romance was in the air in Moreau, Louisiana.

And Adale was here. He understood why she hadn't been approachable, but he'd do his best to make her smile again, just as he'd done his best showing her all the things he loved about Paris.

She'd been a pretty teenager and was now a beautiful woman. With her silvery hair in almost the same chin-length style, artfully curled against her neck and cheeks, and those green-blue eyes that had always held a sense of decorum with a sprinkling of mischief, she looked the same but different. Still the Adale he remembered, only more refined and sharpened, with an edge that he imagined had begun once he'd left her sitting at that sidewalk café long ago.

He had that same edge now too. That same maturity and resolve, that same tempered anger that had mellowed into a simmering memory of what might have been. How many women had he tried to love? How many had tried to love him?

He'd never found anyone because he'd lost the one.

But his papa used to say, "*Nous avons notre temps, et Dieu a son temps.*"

We have our time, and God has His time.

Was this God's time? Had Rémy's time to be with Adale finally arrived?

He said a silent prayer, asking the Lord to show him the way back to her. He'd never forgotten her, so when Cameron Armand tracked him down and invited him to come to Moreau, he knew without hesitation he wanted to see Moreau, but more so, he wanted to see Adale Lavigne-Marchand Broussard.

He'd tried to keep up with her through the years, and when he'd had the opportunity to take a position with a company in New Orleans, he'd done it for his work because he loved that conflicted city, but he'd also done it so he could be near Adale.

He never would have come here while she was still a married woman. Like a coward, he'd waited long after he'd heard her husband had died to make this trip. But Cameron's call had seemed like a sign, so he'd had a good excuse for coming now. Moreau needed to be restored after the devastation of that last hurricane. That was his specialty, restoring historical buildings.

But he and Adale needed some restoration in the relationship department.

Something he'd never been good at with other women.

Because none of them had ever measured up to the girl he'd left in Paris.

Now the challenge had changed. Was she that same girl, or had she become bitter, brittle, and lonely like him?

He sat down on a bench shaded by a mushrooming crape myrtle tree that had lost its summer leaves but gained a garland of colorful sparkling lights. Rémy pulled out his pad to sketch his renditions of the chapel, eager to work on this project. He'd waved to Jolene earlier as she headed under the tents and tarps they'd set up by the wall where she was painting a new mural in the quaint La Petite Chapelle's courtyard.

He also held a new rendition in his mind of himself and Adale together again. One he hoped he could make come true before he went back to New Orleans.

Then he saw the woman herself walking along the riverbank, her arms drawn to her long black sweater, her face turned to the far distance. She still took his breath away—cliché but the truth.

Time to put his musings to the test. "Adale?"

He hurried across the old brick street then down some chiseled steps, about to call out to her again when she turned and stared into his eyes. Then she started marching toward him with a definite implication that they had a long way to go on their personal restorations. A very long way to go.

———◆———

Adale wanted to jump in the river. She'd needed some time and space, and here stood the very reason she'd needed both.

"Rémy," she said as he walked up to her, "what on earth are you doing in Moreau anyway?"

He chuckled, infuriating her even more. "Is that your way of saying you've missed me?"

She tossed her hair off her cheek. "Honestly, I haven't thought about you in such a long, long time. I'm shocked to see you, as you've probably realized by now. No one can explain how you, of all the architects in the world, had to be the one to swoop in and fix Moreau." She wouldn't go into detail about her mother's matchmaking and this being fate. Rémy might agree with Mother.

"I want to help. This town is as lovely as you described it, Adale. Even prettier than I imagined. So romantic, oui?"

"Don't you *oui* me," she replied, wishing that word didn't sound so interesting coming from his lips. "You don't have to stay."

"I wouldn't renege on a promise. Cameron is a good man. He found me and told me with great passion about the needed restoration of this town. I can help if you'll let me. I'm sure you want Moreau to be restored to its former glory, do you not?"

He had her there, and after she'd vetted him half the night, she couldn't deny he'd be an asset to the restoration project. "Well, yes, I want that, but you don't have to help me cochair the ball. Better to stick with what you know. You'd be so bored with hanging Christmas ornaments or draping greenery and garland around doors."

"No, I would not. I often help hang draperies and portraits in homes I design or renovate."

"Don't try to pretend you'd enjoy working with paper decorations. You work with Cameron. He'll take care of you." She pivoted and almost lost her balance, but his next word stopped her.

"Don't."

She'd wish later she'd never turned around, but she did in time to see a deep sadness darkening his eyes. Sadness and a longing that showed her he'd suffered a little bit too.

"Don't go," he said, reaching out a hand. "Can't we sit and talk for a few minutes?"

Oh, how she wanted that. But no! Adale shook her head, causing her bright red bow earrings to jingle. "No, I have a lot to do since my interfering family invited you to dinner." She headed away again, then turned back one more time.

"Oh, dinner is at six sharp. Don't be late." Putting her hand on her hip, she added, "That is, of course, if you even manage to show up."

"Adale?"

This time she didn't turn around.

———◆———

Back home, Adale got on the phone. "Jolene, I forgot this at lunch with all the revelations going on. You and Mattie had better be at this dinner tonight. And bring Cameron and Paul with you, understand? I won't sit here alone with this man you've all inadvertently brought back into my life. I won't let Grandmère steer the conversation into areas I'm not ready to address."

"Mom," her daughter said with a sigh, "why didn't you tell us the rest of the story about what happened between you and Rémy Vachon? He's talented, and he seems like a nice man. He wants to work on the renovations, and he must want to see you. What happened with you two?"

"How do you know anything happened between us?"

"From your reaction, for one thing. You obviously recognized him, but you've never been rude like that before. You acted as if you'd had a run-in with him that left you both upset. Then you ghosted all of us."

"Speak in terms I can understand, please."

"You left without a word. That is so not like you." A sigh. "I understand why you were upset this morning, but you're never downright rude. He must have really done something to hurt you badly."

"He did, but I wasn't rude. Maybe firm, and shocked that you all might think I need a cochair, and him of all people. Whoever heard of such a thing?"

Jolene spoke softly into the phone. "He volunteered after Granny made it sound like such fun. Asked, really, because he recognized Granny, but we knew nothing of this past history until you told us at lunch."

"I'm sure he did recognize my mama." Adale let out her own sigh. "He should have recused himself once they talked. But he agreed, then had the nerve to show up again this morning. Now I have to entertain the man in my home."

"You still care," Jolene replied. "Mom, did you love him once?"

Adale almost said yes. But instead, she retorted, "Never mind. I'll try to work with him, but we need to find a way to keep this from becoming an awkward situation."

"Mom?"

"Be here at five thirty to help serve drinks and appetizers. Wear a nice dress."

Then she ended the call. She shouldn't take this out on her family, but after the girls had seen that portrait of her when she was sixteen, standing with a handsome young man on that bridge in Paris, they'd admitted being mighty curious. Was it coincidence that he'd come here? Her mother had painted that portrait as she'd watched them from her hotel balcony, and suddenly it had reappeared when they were going through Eloise's things. Had it been planted there for a reason? Eloise had implied she didn't know he'd be coming, but she'd obviously remembered Rémy. Remembered, then quickly came up with a grand plan to force Adale to face her past.

Her mother waltzed into the kitchen wearing a bright green and blue floral silk caftan. "I thought I'd offer my help with dinner prep. I can be your sous chef."

Already a bundle of nerves, Adale wouldn't mention Rémy again before dinner. "You can clean and cut the leeks and smash the garlic."

"Oh, I see. I'm in trouble for going along with this. I'll smell like garlic by dinnertime."

Adale felt the swish of her mother's caftan and detected a hint of Chanel No. 5. "Going along with what?"

Eloise stopped like a graceful blue heron spotting a fish, guilt merging with resolve in her eyes. "Going along with this dinner, which I had nothing whatsoever to do with ahead of time."

"You invited him," Adale reminded her. "The game is over, Mama."

Her mother fluttered her hand in the air, her diamond wedding ring winking. "Well, last night I invited a lot of people to stop by to see me in my new studio apartment here in our home. I mean, they were all so kind to show up at my party, I suppose I might have overstepped by suggesting a few things here and there."

"Should I set more plates at the dining table?" Adale asked as she searched the refrigerator and tried to focus on what needed doing. "Did you invite the whole parish?"

"No, sweetheart. Just us."

"If you mean you, me, and Rémy, you're wrong. Jolene and Cameron will be here, as well as Mattie and Paul. I'll get answers to all my questions."

"What questions do you have, darling? I thought we'd cleared all this up at lunch."

"Oh, I gave you a pass earlier, but I'd still like to know why my own mother is scheming against me."

A beat or two went by while her mother started chopping. A halt, a sigh, then more intense chopping. "What are you implying?"

"I don't need to imply. You already know all about this man who's come back into our lives."

The chopping knife clattered against the butcher block island. "What are you saying, Adale?"

"I'm saying that the boy who left me in that café in Paris is now my cochair for the Christmas ball. I think you finagled the whole thing long before your birthday party."

"Oh."

She whirled to stare at her mother. Eloise looked pale and fragile, but she lifted her head to give Adale a direct stare. "He's a good man, Adale."

"So I keep hearing."

"He wants to help us rebuild this town, our town. He's been in New Orleans for a while now. Alone."

"Did you know that?"

"I might have read an article in a *Southern Living* magazine."

"That's what I thought. I'm guessing you put a bug in Cameron's ear."

"I didn't do that. Cameron actually told me about him while he renovated my rooms here. When he told me the man's name, I almost fell out of my chair. But I didn't let on. Old age and all that. I figured no one would listen, and, well, it felt like a good opportunity."

"It's a bad idea, Mother. He needs to go back to New Orleans. Alone. We can make do without him. We always find a way."

"He's donating his time and discounting any work he does."

"That's mighty kind of him," Adale retorted as she again dug through the refrigerator for the vegetables she'd cut up to add to the crackers and baked Camembert.

Her cell rang. Giving it a glance, she saw Frank Miller's number coming up. Dear Frank, editor at the *Moreau Gazette*, Mattie's boss, a friend who wanted more. A companion who she'd finally agreed to have dinner with a couple of times. She let it go to voice mail. She wouldn't be rude to Frank, who was solid and sure and never late. Maybe she should spend more time with him to see where it could lead.

"Why him, Mama? Why Rémy Vachon? There has to be somebody else, anyone else, who can work with us on the renovations."

"He's the best for this particular restoration," Eloise said, her tone demure. "The only one, actually."

Adale turned in time to see her mother wiping at her eyes. "Did you get too much garlic on your hands?"

"Yes, I believe I did." Her mother stood and looked about, then back to Adale. "Let's have a nice dinner. I'd like that more than anything."

Seeing how upset her mother looked, Adale went to her. "Of course. You know I'd never be rude to a guest in my house. But I'll get through this dinner, and I'll find things to keep him busy the short time he's here. Then I won't have to endure his presence too much."

"If you say so," Eloise said. "Now isn't it about time to make the crème brûlée so it can cool a bit before you torch it?"

"Yes. I'll get on that next. Let's get the bouillabaisse going, shall we?"

Her mother looked relieved. Maybe she hadn't pushed for this, after all. Maybe the girls were working to make this easier, despite their grandmére. Or knowing them, they'd probably quizzed her mother by phone when Adale wasn't around earlier, so she'd tell them what she knew about the short time Adale and Rémy had been together. Adale decided she'd need to be courteous to the man about to have dinner with them. What had the minister always said? You can forgive, but you don't have to forget.

How could she ever forget Rémy or the way he'd made her feel, the way he still made her feel?

Chapter Four

Rémy stared up at the beautiful white two-story house in front of him. The inhabitants would probably not call it that. It would be the Lavigne House, as people around here called it. A testimony to the family's legacy, which they'd used for good and giving back to their community. A highly respected family.

He wished he could feel comfortable about how they'd left things. He wanted to tell Adale the truth, but that could only hurt her worse, and he would not hurt Adale again. Ever.

He was rarely nervous, but this was Adale, after all. He knew her, but he wanted to get to know her. Over again. So he admired the elegant Christmas decorations that highlighted the house to perfection and the sleek line of the stately, sturdy home. *Welcome*, it said.

Turn and leave, his head told him.

Go inside, his heart murmured.

When he heard young, carefree voices behind him, he whirled with relief. "Good. Now I won't have to face the music by myself."

Cameron and Paul surrounded him like two young guards.

Cameron gave him the side-eye. "You're not afraid of the Lavigne women, are you, Mr. Vachon?"

"Terrified, really," he admitted. "You see, I knew them before. A lifetime ago."

Paul glanced up at the house. "So we heard today. We all want to hear that story at some point."

"But not tonight, right?"

"They'd chase us out the door if we bring that up," Cameron said with a chuckle. "I do know that much about them. They are not to be messed with or underestimated."

Paul rocked on his boots. "I'm thinking they'll do the opposite. Ply you with so many questions, you won't be able to enjoy the meal."

"Let's get in there and see what happens," Cameron replied. "They can't do any harm if we behave, right?"

"Oui. Got it." Now Rémy's nerves became a tangled thing, like Christmas lights gone bad. "Shall we go into the fray?"

They walked up to the broad porch, the scent of Christmas wafting out of the fresh greenery around them. Then Cameron rang the doorbell, forcing Rémy to enter the world he'd always dreamed of entering.

Adale's world. He only prayed he could find a way to fit in.

The door flew open, and there she stood. Glancing from his young friends to him, she said, "Well, you're on time. That's a start."

He gazed at Adale in her red cashmere sweater, white pearls, slim black skirt, and the same kind of low-heeled pumps she'd worn in Paris. Classic. She would always be a classy lady.

"Hello," he said, after a nudge from Cameron. "I. . .found these two waiting outside." Then he handed her a white poinsettia. "I brought this for you."

"That's very thoughtful. Why do you all look like you're going to an execution?"

"I'm a bit nervous," Rémy admitted. "They're trying to reassure me."

"Actually, we found him waiting outside and dragged him up the steps," Cameron announced. "He's still getting used to all the charm that comes with entering this house."

"Charm?" She actually laughed. "We're loaded with that and more. C'mon, then. The bouillabaisse is getting cold."

They all filed in, but her gaze stayed on Rémy. "We have a lot of catching up to do, don't you think?"

"That we do," he replied, his nerves still jangling but his confidence getting a lift. "It's been a long time."

"Thirty-nine years, but who's counting?"

Paul and Cameron gave him sympathetic glances, then headed in to find support. Adale escorted Rémy, her hands clutching the red paper surrounding the big poinsettia so tightly her knuckles were white.

———◆———

Adale couldn't eat a bite. Rémy had somehow managed to be seated to the left of her. She took her place at the head of the antique mahogany table that had always been in this exact spot in this exact room for at least a hundred or so years. A huge long table that could seat twelve people.

Why did it feel as if the whole thing had shrunken down to just him beside her? His fresh, clean-smelling aftershave wafted toward her each time he passed the rolls or lifted his spoon. His gaze flickered over her like the flames from the tapered candles she'd lit. His presence filled this space, his choppy salt-and-pepper hair as thick as ever, his beautiful eyes still kind and intriguing.

"Mom?"

Adale glanced up to find her daughter and her niece staring at her. They'd both made it home with thirty minutes to spare for dinner. Now they were being extremely prim and proper.

"Yes?"

"This is good," Jolene said. "I've so missed your cooking. Yours too, Granny."

"I didn't help much," Eloise said with a delicate shrug. "My daughter's cooking is renowned, you know."

Rémy lifted his sparkling water. "I couldn't agree more. Delicious."

Adale nodded and tried to swallow her salad. "It's nothing, really." She wasn't being modest. She'd made this dish so many times, it was second nature. Her nerves had been jittery tonight, but thankfully she hadn't made a mess of the whole meal.

"It's a lot of work," Jolene said. "You always bring it all together, the way you do everything. The fish, clams, and mussels, even scallops this time—"

"Not to mention the fennel and saffron. Your seasonings are perfection," Rémy said, his gaze still on her, causing her to grow warm.

"She did allow me to make the salad and cut up the leeks," her mother said, her tone modest. "I also added the garlic. We like fresh garlic. But then, Adale wants everything to be perfect."

"Okay, enough." Adale put down her spoon and stared around the table. "It's nice to have a lovely dinner, especially since my girls are here and my mama too." She smiled at Cameron and Paul. "And you two. I've known you all your life, Paul. I'm so happy for you and Mattie. Cameron, I hope you're feeling more at home here now."

"I am," Cameron said, his grin aimed at her daughter. "Moreau has a lot to offer."

"It sure does," Granny said, her smile beaming. "I love that my immediate family is here at this table and. . .that we have extended family now. Maybe more to come."

Rémy took a sip of his water, the tiny strawberry Adale had dropped in each glass trying to escape as he turned up his goblet. He smiled and turned to her. "*Merci*, Adale."

She inclined her chin, ever the perfect hostess. "You're welcome, Rémy."

"I hope I am," he said quietly before he took a nibble of the crusty bread she'd picked up at the bakery. "It was kind of you to have me for dinner, considering. . ."

"We like dinner guests," Eloise quickly threw out. "The more, the merrier."

They all agreed on that.

"I don't mind an invite from y'all," Cameron said. "But I might have to jog a little more."

Adale softened her prickly attitude. Rémy conversed with ease, a gentleman in every way. He was forward-thinking regarding historical buildings. She listened, fascinated, as he explained how they could repair the chapel to make it even stronger and more beautiful than it had been before.

"I think we can whitewash some old brick to match the original creamy brick walls that are left. You'll never know part of the building is brand-new. The roof and steeple will both be a challenge, but I know a great steeplejack who can make it look perfect."

They made small talk a bit more, steering away from the elephant in the room. But Adale could feel everyone's gaze on her and Rémy. They all wanted to hear the story. A story she'd tried to put out of her mind for most of her life.

"What about the Christmas ball?" Mattie finally asked, always the one to stay on point. "We do need to discuss the details."

Adale stood. "Let's move dessert into the sitting room."

The girls took that as their cue to follow her into the kitchen. Jolene shot her a glance. "He's really nice, isn't he, Mom?"

Mattie grabbed a tray and filled it with the vintage floral Dresden cups and saucers, her gaze hitting on Adale. "Are you upset about him being here?"

Adale stopped with the ramekin of crème brûlée she'd been about to place with the others on another tray. "We will discuss this later, after everyone is gone."

"But are you upset?" Jolene asked, giving Mattie a silent glance.

Adale took a breath. "I'm surprised, confused, and curious. As I'm sure you all are. Curious, I mean. None of you seem surprised. I guess that's what hurts the most, that my mother could spring this on me when I'm already so busy. . .remembering other Christmases."

"It can wait, Mom," Jolene said, her dark messy bun sprouting out on her head in little shoots. She'd worn a pretty maxi dress, floral and flowing, over buttery soft boots. "It'll wait until later, okay?"

"Okay," Adale said, smiling, refusing to cry or even think beyond dessert. She had to do this. She wouldn't break down now. But it had been his sweetness, his kindness, that took her back to that time when they'd stood on the bridge and promised they'd find a way to be together.

But that promise had been broken.

Well, now here he sat in her home. What was she to do about that?

"Mom?"

She whirled to see Jolene standing there, her beautiful face etched with worry. "What, darling?"

"Did you love him long ago? He's the boy on the bridge. We know that now. But did you love him more—"

"Let's get this dessert out there while it's still pretty," she said, taking in a deep breath as she managed a smile. "Go on you two. Take the coffee to the table by the tree. I'll be there shortly."

Mattie and Jolene did as she'd asked, thankfully.

Adale stood there in the butler's pantry, the memories of other Christmases sparking through her mind. Her heart ached for Pierre. So much.

Then she felt a hand on her arm. "Let me help with that."

Rémy.

"No, you're a guest," she managed to say, seeing him there only startling her more and making her feel strange and guilty. She hadn't been interested in meeting other men. At least not until now.

"Let me, please," he said, lifting the tray. "It will be okay, Adale. If you don't want me here, I can work on things from a distance. I've been doing that anyway."

She came out of her stupor then. "What does that mean, Rémy?"

"It means I've waited for a long time. I can wait a bit more if you need me to do so."

Adale lifted her chin and took a deep breath. "For now, let's get through the rest of this dinner."

He nodded, silent, his dark eyes full of a fledgling hope.

Adale had to decide how much of that hope she could handle.

———◆———

"So we came up with the idea of a black-and-white Christmas Eve ball," Mattie said, apparently for Rémy's sake. "Everyone dresses in either black or white or both, all fancy and elegant. You still like that idea, don't you, Aunt Adale?"

Adale felt a headache coming on. "I liked that idea in November when we started ordering supplies. But we're days away, and I've already been meeting with the whole committee on how we will create this. Bringing in a new voice at this late date will not be easy."

She waved a hand in Rémy's direction, then took a big bite of her dessert, her stomach nervously protesting.

Rémy sat still, watching her, his half-eaten crème brûlée on the table beside his coffee. "This brûlée is perfect," he said. Then he turned to Adale. "I don't want to change your plans or your choice of decorations. When Cameron told me about the theme, I got excited. Overly excited, I think. I suggested a few things then after I met Eloise. She loved the idea of my assisting you." He sent Adale a solemn stare. "I had hoped to speak to you about it."

Eloise gave her daughter a raised eyebrow. "We did try to find you, several times. I've never known you to leave a party early, even when you're not having a good time."

"I got tired."

"We really wanted to tell you all about our ideas," her mother went on.

"It would have been wise to speak to me *first*. And maybe mention the one big thing you managed to keep from me."

"You mean Rémy?" her mother asked, her stare turning into the mother stare. As in *Do you not understand what I'm trying to say?*

"Of course I mean Rémy."

Eloise did her infamous shrug. "I wanted you to have a chat with him. I wasn't sure it was our Rémy at first, of course."

Adale glanced at Rémy. "I'm now very aware of him, Mama."

His gaze held her still. "I ruined the party. That's why you were avoiding me."

"Well, here you are." Adale leaned forward. "We have a few days, Rémy. I've told you to bow out, but if you're determined to follow me around and take orders, then so be it. I won't fight you anymore. I don't have time to fret about you being here. The theme is locked in, so any ideas you have will have to work with the black, white, and gold we've put together."

"That sounds like a perfect black-and-white ball to me," he said, nodding. "I'll do whatever you tell me. I hope to meet a lot of the people who live here and want to rebuild. It will be an honor to contribute to that cause."

Adale had to admire his spiel, but could she trust him to follow through on any of those pretty promises?

Her mother, daughter, and niece were watching her with bated breath while Cameron and Paul tried to decipher the crème brûlée, their heads down while they shoveled it in. Adale decided she'd be the one to take matters into her own hands.

"You *should* meet the people of Moreau, and you *should* know I won't let them down. They look forward to the ball each year. Most of the townspeople donate their money to have one night of Christmas glamour and fellowship to continue raising money for everything from art and literature to the Christmas market or our many other festivals. Of course, this year is all about renovation after the hurricane. We all love our little town. I can't let them down, even if you're pestering me."

Her mother gave her what might have been a proud nod. "I knew you'd find a way to make this work, Adale. You've always been industrious and determined."

Mattie and Jolene glanced at each other, then back to her. "We'll help, Mom," her daughter said. "I'm looking forward to the ball." She smiled over at Cameron. "The decorations are here, ready to be put out. The touch of gold on the tables will make it so festive. You don't have to worry about anything."

Adale nodded, but she couldn't stop her concerns. So she chose to talk about the ball—her main event. "Okay, so let's go over the plans for tomorrow. I've got the food ordered, and the caterer is the best with food for large groups. I even convinced Chef Ernie Perot to make mini muffies. We'll have prime rib stations, with all the trimmings, fresh shrimp from the Gulf, along with hush puppies, lots of dips and vegetable trays. Dessert will be mini bread pudding cups, crème brûlée, plus little slices of dark chocolate doberge cake with cream cheese pudding layers."

Everyone clapped and smiled.

"Yummy," Eloise said, her eyes dreamy. "There is nothing better than a good doberge cake. Unless it's mini muffulettas, of course." Then she leaned in. "But don't tell Chef Ernie I said that. His ego is big enough."

"I'm glad you approve, Mama."

She went on, seeing Rémy's interest in the way his eyes lit up. "We'll set up serving stations all over the community center but have both sit-down tables as well as cocktail tables here and there. People can stand, mingle, or sit and visit. So I'm not worried about that. But we need to start putting up the decorations tomorrow or we'll be behind. I don't like being behind."

Rémy's laughter caught her, so she stopped to turn toward him. "What exactly do you bring to the table?"

He looked surprised but got it together after a quiet moment. "I can hang garland, build props, paint wooden trees, or create any type of scene or prop. I can create the Eiffel Tower out of papier-mâché." He stopped, stared over at her with those deep blue eyes. "I can recreate bridges and paint small murals. You'll think you're back at a ball in Paris."

"I'll never be back in Paris," she said, getting up to dismiss her guests. "My heart belongs here in Moreau."

Chapter Five

The crowd scattered. Mattie and Jolene took their fellows to help with the cleanup. Granny yawned with all the drama of an actress and bid a rather flamboyant good night.

That left Adale with Rémy, who had not taken the hint.

"You can go," she pointed out while she ran a hand over her hair. "It's been a long day with a lot to absorb. You're probably tired."

"I'm wide awake," he said. "Why don't we go for a walk?"

"It's cold out there, and I'm exhausted."

"Just around the block. I like looking at the lights."

"You mean, like the Paris lights? You said you loved the way the city lit up at night."

"I believe I said I liked the way *you* lit up the city."

Adale had to hold her breath and let it out to center herself. He still held that charming attractiveness she could never forget. "These days I don't light up anything except candles."

"Your razor wit has gotten even sharper."

"Don't forget that."

He'd somehow found her a coat and slipped it over her shoulders. Then he called to the kitchen to tell Cameron they were stepping outside for some air. Soon they were out on the front porch.

Adale tried to protest by standing close to the door. "You should go on without me," she said. "My mother and the girls are probably all standing at the window watching."

He glanced at the windows. The kitchen had huge windows, and yes, the girls and their significant others were glancing out the window. "It's only a walk, Adale. Nothing more."

She checked around. These old houses were like gingerbread all dolled up with pretty decorations. Some reminded her of wedding cakes, some were made of grainy brown or red bricks trimmed in white twinkling lights. All beautiful and in the Christmas spirit. She had to find her Christmas spirit again somehow.

"Okay," she finally said. "Let me show you my town, Rémy."

He placed his hand on her arm. "I've been waiting to see it for a long, long time."

Adale knew she should turn and go back inside like the sensible woman she'd learned to be. But her heart didn't want to be sensible tonight.

Non, tonight she wanted to feel young again, wanted to walk with a nice man beside her. Wanted her memories to fade, to be replaced by new images. Maybe no longer what might have been, but more what might become if only she could forgive Rémy Vachon.

Did You bring him here, Lord? Should I follow my heart or pray hard to resist temptation? Should I forgive and let him into my life again or avoid another heartache?

Too late, she saw the temptation and worried about the heartache. But a walk around the block wasn't scandalous, was it?

———◆———

"It's a beautiful night," Rémy said as he held Adale's arm. They walked up her street, then turned back toward the river that ran down below the gently sloping backyard. "Just enough snow to make everything so peaceful and pretty."

"But we both know everything is in chaos, don't we?" his lovely companion retorted, pulling her arm away. "In my wildest dreams, I never imagined you'd show up in Moreau, or even in the States for that matter. Now I find out you've been living a stone's throw away in New Orleans."

"You've been caught off guard."

"That's an understatement."

"I wanted to see you, Adale. I've been respectful of you being a widow and having obligations, but when Cameron called me, I felt it was time."

"Time for what, Rémy?" she asked, turning to stare at him as they reached the river, where the bright lights lined the historical part of town. "Time to make amends, time to apologize, time to explain?"

Rémy turned to her, wanting to tell her the truth. "All of the above."

"Now's your time. We're alone, and I'm listening."

"Not yet," he said. "I think we need to get to know each other again. I'll be here through Christmas. Can't we enjoy this wonderful second chance?"

Adale whirled like a ballerina in the wind. "Is that what you think? That if you came here, donated your services, and endeared my entire family to you, that we'd have a second chance?"

"I came here for you, Adale," he said, frustration coloring his words. Frustration and a longing that had followed him around for his whole life.

"You'll have to do better than that," she said, her eyes flashing every bit as brightly as the lit-up alligators guiding Papa Noël across the river on a pirogue. "Before anything happens between us, you owe me an explanation. Until then, I'll abide you being here for the sake of charity. I want to stay in the Christmas spirit." Then she pivoted back toward her house. "The next committee meeting is at nine in the morning. It will be short because we'll begin with setup. Mr. Tatum and the whole crew from Majestic Tents and Tables will be there. Come ready to work all day tomorrow. Good night, Rémy."

"Adale?"

She turned, stared at him. "What?"

"Let me walk you back home."

"No, thanks. I know the way."

Then she was off, her shoes clicking on the sidewalk with the same cadence as all the moments he'd lost and hoped to gain back, clicking away like a clock's second hand.

Rémy found a bench and listened to the river, the soft gurgles and ebbs reminding him of how long he'd wanted this. Now that he'd arrived, everything had gone wrong. Adale didn't care about him in the same way she had when they were teens, and how could he blame her? He'd left her there waiting. He knew her agony because he'd stood on a bridge down from the café and watched her for at least an hour or so. He'd felt that same agony.

Watched her sitting, waiting, wondering, when he'd promised he'd be there. But he had not been there because of another promise—not so much a promise as an ultimatum. So he'd watched her walk away, her head down, her steps slow, until she'd walked out of sight.

Out of his life.

Rémy said a silent prayer there by the river.

Let me be the man she wants me to be. Let me show her how much I care about her still. Lord, show me the way. Show me a sign that now is our time.

He'd always loved Christmas, and this town held Christmas like a snow globe full of hope. Rémy held to that hope too. He wouldn't give up.

He was, after all, a patient man.

***

The next morning, Rémy arrived early at the community center, ready to do hard labor. If that gave Adale some satisfaction, then he'd gladly work all day and night. He'd stopped at the local coffee shop—Le Petit French Press—or the Press as the locals called it—to order one of every kind of coffee and one of every kind of Danish and croissant. The big bag he held in one hand smelled as scrumptious as the coffee tray he balanced in the other hand. Now to get the front doors open.

"Let me help."

He turned to find Adale walking toward him with a huge briefcase of a purse in one hand and another tray of coffee in the other. "I see we had the same idea. I called mine in, so I must have just missed you." She slung the tote bag over her leather coat, then tugged at the industrial door handle. "Enter at your own risk."

He entered, risking everything by crossing this threshold. "Merci." Then he smiled at her. "But aren't I supposed to open the door for you?"

"You're in my territory now, Rémy," she replied. "No need to be polite."

He followed her in and placed the food and coffee on a high counter opening to a big industrial kitchen. "Oh, I meant to ask you about the parade? Does that still happen?"

Adale's eyes went dark for a moment. "You remembered that?"

"Of course I did," he said as he made sure the coffee felt warm to the touch. "You looked so alive when you talked about that and the lights along the river."

"We got the new lights this year," she said. "Had the parade the Saturday after Thanksgiving. We hope people will start coming back if that day is in their memories—having it the same day each year makes for a new tradition."

"I'm sorry I missed it."

"It was smaller this year since we're practically starting over." She turned and waved to the event manager. "Hi, Mr. Tatum. Is Jackie with you?"

"On her way," the man replied. "She wouldn't miss this one."

Adale laughed. "How's that new grandson?"

"Jameson is growing like a weed and keeps us on our toes. Best fun I've had in a long time."

Adale nodded then turned back to Rémy. "You see what I mean. Good people who want to rebuild our town. That's the focus."

Meaning he wasn't, he decided. "I'm glad I can help with that. I've always loved bringing quaint historical buildings back to their former glory."

She turned to face him, her porcelain skin bright from the cold. "That's the reason I can't send you away. I've read up on you, Rémy. Quite impressive. I'm surprised I didn't know more about you."

"Maybe because you didn't want to know more about me?"

"Probably right on that. I've been clueless regarding you—so near, and yet I had no idea you'd moved to Louisiana."

"Adale—"

People started coming in, so she gave him an apologetic look of relief. She didn't seem ready for the deep discussion yet even if she did want answers. She took off to greet her volunteers, giving out commands like a drill sergeant. Rémy could only smile and follow orders. But he didn't mind. Soon they were all drinking coffee and nibbling confections as they moved toward the storage room to retrieve the decorations her committee had ordered.

Adale ticked off tasks as the two dozen or so people there hung on her every word.

He could certainly understand. She was a good person, a classic community volunteer, someone who loved fiercely and wore her pride like a tiara.

"You," she called to him, looking cute in her tan suede boots and a festive poinsettia-embossed sweater over worn jeans. Cute and young and ready to get this done.

"Oui?"

"You can start by helping Mr. Tatum and Cameron set up the round tables, eight chairs to each table. Make sure they look symmetric so our guests can pass through without people having to move their chairs." She shrugged. "A lot of full-skirted gowns at this ball."

"But of course, *madame*," he replied, loving every second of being in the same building as Adale. He could hear her sweet, cultured Southern voice echoing through this huge rectangular community center. Like music to his ears.

Once they got going, someone turned on the radio to Christmas music. Everyone began to hum and sing. Cameron and Jolene did a little jig to "Here Comes Santa Claus."

Adale walked by during a rendition of "I'll Be Home for Christmas," and Rémy grabbed her arm. "Care to dance?"

She glared at him until Jolene and Mattie tugged her into their casual waltz. "C'mon, Mom," Jolene said. "It's Christmas. Lighten up."

Adale huffed and joined in, Rémy taking her into his arms. They swayed and sang until they were giggling. Then the music stopped.

Chapter Six

Adale whirled through the rest of the day, her mind all over the place between mellowed long-ago memories and her current raw raging feelings. What had she been thinking, dancing like a teenager with Rémy while her family and friends watched? She hadn't been thinking—that was the problem. Rémy seemed to do that to her, make her lose her senses, make her remember being young, in Paris, and in love. Now they'd surely be the talk of the town.

She didn't stop for the next few hours, but rather focused on getting the building to look elegant and sparkling. Now Adale stood in the kitchen, her mind choreographing how the caterers should set things up.

Jolene slid up next to her. "Mom, we're going for pizza. Miss Mary Ann's going. She asked if you wanted to join us."

Mary Ann was one of Adale's best friends. She'd worked hard all day, so they hadn't had much time to chat. She'd be a good person to talk to in confidence. "I might. Let me freshen up."

"Before you do, what do you think?" Jolene asked, in her reindeer-embossed sweatshirt down to her knees over dark leggings and flat furry boots.

"You look adorable. Don't bother changing for pizza."

"Mom, not about me. What do you think about the decorations?"

Adale blinked and turned to stare at the entire room. The sparkling lights they'd hung shimmered everywhere.

"Oh my word." She grabbed Jolene's hand. "It's so beautiful. Even more than I imagined."

The place shined, all decked out in black, white, and gold balloons, with black tablecloths and gold runners, and dinnerware to match. The centerpieces were white feathers, white sprayed tree branches, and golden sprayed magnolia leaves tied with elaborate bows, and a bit of greenery winking from each tall glass vase full of black, white, and gold sparkling balls. The ceiling held sheer white sheets of gauzy material draped with big sparkling bows. The chairs were covered in black-and-white plaid felt covered with sparkling gold stars, shimmering as if they'd been thrown there.

The side tables carried out the theme. Then she spotted the fleur-de-lis symbols decorating the smaller cocktail tables. "I don't recall ordering those."

Jolene shrugged. "Rémy found them in the back of the storage room here. He thought they'd look nice—like flowers—in the smaller vases."

Adale almost objected, but true to his word, Rémy had worked as hard as anyone today. Now she didn't see him. She'd thank him later. She didn't want to look too obvious. "That's a nice touch," she said, tamping down her earlier thoughts.

The light gold fleurs-de-lis were centered in the middle of what looked like white lilies with gold-tipped leaves. Seemed Rémy had a flare for the dramatic.

"Amazing, and so perfect." Then she laughed. "We could also have a Saints football team party in here."

"We do have their colors, but this is so Louisiana." Jolene brought her back to the present. "So, pizza? Miss Mary Ann is waiting."

Distracted, Adale nodded. "Of course. Let me clean up a bit and get my bag."

"We'll wait outside and walk to the Pizza Café."

Adale rarely ate pizza, but the Moreau Pizza Café had the best around, made fresh and cooked in real pizza ovens. They had great pasta too. "I'll be right there, honey."

Adale washed her hands, then freshened her lipstick. She really wanted to go home, get into her pajamas, and go to bed early. Exhaustion clouded her clarity.

When she got outside, that idea sounded even better. Rémy stood waiting with the usual suspects. Adale nodded to him but walked up to Mary Ann. Her friend had a knowing smile on her face that outshined the grinning snowman on her black sweater. "He's handsome."

"Not you too?" Adale said, shaking her head. "Does everyone in town know about our history?"

"You two have a history?" her redheaded friend asked, a shocked expression on her face. "Do tell."

Adale sent her a mock frown. "I think you already know."

"A little," Mary Ann said. "But I want details, girl. This is big news."

Before Adale could reply, Rémy came strolling over. "May I walk you ladies to the Pizza Café?"

"Well, of course," Mary Ann answered for both of them. "We'd like that, wouldn't we, Adale?"

Adale could only nod and glare at her smiling friend. While Rémy looked rather pleased with himself.

"It's a lovely night," he said. "I had a great time today."

"Aren't you tired?" she asked, wishing he'd take the hint.

"Non. These young people make me feel alive and youthful again. I did as you suggested. I got to know some of your friends, Adale. You were right. Moreau is a special place."

"It used to be," she said. And she wasn't talking about before the hurricane.

———◆———

They got a big round table in the back corner, everyone scrambling for spots.

Rémy somehow found one right by her, with Mary Ann on her other side. Blocked in by Jolene and Cameron, then Mattie and Paul, and a few other volunteers, Adale couldn't escape without making everyone get up.

"You don't look so happy," Mary Ann whispered, her green eyes bright. "I imagine you're tired."

"You could say that," Adale replied. "This is always a major undertaking. I can't help but think of Pierre. He loved helping me with the Christmas ball. He always said we had more fun than Mardi Gras, but we did it without all the hard drinking."

"Your Pierre was a keeper," her friend said. "I'm sure it's always difficult during the holidays."

Adale nodded. "It is, but we carry on, don't we?"

"Yes, we do," Mary Ann said, glancing toward Rémy. "We should have lunch soon. And really talk."

"I'd like that," Adale said. "I need that."

Her friend gave her an understanding look. "He seems so nice, Adale. But you know him better than the rest of us, I reckon."

"I used to know him," Adale admitted, keeping her head turned toward Mary Ann, her voice low. "Now I'm not so sure."

The waitress passed out the menus. Rémy handed Adale hers. "You don't want me here, right?"

"I didn't say that."

"Your expression told me."

She let out a sigh, her smile for the benefit of the others at the table. "Rémy, you worked hard today, so you can eat pizza with us. I don't mind, really." After she'd ordered her favorite metropolitan pizza, she turned back to him. "I do appreciate your help today. The fleur-de-lis centerpieces are beautiful. I'd forgotten we had some centerpieces stored away."

"I told you I like to restore things, or in this case, find something beautiful and bring it back to life." He gave her a steady gaze. "I wish I could do that with you."

Adale balked. "Are you saying I'm old and need restoring? That I'm not alive but just an empty shell?"

"Non, you know that's not what I meant." He leaned in. "I want to restore our friendship at least. I had hoped—"

"—I had hoped once too, Rémy. Sometimes we can't get the things we hope for."

He didn't respond. He only inclined his head. "Can't we bring about a Christmas truce? Peace on earth, forgiveness between you and me?"

Adale glanced up to see her daughter watching them. She wouldn't upset this time with Jolene, a time she'd prayed for many times over. So she smiled across the table at her daughter, then turned to Rémy.

"You know, you're right. We can be civil, and we might become friends. What happened a long time ago is over and done. I've had a good life here, and I hope your life has been blessed too. Besides, you won't be here much longer. I think I can make peace with you for the sake of Christmas."

He raised his goblet of mineral water. Adale did the same. They toasted to their new truce. Soon everyone began toasting each other over chatter and Merry Christmas wishes. Jolene's smile was worth that little bit of discomfort.

"See what a little give-and-take can create?" Rémy said in her ear. "I'm glad we had this discussion."

Adale gave him her best smile. "Don't push things. Your pizza is coming out of the oven. Prepare to be amazed."

Rémy chuckled and grinned at her. "I'm already amazed, Adale. You're smiling at me, and that is the best gift of all."

"You haven't tasted the pizza yet," she quipped. Suddenly, she was starving.

Adale was still smiling the next morning.

"Well, you're certainly in a good mood," Mama said as she entered the kitchen like a queen waiting to greet her court.

Adale turned from the bacon she'd fried crisp. "I feel good about things."

"What things?" her mother asked as she patted her fluff of white hair and adjusted her big black reading glasses. "I hear the decorations for the ball are spectacular."

"And who might have told you that?"

"The girls when they brought me pizza last night. You were conspicuously absent, so we speculated about you."

Adale decided to go with it. "Rémy and I went for a walk along the river. A nice night, chilly but pretty. We had hot chocolate."

Eloise stood very still, surprise making her eyes go wide. "I don't think I heard you clearly, darling."

"You heard me, Mama," Adale said. "We've agreed to a truce—for the duration of his stay in Moreau."

"A whole month?"

Adale stood still now. "What do you mean, a whole month?"

"Oh, nothing. My, that bacon smells so good."

"Mother?"

Eloise looked caught and confused. "I mean a week or so."

"You said a month, Mother."

"You know I have memory issues."

Adale didn't know whether to laugh or cry. She prayed for patience. "Mother, is Rémy going to be staying here for a month?"

"I thought you knew. He rented the big suite in the bed-and-breakfast—you know the Maison Beignet. The top floor suite that has that cute little galley kitchen."

"I'm so happy for him, but I want to know how long he'll be here."

"I don't recall."

Adale's good mood faded like the fog over the river. "He's staying a month, and no one told me."

"At least," her mother said in a matter-of-fact way, "it will take that long to get things moving on the chapel. You know, God had to have seven days to create the earth. So a month for our tiny beloved chapel is a small sacrifice, don't you think?"

"I'm trying not to think beyond Christmas Eve," Adale said. "If he's still here on Christmas, am I expected to invite him to our family dinner?"

"That sure would be the polite thing to do. We can't let him get stuck with Nadine Collins. You know she's single for the third time, so she likes it when single men stay at her B and B. I mean her front door is constantly open to visitors."

"Mother!"

"See, even you're horrified at the thought of him being at the mercy of that flirt all day long on Christmas. She can't cook very well. She has hired help to do the breakfast part of her livelihood. That means they'd sit there all alone, and mercy knows what ideas she'd put in his head."

"Okay, enough. Please let me drink more coffee before I absorb this new revelation. I think all these surprises will be the end of me."

"You'll be fine. You've managed to have meals with Rémy as well as nice walks with him. People have seen you together. Soon you'll be a thing."

"We are not a thing. It's a truce. One that I thought was short-lived."

"A month isn't that long, sugar. A few days have already passed. It'll go by like that—" She snapped her fingers. "Of course, we need to consider New Year's Eve, don't we?"

"I'll be in my pajamas and in bed at midnight," Adale retorted.

"What about the other few hours of the night?"

"Your mind is in better condition than you let on," Adale replied. "Mama, stay out of this, please."

"I have stayed out of it," her mother said with a firm tone. "For too long now."

Adale gave her mother a stern stare. "What does that even mean?"

"I'm hungry," her mother said. "Can I be fed? I thought meals came with this new setup."

"You're avoiding the issue, but yes, here is your bacon, and I have a quiche coming out of the oven."

"That's more like it," Eloise replied with a prim smile. "Adale, all of this will be okay if you'll relax and try to see him in a new light."

"What light would that be, Mama?"

"One where you let go of that chip on your shoulder and let nature take its course, darling."

Too tired and mixed up to keep up with this discussion, Adale didn't argue. "I have to hurry. I'm working at the Christmas market today until at least lunchtime. Schoolchildren. Field trips. They buy presents for their parents. I somehow got stuck with this day till noon. I'll come home with a migraine, I'm sure."

"That's a great idea. Not the migraine, but letting them enjoy the market in the daylight on their own." Eloise looked lost for a moment. "I miss those days."

Adale felt bad now. "Would you like to go sit in the booth with me?"

Her mother perked up. "Depends on the booth. I can't abide that booth where Paul Bunyan creates animals out of tree stumps. Too loud and too much sawdust, although his creations are right pretty."

"His name is Robby Pickett, Mama. You know his wife, Margie. It's Robby's Rustic Creations."

"Yes, but that doesn't mean I have to endure that noise for four hours."

"We will be in one of the food booths. Muffulettas from Cajun Cooking."

"Oh, I'd be happy to help there. I can aggravate Chef Ernie, and that always makes my day. And we can share a muffuletta for lunch."

Adale nodded. "We can do that. Finish breakfast, and then put on something warm. It's still chilly even though the sun's shining a bit."

Eloise reached for her hand. "You know I want the best for *you*. I won't always be here."

"Mama, don't talk like that. I'll figure out things with Rémy. Please tell me there are no more surprises."

Her mother looked thoughtful, her brow furrowing. "None that I can remember right now, sugar."

Adale took that to mean more to come. But she also realized that, in her own sweet way, her mother wanted to make amends for the past so she could leave Adale with a possible change in her future.

Was she ready for that kind of change?

Chapter Seven

The Christmas market usually opened at night so everyone could enjoy the pretty lights strung across each booth. Adale loved working in the food booths because they stayed so busy and provided instant meals to take home for dinner. Today, once the dozens of schoolchildren had been fed, she'd be off in time for the muffuletta she'd promised her mother for lunch.

Eloise sat in a comfortable folding chair with a cat-embossed Christmas throw over her warm flannel-lined slender pants, a light sweater and wool walking coat keeping her warm. She'd thrown on a black beanie that had fake jewels in the shape of a flower on one side. Mama always managed to look sassy and chic, as if she'd just stepped out of a sedan in Paris. Now she held court with friends who happened to pass by.

Paris. Always on Adale's mind these days. Rémy had been nice at dinner last night, but their walk back to her car had been quiet. He'd insisted on walking her back to the community center, but when he'd turned to her like a young beau about to kiss his girl, Adale had smiled up at him. "Truce, remember? That doesn't mean everything is okay between us, Rémy."

"I know," he said. Then he kissed her gently on her cheek. "Good night, Adale."

She'd expected a little more of a protest, but that chaste kiss had stopped her in her boot tracks. Now she had to wonder if he could be growing weary of her putting him at arm's length. How would she feel if he did that?

Coming back to the here and now with the sounds of children laughing and calling out, she decided she wouldn't think of Rémy today.

A few minutes later, Adale turned from helping Mary Ann serve a family of four to find her mother laughing and chatting with one of the neighbors. "Yes, we know Rémy. We met him years ago, and he lives in the States now."

Adale glanced at her friend. "See what I mean. It's like I'm a teenager again."

Mary Ann shook her head, then called to Chef Perot that they were running low on muffulettas and shrimp-on-a-stick.

Then she turned back to Adale. "So you two knew each other in Paris?"

Adale had tried to explain between waiting on hungry people. "We did. I was sixteen, and he was eighteen. My parents were okay when we talked all night at the party we'd attended. But once we started going around Paris together, my dad got worried."

"Couldn't have his firstborn staying in Paris," Mary Ann said with one of her knowing smiles. "Is that what you planned to do?"

"We weren't sure," Adale admitted, keeping in mind her mother might start listening. "We only knew we were madly in love and had to be together. We talked about me taking a foreign studies year there or him spending a semester at LSU. We were to meet that last night to form a plan and, well, say goodbye until we could get together again in one country or another."

"But he never showed up?"

"No."

Adaie glanced around, glad the crowds for the market were heavy with families today. The sound of zydeco music down on the main stage wafted through the late morning. The band always played fun songs for the schoolchildren. The sun wobbled between clouds as the last of the snow held on in shady spots.

"That must have hurt," her friend said after taking a sip of her latte from an insulated red Christmas cup that said: EAT, DRINK (COFFEE), AND BE MARY ANN.

"You can't imagine. Heartbroken. I'd never felt that way before, but as my mama kept saying, I was only sixteen. I had one more year of high school. I'd barely started dating." She shrugged, seeing the things she hadn't seen back then. "I only knew I loved him and didn't want those two weeks to end."

"But they did." Mary Ann waved to someone they both knew from church. "So you never heard from him again until now?"

"No." Adale glanced at her mother, who now stood talking to her crafting friends. "Mama says it's a God wink, but I think she orchestrated the whole thing."

"Maybe she had a sign or God did wink at her, so she went with it," Mary Ann suggested. "You have every right to meet someone, Adale."

Adale thought about that. "You know, it's strange. No word about him or from him. But she said she'd read an article in *Southern Living*—that's how she found out he'd moved to New Orleans. She never mentioned it—citing letting bygones be bygones."

"Again, a good point. You were a married woman for close to thirty years."

Adale nodded. "See, this is why I'm telling you all these things. I need someone levelheaded and not fully involved to set me straight."

Mary Ann burst out laughing. "I've never been called levelheaded before."

"But you will set me straight, right?"

"You want my honest opinion?"

"Always."

"I think your mother saw Rémy at her party and took that as a good sign, just like Rémy heard from Cameron and took that as a sign. It all came together, and while you were ambushed with a surprise you'd never seen coming, that could be the only way for it to happen."

"Okay, I get that," Adale admitted. "But what kind of sign should I look for now?"

Mary Ann glanced around. "How about this one? The man in question is walking our way, and he's smiling to beat the band."

Adale whirled to glance down the food corridor. Sure enough, Rémy strolled toward their booth, determination on his handsome face.

"That's not a sign," Adale hissed as she straightened her hair. "That's just Rémy being annoying."

"And looking fine doing it," Mary Ann said before popping a hand over her mouth. "I'll have my lunch over there with your mama."

"No, don't leave me."

But too late, her friend had whirled like a tornado to the back of the booth.

"Hello," Rémy said, waving to Eloise and Mary Ann before looking toward Adale. "This is a nice festival."

"Have you toured every booth?"

"I have," he admitted. "I shopped a bit; then I saved the best for last. I hear the Cajun Cooking muffulettas are the best around."

"Everything in Moreau is the best around," she said with pride. "We do know how to eat good food."

"Well, it seems that's all you and I do, but I'm not complaining. When is your shift over?"

"Who wants to know?"

"I thought we could bundle up and take a nice drive out into the countryside. I have a small car, but we can put the top down. You'd need a hat."

"I haven't agreed to go."

"We need to be away, Adale. Alone so we can really talk without any outside help."

"You do have a point there." Her mother and Mary Ann were pretending to talk to Chef Perot, but she knew all three were discussing her and Rémy. Or possibly arguing about crawfish étouffée.

"My shift ends at noon, but I promised Mama we'd share a muffuletta. Can you wait?"

"I can wait," he said, as if he'd been doing that a long time. "Or if you don't mind, I could eat my lunch with you two, and after you get Eloise home, I'll come pick you up."

"I should be at the community center doing things."

"Your crew has taken care of today's to-do list," he said. "I've been there most of the morning. The volunteers are ticking off each task."

Thinking that was thoughtful of him, she said, "The ball is coming up fast. Only a few days now."

"It will be perfect." He studied her. "Or are you looking for an excuse to stay away from me?"

"Maybe. It's still surreal, having you back in my life."

"Let's pretend. How would you see me if you'd just met me?"

Adale had to admire that bold question, but her heart pinged away in a warning. However, she had to be honest. "I'd get to know you. Ask you what you do for a living. Who your people are, of course. Then I'd invite you to dinner with my family and show you our beautiful town. I'd consider you someone who might become a good friend."

"I think we can agree to check all those things off your list. We can be friends, Adale. If that's all we'll ever be, it will be more than I ever hoped for."

His gaze moved over her face again. "What are you thinking?"

"I'm thinking we do need to go for a drive to really talk, Rémy. We're not teenagers anymore. Now there's no one to stand in our way."

"Exactly," he said, a frown clouding his expression. "So we'll take things slow and enjoy the ride."

"I can live with that," she said. "But I can't stay gone too long."

"I'll have you home long before dark."

Adale ordered their food. When the next crew came in and the booth got busy with the lunch crowd, she waved to the chef, then walked with Mary Ann, Mama, and Rémy to find a picnic table with a tall heater sending warmth out into the air. They all settled in to eat. She was glad for the company.

Then Mary Ann surprised her by saying, "I can take Eloise home, Adale. That way you and Rémy can leave from here for your drive."

Eloise winked at her. "I asked her for a favor."

"How thoughtful, Mama," Adale said.

"Signs, darling," her mother whispered. "They are everywhere."

Adale chewed on a mint and fluffed her hair. She'd worn a wide warm quilted band across her ears to keep the chill away, so now she had hat hair. She placed that same grayish band back over her head. Rémy had said she'd need a hat.

After leaving the public bathroom, she threw on her navy walking coat over her jeans and boots. Her turtleneck would help with the warmth.

The market had settled down now that the lunch crowd had come through. It would close soon but reopen tonight. She searched the entryway and saw Rémy talking to Frank Miller.

Oh dear.

The two men greeted her with awkward half waves.

"Adale," Frank said, his smile forced, "I heard you're going for a ride with our distinguished visitor. I'd hoped to interview him for the paper."

"I'm surprised our Mattie didn't beat you to that, Frank," she said, smiling at her friend. "She'd love that opportunity."

"Either way, we'd have an exclusive."

They all stood silent for a moment.

Rémy reached for Frank's hand. "I'll be happy to talk to you and Mattie about our plans, as long as it's approved. I don't want to overstep."

Frank shot him a look that indicated he'd already done that, but her friend remained professional. "I'll let Mattie know. She's like a dog with a bone once she gets on a story. I know she'll want to hear this one."

His eyes danced over Adale's face. "Good to see you. Take care."

"Good to see you too, Frank."

The newspaper man walked away, his big shoulders slumped.

"I see you still have it," Rémy said as he guided her to a tiny white sports car.

"Have what?" she asked, distracted by how close together they'd be in this go-cart.

"That charm that attracts people to you. Frank has it bad."

"He's a friend," she said, hoping her blush wasn't showing. "We've had dinner together once or twice."

"He's not happy that you're with me, but then not everyone is."

"He wants a story, and he thinks I'm part of your story."

"Exactly," Rémy said as he opened her door for her. "He's not happy that we have a past."

She slid in and adjusted her knees away from the dashboard. "Well, he's not the only one."

She might get claustrophobic in this munchkin of a car where she'd be too close to Rémy.

Rémy got in and cranked the engine. It purred like a little kitten. "It's chilly still. Top up or down?"

"Down," she said, gasping for breath. She'd be okay with the cold air flowing over her. It could knock some sense into her head.

Not a good idea. Not good at all. When would she learn to say no to Rémy Vachon? Maybe she should consider another date with Frank. But Frank, as dear as he was, didn't make her heart flutter or her pulse race.

This man did. Still. Maybe even more so now. That realization made her want to open the door and run.

Too late. The little car took off like a rocket, and soon the sun heated her face and the wind whipped at her hair. Adale forgot the rest of the world, even if her mind shouted this had been a bad idea.

Rémy drove the car along the river road, heading out of town. Winter had stripped most of the trees bare and tossed the live oaks here and there, but those giants still mushroomed a nice canopy over the two-lane country road. The sun shone like a Christmas tree ornament overhead. Rémy turned on the seat warmers and raised a heavy see-through screen behind them to knock the wind off.

"Fancy little machine," she said, admiring the black leather and the clean lines. "You obviously live the good life."

"I have a good life," he admitted, his smile soft, his eyes intense. "I have friends all over the world, and I've helped renovate some amazing buildings and homes. I can't complain."

"Me either," she said. "Although I do at times."

When he spotted an overlook with a picnic table, he pulled the car off the road. "It might be easier to talk without the wind in our faces."

Adale opened the door to get out, her earlier fears about being close to him now simmering. Having the top down helped, but mercy, the man smelled like sunshine and a forest and looked like he should be in this car on the cliffs of Monaco, not some bumpy country road near Moreau.

He was still so handsome and charming. Didn't that go away with age? Or did it just mellow into perfection?

Adale tried to fluff the hair underneath her headband. Not much to do but smile and work at staying calm.

They walked toward the table, not touching but not too far apart.

Rémy turned to lean against the old, worn wood. "Are you still mad at me, Adale?"

"Yes," she said without any fanfare. "I think I have that right."

"I'm sorry," he said, his head down. He lifted his gaze to her. "I'm so sorry. I was young and stupid and. . .confused."

"That's too bad," she replied. "I believed in us. But it's okay. I had a good life. I loved my husband. I miss him every day."

"I'd expect no less from you," he said, his hands in the pocket of his buttery-tan leather jacket. "I'm so glad you had a happy, good marriage. Jolene is a joy. Such a talented intense girl but with that same *joie de vivre* you had when we met."

Adale took that in, remembering how young and carefree she'd felt in Paris. "I guess I had to outgrow that? Or. . .I lost it that night."

She saw the anguish in his eyes but continued. "Are you ever going to explain to me, Rémy?"

He looked thoughtful. Then he looked defeated. "I can only say that I had no choice at the time. But I should have let you know, sent word, left a note at your door. Something. Chalk it up to being young and unsure—"

"—unsure of us?"

"Non. It wasn't like that. Very much sure of us. I was not so sure of everything else. It's hard to explain all the feelings I felt being with you, getting to know you, watching you walk away."

Adale zoomed in on that. "You watched me walk away? Is that a metaphor, or were you there that night, after all, Rémy?"

Chapter Eight

Rémy saw the hurt in her beautiful eyes. He'd done it again. He'd hurt her, but if he told her the truth—that her father forced him to let her go home—she'd be angry at her father. Rémy knew in his heart, Oliver Marchand had confronted Rémy because he wasn't ready to let his little girl run off with a man she barely knew. A man who might not be able to give her the life she deserved.

"You were nearby then?" she asked, her tone firm, her eyes devoid of any emotion.

"I stood on the bridge down the way—our favorite bridge—and I watched, hidden, so you couldn't see me."

Adale moved away, whirled around. "Hidden because you were a coward."

"I wanted to go to you, tell you how much I loved you, but I couldn't."

She nodded, her eyes moist now. "Was it my age, Rémy? Or that I'm Southern and I wouldn't fit in?"

"You'd have fit in, Adale. You can charm anybody, anywhere, and I loved—*love*—your accent. Your age did factor in." He sighed and tapped a boot against a rock. "I didn't want you to give up some of the best years of your life for me."

More so, her father hadn't wanted her to waste the best years of her life on someone who might hurt her. Yet, they'd both wound up doing that very thing.

"The best years of my life?" She looked shocked, anger flaring in her eyes with firework intensity. "For the next few years, I thought of you and only you. My daddy brought Pierre home for dinner one night, and well, I knew I needed to find a good man to marry. Pierre was that man. We'd known each other all our lives, so it just fell into place. He was older and in law school, and I had my senior year at LSU. I planned to teach school or find an office job. We fit. We made it work. I truly loved him, but we both worked hard those first few years. Then I found the *best years of my life*—my family, my church, my community. My world. You weren't in it."

"I didn't belong in it." He pushed off the tabletop and stared out over the trees. "Maybe I don't belong here either."

"You might be right," she said, wiping at her eyes. "If you felt that way then, why would you come here now? Did you come for the work, knowing you might run into me? Or did you come for the work and had no choice but to seek me out once my mother set this up?"

Without thinking, Rémy walked up to her, then put his hands on her arms. "The work is important to me, but Adale, make no mistake about it. I came here for you. I want to be the man I should be, the man you can forgive. I want a new start, not one where we left off. I want—"

"—forgiveness?" She stepped back, away from him. "I know I'm supposed to forgive, and looking back, I can see we might have been impulsive and irrational, but what I'll never understand is why you didn't have the courage to tell me these things to my face."

"I have the courage now," he said, weary with wishing for so many things. "I've prayed about this, asked God to grant me grace. I was young and foolish, and I loved you enough to let you go. The hardest thing I've ever done."

"Worse than letting me leave without any answers? Without so much as a goodbye?"

He wanted to say yes, the worse few months turned into years of poring over his studies, learning his craft, and yet still aching with regret. But he knew she'd suffered because of his actions. Because of her father's threats and intimidation. Because of Rémy's fears and doubts. He'd often wondered if her mother knew what had happened. He'd prayed Eloise had told Adale the truth. He didn't doubt now. No one had explained any of this to Adale. That much was obvious.

"It was tough on both of us in different ways. You got married, and you have a beautiful, creative daughter. I, on the other hand, never found the right person to spend my life with. I tried, several times, but it never worked out."

"And that's my fault?"

"No, it's all my fault," he replied. "No one else would do."

She stared over at him, shock shifting to disbelief, anger softening to surprise. "You dated, tried to meet someone special, and yet you didn't?"

He tugged her back. "I did meet someone special when I was eighteen and stupid. Now I'm pushing sixty, and apparently I'm still stupid."

Adale sank down on the picnic table. "Unbelievable. You aren't saying what I think you're saying, are you?"

Rémy sat down beside her and took her hand. "I'm saying that exactly. I never found anyone I wanted to spend the rest of my life with. I always compared any woman I dated to you, Adale. You're a tall order."

"I'm just me," she said. "I'll always be just me."

"You'll always be that girl to me, though. The girl I enjoyed taking around Paris. The girl who could light up a room with charm and manners and such a sweet soul. I like that girl. I like just you."

She got up and crossed her arms over her coat. "The girl you left sitting there while you stood on a bridge and watched. You do realize this is even worse than not showing up. Standing there. So close and so distant." Taking off toward the car, she called back, "I'm not that girl anymore, and I won't be fooled again. I need to get home. I have a million things to do before the ball Saturday night."

Rémy had no choice but to follow her. She'd been so close to understanding. But how could she forgive him if he couldn't even tell her the truth? He didn't want to break her heart all over again by confessing her powerful father had told him to get lost. Told him he wasn't good enough for Adale Lavigne-Marchand. At the time, Rémy didn't *feel* good enough. He had very little money just starting out in his chosen school of architecture. He had to work to help pay for it.

His family put on a good front, but they came from old money that had long run out. Then his father had started drinking to soothe his shame, and they'd finally had to let go of the home that had been in their family for over a century. He'd been too ashamed to tell her the truth. Even now, he was still ashamed. And the reason he tried to save old historical homes. Saving houses meant one thing, but having a home meant quite another. Would his past ever let him truly have a home of his own again? Or the one woman he'd loved for most of his life?

Standing here, watching her walk back to the car, Rémy accepted that he'd never be able to tell her the whole story without hurting her even more. Without the shame of his life laid out in front of her.

He got in the car and put the top up. A cloud had brought the chill back.

The way Adale hugged the passenger-side door held the cloud over them until he dropped her off where she'd left her car.

He got out and walked around, but she was already walking away.

"Adale," he called, "can you at least consider forgiving me?"

She pivoted to face him. "Like I always say, I can forgive, but I can't forget. You stood on that bridge and watched me sitting there alone, waiting, wondering. Now that I know that, I surely won't ever forget it."

Then she got into her car, slamming the door before he could say anything more.

The rain started falling all around Rémy, reminding him of the mist he'd walked through on that horrible night so long ago.

———◆———

Adale poured herself into finishing up with the ball preparations. She had to pick up her dress on Friday, so Thursday she went over the food again and made sure the community center was clean and sparkling and that they had several members of the Moreau football team to help with valet parking. They worked every year to raise money for the team, then got to take turns bringing a plus-one into the ball once most of the cars were parked. They had to leave early, but she loved watching the coach round the boys and their dates up so they could get home early for Christmas Eve.

The tradition in the Lavigne home had always been the ball, then opening one gift when they got home—all gussied up, as Mama liked to say. Adale remembered Jolene and Mattie, along with Adale's sister, Claudia, and Mama—even Daddy way back—entering the house in their finery, the girls usually wearing pink or blue, tugging off their dress shoes, plopping down to open one gift, and then having hot chocolate and cookies before going to bed. As the years passed, Adale and Pierre moved into the big house, where this tradition always took place. Once it got late, Claudia and her no-good husband would hurry Mattie to their house down the street. Later, after Daddy died, Mama would walk to her cottage.

Then Pierre and Adale would tuck Jolene in and go back to dance in front of the fire or sit and cuddle.

Now as she nursed a cup of coffee in the empty kitchen, she remembered those special times while she tried to forget being with Rémy earlier in the week. She hadn't seen him yesterday, but she knew he'd worked on plans for the chapel and managed to get in some last-minute work at the community center. Jolene had told her that much.

Adale had done some heavy praying, which made her decide she'd forgive him. He'd be gone in a few weeks, and she could tolerate him until then. She *would* tolerate him. After all, forgiveness worked more for the forgiver than the one needing the grace. What did it matter now, when she'd had a good life, a life she'd never change if she had the choice. They'd thought they were in love, but things might have taken a different turn once they'd gone back to living in different countries. Could she really blame Rémy for letting her go? He must have thought the same, standing on that bridge so close to her.

Maybe it had been the noble thing to do.

Her heart had cracked an inch or so, trying to reason why he'd done what he'd done. But oh, they were so young. Had she held this grudge for too long?

Jolene came in and yawned, her long hair rumpled, her robe worn but a bright turquoise that made one blink.

"Hey, honey," Adale said. "Coffee's fresh."

Jolene walked like a zombie toward the coffeepot. "Thank you."

After she had a few sips, she walked over to Adale. "You love to stand at this window and watch the river flow, don't you?"

"I reckon I do," Adale said, forcing a smile. "How are you doing?"

Jolene ran a hand through her hair. "I'm okay. The mural is finished. I hope everyone will like it and see it the way I see it."

"I'm sure your artwork will shine, honey. It's always good to have a fresh perspective on things. Allowing the whole community to help is a genius idea."

Jolene stared at the river, her expression somber. "I hope so." Then she perked up. "I'm looking forward to the ball, then cinnamon rolls on Christmas morning."

"So you did miss the cinnamon rolls?"

"Always." Jolene grinned, then turned serious. "Mom, tell me about you and Rémy."

"Oh, mercy. I'll need more coffee," Adale said, wondering how she could explain. "And if anyone comes in, we will finish later. I don't need the peanut gallery hearing all of this."

Jolene refreshed her coffee, and they sat at the corner of the breakfast table, facing the stairs so they could watch for any incoming stragglers. "I like Rémy, but I won't like him if he hurts you."

Adale wanted to blurt out that he'd done just that, but she'd had a long talk with God last night, her mostly talking and the Lord listening, so she was better prepared to speak to her daughter about this now.

"We were both hurt, but we were also very young. When I look back now and think how young, I'm surprised your grandparents didn't lock me in the hotel room."

Jolene smiled, grabbed a piece of sweet potato bread with walnuts, and slathered it with butter. "Granny would be good at that. Grandpa, not so much."

Adale let that slide too. "They were both very protective, but actually, your grandmother understood young love. She let me sneak out during the day. Not after dark, however."

"Wow, a new revelation. Imagine Granny going rogue on Grandpa."

"She's always been a rogue, darling, and the only one who could ever stand up to Oliver Marchand."

"Back to Rémy, Mom."

"What can I say? We met at a boring adult function, and we talked all night. He was so handsome and charming, and that accent—" She held her hand to her heart. "Not drawling and sweet like your daddy's but. . .all the same."

"I get it," Jolene said, no judgment in her eyes. "You fell for him?"

"I did. And he fell for me, or so I thought."

"Paris and young love. I think that's still a thing."

"Always a thing, yes. We were together for hours at a time almost every day. His parents didn't approve either. They had an old name attached to old money. They expected him to marry someone within his social standing."

"But how does that song you and Daddy liked go?" Jolene tried to quote the Eagles. "All the debutantes in Texas, baby, couldn't hold a candle to you."

"The Long Run," Adale said, laughing. "Well, they could, but the Moreau debutantes sure had a run for their money." She waved her hand in the air. "Your daddy and I had our own long run. Anyway, our parents did not encourage Rémy and me because after my senior year of high school, I'd head off to LSU and he'd start design and architectural school. We had a lot between us, starting with an ocean."

"So you broke up?"

Adale nodded. "He never showed up on my last night there. I waited at our favorite sidewalk café, but. . .Rémy never came. I had to leave the next morning."

She couldn't bring herself to tell Jolene he'd been there on the bridge not far from the café. The same bridge her mother had painted in the picture of them.

"I never saw him again until the night of Granny's party."

Jolene lowered her eyes, her long lashes hiding her shock, then she looked back up at Adale. "I asked you once, and I need to know. Did you love Rémy more than you loved my daddy?"

Chapter Nine

Adale wasn't sure how to answer that, but she knew the truth. "I loved your daddy, Jolene. With all my heart. I miss him every day."

Jolene bobbed her head. "I know you loved him, but were you in love with him? In that way that Rémy made you feel?"

"That's a tough comparison. I loved your daddy for most of my life, still love him. I knew Rémy for two weeks when I was sixteen."

"But you loved him then."

"I did, as much as a teenager could love anyone."

Saying these things out loud sure put a new perspective in Adale's head.

"But now you love Daddy more."

"Yes, honey. I fell for your daddy once we started dating. I'll admit I was still hung up on Rémy when I started college, but I dated, had fun, and the sting of his rejection lessened. Once I got to college, I saw Pierre Broussard around campus, but he was about to graduate and head right into law school. I figured we'd pass each other and wave. But your granddaddy had seen us flirting at a pool party on spring break, so he had Pierre over for dinner one night."

Jolene finally smiled. "That's when you fell in love. That's the story you both always told everyone. Is it true?"

"Of course it's true." Adale wanted her daughter to understand. "You know, people can have more than one love in a lifetime before they find the one."

Jolene finally let out a sigh. "Daddy was the one, then."

"The one and only," Adale said. "But now Rémy is here, and I'm not sure how I feel about that. It's brought back all the old feelings."

"Even the love feelings?"

"I don't know. Maybe. But it's hard to forget how we left things, and now we really don't know each other. We're not the same, of course."

Jolene sat back in her chair. "You know, when I first got here, I felt all the old feelings. Not being good enough or perfect enough, a failure, you name it. But the more I hung around and let go of my guilt over Daddy's death, the more I wanted to be forgiven for leaving. Cameron helped a lot with that. I'm here to stay now, Mom. All those misconceived notions are gone. Maybe you should consider that with Rémy."

Adale let out a gasp. "I'm so thankful that you're staying and that you have Cameron now. Earlier, you seemed concerned about all of this, and now you want me to give Rémy a second chance?"

"You gave me one," her daughter pointed out. "You always forgive people, Mom. The fact that you can't forgive Rémy for something that happened last century means you still have feelings for him. Feelings you might have pushed away because you loved Daddy and me so much."

Adale poured her cold coffee in the sink. "When you put it like that—"

"So it makes sense, right? You need to forgive Rémy or at least stop fretting about him being here. He's a good man, a well-established faithful man who is comfortable in his own skin. Until you walk into a room."

Adale tried to hide her smile. "I haven't noticed."

"Yes, you have," Jolene said. "Go for it, Mom. I miss Daddy every day, and I know you do. But. . .you deserve a second chance too, don't you think?"

Adale studied the Christmas runner she'd placed along the old counter. Poinsettias and sparkling gold danced before her eyes. "I reckon I've been a pill about this."

Jolene held her thumb and index finger together. "Just a little bit."

Adale nodded. "I'll do better. I'd already decided that myself after a long night of praying. I can forgive Rémy and I can put up with him being here, but the forgetting, honey, that's the part I struggle with."

"It's a new start, Mom. You're never too old for that, are you?"

"No, I suppose not. But I'm scared."

"Of what? Being alone? Or loving again?"

"Both," Adale admitted. "Both."

Granny walked into the room and stared at them. "Who died?"

Jolene burst out laughing. Adale did the same.

"Well, it must have been someone neither of you liked."

"Mama, nobody died. We were having a mother-daughter conversation."

"I see," her mother said with a sniff. "Well, I'm a mother. I have a daughter. Shouldn't I have been in on this conversation?"

"Do you have to be in on all conversations?" Adale asked, giving her a warning glare.

Eloise grabbed at her white tufts of hair sticking out in all directions. "I suppose not, even if I am the old wise one around here." She headed for the coffee. "I probably don't even want to know anyway," she said with her nose in the air.

Jolene glanced at her watch. "I have to go to work. I don't want to be late, because Cameron and I are going to go over the finished mural and make sure it's as near perfect as possible."

"Bye, honey," Adale said. "I sure enjoyed our talk."

"Me too, Mom." Jolene threw her an air kiss and then actually kissed Granny. "Love you, Granny."

"Love you too."

Eloise waited a beat and then turned to Adale. "What just happened?"

Adale wasn't ready for a heart-to-heart with her mother yet. "We had a nice girl talk about her being back for good."

"Back for good." Eloise smiled. "I'm so glad to hear that. We're gonna have the best Christmas!"

"Yes, we are," Adale replied, her mind on Rémy. "All of us, I hope."

———◆———

Adale went to the community center for one last walk through. Her dress was ready. The caterer would start bringing in the food early Saturday morning.

The local weather forecasters had said the snow might return in time for Christmas, but she doubted that. One early snow in Louisiana had been a rare treat. Another one in the same month would be too much to expect. But then, this Christmas had been full of surprises.

One being the man who glanced up at her as she entered.

Rémy looked great in worn jeans, an old navy-blue sweatshirt, and work boots, his hair all tossed and messy.

Give me strength, she silently prayed.

He nodded and went back to his work.

Oh, so that's how it was going to be now.

Well, she deserved a brush-off or two. She'd tried to be polite, but sometimes being polite could be the worst insult of all.

"Hey, Miss Adale," Cameron called out as he walked pass. "Looking festive."

"Thank you, Cameron," she said, taking the brownies she'd baked after breakfast to the snack table. "I'm looking forward to seeing you tomorrow night."

Cameron looked a little bashful. "I'm looking forward to having Jolene as my date."

Adale laughed. "She's excited about that too."

She walked right on past Rémy, who now ignored her, then whirled around. "Hello."

He stopped his hammering and looked behind him. "Oh, were you addressing me?"

She put her hands on her hips. "Maybe."

He moved around one of the Christmas trees they'd made from shipping pallets.

Adale admired the white dusted trees with gold painted stars sparkling on them. Someone, Rémy she guessed, had trimmed the tips of each cut-out branch with heavy white that looked like snow.

"Those are pretty."

"Thank you."

"Can you take a break?"

He didn't even look up. "I don't know. The chairperson is a tyrant."

Adale finally got humble. "Rémy, I need to speak to you in private."

That got his attention, along with every else's. It had been a long time since Adale has turned so many heads. She kind of liked it.

He wiped his hands on a towel, dusted the gold off his blue jeans, and lifted an arm, but he didn't look happy. "Lead the way, Madame Chairperson."

"Let's take a walk," she said. She still had on her coat, but she waited for him to grab his from the counter.

He didn't speak. He wasn't going to make this easy.

Finally, he said, "What's this about, Adale?"

"A lot of things," she said as they strolled along until they reached the river. "I wanted to apologize."

Rémy stopped dead still. "I'm sorry. Would you repeat that, please?"

She tapped his leather jacket sleeve. "You heard me right, Rémy. I've been bitter and mean and way too polite."

"Polite?" He nodded. "You had a duty to fulfill, Adale, and you handled it with class and grace. In fact, I think I can safely say you are the politest woman in all of Louisiana."

Adale frowned at his tone, then found her favorite bench. Leaving room for him to join her, she sat down. He did too, but with caution.

The river gurgled and curled, ever moving, ever changing.

"No, I haven't handled you being here with any class or grace. I ran from you that first night, remember? I'm the coward. Then I pushed you away and really showed myself. I wanted to say I'm sorry and, well, the past has to be the past, doesn't it?"

Rémy gave her an unsure once-over, probably thinking she'd hit her head or had a serious fever. "I would like that, oui. Our two weeks together were special, but you're right—you're not that girl anymore and I'm not that boy. We're adults now. We can make our own decisions. I will abide by whatever decision you choose to make. I've run out of excuses, and I don't expect forgiveness."

She let that settle over her with a chill. "But you still haven't told me the truth."

"I've told you what I know to be the truth," he responded. "But last night I went over everything in my head, and I understand you can't accept my flimsy apologies. So I will have to accept that it's over between us, Adale. The past and the here and now."

"What about our truce?"

He turned, his eyes full of torment and regret. "I want more than a truce. I want us back. No, change that. I want to get to know *you*. We didn't have enough time then, and we don't have enough time now. I came here for good reasons, but my hope for us might be the one wrong reason."

Afraid he was about to walk out of her life again, Adale took a long breath, held it, and then let it go. "I want peace, Rémy. That's my decision. Things are good for me right now. My daughter is home, and she's found a wonderful person to spend her life with, if that's her choice. My mama is safe and comfortable in our home, so I don't have to fret about her anymore. We have always had a relationship that's like a tug-of-war. But we make it work, and I respect her and love her. Now you're here and it's so amazing, but I got so caught up in being angry with you that I forgot to enjoy the amazing part."

She lifted her hand to the sun. "It's like when God gives you a perfect sunset, but you miss it because you're on your phone or not in the moment or not even listening. You forget to look at the world's beauty. You finally glance up, and the sun has set. It's dusk, and the gloaming shows you only part of what you could have seen." Then she shrugged. "I'm not making any sense, am I?"

"You're making perfect sense." His eyes held resolve now "We only had the afterglow in Paris. We saw the tip of the sunset before it vanished behind the buildings and trees. We couldn't see the whole beauty of it. Here, we could have been able to see the sunset in all its glory for a long time." He stopped, stared out at the water. "And possibly the sunrise too."

"We might have," she replied. "But if I'm being honest—and I'm trying hard to enjoy the beauty and the blessing of seeing you again—it will take some time. I'm scared. I'm doubtful. I'm old and ornery, set in my ways. I don't like change or surprises or remembering things I've tried so hard to forget. But. . .for now, I'm glad you're here. It's been an exciting few days, so I don't want to ruin Christmas, the ball, or anything else with my pouting and fuming."

"I never wanted to ruin Christmas either," he said. "I had thought this might be my best Christmas in a long time. Because I'd be with you and your family here in Moreau, which I really do love, by the way."

"That's important to me, that you understand this is my home and I do care deeply about it."

They sat silent for a moment, then she turned to face him. "So here's what I'm proposing." She took his hand. "I'm sorry. And I mean it this time."

Rémy grabbed her hand and held it in his, his gaze wandering over her rings and bracelets. "I'm sorry too. None of us should have surprised you the way we did at your mother's party. When I look back on it, I cringe."

"So do I, but for different reasons. Surprise is an understatement," she said, her heart feeling light and free now. "I didn't handle it very well, but that's all behind us, and so is Paris. I'd like to start over—no promises—just hope."

"I don't know if I can stay," he said, his gaze holding hers. "It's hard to see you when you still seem so dead set against me."

Adale's good mood vanished. She felt foolish for acting like a silly schoolgirl. "I'm trying to do better, Rémy. Are you saying you don't want a friendship or anything to do with me?"

"I'm saying I won't push you anymore. I won't ruin your Christmas. I won't even bother you for a walk."

"But what about your promise to help with the renovations?"

"I can do that and avoid you. I'll be so busy, I probably won't think about anything else. I booked the room at Nadine's for a month at least, but I plan to go back to New Orleans on weekends."

"I see," she said, her heart dropping like an elevator hitting the final floor. "That's fine, then. So be it." Her pride made her sweat underneath her jacket. But she held up her head. "We should get back. I've got things to do, and time is ticking away. You know, a manicure, getting my hair trimmed. Got to put on some color, or as Mama would say, paint the old barn door."

Rémy turned to her. "You look beautiful right now."

Adale patted her windblown hair while she tried to gain control. "As I said before, I'm just me. But the Christmas Eve ball calls for one looking one's best. I hope you have a tuxedo."

"I don't know if I'll be attending the ball. I'm going back to New Orleans this afternoon. One of the renovations there had some permit issues. I have to take care of things."

"Now? You have to go back now? People are expecting you at the ball."

She'd been expecting him at the ball. But she'd treated him so horribly, he didn't want to be around her now.

"No one will notice if I'm not there."

She chuckled at that. "Oh, I think a lot of people will notice." She wouldn't tell him she'd notice. Or that she'd been looking forward to being with him there. "Jolene talked about you this morning."

His smile was bittersweet. "She's a smart, accomplished woman. Like you in many ways."

"Why won't you stay? We can't waste any more time sparring with each other when we need to stop and enjoy the holidays and the meaning of this season. It's a time of joy and. . .forgiveness."

"Because while you might be willing to forgive me, you're not ready to actually tolerate me or. . .take the next step. The step we missed all those years ago."

"Rémy," she said, her words wobbly and unsure, "is there something else between us, something you can't tell me?"

He gave her a look that shattered the rest of her dignity. "I don't want to hurt you anymore, Adale. You were very clear last night. It's better this way."

"If that's how you feel, then I'm glad we reached this understanding," she said, starting back toward the community center. "I need to go."

She hurried away before she burst into tears. She should be relieved, since she knew he'd been holding something back. But her feet felt weighed down, and her heart pumped with a bruised pace that took her breath away.

She'd lost him again, and this time it hurt even more because she still loved him and she still didn't know the truth.

Chapter Ten

The weather took a turn for the worse on Friday. The temperature dropped after the rain passed through overnight. No ice or snow yet, but Adale worried it might hit again soon. Most of the people could walk to the community center, but not if the sidewalks became icy and slippery.

Even that possible scenario didn't worry her as much as what Rémy had said to her last night. She'd gone straight home, told her mama she was exhausted, and then went to bed. And cried and wondered and prayed.

Why had she been so foolish? If he really wanted to make up for the past and be with her now when they were both beyond mature, why couldn't he open up to her? How could they move forward with so much still between them?

She had to focus on getting through this ball, because instincts told her Rémy wouldn't show up tonight. He was right about one thing. He had hurt her after all.

She left early and went to the community center to take her mind off Rémy. The caterers began bringing in the food prep supplies and started setting up in the kitchen so they could carry food to the tents out behind the kitchen. Mr. Tatum went over the last-minute details, assuring Adale he'd have heaters set out to keep the staff warm in the tents.

She went through the motions, her smile pasted tightly on her face, her eyes still puffy from a sleepless night. Her mother had taken one look at her this morning and asked, "What happened?"

"Not now," Adale had replied. "Not now, Mama."

Adale and her mama still needed to have a heart-to-heart talk, but Adale didn't want to make her own mood any worse before the ball or Christmas. Monday would come soon enough.

Now Adale's nerves were tangling themselves into a hissy fit. She glanced up as a certain person entered with a lot of fanfare, her earthy perfume announcing her from ten feet away.

Nadine Collins yelled hello in her nasal voice as she pushed a worker out of the way to head toward Adale. "Rémy told me he might not be back for the ball, Adale. What did you do to that man?"

Adale thought of speaking her mind, but instead she said, "I don't control him, Nadine. He can come and go as he likes."

"Oh, I see. So all the rumors might not be true after all. Rémy was sure in a mood when he told me goodbye last night. Trouble in paradise, I reckon."

Adale looked past Nadine's smug face. "Excuse me. Unless you're here to work, I can't help you." Then she took off to the back of the building.

Nadine, all glittered up in an undersized furry top rimmed with red sparkling ornaments that begged to win an ugly sweater contest, made a face. "You must have bored him to tears." Then she shrugged and walked out the door.

Adale's mind reeled just thinking about Nadine being the last person to tell Rémy goodbye. But she reminded herself this couldn't last, and now that he'd realized that, same as her, things would be easier. He'd be busy with renovating the chapel. She'd go back to her volunteer work and helping her mother get acclimated to being back in the big house. Not to mention, enjoying time with Jolene. A great new year. Rémy would be gone soon, so they couldn't get attached. Not this time. Not in the same way at least. They'd dodged a bullet, no doubt.

But she did doubt.

"You're thinking," her friend Mary Ann said, dragging her out of her musings. "Something on your mind?"

Mary Ann had helped so much this week, but Adale found it hard to share this hurt, even with her best friend. "No. Just considering how life will be after the holidays."

"You mean, once all of this is over and you have to go back to reality?"

"Yes. Rémy and I had a talk yesterday. We both feel it's best to go our own ways, not get too close again."

"Oh no. Are you sure that's what you want?"

Adale took a deep breath. "It's what I've wanted since he walked into this building a week ago. One week, and now—he might not come to the ball."

Mary Ann's green eyes widened. "You don't need to explain. You have feelings for him, and he obviously adores you. Maybe things happened too fast and he's rethinking."

"Or maybe he got tired of my rude remarks and how I pushed him away at every turn. I apologized and told him I'd forgiven him, but he'd already decided he'd had enough. He's doing the same thing he did long ago. He's running away."

———————

Rémy had only been there a week, but he liked Moreau. It held a mix of French and Cajun heritage that blended well and reminded him of the small villages back home. He'd traveled a lot in his career and gone back to Paris many times. He'd always visited the bridge where he'd stood so long ago as he watched Adale walk out of his life.

Now, back in New Orleans, he almost felt a relief. Had it been a mistake to pursue Adale? He hurt worse now than he'd hurt standing on that bridge in the mist.

He hadn't planned to live in America, especially not New Orleans, but God knew his path while he was making other plans. Now he stood watching the Mississippi River flow, wishing he could have had one dance with Adale at the ball. Because being with Adale and her family felt like home to him.

Cozy, loud, unassuming. Not distant and strained, the way his family had always been. His mother was dead, but his father, ever the prideful curmudgeon, had been living in a retirement facility in New Orleans for the past four years, paid for with the checks Rémy sent once a month. He tried to go by there as much as possible, and he knew his father was in good hands. Yet he worried and wished they could have been closer. He basked in the glow of Adale and her family. A faith-filled life with loved ones who weren't afraid to speak what they felt or to fight against their pain and problems by turning to God first.

He turned from the river and the chill of the wind. If she'd have him, he'd make a life with Adale. They could start fresh, with more wisdom and understanding, and have many good years together.

She hadn't made any promises, but she had changed her attitude toward him. But he didn't want to be a friend only. He didn't want a strained truce. He wanted love and all the complications that came with it. He'd always run away from love before, could never fully settle down. It hit him like a rogue wave from the water, that he could have been using his love for Adale as a shield because of his fear of loving anyone.

Even her. What if he told her everything and gave her the chance to really forgive him?

————◆————

That afternoon Adale stood in her kitchen making gumbo. With the cold weather coming on strong and her emotions roiling like a storm cloud, she needed comfort food.

Her mother walked into the kitchen after taking a nap. "Oh, gumbo. Is Rémy coming over tonight?"

Adale stirred the gumbo then turned to face her mother. "No. He had to return to New Orleans to check on one of his other renovations. Permits, or so that's the excuse he used."

Her mother gave her a long appraising stare. "I see. Well, he is a busy man, but surely he's coming back for the ball."

"He said he might not make it in time."

Eloise saw the corn bread waiting to go in the oven. Shaking the bread pan to help it settle, she said, "Rémy told me the night we talked that he had brought his father to New Orleans. He's in an assisted living facility, in the Alzheimer's wing. He might have gone back to check on him too."

Adale put a hand to her mouth. "He never mentioned that, and embarrassingly, I never asked. We really did have a lot to catch up on, but I think we're done with all that. We had a talk earlier today, and he's decided he's had enough."

"I see," her mother said. "Still, you're worried. Or maybe disappointed?"

"Both," Adale admitted, her nerves caving in. "I know he has to go, but I really want him here."

"Ah," Eloise said. "You have feelings for him again?"

"I do," Adale said. "I only now realized I've been fighting this with all I'm worth and I've failed. I thought this time things might go better. I can't even be mad, because this time he might have a legitimate excuse."

"And he didn't last time."

"No, except our age and the distance between us. But I know there's more, and that is the one thing holding me back." She shrugged. "He knows that too, but he refuses to be honest with me."

Her mother took her by the hand and tugged her toward the table. "We need to talk, darling. I'm the only one who can give you the answers you need on why Rémy didn't show up that night. I have to say, I'm glad this day has finally arrived. You need to know the truth, Adale."

———◆———

Adale got a glass of water with lemon and motioned toward the den. "We might as well enjoy the fire. We can eat our gumbo after we talk. That is, if I'm still hungry."

Her mother, dressed in a peach-colored tunic over light gray fleece lounging pants and furry booties, sank down as if she was about to be interrogated, her eyes full of something Adale rarely saw there. Regret. A true, deep, sad regret.

"Mother, you're beginning to scare me."

"Nothing to be scared about unless you dislike me afterward."

"Okay, stop with the drama, please, and start talking."

Her mother put down her drink. "Well, you were young and innocent and so full of life. Rémy was handsome, available, and a little older. At first we thought it was kind of sweet, but the more your father got to know Victor Vachon, the more worried he became."

"Why?" Adale had been so single-minded about Rémy, she hadn't thought much about his parents. "I thought the Vachons were a suitable family."

"That's what your daddy thought too. But trying to negotiate a business deal with them became difficult. The more he dug into their personal records and finances, the more Oliver understood that you couldn't be a part of that family."

Adale stared at her mother in shock. Her palms grew moist, her breathing harsh. "What are you saying?"

"The Vachons had no money, darling. They had their name, their lineage, and the home they inherited, which was falling apart around them. Your daddy went over there in good faith to negotiate a business deal on some property Victor needed to sell—not their home but still a nice commercial property. But the property didn't live up to the hype, so Oliver had to turn down the deal on behalf of his client. Things got ugly between the two of them."

Adale began to see the scenario. "So because Rémy's family was broke and his father drove a hard bargain, Daddy decided I couldn't be with Rémy, and you agreed?"

"It's a lot more complicated than that, Adale. Let's say we had agreed to you and Rémy continuing to be involved. Would you have given up your college education to stay there in France? Or go back there for an education? How would that work? We had money, but that's a lot to deal with, especially since Rémy had told you he might take courses at LSU. He would have had to find a job or take out a loan. A burden on him and you if you married him. Victor flat-out told your daddy they had no money for Rémy's schooling. He even implied we could help with that if we wanted Rémy for a son-in-law." Her mother paused for a moment. "Rémy's father had a drinking problem."

Adale stood and went to the fire, a chill coming over her. "I don't understand. Did Rémy give up on us because of this? Is that why he didn't show up to even explain? Because his father tried to barter a dowry from Daddy?"

Eloise brushed a hand over her hair. "No, darling. Rémy didn't show up that night because your father forbid him to do so."

Chapter Eleven

Adale went still, her head filling with scenes like a movie rolling by. Following that, she remembered conversations and things people had said to her.

> *"It wasn't his fault."*
> *"I never wanted to hurt you."*
> *"I had to let you go."*
> *"We were both so young."*
> *"You were both so young."*
> *"I had to do the right thing."*

Both her mother and Rémy had tried to tell her the truth, but neither of them had actually told her the whole truth.

She went to the kitchen window and stared out toward the river. "My daddy told Rémy not to meet me at the café that night?"

Eloise followed her back into the kitchen. "He met with him earlier and explained what he knew about the family. He wouldn't tell anyone, of course, but he wanted Rémy to understand. We liked

Rémy, thought he was a fine young man, but you couldn't walk into that tangled mess."

"You decided this on my behalf, or on the behalf of daddy losing this account."

"We decided this in your best interest," Eloise said. "In the end, your father did help finance Rémy's education."

· Adale whirled, dizziness overtaking her. "As a bribe? Did Rémy break my heart over money?"

"No." Her mother held up her hand. "No. He only told Rémy he had to do the right thing. That you were young and impressionable and about to go off to college in a year. You were still in high school, Adale. It became an impossible situation, but we thought you'd both get over it."

"Yet Daddy made it convenient for Rémy to agree? Offering him what he needed more than he needed me—money."

Eloise shook her head. "Your father didn't bribe Rémy. Rémy never knew about his father's suggestion to Oliver. We came home, and then the years went by. Oliver kept in touch because he liked Rémy. He found out where he was going to school, and, well, he helped finance a scholarship for that particular school of architecture. You see, our ancestors had helped start that college. It was easy to send money and nominate Rémy for the scholarship, and three years after Paris, honey."

Adale turned off the simmer on the gumbo, her appetite gone. "Then a year later, Daddy brought Pierre home for dinner."

"Yes, and that was that. We were so happy for you and Pierre. But I never forgot Rémy, and neither did your father. Rémy probably hasn't told you this, but they finally lost their home while he kept at his schooling. He worked his way through school, and renovating his family's estate was one of his first projects. They never got it back, but his salary helped his parents live comfortably in a small town in France for many years. He did the right thing, Adale. He did it out of love."

Adale sat down at the table, too weary to stand any longer. "All these years I blamed Rémy, held a dark place in my heart dedicated to hating him, being humiliated by him, left alone by him. When really, the whole time he was being noble and loving, only for all the reasons I never considered. Yet my own parents didn't have the strength to set me straight."

"I know," Eloise said. "I wanted to tell you so many times, but you were happy and thriving and living in our home, so I had you close by. I became selfish in my omissions. I didn't want to stir the pot. I didn't want to mess with a good marriage. It wouldn't have changed anything."

"Except my attitude," Adale said. "I wallowed in self-pity, Mama. I hated Rémy because I never knew he'd been manipulated, same as me. You all controlled our future."

Eloise sat down beside her and took her hand. "Not controlled or manipulated, Adale. Protected. Parents do that, as you well know. They protect their children as much as they can. You are a fine woman, a good woman who has a strong faith. That got you through the hurt of what we had to do. Your father's faith in you and Pierre, and in Rémy too, got you where you are today. Don't be mad at your daddy, honey. He loved you so much."

Adale felt a tear streaming down her cheek. "I loved Daddy. I did. Somewhere in the back of my mind, I blamed him though. I figured he'd had something to do with this, but Rémy never let on, never once accused him or told me what Daddy had done. To think of how horribly I treated him when I saw him here. I need to let all of this soak in, but now it might be too late. If he does happen to come back, I'm going to tell him the one truth I've discovered this week."

"That you love him again?"

She bobbed her head. "That I love him now and forever." Then she glanced out at the twinkling lights on the street. "In a way, it's as if Daddy and you with the meddling, then finding that portrait of Rémy and me, and Jolene coming home all happened exactly the way it should have happened." Then she let out a chuckle. "I did love Pierre, and I will always love him. He made me forget Paris."

"That's why I couldn't tell you this until now," Eloise replied. "I knew the night I saw Rémy standing there the time had come."

Adale shook her head and wiped at her eyes. "Really, what took you all so long?"

Eloise hugged her close. "Sometimes, sugar, we just have to wait on the Lord. He will never leave us comfortless."

Adale held tight to her mama. "He has never let me down, and having Rémy back proves we all did the right thing back then."

They sat like that for a moment. Then Eloise said, "Now, how about that gumbo?"

"And *It's a Wonderful Life*?"

"That would be lovely, darling."

The front door opened. They heard chatter and laughter.

Jolene and Mattie walked in with Cameron and Paul.

"Uh, we heard there's gumbo in this kitchen," Paul said with a grin.

"Sure is," Eloise said, getting up with a flourish. "We were about to eat. Then we're watching our favorite Christmas movie."

"*Die Hard?*" Cameron asked with hope.

Adale shook her head. "Not exactly."

Jolene glanced from her mother to her grandmother. "What did we miss?"

Eloise danced around. "Nothing for you to worry about. We had us a good heart-to-heart talk, is all. But it will remain between us."

Mattie threw down her big tote. "Oh, we'll get it out of you soon enough, won't we, Jolene?"

"You will not," their granny said with a lift of her eyebrows. "If you don't behave, you will not get any of the red velvet cake I ordered from that bakery in Hawkins."

Mattie and Jolene both nodded. "Okay, cake it is, then," Jolene said. Then she whispered loudly, "But later, after cake, we'll find out what's going on."

Adale laughed when she wanted to sit and cry. Now she really wanted to see Rémy at that ball so she could tell him she was sorry she ever doubted him. And that she loved him.

———◆———

Rémy finished up his business with time to spare, so on Saturday he'd gone by to see his father after meeting with his entire crew. The permit problems had been cleared up after he'd gone through several phone calls and different avenues up the line. He was frustrated, especially since one of his crew members hadn't filed the proper permits. Rémy didn't like firing workers, so he'd had a long talk with the man. One of his children had been sick, and the doctor bills and stress were both mounting. Rémy decided to give him another chance.

Rémy thought about Adale and wished she could give him a real second chance, not a polite pass while she had to be around him. Oh well, this might be for the best anyway. Maybe they were never meant to be together after all.

Now, after cleaning up some things that needed his attention, calling the client to assure her he'd get her job back on track, and having a quick meeting with all his employees on this job to remind them of what he expected, he'd finished up then hurried out the door. He wasn't sure if he should go back to Moreau. When he got in his car, he saw the bright red box he'd left under a stack of files. His gift to Adale—one he'd started on long ago. Last week he'd added one more layer to this special gift. Should he at least make an appearance and give this to her? Would that help soften her heart and open her trust?

He prayed for an answer to that question, an affirmation that his prayers had been heard. When he considered how she'd come so close to truly forgiving him, Rémy wished he hadn't told her things were over between them.

Another lie he'd told himself. Could he walk away again? He glanced at the little box and knew the answer to that. He would go back for one last try and one last dance.

A winter storm hovered to the west, but he had a few hours to get back on the road before the worst hit. He checked for any road closures and found the interstate roads were still open. If the state got any more snow, it would be late this afternoon or tonight at the earliest. He had a slim window of opportunity.

He'd left the French Quarter, headed for I-10, when his phone rang. "Rémy Vachon," he said after hitting the car's phone connection.

"Mr. Vachon, it's Linda from Dupont Assisted Living. Your father had a fall today after you left. He's all right, but he's asking for you. Are you still in town?"

"Yes," Rémy said, already looking for the next exit. "When I saw him earlier and told him about my next renovation in Moreau, he seemed in good spirits. What happened?"

"He got out of bed and came looking for you," the nurse explained. "He keeps saying he needs to make amends."

Rémy had no choice but to turn and hurry through the afternoon traffic to see his father again. He only prayed everything was all right and his father was just confused. He hoped he'd still be able to get to Moreau before dark.

He couldn't let Adale down a second time.

The Dupont Assisted Living Facility, located near I-10 in Metairie, wasn't hard to find. One of the reasons Rémy had chosen the Dupont. Close to New Orleans but easy to access by back roads if necessary.

He pulled into the winding drive, parked under a mushrooming live oak, then hurried inside. The nurses waved to him as he turned right to get to his father's apartment.

When he entered, a nurse was with his father. "Dad, are you feeling better?" Rémy asked as he approached the bed.

His dad had a dark bruise on the left side of his face. "I took a dive," he said, his voice weak. "But I was trying to find you."

At least Victor knew him today, Rémy thought as he glanced at the nurse.

"Mr. Victor's got something on his mind," she told Rémy. "I'll be nearby if you need anything."

Rémy nodded, then sat down beside the bed. "Why did you need to see me again, *Père?*"

Victor Vachon lifted his dark eyes to his son. "I wanted to say I'm sorry."

"Sorry?" Rémy thought of a million things that his father could apologize for, but he'd never heard Victor say he needed to apologize to him. "About what, Father?"

"Your girl," Victor said, his accent more noticeable with his anxiety. "Anna, Abigail, no, Adale, correct?"

"Oui," Rémy said. "Adale. What made you think of her today?"

"The television," Victor said, his eyes watery. "I saw the Eiffel Tower. I remembered Paris and our home."

Rémy nodded, unable to say anything. The home they'd lost, the life they'd lost. He hadn't handled it very well. Especially after losing the girl he loved too.

"That was a long time ago," he said. "You don't have to worry about all that now."

"But I do. Now is the time," Victor said. "Moreau is where she lives. You need to go to her, son."

In a winded voice, with many pauses and sips of water, he told Rémy the truth of what had really happened in Paris almost forty years ago. When he'd finished, his skin withered and pale, his hand clutching Rémy, he finally said, "Can you ever forgive me?"

Rémy sat numb with shock, regret, and a new understanding. He glanced out the window to see snow falling. The afternoon had turned dark, the skies a grayish white. What could he say? What did it matter now that his father had bartered with Rémy's heart, trying to get money in a horribly desperate way? No wonder Pierre Broussard had told Rémy to leave his daughter alone. Rémy had long wondered if this had something to do with his father. Victor drank too much, dreamed too much, and failed at every attempt to save their estate. Rémy had left, had gone off to college to get away from the chaos of his family's daily trials and fights. The guilt of that and how, for a few years, Pierre Broussard kept in touch, even though he didn't want Rémy to marry his daughter, still ate at Rémy.

He finally told his father, "I'm the one who should be asking for forgiveness. I did nothing to help you."

"But you made up for that," Victor said, his tone insistent. "You helped rebuild our home, and now it's beautiful again. You saved your mother and me and took care of us. She was so proud of you, Rémy. And I'm proud of you now. Go to your girl, son. She's waiting."

His father drifted off to sleep, leaving Rémy once again caught between two worlds. He didn't want to leave his dad, but he did want to find Adale and tell her everything. God had given him more than a sign. The Lord had finally answered his prayers with this explanation. It all made so much more sense now.

The nurse came in to check Victor's vitals. "He'll sleep the rest of the night. He doesn't have a concussion. Our doctor made sure of that. He needed to see you, is all."

"Should I stay?" Rémy asked, resolve in his question. "Is this it? Is he near death?"

"Mr. Vachon, you heard the man, and so did I when I came to the door. I don't know what all he said, but today's a lucid day. I think he needed to get some things off his chest. So go get your girl. That's all he's wanted all day long. He kept trying to remember so many things."

"I'm afraid to leave him," Rémy said. "I should stay."

"I promise I'll call you if anything changes. Your daddy's tired. Now that he's had his say on this matter, he can rest. You know, tomorrow he might not remember any of this, including you."

Rémy waited a few minutes; then he kissed his father's forehead, told the nurse to keep him posted, and turned to hurry back to the woman he'd been waiting for all of his life. Snow or no snow, he'd get back to Adale. Now that he knew the truth, he only wanted to hold her and tell her they were free and clear. And he'd do his best to be on time.

Chapter Twelve

A dale stared at her light pink manicure and wondered what to do next. She'd gone by the venue early this morning on her way to get her manicure. The whole place looked beautiful but not too overdone. Elegant and lovely.

They'd hired a DJ who would play both current and old songs along with Christmas music. She couldn't find anything left to do except get her hair to behave, but Kimberly planned to pull it back in a chignon of sorts.

When her phone buzzed, she tugged it out of her jacket pocket and saw a message from Rémy.

HAD TO MAKE A SIDE TRIP BUT ON MY WAY BACK. I HAVE A LOT TO TELL YOU.

He was coming back!

Adale texted back, her hand shaking as she tried to type. SAFE TRAVELS. THE SNOW IS COMING. I HAVE A LOT TO TELL YOU TOO.

She went home and sat down in the den by the fire, everything her mother had told her moving through her mind over and over. Adale wanted to be angry, needed to vent or rant or maybe have a good cry.

But she couldn't. Because despite her parents interfering and Victor's desperate try at manipulating them, she knew she'd had the life she'd been meant to have. She loved her little town here on the river. Loved the mix of Cajun, Creole, French, and everything in between. She'd loved her life here with Pierre, Jolene, and her over-the-top mama. She'd loved helping to raise Mattie. She'd loved her daddy, even when they'd disagreed. And she loved and missed her sister, Claudia, who'd helped her through the heartbreak of losing Rémy. She'd be laughing her head off right now.

Mattie and Jolene came down the stairs.

"Mom, there you are," Jolene said as she took a seat on the ottoman in front of the sofa. "Have you heard from Rémy?"

"Yes. He's on his way." She didn't elaborate.

Mattie went to one of the windows by the fireplace. "It's snowing, but it's light. The forecast says it could get worse later tonight. Snow for Christmas." She grinned big, reminding Adale of Claudia.

"You look like your mama with that big grin. She loved when storms would come, until she saw the lightning. Then she'd run into my room and crawl underneath the covers. We'd count the seconds after the lightning. We always knew the thunder would come next."

Mattie came to the sofa and sank back against it. "I miss her. I wish she could be here tonight. She loved getting all dressed up."

"That trait seems to run in this family," Adale said. "Mama taught us to never leave the house without some color. She refused to let us get the mail in a robe and pj's. She said when you leave the house, you need to be prepared for anything."

"She's right about that," Jolene said. "Anything can happen, and you might as well look good when it does happen."

"Mama was the same," Mattie said. "No wonder I'm a perfectionist. I guess that trait runs in the family too."

They all smiled then sat there, each with her own memories, each with hope for their futures. The fire popped and sparkled, keeping them warm.

"Tonight, let's remember those we've lost," Adale suggested. "And those we've found."

Mattie nodded. "This has been an amazing time—Jolene is home, the Christmas market is thriving, and the mural is beautiful. And Paul and I are together after all these years. Who would have ever guessed that one?"

Jolene pointed at her mother. "Not to mention, the talk of the town. My mother and Rémy Vachon, reunited after almost forty years of what-ifs and what could have been." She smiled at Adale. "Now you can focus on what's to come."

Adale nodded. After seeing Rémy's text, she felt better about the future. "I am excited about what's to come."

"And you have Cameron," Mattie reminded Jolene.

"I do, and I didn't have to wait for him. He was here waiting for me, except we didn't know he was waiting for me."

They all laughed at that. Then Eloise entered and read the room. "Oh no. Are we having another heart-to-heart to which I wasn't invited?"

Adale patted the sofa. "You're invited, Mama. We're remembering the people we love—the ones who've gone on, and we're rejoicing for those new and found."

Her mother put her hands on her hips and shook her head. "Y'all each got new fellows, and I'm left all alone. How fair is that?"

"Chef Ernie Perot likes you, Granny," Jolene said. "I think he'd love a dance with you tonight."

"Humph, that old geezer. He still thinks his gumbo is better than mine because I don't use okra. I don't like that slimy stuff, and he knows it. What does it matter when my roux is dark and rich and smoky? He can't stand the competition."

"Oh yeah, y'all have it bad," Mattie chimed in. "Def a dance coming in your future, Granny."

"Def not," her grandmother said, throwing up her hand. Then she gave them a prim smile. "But he will be blown away when I strut in wearing my stunning black chiffon pantsuit and my best string of pearls."

"There you go," Adale said. Eloise finally sat down and started laughing. Then they all told stories of past parties with the disasters of wearing the wrong dress or eating too much food. Soon they moved on to the ball tonight.

"I guess I'll have to wear orthopedic pumps," Eloise said, "but I'll still look fine. Isn't that what y'all say these days?"

Mattie and Jolene collapsed into giggles. Jolene nodded. "You're fine, Granny. I'm fine. We're all fine."

"What did you put in their hot chocolate, Adale?"

Adale stood and straightened her jacket. "We haven't had hot chocolate, but that might be nice. As long as I can still zip my dress tonight."

She hurried to the kitchen, her mind full of a happiness that transcended being content, a happiness full of the joy of Christmas, when Mary and her newborn had basked in love and peace. Christmas, a time when mothers everywhere celebrated their own children and everyone they loved.

Happiness. In this house again. True happiness. Tonight she and Rémy would be together, whether they danced or sat in a corner and whispered plans for the rest of their days. A happy day and a very merry Christmas.

His text hadn't promised anything, but Adale felt it in her heart. She hummed a song while she made the hot chocolate.

"All we do is eat," her mother declared while she grabbed a cookie. "I like it here. I think I'll stay a while."

"Me too," Jolene said. Then they all started giggling again as the conversation turned to their gowns and jewelry for the ball.

Adale listened while her heart lifted. Now if Rémy could get back in time for the ball.

Seven o'clock.

Adale glanced at her watch again. Rémy still wasn't here. She'd waited as long as she could at the house, but she needed to be here at the community center to greet people. The weather had gotten worse, so she guessed he'd been caught up in traffic or had to take back roads. He said he'd be here, but she had to wonder about the side trip.

A new anxiety settled in her stomach as she walked the perimeter of the decked-out ballroom. People were beginning to arrive. Mary Ann came by with her husband, Jimmy.

"Look at you," her friend said. "Adale, you're gorgeous."

Adale hugged Mary Ann. "You look pretty in your classic black dress. Love the magnolia blossom brooch too." The big creamy flower on her friend's shoulder shimmered with yellow and green gemstones in its center.

"Why thank you," her friend said. "Let's chat later. Where's Rémy?"

Adale explained, thinking she should hold up a sign saying he'd be late.

She waved to Mayor Ammons and his wife, Barbara. They looked festive, him in a nice tuxedo and her in a flowing ombré white and black gown. Frank Miller came strolling in. He had on a nice tuxedo, but he tugged at the bow tie as if it were a pinching crab.

"Frank," she said, trying to calm her worries, "you clean up nice."

"Well, this is the event of the year," he replied. "I hope our photographer can get some good pictures. You know how folks love seeing their pictures in the paper."

"Yes, we need that publicity," she said, glancing around and waving to people. "It will make a nice front-page story."

"Where's Rémy?" Frank asked, halfway with hope and halfway with dread.

"He's running late. The weather."

"Oh. Well, I heard the interstate's about to be shut down."

Adale refused to panic. She touched a hand to her hair, silently thanking Kimberly at Kimberly's Kurls for making this chignon work. "I'm sure he'll be here soon," she told Frank. "Meantime, take all the photos you want. Go enjoy the serving stations."

Frank glanced over her. "You look real nice, Adale. Save me a dance?"

"I'll do that, Frank." She smiled at him. "I've enjoyed our dinners, and I appreciate that you ask me to share meals with you, but—"

"But I'm just a friend," he finished for her. "I understand, Adale. You know, Mattie kept telling me I needed to get to know you better. I wish I hadn't waited so long."

"Frank, you'll always be my friend."

He took her hand. "I sure hope so. Now I'd better make the rounds. Hope you hear from Rémy soon."

After he walked away, she looked down at her black gown. The bodice and elbow length sleeves were made from sheer lacy black that worked for modesty's sake, while the fitted waist and tulip-shaped skirt worked in the comfort department. She had on her favorite black kitten heels, tiny pearls gracing the vamp.

She'd dressed to enjoy herself and to look nice for Rémy. Vanity, much?

Now she could only focus on the fact that he wasn't here yet. A side trip? To where? A week ago she didn't have any reason to worry about Rémy Vachon, but now she couldn't stop worrying. This felt the same as when she sat at that café and waited. She didn't like feeling helpless, but he had said he'd be back. What if that meant he was returning out of obligation, to finish the chapel repairs?

"Honey, you need to smile," her mother said as she passed Adale. Then she stopped and turned around. "What's wrong?"

"Rémy is late," Adale said. "I know he's on his way, but he hasn't texted me since earlier today. I'm worried. I'm trying not to panic, but Mama, we had words yesterday and he implied it was over. He wouldn't stand me up again, would he?"

Eloise looked toward the people flowing into the room, then back at Adale. "If he's late, it won't be because he's standing you up. This weather is nasty, and by midnight the roads will be frozen. You know we Southerners are famous for not knowing how to handle icy roads. He might have no other choice but to stop for the night."

Adale didn't want to sound petty. "You're right. I can't blame him this time. Mother Nature isn't to be messed with."

"Well, we can still have a good time," Eloise said. "You've always enjoyed the ball before."

"I managed to get here the Christmas after Pierre died, even if I felt so lonely I wanted to go home and curl up in bed and cry."

"But you didn't," her mother reminded her. "You're made of stronger stuff."

"Well, that stuff is making me doubt myself."

"Never doubt. Hold tight and everything will work out."

Adale smiled. "I will, Mama. I'll be okay."

She saw Jolene and Cameron coming in and tried not to gasp when she saw Jolene's dark green dress. So like her gloriously free-spirited daughter to ignore the black-and-white rules tonight.

"Honey, you look so pretty." Jolene did look pretty with her hair caught up in a curling bun that brought attention to a pair of black diamond earrings. "That dress was made for you."

"You're not mad, then?" Jolene asked.

"How could I be mad? You're here, and that's all I could ask for."

Cameron smiled and gave Adale a chaste kiss on the cheek. "You look pretty too, Miss Adale."

"Well, you look mighty handsome," she replied.

"Where's Rémy?" he asked, glancing around.

"We don't know," Adale admitted. "On his way, we hope."

Jolene shot Cameron a cautious glance. "Let's go find some punch."

"Good idea," he said. Then he turned back to Adale. "I hope he gets here soon."

"Me too." Adale looked around, determined to put on a good front even though her heart ticked too fast and her pulse had taken off after it. Did the side trip have to do with him wanting to tell her something, same as she wanted to tell him what she knew now? He could already know all that her mother had told her. Did he resent her family? Was that the part he'd left out?

No, she told herself. *Don't go down that road.*

He said he'd be here. She'd wait.

Nadine Collins waltzed in wearing a white gown that glowed with sequins, her blond hair cascading in wild ringlets down her ponytail, her lipstick a bright red. Making a beeline for Adale, she practically squealed with delight.

"You look amazing, Adale. So matronly."

Adale took the backhanded compliment in stride. "And you look like a Hollywood star," she quipped back to Nadine.

Nadine smiled and struck a pose. "Where's Rémy?"

The question of the night. "He's on his way."

"Is he driving in this weather? He told me before he left yesterday that he had business in New Orleans. Among other things."

Adale wouldn't take any bait. "He texted he's on his way." Then she spotted the police chief. "Tom, over here," she called.

Tom Manning came up to greet her and Nadine. "You two look like red-carpet movie stars."

"Thank you," Adale said. "Tom, be a dear and take Nadine around to the food stations. She seems to be hungry."

"I'm not so—" Nadine stopped and took in Tom Manning in his tux, his hair combed and his official uniform at home. "Well, maybe a few bites and something to drink. How 'bout it, Tom?"

Tom grinned big. "I'd be happy to escort you, Nadine. I figured you'd be here with a plus-one."

"You can be my plus-one," Nadine said, slapping her red finger-nails against his lapel. "You look so different wearing black. I need to pay attention."

They walked off arm in arm, saving Adale from trying to choke dear Nadine. Rubbing her forehead, Adale pushed away the headache she felt coming on. Then she said a prayer, asking for the Lord to keep Rémy safe.

Mattie and Paul walked up, and Adale clapped her hands together. "You two—how precious."

Mattie smiled and twirled in her strappy black full-skirted gown, her blond hair in retro waves pulled back at the side with a sparkling comb. Paul looked mysterious in his tuxedo, his dark hair crisp and combed.

"Make sure the *Gazette* photographer gets pictures of you two," she said as she hugged Mattie.

"Oh, we plan to do that," her niece said. "Maybe one of the whole family together, including Rémy." Mattie glanced around. "Let me know when he gets here."

"I will," Adale replied, hiding her worries. "Now go have fun. I have to mingle a bit."

Soon the place became packed with people, most of whom had managed to walk here wearing boots or sneakers, then putting on their dancing shoes once they were inside. Adale heard things ranging from "I didn't want to miss this" to "Well, we live around the corner. It wasn't a bad walk." Several people had complimented her on the decor and thanking her for "bringing snow to Louisiana."

"I'm not that powerful," she'd said on a laugh.

Her mother kept checking on her. "Adale, you should eat something."

"I'm not hungry, Mama."

"He'll be here. He said he'd be here, and I believe he will."

"I need to know he's okay and safe," Adale finally told her mother. "I need him to be safe."

Eloise hugged her close. "I know what you're thinking, but he wouldn't stand you up like he did in Paris, not after everything he's done to be with you, sugar. Let's pray he'll be here soon."

After an hour or so of chatting with everyone and greeting people, Adale wanted to go outside and scream into the wind. Where was Rémy? She'd tried to call, but his phone only went to voice mail. As she walked around with a smile and tried to nibble food, she worked to put all the horrible scenarios out of her head. But as the night progressed with stunning success, considering the weather, she had to accept that Rémy might miss the ball.

And this time there was nothing either of them could do about it.

Chapter Thirteen

Rémy couldn't believe what had happened, but here he sat in the back of an ambulance, his sports car a crunched mess on the side of the road. Black ice and a guardrail did not mix very well. The tow truck could take longer due to the weather.

He was only two miles from Moreau on one of the old parish roads—a shortcut an old-timer ten miles back had shown him. He'd tried to call Adale, but the phone reception in this particular spot barely had a pulse, and she was in a noisy, busy room with lots of active phones. Thankfully, he'd been able to call for help, and he wasn't hurt badly. Cuts and bruises. Now he had to get to Moreau and get into his tux.

One of the first responders, who'd called in a tow for the damaged car, came walking up. "Mr. Vachon, you're clear to go."

"That's great," Rémy said. "But I'm waiting on the tow truck. My car is a mess, and I'm late for the Moreau Christmas Eve ball. My date is waiting on me."

"Really now?" the young man said. "We're headed back that way. Not for the ball, but once we get back, our shift ends." Then he held up the red box. "Did you by any chance need this?"

"Yes," Rémy said, taking the box. "I sure do need that."

Rémy glanced around as he saw a heavy truck barreling toward them. "Well, at least my car has a ride." He stared at the man's name tag. "So Sam, since I'm technically a patient, can you give me a ride into Moreau?"

Sam grinned, then looked at the sky. "Unless you feel like walking."

"No, I don't feel like walking. I might run though."

"How late are you, sir?"

"About forty years or so."

"And who is your date?"

"Adale Lavigne-Marchand Broussard," Rémy said, hoping a little name-dropping would do the trick. "I also need to get my tux out of the trunk. I'll get dressed in the ambulance if you don't mind."

"Say no more," Sam said. "You can ride up front with me—once you're dressed, of course. Miss Adale would have my hide if I left you standing in the snow."

Rémy didn't argue, although they were probably breaking a lot of rules. He figured it being Christmas Eve meant they could let that pass. He wouldn't turn down a ride, but he could have run all the way if need be.

The tow truck driver made quick work of getting his two-seater up onto the towing platform. "I'm headed in the other direction," the burly driver explained after handing Rémy a card. "Here's where you can get 'er back or send someone to file an insurance claim."

Rémy got in the ambulance, his head sore and a cut down his cheek, but he had to get to that ball or Cinderella would leave without him.

—◆—

Nine o'clock.

Adale had given up on Rémy. He had to be in a hotel some-where on the road, but why hadn't he at least called? She'd checked her phone so many times even her mother looked worried. Jolene told her with a lot of people here on their phones, service could go haywire. Or not work at all.

Now, as Adale sat at her table listening to "I'll Be Home for Christmas," her mind felt numb and her heart heavy. She'd had a lovely enough time, considering that everyone in the room kept casting sympathetic glances at her. Even Nadine, who had not let go of Tom Manning's muscular arm all night, had given her a smile that was a mixture of *I'm sorry* and *thank you*.

"It's really bad when Nadine starts feeling sorry for you," she whispered to her mother.

Eloise had been talking to everyone in the room, charming them with her wit, explaining her love of art, arguing with Chef Ernie if he even looked her way, then dancing with the man when an instru-mental waltz had played. But now, like a mother hen, she sat with her daughter, trying to make Adale feel better.

She glanced around and made a noise that sounded like a snort. "I imagine Nadine had plans for our Rémy. When he didn't show up right away, she latched onto poor Tom." Tapping Adale's shoulder, she said, "Clever on your part to match them."

"I think they make a great couple," Adale said, her forced smile beginning to add to her headache. "I don't know why I didn't think of that matchup years ago."

"Well, you've never been in competition with her before, darling. You're not in competition with her now. You're already won your man." Her mother gave an eloquent shrug. "Nadine is a tempest in a teapot. She's obvious and flirty, but she'd give you the shirt off her back—I mean, she has a heart of gold. She's the first person in the church doors every Sunday. I think she's just lonely."

"I agree," Adale replied. "Her first husband left her years ago, and she's been a mess since, bless her heart of gold."

"You have nothing to worry about. Not that I'm judging too harshly, mind you."

"I'm not worried on that account," Adale said on a whisper. "I wanted one night with a man I haven't seen in thirty-nine plus years! Is that too much to ask?"

Her mother glanced over Adale, her gaze centered on the entry-way. "I don't think it is," Eloise said with a smile. "Turn around, Adale."

Adale pivoted in her chair. Rémy stood there in his tuxedo, his hair windblown, his bow tie a bit crooked, his gaze searching the room. She stood, her knees wobbly, her heart both broken and mushed back together.

"Oh mercy," she said. Then she noticed his face. "Mama, he's been hurt."

She didn't wait to hear her mother's questions. She walked toward him with purpose and intent. She didn't plan to let anyone get in her way.

"Rémy!" she called out, her feet picking up speed as she got near him. "What in the world happened?"

He didn't say anything. Instead, he pulled her into his arms and held her close. "I hope you saved the last dance for me."

Adale stood back to study him. "You're hurt."

"I had a minor accident out on the river road, a few miles from where we stopped the other day."

She gingerly touched the scratch along his jawline. "That's awful. Are you sure you're all right?"

He heaved a sigh. "I'm fine. A few bruises. My car is not so good."

Adale's heart started beating again, faster but with a steady pace. "I was so worried. I thought—never mind what I thought. I'm glad you're here."

"I know what you thought," he said. "That I wasn't going to show up? Right?"

She couldn't deny it. "It crossed my mind after the last time we talked, but I did consider the weather. I thought you'd had to stop somewhere."

"Non, I drove a little too fast." He shrugged. "I made it thanks to the EMTs who came to my rescue."

Then while everyone in the room watched, he tugged her to the doors. "I invited them to come in and get warm. I also invited the firefighters and other first responders who've been out there helping people all night. I hope you don't mind."

Adale put a hand to her lips. "Mind? I'll be the first one in line to thank them." She rushed out and waved. "Y'all get in here."

Several men and women, all still in uniform, hurried up to the community center.

Adale grabbed the DJ's mic and explained what had happened. "This is why we volunteer and work hard to keep our town updated and restored. This is why we love Moreau. So let's keep celebrating."

Everyone clapped, and soon she and Rémy were surrounded by well-wishers and people who wanted to hear about his accident. After that, Adale got her dance with Rémy, Jolene held tight to Cameron, and Mattie smiled while she danced with Paul. Her mother even did another jig with Chef Ernie.

Near eleven, everyone started toward home, some catching rides with the men and women who always came to their rescue. As the crowds dwindled, Rémy took Adale by the hand. "Let me get your coat. We can take a walk."

She didn't protest. "I need to make sure Mama has a ride home."

Adale ran up to Eloise. "I'm going for a walk with Rémy. Do you have a ride?"

Her mother grinned. "Chef Ernie has a big old truck with something called a Hemi in it. Apparently, that can get a woman home in one piece if we don't get into an argument."

"Behave, Mama."

"You too, Daughter."

Adale hugged her girls and their handsome escorts. "Get them home safely. Y'all wait until I get there to open gifts," she told Cameron and Paul.

"Yes, ma'am."

After they'd shut down everything with the intent of cleaning up tomorrow after church, she followed Rémy. He held her hand as they strolled alone, careful to walk slowly. Adale snuggled into her long black wool dress coat and the boots she'd worn earlier.

"I was so worried," she said as they strolled toward the chapel. When he took her back to the courtyard, she smiled at seeing the white tarp covering Jolene's mural. They'd see the final reveal tomorrow. "I'm glad you're okay."

Rémy tugged her close. "I'm better than okay now." He kissed her on her forehead. "I thought this would be a good place to give you your Christmas gift." Then he reached inside his suit pocket and brought out a long red velvet box. "For you, *mon amour*."

Adale opened the box and gasped. "Rémy—"

She stared at the beautiful charm bracelet. The streetlights and the mural's spotlights showed her the gleaming tiny diamonds on the Eiffel Tower charm. Then she noticed a Louisiana-shaped charm with an emerald sparkling there. Next a bridge with a sapphire shimmering like water. Then two hearts merged together with two tiny diamonds winking at her. "This is beautiful," she said, tears in her eyes. "But how, when, where did you find this?"

Rémy took the charm bracelet from its nest. "Adale, I had this made to give to you before you left Paris. At the time, it only had the Eiffel Tower on it. I. . .added things through the years, hoping that one day I could give it to you, as a friend, as a token. I never wanted to interfere with the life you had here. But time and circumstances changed that. Yet now, here we are. I added the last charm recently. I found it in a shop in New Orleans."

He lifted her arm. "Let me."

Adale nodded, too overcome to speak. Once he had it clasped, she held up her hand and dangled the charms. "I love it, Rémy."

"*Je t'aime*," he said. "Can we make this work?"

"I believe we can," she replied. "I love you—again. I never dreamed I'd see you—again. My mama said God is in the details. She thinks we were meant to be together now, here, in this time."

Rémy kissed her and held her close as the last of the snowflakes danced around them. "Your mother is a wise woman."

Adale laughed after savoring the kiss that merged her sweet memories with her hope for what might come. "Yes, but let's not tell her that. She'll get a big head."

They stood there while Rémy poured out his heart to her and told her what his father had revealed. Then she did the same.

"Our parents held their secrets close, didn't they?" He touched a hand to her cheek. "I was so ashamed, so confused. I should have stood up to your father, or at least I should have come to you. But I had nothing to offer with my family falling apart. We even lost our home."

Adale put a finger to his lips. "Rémy, you had my heart. What happened is terrible, but in God's own time we've found our way back to each other. That is the truth. Our love is the truth—no more shame, no more worries. Here we are."

Rémy laughed and kissed her. Then he escorted Adale home, where they had hot chocolate with Christmas cookies and enjoyed watching her mother along with Jolene and Cameron, and Mattie and Paul, all open one gift. She'd already shown them her gift from Rémy.

"I have something for you, Rémy," Adale said, standing. "I'll be right back."

She returned and handed him the portrait her mother had painted of them on the bridge over the Seine. "You're home now," she said, smiling over at him.

Rémy studied the portrait, then stood and hugged her close. "Thank you. I'm home because I'm with you. At last."

Granny clapped. "You and Rémy can have the top floor to renovate. The girls can take the cottage." She shrugged. "My family all around me."

"I love that idea," Mattie said. "As long as Jolene is okay with it."

"I'm good," Jolene replied, bobbing her head. "The bathroom is bigger!"

Adale looked at Rémy. Her heart swelled with love and gratitude. "Rémy and I are going to take things slow and enjoy getting to know each other again."

"Oui." Rémy glanced around. "But I'd love to renovate the upstairs—one day."

Mattie laughed. "Granny, now you need a fellow of your own."

"Don't worry," her grandmother said. "Chef Ernie and I are planning a gumbo cook-off for Valentine's Day to raise more funding and to have more fun in our old age."

Mattie squealed then got out her phone, already making a list.

Jolene laughed and held Cameron's hand. "It's so good to be home."

"I agree." Adale glanced at Rémy. "Now we're all home, where we belong."

"Merry Christmas," Rémy said. "Merci."

"A Christmas to remember," Eloise added, tears in her eyes while she smiled at everyone. "A *Louisiana* Christmas to remember."

A member of the American Christian Fiction Writers Honor Roll, **Lenora Worth** writes romance and romantic suspense for Love Inspired and sweet romance for Tule Publishing. She also writes for Kensington Books. Three of her books have finaled in the ACFW Carol Awards. She received the *Romantic Times* Pioneer Award for Inspirational Fiction. Lenora is a *New York Times*, *USA Today*, and *Publishers Weekly* bestselling writer and a 2019 Romance Writers of America RITA finalist. With one hundred plus books and novellas published and more than three million books in print, she enjoys adventures with her retired husband and loves reading, baking, and shopping—especially shoe shopping. Go to www.lenoraworth .com to sign up for Lenora's newsletter and find her book list and upcoming releases.

JOIN US ONLINE!

Christian Fiction for Women

Christian Fiction for Women is your online home for the latest in Christian fiction.

Check us out online for:

- Giveaways
- Recipes
- Info about Upcoming Releases
- Book Trailers
- News and More!

Find Christian Fiction for Women at Your Favorite Social Media Site:

 Search "Christian Fiction for Women"

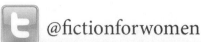 @fictionforwomen